A Heart On A Sleeve
Kelli Cooke

First Edition August 2025

Developmental Edit: Annie Meagle (Spare Words Novel Editing)

Copy Edit: Briana Ozor (Ozor Edits)

Proof Edit: Sarah Taig & Cassandra Moll

Cover Design: Sam Palencia (Ink & Laurel)

www.kellicooke.com

A Heart On a Sleeve
KELLI COOKE

Praise for A Heart On A Sleeve

"A cozy, heartwarming tale that will make you laugh and swoon! Cooke has crafted the perfect blend of magic and sweet, slow burn romance, relatable characters that burrow into your heart, and a charming town you want to live in. Filled with forgiveness and healing, A HEART ON A SLEEVE is the light-hearted but deeply feeling romance of your dreams and will remind you of the beauty of believing in love and wearing your heart on your sleeve." – Breanne Randall, New York Times Bestselling Author of The Unfortunate Side Effects of Heartbreak and Magic.

"A delightful, romantic escapade full of cozy moments, pumpkins galore, and lots of tension-filled magic." – Margaret Rose, Author of the Love at The Lake Series & Sink or Sell.

"A Heart On A Sleeve is a magical story in more ways than one! The characters are real, the setting's alive, and the plot will permanently ink itself into your mind. Cooke brought the perfect combination of sweet, spice, and sass that will make you fall in love with Mage Hollow and the people who live there, not just in autumn, but all year long." – Cassandra Moll, Author of The Golden City Series & The Maple Grove Series.

Author's Note

Dear Reader,

Have you ever had a dream that you just couldn't let go? Something that played on repeat in your mind and felt so tangibly real you could almost reach out and touch it? That's what this book is for me. It started as a simple dream that woke me up from the depths of sleep at three in the morning (the audacity). What started as a picture in my brain bloomed into the story you are about to venture into. And while I normally use this forum to note trigger warnings (don't worry, they are below), I am also going to share a little here about what I hope you take away from this experience.

Life is so busy! It flies by for most of us with some days seemingly longer than others. But there are some experiences that we just have to stop and take in. Moments in time that would otherwise be a mere blip on our radar. For me it's driving through a new small town or walking through a festival in the city closest to where I live. I find myself getting lost in those moments, dreaming of the people who live there, the stories and lives unfolding around me. Because of that, Mage Hollow (the town in this book, if you didn't already know) is crafted to feel in a way like its own character. If I'm being honest, I wrote this with the hope that when you are finished reading, you want to pack up and move there—I definitely do!

This book explores themes that bridge the gap between a magical world and the very real one we live in. No matter what you believe, I hope this book resonates in that wearing your heart on your sleeve and being open to love is always scarier in our minds than in reality. Take the leap and walk through this life being your most vulnerable and authentic self—you are perfect and beautiful just the way you are.

As always, your mental health matters to me more than pages read or books sold. The below potential triggers are in this work, please opt out if you feel inclined or proceed with caution if the following could be troublesome for you.

- On Page Sexually Explicit Material

- A Complicated Parent/Child Relationship

- Hospitalization of the FMC (brief and non life threatening)

- Magic/ Witchcraft

Love Always,
KC

Everyone is worthy of love.

Take my hand as I lead you into a world where it's always safe to wear your heart on your sleeve.

Prologue

Where It All Began

Salem — October 1692

"Cucumber, shoo. Go on. Out!" I've been working the buttons on my petticoat for the last few minutes, racking my mind for anything else I might need, and this stupid cat won't leave me alone. He's not very bright. I found him munching on John's garden, and I rescued him despite the many protests from the man whose radishes I saved. I guess that makes me not very bright, too.

I'm startled by a loud rap at the dilapidated cottage door, and it takes me a minute to gather my thoughts. I'm not expecting anyone, we are supposed to meet at Proctor's Ledge—one last chance to bid our sisters goodbye, and an attempt to ensure we aren't spotted sneaking off. I haven't finished readying myself for my adventure. My stomach sinks at the thought that I've come so close but maybe I'm too late.

Moving nimbly toward the small window, I peek at the front porch. Surely they wouldn't come to take us at night, we didn't do what they're accusing us of. Not completely, anyway—I do have the gift, but I've never used it to cause harm. John waits patiently, raising his strong, callused knuckles to knock again.

Rushing to let him in, I sweep the door open quickly, and he slides inside kicking it closed. "Irina, I . . . I can't just leave." My heart bottoms out low in my belly as I try to wrap my head around the words he's saying. A sweeping tingle races up my spine burning each nerve ending as it goes. It's a tell tale sign of bad luck—at least for me.

"What? We have to go." I dismiss his statement. John and I are in love. Meant to be together—create a life together. I can't do that here, and he knows it. I begin to pace—one step, then two, before turning and repeating the motion.

He stops me by placing his hands on my arms and looking deeply into my eyes. "I love you. I will not let them take you from me." He runs his fingers through my long golden locks. "You have to stay, for me, for us."

I press up onto my toes, placing a kiss on his lips. I know it'll be the last. "John, no. There's no way." I shake my head in disbelief. "You saw what they did to Trudy." When he stares at me blankly, my mind corrects that statement: he saw what he allowed them to do to Trudy. He knew her, he knew my sister was good, nary a mean bone in her body—he still let them take her. The pain of that decision has plagued my insides like a festering wound that refuses to heal. But instead of eradicating the problem—John—I keep smoothing it over, and hoping it'll eventually be so covered up I'll forget. My sisters don't like him, don't approve of him coming with us. This is exactly what Josephine warned me about. She knew it would happen, and I refused to listen. *How could he be so blind*? Staying wouldn't mean only the same fate for me. They'd hang us both if they knew what we meant to each other.

He runs a hand down his face, combing through his jet black beard with his fingers. "I won't abandon my family. Choose us, stay with me, and live honestly."

If I stayed, it would be the furthest thing from living a truthful life. I would have to hide who I am. I'd have to bury my heart so deep it would never see the light of day. Although my dreams are scattered like the leaves that dust the ground outside, I know my choice. "I can't stay. I refuse."

For a moment, everything is still. Even Cucumber sits patiently, like he's waiting for us to find a way through this impasse. But there is no way out of it. We both know it, yet neither of us wants to make the first move. The last embers on the fire burn out, an owl hoots in the cold night air, and in the stark blackness that envelops me—John walks away.

"We've been trudging through this forest forever, can we please take a break?" Beth whines. She's the youngest of us at no more than ten plus three. She's also the most powerful.

"Just a little while longer child. We need to be sure they didn't follow. When we didn't show, they probably started searching," I explain unnecessarily. She knows how this works. We've watched our entire coven picked off one by one over the last six moons. Our time was coming, John told me.

At the thought of him, a sharp pang buries itself deep in my heart. I never considered him not joining me. It wasn't an option after everything I'd swallowed, everything I chose to overlook—until it was. When I showed up alone, my sisters weren't surprised. But they didn't rub my nose in it. Instead, they looped their arms through mine, and carried me off—broken and numb.

"I see it. I see the place I dreamed about." Josephine grabs our arms, tugging us forward more swiftly now. "I knew we were close. Mother guided us." My oldest sister has dreams, premonitions, really. She knew where to go because she's seen it countless times over the last few months.

When the water is to your left, walk until you pass our place of rest, but don't look back. Keep going until the new moon shines like golden drops on the roof. The plan is foolproof.

As we step over fallen leaves and crunch branches with our shoes, a small cottage appears. It's covered in moss and ivy, nearly invisible to the untrained eye. We rush toward it, desperately working to gain shelter. Pushing through the haggard door, the possibility of a beautiful new life blooms before my very eyes.

It's small and abandoned, but everything we need is here: a place to cook, a chair to rock in, and best of all—a cauldron. Beth slips to the floor in exhaustion and glee; happiness radiating off of her in waves. Josephine sets her pack down on the wooden table, untying it, and retrieving her spellbook. I lock eyes with Beth, both of us snickering over how responsible she is. We want to relax, and she is getting right to business.

Approaching, I cautiously glance at the pages as she turns each one thoughtfully. "What are you searching for?"

Jo doesn't look at me when she responds. "Mother said to find the one that will protect us." Her fingers delicately trace the words on each page, searching . . . more searching . . . and then, she stops. "I've got it. It says here we must name this place. We must set boundaries."

"Come on, Beth." I nod my head toward my sister, motioning for her to come help as Josephine quickly jots down our chant.

When Beth joins us, we link hands with the book in the center of our triangle and read the words she has scribbled aloud.

"From east to west and north to south, where the ocean meets the coast, and the trees dwindle out. We name this land the home of Mage. It's hollow our shelter, and its abundance our liege. May we spend our days free to roam and free to do as we please."

The three of us, in perfect sync, repeat the phrase two more times. But as we finish the last of our chant, I belt out, "Never again will we wear our hearts on our sleeves."

One

Olive

The Flasher

The wind blows softly, sweeping through the trees and creating a low whistling sound as I step off the front steps of my rental cottage and push through the gate of the white picket fence. The first signs of a new season pepper the ground as I walk carefully toward Mage Square. I have only a few blocks to take this place in before I'll be stuck behind a desk with my nose in a book, not that I'm complaining. Books are better than people. They don't judge, don't expect anything, and most of all they provide an escape. The low rumble of a motorcycle vibrates through my ears. Normally, I would look up and search to see who's brave enough to ride such a thing. Instead, I remain mesmerized by the brightly colored leaves that rest at my feet.

I attempt to sidestep the freshly fallen pile—the leaves are too beautiful to crunch, with their burnt oranges, scarlet reds, and crisp yellows. But as I admire the foliage, a whoosh hits me like a cool slap to the face and my dress wraps itself around my head. Flailing like a baby bird leaving the nest for the first time, my arms fly in every direction, and my purse launches like a rock from a catapult, landing with a thud. I twist in an attempt to right myself. Seconds feel like minutes while my undies are exposed to God knows who. I struggle to find it but finally grip the hem of my dress and pull it down, desperate to maintain some sense of decorum.

I'm starting a new job today, my first real job since I graduated from college, and isn't this just my luck? The irony of my new beginning starting with no less than a hearty dose of embarrassment and indecent exposure isn't lost on me. If I thought I was nervous before, there's a good chance my new boss, and everyone else in this sleepy little town I now call home, just saw my granny panties from across the street.

Freaking perfect!

Like any semi-sane person would do, I glance around furiously to see who might have lain witness to this tragedy. My heart thumps, and my cheeks heat in that same embarrassment that comes with waving to someone who doesn't see you or doesn't wave back. You know the kind, an embarrassment that leaves you mumbling under your breath—*hello to you too*—before promptly playing it cool.

There's only one voyeur, *thank goodness*, a man on a motorcycle dressed in all black with a dark helmet that has an iridescent quality to it. He's halted mid-street, staring. Red flushes over my already-heated skin, crawling up my neck and painting my face the same color as the crimson leaves that got me into this mess. We didn't have the same seasonal changes back home in Alabama, so basking in the beauty of it stirs something in my soul. And apparently, distracts me enough to flash the whole town on my first full day here.

Rather than give into the strong desire to crawl into a hole and never return, I straighten my proverbial crown—like the good pageant queen I am—and give the rider a brief wave before continuing across the square. By playing it coy, I'm hoping that this will be one of those things that I can shove into a tiny box in my mind where all the mishaps I want to forget go to die. As if my wave snapped the stranger back to life, there's a dramatic squeal of tires, and the rider zooms off. Shaking my head, at them or maybe myself, I stop on the sidewalk to take in my new place of business.

Black Kettle Bindery is a unique establishment. It opened its doors nearly fifty years ago with a mission of restoring old books and historical texts to their former glory. Now, while they still restore and preserve works, they also sell a variety of new releases, kitschy trinkets, and custom-order or rare-edition books. As a person who specializes in historic restoration work, it's the perfect gig for me. It allows me to live close to my best friend, and it's thousands of miles from my mother's endless mission to marry me off to the highest bidder.

Black Kettle has a magnetic curb appeal, much like everything in Mage Hollow. Calligraphic gold lettering adorns the stark black wood sign hanging above a picture window. The entrance is tucked away off the street with historically accurate oil lamps hanging on each side of the doorway. A reading nook is visible through the glass, sitting off to one side with tufted bench seating for patrons to linger with their books.

This store is a perfect match for Mage Hollow, the austere town that may be a little more *Hocus Pocus* than *Gilmore Girls* but is charming all the same. Here the streets wobble and sway with the ebb and flow of the hundreds-of-years-old cobblestones. The houses are styled in a mixture of Victorian-era Second Empire, with mansard roofs and intricate adornments, and the more well-known Greek Revival style that one typically imagines when picturing coastal Massachusetts. Quaint shops mark the uptown square as a bustling yet relaxing place to be.

The town is ethereal in all the best ways. Like a snapshot in time, an ode to history. Lingering signs of summer lurk amongst the blossoming colors of fall. It's the perfect mix of old plants withering while new ones bloom, as if the change of seasons is as transformative as the seasons of our lives.

I pull in a deep renewing breath as I close my eyes and smell the sweet scent of the swiftly dying limelight hydrangeas that surrounds the tree-lined street. Peering up at the sign once more, I smooth my hands over the tea-length gingham dress I'd selected in one final attempt at making sure I'm wrinkle-free—especially after what just happened—before first impressions are made.

Reaching for the door handle, I press down on the vintage lock and pull it open swiftly. The comforting smell of old books melded with vanilla candles envelopes me as I step into the place I plan to spend most of my days. Behind the stately counter, fashioned with a gold-leaf cash register, sits a man who must be Beau Brooks, my new boss.

"Well, you must be Olivia," the portly man in his sixties with round-framed glasses and a tweed vest greets me.

"How do you do, Mr. Brooks? It's a pleasure to meet you. Please, call me Olive." I muster up my award-winning smile, attempting to charm him. I spoke to him on the phone briefly once, but securing this position had been mostly handled through a backroom deal with my best friend's father. It took calling in a favor to prove to my parents that my degree actually meant something. That the tiny piece of paper went beyond another box to check on the list making me, as they would say, the perfect wife.

"Oh my. Tony said you were a Southerner as sweet as smooth molasses, but I never imagined this. Are you sure you know what this job entails?" His eyes are narrowed, deep frown lines evident as he takes me in.

"Uh, y-yes. I'm not sure I know what you are asking. I apologize."
How am I already messing this up?

"This job requires you to lift heavy boxes, clean dusty, old books .
. . I can't imagine a beauty such as yourself getting her hands dirty."
He's confused because he thinks I'm pretty? I mean, this is better
than him being scandalized by my latest mishap, but still. Where I
grew up, I'm not far from underdressed.

"Mr. Brooks, I assure you that while I do appreciate fashion, I'm
prepared with what it takes to do great work here. I have completed
my education, and I can promise that I value history far more than
appearances." Pouring every ounce of conviction I have into my
reply, I try to soothe whatever misgivings he has about me from first
glance. I need him to like me, to want to keep me in this position.

"Very well, then. Come with me and I'll show you your desk," he
says, nodding and motioning for me to follow him toward the back
corner of the shop.

I set my bag and tools down at the worn wooden desk and am
pleasantly surprised with the tour he takes me on. Beau, which I
have been given strict instructions to call him from now on, shows
me the various books, ranging from contemporary romance to an
elite selection of treasured first-edition classics. He gives me a brief
overview on pricing and how to run the ancient cash register, as well
as a glimpse into the handwritten schedule of appointments for the
restoration work that I am now solely responsible for.

Of course, Beau reminds me that restoration projects only get worked
on before we open and after we close. It was the very first thing Tony told
me when describing the position, and I've made my peace with it. Taking
this job was the only way to escape my mother and her expectations. Not

to mention, the onslaught of suitors she always has at the ready. There's not much I wouldn't do to finally have that freedom.

During "customers' hours," as Beau lovingly calls them, it is my responsibility to serve them, answer questions and make recommendations. I wouldn't love that aspect of the job as much if it meant long hours; however, as in most small New England towns, shops here are only open from ten to four with an hour lunch break in between. That makes for a total shopping window of just five hours—it's a wonder Beau makes any money at all.

Adding to my suspicions about Beau's management skills, apparently he also takes a long lunch each day from eleven to two so that he can spend time with his beloved cat, Mr. Pickles. Managing the store part-time was not in the job description. For the next three hours, I'm on my own. Thankfully, there isn't a customer in sight when Beau grabs his messenger bag and bike helmet and heads for the door.

"One more thing before I go. You should look over this and learn all you can. We will have many shoppers interested in the histories this week." Beau shoves a flyer at me. Turning on a dime to push his way out the front door, his own clumsiness causes him to slightly catch a toe on the threshold. I purse my lips tightly, attempting to stifle the giggle that overwhelms me—my new boss is adorable, but it wouldn't be proper to laugh at his misfortune.

Opting to look at the now-crumpled flyer in a bit, I take in the shop. It's stunning and historic with handcrafted built-ins to house the many books on display. Cherry-wood tables line the center of the room for guests to work quietly, a variety of seating choices sprinkled throughout. The trinkets are more giftable than cheesy: greeting cards with poetic sayings detailed in calligraphy, beautiful hand-painted journals, and of course, a curated collection of coffee mugs. One wall is lined floor to ceiling with books, adorned with a sliding ladder for easy access to those out of reach. If I had to create my very own library, this is exactly what I imagine it would be.

The door chimes, alerting me to my first guest. *Here goes nothing.*

I swiftly make my way to the front, plastering on my brightest smile, prepared to woo the unsuspecting person into purchasing something. Beau left me alone. I have to prove I can handle this role, despite the very limited training he gave me.

I'm on a mission to make my new boss proud, walking with a purpose until my gaze lands on the same dark denim pants from before, leaning against the open front door. I stop, frozen, confronted with what is likely the most beautiful yet panic-inducing man I have ever seen staring back at me with what seems like a mixture of intrigue, and maybe annoyance? His cobalt-blue eyes hit me first, pulling me in like a rip current paired with a strong jaw that's dusted with a neatly kept beard, and short brown hair that's a bit too long up top. He's sporting a casual look with a white V-neck tee and those pants that unfairly accentuate his powerful thighs.

The panic-inducing part is . . . he's the one and only (known) witness of my Marilyn Monroe moment. The man's covered in tattoos. Every inch of his exposed skin, from the top of his chest, peeking out of his shirt, to his forearms, has ink. His appearance screams, *I'm a walking sex symbol.* Of course, he would be the one who holds the cards of my first and only foray with indecent exposure.

This stranger witnessed the single most mortifying moment of my life, and that's saying something. I haven't exactly had a shortage of mishaps over the years. I know how to manage them, how to plaster on a grin and pretend it didn't happen. How to wear my crown proudly, keep my chin up, and move forward, rather than embarrassing my family. What I don't know is what to feel other than dread over him staying either too long or not long enough. I can't be sure which, or why I even care, but there's a brief skip in my heartbeat and a sinking feeling in my stomach that nags, *He's someone important.* I'm desperate to pretend he didn't just see the full-coverage white briefs I chose to wear today. Note to self: only leave the house in magazine-worthy panties from now on.

Forcing my smile to stay firmly in place, I muster my courage, fully believing he's going to be either unbearably smug about our earlier encounter or incredibly lost at having accidentally found himself in a quaint bookstore, face-to-face with, for all intents and purposes, a flasher. He's definitely not going to mention what he observed . . . right?

"H-hi there, can I help you?" My voice squeaks a bit with nerves and a Southern twang I've spent too many years trying to eradicate from my diction. At this point, it only escapes if I'm on edge or upset about something.

"You must be new in town." His voice is gruff as he moves closer, allowing the door to close with a click. A smirk lurks at the corner of his full, deliciously edible lips. *Do not, I repeat, do not look at his lips. Why on earth is this man affecting me so much?*

"Observant," I mutter quietly to myself while raising an eyebrow. "I'm Olive. Can I help you find something?"

"If I have observed anything, it's that you"—he points his index finger at my chest—"are new in town."

Shoot! He heard that. "Yes, I am. Does it matter?"

"Not particularly, I just didn't want you to think for even a single second that it wasn't painfully obvious." A cool and impartial tone laces his words.

"Okay. Are you on the welcoming committee or . . . something?" I ask, trying and failing to tamp down a small huff as I cross my arms. It's out of character for me to be this worked up, but in my defense, he's acting like there should have been a flyer passed out introducing me. I know this is a very small town compared to Mobile, but I really don't believe it's *that* tiny. Also, can we address the elephant in the room? I'd rather we don't, but if I have to deal with it, then let's just get on with it.

"No, Olive, I'm not. But I do know almost everyone here, and there is zero chance that if you were a local you wouldn't have held certain things in place while coming around that corner." A smirk paints his face amused. "Everyone that's local knows it's a brutal crosswind." *There it is. Jerk!*

"I-I'm . . . well, now you have me flustered. I'm going to pretend that didn't happen, and I would be really grateful if you did too. Now, is there something I can do for you, sir?"

He flashes me a smile so breathtaking that heat zaps up my spine, releasing a wave of shivers across my skin. My cheeks warm, turning what I can only imagine to be an embarrassing shade of pink.

He steps closer, yet again, nodding toward my strawberry blonde hair. "Still a little mussed, if you ask me. Heck of a first impression, princess." His gaze lingers on my face. "But I'm here to pick up an order, not talk about your hobby as the new town streaker. Name's Sam O'Reilly."

Holy mother of Pearl. The sound of his name tumbles around in my head turning it to soup. I should be pissed that he's outright mocking me, but I've never had such a visceral reaction to someone. I'm a little out of my depth.

"I-I hardly think that qualifies as streaking. If I was planning to make a name for myself, I'd like to believe it would have been a better show. And, uh, please don't call me princess." I smile as sweetly as I can—fake it till you make it and all that.

"Sure, princess. Whatever you say. Now my order . . ." It seems like Mr. Smug, motioning toward the counter, would like to end this conversation, maybe even more than I would at this point. I take back what I said about there being something important about him. He's like every other man, managing me and telling me what to do.

"Um, one second. Let me find it." I dash behind the desk to look on the shelf reserved for pickups. He clearly isn't going to let my morning mishap go or stop calling me that ridiculous nickname, so I need to get him to leave pronto while still being polite. The last thing I want is Beau catching wind of me being anything less than helpful to a customer.

I start pulling books out and placing them in my free arm. Each one is labeled with the customer's name, but I don't see any marked Sam. "Are you sure you have an order?" I ask, the pile in my arm growing more difficult to hold by the second.

"Yep." One word, that's not helpful at all.

I dip my head lower, checking to see if I missed any books shoved to the back of the shelf, and at the same time the pile in my arms starts to falter. In my moment of panic—*I can't let these fall, they are fragile and Beau will literally fire me on day one*—I lean forward, wrapping myself around them to make somewhat of a cocoon. I'm so focused that I don't notice Sam moving toward me until he growls out, "Jesus, let me help you." My eyes jump to his, horror most certainly painted across my brow.

"I, uh, maybe just—" I don't have to finish. He wraps his arm around my front and slowly pulls each book out of my grasp. My breathing is unsteady in this close proximity, but it worsens when he reaches for the last book and his fingers lightly graze my forearm.

Good gravy.

When the books are lined carefully on the counter, Sam grabs one, clutching it in his long fingers. "Here it is . . . O'Reilly, just like I said," he quips, smirking at me. I glance at the label. It reads Mabel not Sam.

"It doesn't say your name. I'm sorry, I can't let you take that," I protest, my stomach queasy with the idea of giving someone the wrong purchase right off the bat.

He ignores me. "It's my mom's. I'll see you around town. Oh, and a word of advice. Wear something a little less breezy next time." Sam turns and walks confidently out the door—as quickly as he arrived, he's gone. And me? I'm left wondering who the hell Sam O'Reilly is and how the heck I'm ever going to live this one down.

Shaking it off after a hearty dose of self-deprecation, I decide that I can't let this ruin my day. And I should probably tell Ariella before word gets out. I can assume I'll be the talk of the town in record time, if I'm not already, and that's the very last thing I need. I grab my phone and shoot off a text.

> Sooo . . . first day's going great. I flashed all of Mage when the wind blew my dress over my head and Beau already left me to run the shop.

Ari

> OMG! Was it when you turned the corner by the candy shop? Sorry, babe . . . should have warned you. Tell me you don't have on period panties, puhleeease.

> They are the only ones I could find in all my boxes.

Ari

> Did anyone see?

I leave her on read. She deserves it. These are things that best friends are supposed to share when you move to their hometown at *their* urging. Ariella Marino is my kindred spirit, the yin to my yang, yet she often gets caught up, conveniently forgetting to mention the, let's call it, small details.

When I first met her, at St. Christine's University in northern Alabama, the pint-sized spitfire had burst through the doorway of our tiny dorm room shouting at her mother just a few steps behind her in the hallway. With her accent thick with the Boston *r*, and her dressed in casual cut-off jean shorts, an AC/DC concert tee, and Chuck Taylors—she was my exact opposite. Ari had forgotten to mention to me that her entire family would be helping her move in.

In minutes, our tiny dorm room was flooded with a slew of Italians shouting about decor, tossing boxes, and scaring the living daylights out of Anne Bowman, otherwise known as my snooty, old-money mother. A heads-up would have saved me so many lectures from Anne, but I couldn't help it—as an only child with zero freedom to express myself, I found Ari's family fascinating. Ari may be unreliable at times when it comes to the details, but when it counts, she's always there for me.

Tossing my phone back in my bag, I grab the flyer Beau gave me. A once-over tells me there is a big town festival this weekend to kick off the fall season. It's called the Hollow Hearts Festival, and it's a celebration of love for the famous witch, Irina Hallowell. The flyer doesn't really give much detail as to what the fuss is about, it sounds like the festival will be a fun fall-themed activity regardless. I don't have a ton of experience in witchcraft or know much of the history of it, but I figure that worst case, I can make up some swoony unrequited love stories for the tourists who might ask about it this week.

I toss the flyer in my bag, getting back to actual work and planning for upcoming restorations. That's the whole reason I'm here, after all—to breathe new beginnings into books that bring life to a beautiful past.

From what I can tell, Beau hasn't been able to keep up with the workload. I'm going to be busy for the next, I'd wager, six to eight months.

Two

Sam

The New Girl Next Door

"Order for Sam," the barista at the Brewhouse calls from behind the busy counter. I make my way around a couple of locals, smiling halfheartedly and avoiding eye contact. The last thing I need this morning is a conversation about the weather or someone (the elderly Beatrice Bushnell) giving me their unsolicited advice on how to make my business more family friendly—when you're covered in tattoos like I am, those are the two most common topics with a crowd like this. I hate both of them.

Wrapping my fingers around the steaming cup of black coffee, I head out the back, pushing the steel exit bar. I make my way into the alley behind the row of businesses lining the west side of Mage Square. There's nothing but a few dumpsters, a stray cat, and a line of trees that disguise this alleyway from the cozy neighborhood behind it. I take a deep breath and a long sip of my drink before turning toward my shop, thankful for a moment alone.

A few steps in, it dawns on me that this is my third cup, and while my first client of the day isn't for a couple more hours, it's not going to do much to steady my hand or allow me to get my stencils drawn up. I shouldn't have stopped for it, but it's been a weird morning. I was up early throwing weights around in the gym, hoping to get last night's text from Bridget—my recently dumped little sister—out of my mind. When that didn't help relieve the urge I have to throttle her ex, I went for a ride.

The quick spin on my bike was supposed to clear my head, to ground me in the cool breeze coasting across my skin, to tamp down the anger and protectiveness coursing through my eldest-brother veins. Instead, it led me to the center of Mage just in time to watch the most beautiful woman I've ever seen all twisted up with a fancy dress around her head and white panties that covered nothing and everything at the same time, on display for all to see. To be fair, I was the only creep that stopped to gawk. I'm not sure anyone else even caught wind of the show, and part of me is thankful. I can't really say why—apart from the way the sight made my jeans feel entirely too tight behind my zipper and sent my heart racing wildly.

I'd shamed myself for being gross and quickly moved on, but then when I finally got my mind to a place of acceptable denial, Mom called and reminded me to pick up the book she had Beau restore. Beau is an old family friend, and he's often polishing up some random find that my mom digs out of the attic. We assist him in keeping his shop in working order and help him with moving boxes from time to time—working for Beau is an even exchange when you consider my mother's ability to lay on the Irish Catholic guilt. Mabel is our matriarch, the mother everyone else wishes they had. My siblings and I love her endlessly, but she has an uncanny ability to insert herself into all kinds of situations, routinely finding tasks for us to do. Supporting Beau is the easiest of those tasks, no doubt.

Come to think of it, she probably knew that I'd stopped and stared at the new beauty and sent me into Black Kettle on purpose. My siblings joke that she has magical powers since she comes from a long lineage dating back to the founders of our town. It's bullshit just like every other legend or tale—there's no such thing as magic. It's more so that the woman has eyes and ears everywhere; nothing happens in Mage Hollow without Mabel O'Reilly knowing about it.

I need to let it go, but I keep thinking about the way Olive called me sir like it was the most natural thing in the world. It pissed me off and turned me on. On the outside, Olive is the total package. But there's something about her demeanor that makes me doubt that what I feel is anything more than physical attraction. It might be the way she wears her confidence like a suit of armor, like she's practiced keeping her poise at all costs. Just when I thought I had her rattled enough to react, she'd blush, then snap right back into smooth Southern belle mode. I'm not used to anything or anyone being *that* polished.

The new girl couldn't be more different from me—so why does she make my heart race and my stomach flip simply from sharing the same air? There's never been a shortage of women to choose from in my life, but with this one, my fingers still itch from the desire I had to wrap them around her long strawberry blonde locks. My skin flushes at the memory of her cheeks turning a dusty pink when I spoke to her. I should have been nicer, but the urge to run my thumb along the freckles dotting the bridge of her nose was as all-consuming as the peculiar need I felt to protect her.

Max, my brother, would say I have a savior complex. And that she's under my skin because I caught her in a vulnerable moment. Maybe that's true, but as much as a part of me wouldn't mind being her knight in shining armor, I couldn't flirt when she was so clearly riding the line of prim and proper and I'm not.

Pulling myself from my thoughts, I slide my key into the lock and let myself into my shop, Eerie Ink. I started tattooing when I was eighteen, a side gig while playing hockey for the local AHL team. But when I realized six years ago that I wasn't ever going to get called up to play at the next level, and that aging out is real, the art of marking skin became my passion.

I sip my coffee, scanning my appointment book. I have a few clients scheduled this afternoon, and I need to draw Jimmy's latest addition on transfer paper so I don't get behind. Taking a seat at my desk, I pull open the drawer and snag a few supplies to get started when the front door jingles. The only people with keys are my sisters and my mom, so it has to be one of them. I take a deep breath and wait patiently to see who's coming to give me hell today.

Bridget pops her head in the doorway of my office. "Hey, Sammy . . ." she says, a shit-eating grin on her face. "Is it just me or did an angel get dropped into Black Kettle Bindery out of nowhere this morning?" *How the fuck does she already know?*

I take another sip of my coffee, ignoring her and beginning to draw. I make three unsteady lines before Bridget plops down on the high-back leather chair in the corner of my office. "I don't know what you're talking about."

She laughs, kicking her feet up over the arm of the chair and pushing her head into the crook of the black leather. "Yes, you do. You're a terrible liar." Bridget narrows her eyes at me. "What do you know, and what aren't you telling me?"

"I don't know anything." I shake my head and try to focus on the task at hand. "Olive is the new girl Beau hired," I mutter under my breath.

"I don't know anything, Bridget, just her name and where she works," my sister mocks. I look at her from across my desk, flattening my lips into a thin line. She holds her hands up in surrender. "I'm just saying, how the hell do you already know her name?"

Before I can open my mouth to answer, her eyes get that twinkle, and she shoots me a knowing look. "Mabel," we say in unison. Bridget tumbles into another bout of laughter, and I shake my head. Leave it to our mother to already be up in the new girl's business not five seconds after she skips into town.

"So, you gonna tell me about how our mother put you in the same room as her, or are we going to pretend that I missed the way your voice went up an octave when you said Olive?"

I pull in a breath, slowly releasing it and trying to play it cool. "Had to pick this up." I point to the carefully wrapped book that I picked up from Black Kettle.

"Of course, Mom would use one of her random attic finds as a tool for setting you up with your next girlfriend." Bridget shakes her head, seemingly in disbelief. "You know, sometimes I don't know how she does it."

"She's a busy body."

"Maybe it's magic."

I suck my teeth, practically hissing at the words. "Let's not get carried away, Bridg. We both know magic isn't real, and she's not my next girlfriend. Olive is way too proper for me. I doubt she's ever even stepped foot in a tattoo shop. Not interested. She's more Max's type anyway," I lie, something I strictly avoid, and a lump hits the back of my throat as a result.

I don't even know her well enough to determine if she is or isn't a match for anyone, but since the moment I saw her, I wanted her for myself, not my baby brother. I've never believed in love at first sight or that magical connection people reference, but something happened when I saw her this morning. It's like my brain rewired itself, and now after one flashing (which she handled like a champ) and a three-minute conversation, she's all I can think about. It's unsettling.

Bridget stares at me with her mouth hanging open. "You're so full of shit it's not even funny. I can just picture it now, you calling Mom and encouraging her to set Max up with Beau's new beauty. What's she like anyway?"

She's not wrong, but the whole thing is so fucking weird. I'm not like this. I don't fall for anyone, even if deep down I want to find my soulmate, to have that profound and unwavering love that my parents have shared for more than thirty years. "Uh, she's Southern and easy to rile up, but it's also like she stepped right out of the country club. Didn't really learn much about her." I shrug and resume drawing.

Bridget shifts in the chair, putting her hands on her knees and leaning forward. "A debutant, really? Interesting. I wonder what she's doing in Mage Hollow." She lifts one eyebrow. I know she's pushing me. Bridget and I are the closest in age in our family, and she's always been able to read me.

I drain the rest of my coffee, throwing the empty cup in the bin that sits under my desk. "Look, I know you're fishing. It was a brief conversation, nothing to tell. How are you holding up? You never texted me back last night." I level her with a look, changing the subject.

"Mmmk, big brother. We'll see." She stands and moves toward the door. "But don't forget that Mom knows everything, and I can tell from your face that you're still picturing her panties."

With that she leaves my office, cackling the whole way to the front door, completely disregarding my question about her breakup. Last night it was the end of the world, and today we are apparently avoiding it all together. It isn't until I hear the familiar jingle and the shop door closing behind her that I realize I never mentioned the flashing. *God damn it, Mabel!*

"Make sure you clean this with antibacterial soap a couple of times a day, then put this on it after so it stays moist," I say, handing Bill a tube of tattoo jelly. I just wrapped up a traditional piece on his forearm, a horseshoe accented with gold and red. It's a cool piece, but I know from experience he's not the best at keeping things clean.

I've learned through years of practice that tattoos with fine details will look like shit if they aren't cared for properly. It doesn't matter how good I am or how precise the lines are. The healing process is critical. My best clients take it seriously, and the ones who don't inevitably return for multiple fixes. I should be grateful for the extra cash, but it's more important to me that they have a quality result.

I finish ringing up Bill, my last appointment of the day, and he makes his way toward the door, stopping next to the window. "Holy shit, who the fuck is that?" he asks, staring at someone across the street.

I move so that I can see around him and am once again paralyzed by her beauty. Every bit of her is stunning. From the blue-and-white dress she's wearing, to her long strawberry blonde hair that's swaying in the breeze. Olive looks like she stepped off the pages of a magazine and landed right on my doorstep.

"That's, uh—she's new in town," I mumble. Shaking my head in an attempt to rattle the thoughts of her out of my brain.

Bill sighs heavily. "She's going to give everyone in this town a run for their money." His assessment makes me chuckle a little. He's not wrong, there is something magnetic about her. I can't help but wonder, like Bridget, why she would even come to Mage. What could have been so appealing about this place that she would willingly work for Beau?

I clap Bill on the shoulder a little too hard. "You better get home to Tracy before word gets back that you were staring at the new girl."

He turns and looks at me, a slow understanding seeming to sink into his features. "Don't worry, Sam. I'm sure she has a thing for guys with tattoos," he says sarcastically.

And that's just it, he's probably right. It's not that ink in your skin makes you an immediate bad boy, it's more that other people assume that's true. I could be the most religious, Bible-toting, saves-kittens-from-trees kind of guy, and it wouldn't change the way people like Beatrice Bushnell, and maybe Olive, see me.

Three

Olive

A Bright Yellow Vest

My feet pound the pavement, the wind whistling through the trees as I run. The sun hasn't risen yet, streetlights cast dark shadows around every corner. There's something exhilarating about the feeling of sweat dripping down my body, the heat in my lungs like a hot-air balloon burner propelling me forward. I'm basking in the warmth of my working muscles, a contrast to the crisp air of early fall in the Northeast. I should be scared by the number of mysterious things lurking just beyond my reach, but the need to feel a rush of adrenaline, to push myself out of my safety net, is freeing.

I round the winding road leading into Mage Square, and my pace slows. The dim glow of the Victorian oil lamps brightens the usually busy center just enough to emphasize the parts of this town I'm beginning to love most. There's the quaint gift shop that's outfitted to supply shoppers with a myriad of magical-themed toys, freakish candy, protective sage, and ancient spell books a plenty. Or Union Tavern, which

I've come to know serves the best turkey Reuben to ever touch my taste buds and beer served at exactly the right temperature in a frosted mug so cold you can almost hear it crackle. There's no shortage of interesting yet slightly corny things to find here. Mage Hollow goes big on playing into their supposed "witchy" past. They claim to be a more accepting version of Salem, the original home of those who prefer black cats and broomsticks over perfectly appointed linens and ocean-themed decor.

A bright glow emanates from the far corner of the square affirming one clear truth: Beau Brooks is no slouch. Despite my initial suspicions about his extended lunch breaks and seemingly ridiculous working hours, the man gets down to business. I've always been an early riser, waking before anyone else to run, ready myself, and of course have coffee—Mom always says a good Southern woman is never seen without a full face of makeup and a smile. That means, getting all the unsightly stuff done before the sun comes up. For the past four days, my morning jog has led me here, only to find the lights illuminating the windows of the Black Kettle while Beau scurries around inside, stocking shelves.

I've offered to come in early to assist, but he always says the same thing: *The morning is my special time, the early bird does not get the worm here, Olive.* I'm tempted to ignore him and show up early anyway. But I don't want him to be annoyed by me just a few days in. I'm trying to make a good impression, to start my career on the right foot. And that's just it, to me it's so much more than a career—it's freedom from the flashing red sign held over my head by every wannabe suitor that reads: *her father has money.* Not to mention my mother who trails behind them ready and willing to sell me off for what is practically the modern-day version of a goat.

Checking my watch to note my mileage and the time, I whip around to head back in the direction I came from. Running past the shop might make Beau squirrely; it's not worth the scolding. I tap the volume on my AirPods up, running quicker to pace with the beat. Darkness encroaches on me, slightly impairing my vision as I make my way back out of the square, carefully watching each of my steps on the cobblestones. I'm making swift progress until I run into a brick wall, or what feels like one, with a thud.

I rip my earbuds out just in time to hear a somewhat familiar and irritatingly sexy voice growl out, "Jesus, the fuck are you doing out here." *Nope, not a wall. Just Sam.*

"Running?" I say, a bit of sarcasm in my tone. It's too early for niceties even if I'm swallowing down the lump of guilt that lodged in my throat as soon as the words left my lips.

"It looks like you're asking to be mugged." He shakes his head at me, or at least I think he does. It's hard to tell as I'm still plastered against his broad chest, his cedar-and-cinnamon scent overwhelming me with every breath I take. I shove off, peeling his grip from my biceps.

"Nope, not that." I glance around to see if anyone is watching, a force of habit from years of learning not to cause a scene. The only thing I notice is a pile of boxes in the back of a truck. Maybe his truck?

Sam shifts his weight back and forth, almost like he's the one who's a bit nervous. "Uh, yeah . . . it was a joke. What would compel you to be out here alone?"

"Running," I repeat. "You know, it's that thing people do for exercise." I try and fail to mask the nerves in my voice.

"Yeah, I've heard of it. But most people that look like you do it in the safe confines of a fancy gym with towels and those disgusting green drinks or whatever." His face turns sour.

I muster my sarcasm, simply to repay the favor of his rudeness. "And here I was thinking you were bringing me a towel, my mistake." I look at him from under my lashes, feeling my stomach twist in guilt again when I notice his face sink just slightly. "Actually, I prefer running in nature." I don't know what's gotten into me, I'm usually a lot better at playing pageant nice. Maybe it's his general air of cockiness that flusters me.

"Sure you do, princess. And I drink pumpkin spice lattes." His ever-present scowl pops back into place, as if my wanting to take in the fresh morning air is offensive. "No need to pretend we're something we aren't," he snips out.

I'm growing tired of his dirty looks. Every time I've come remotely close to him over the last few days, I'm accosted with that glare. At first, I thought maybe he was staring at me, but his gruff tone tells me he has a distaste for my personal brand of being. The feeling's mutual, at least when he speaks. I can't deny his ranking on the lickability scale, much to my dismay.

"Well, this has been . . . delightful. I'm gonna go." I spin on my heels, running briskly toward my cottage. I can feel him watching my retreat and it makes me nervous. There's something about him that seems to get under my skin. Every time I walk (or run) away, I tell myself the next time it'll be different. The next time he won't rattle me.

My morning has been as predictably boring as it could be for only having been here less than a week, anyway. After returning to the cottage and readying myself for work, I stopped into the Brewhouse for a pumpkin spice latte. I second-guessed my coffee choice after the snide remark Sam made, but only for a brief moment before the drink's glorious scent filled my nose and feminism reminded me I have the right to order whatever

I'd like. I didn't walk away from a cushy life and a trust fund just to let another person dictate my every move.

As I push through the door of Black Kettle, a small jingle bellows my arrival at the same time Beau announces, "There's an odd gift waiting for you on your desk." He looks up from where he's seated behind the register, his usual perch, and eyes me over the rim of his round spectacles.

Ignoring his announcement, and assuming it's a euphemism for another restoration to work on, I sing song, "Good morning to you too, Beau," waving my hand in the air smoothly as I walk past the center tables toward my desk. "What in the . . ."

An offensively bright neon yellow vest and matching headlamp greets me, draped on my chair with a note pinned carefully on the fabric:

So you don't run into any more unsuspecting men in the dark.

-S

I don't get him. One minute he's a complete stranger in the middle of the street staring at me like he might enjoy the view, and the next he's grumbling about my lack of self-preservation and leaving me gifts he has to know I'll never use. He doesn't seem to like me. But then again, why the hell would he care if I run in the dark, and why does the whole thing bother me so much?

"I told you it was strange . . ." Beau trails off, walking past me to refill his coffee mug. He shakes his head and lets out a barely audible chuckle before taking a sip.

A heavy sigh escapes me as I clutch the vest in my hands, holding it to my chest. Sam's familiar cedar-and-cinnamon scent creeps into my airspace, momentarily intoxicating me. Snapping out of it, I ask, "What's his deal?" Beau looks at me like he doesn't have even the slightest idea what I'm talking about. "Sam, that's who left this, right?"

He smiles softly, one dimple appearing in his round, rosy cheek. "Sam is a good boy. Owns the tattoo shop across the way. Nothing to worry about with that one, Olivia."

"Okay, but did you see him bring this in? Did he say anything?" I need the elderly man standing in front of me to give me details, to tell me something I can work with.

Where I'm from everyone knows everything—nothing is a secret at the Mobile Country Club. I mean, come on, what would a tattoo artist be doing hauling boxes in the wee hours of the morning or sneaking in to deliver random presents?

"Nope."

One word, that's it? How would Beau not see him? I'm so confused and slightly annoyed. "Look, there's not much to say. I'm not a gossip, young lady. I need you to do something for me this morning."

Choosing not to irritate him with more questions, I nod, letting him know to proceed. "There's a town meeting this morning, in about"—he checks the old-fashioned gold watch dangling from his vest pocket—"five minutes ago. I need you to go in my place." I open and close my mouth a few times, unsure what to make of him asking me to attend a meeting when I'm apparently already late.

Grabbing my bag and stuffing Sam's gift inside, I finally nod before answering, "Okay, uh, where is it?"

"Just over at the library this time. We normally meet for brunch on Sundays, but with the festival, they moved it up." Beau walks back toward the front, setting his mug on the counter and grabbing his book.

"Is there a reason you aren't going? Or is there something you want me to find out? I can take notes," I offer.

He shakes his head. "No need. I just don't feel like listening to it. Let me know if anything interesting happens." Beau dives back into his book, and I make my way to the door. When I have one toe on the threshold, he chimes in again, "Maybe you can thank Sam for the gift."

My stomach flips. I didn't take Beau for a meddler, but I guess he's more of a gossip than I originally thought. I shake my head and scurry as quickly as I can to the large brick building two blocks away.

I haven't had the chance to explore this one yet, but from the outside, the library perfectly matches the rest of Mage's aesthetic. The handle I wrap my fingers around is wrought iron, cool to the touch as I pull it open. The black wooden door is heavy, and I have to throw my whole body into the effort to open it, causing my attempt at a quiet entrance to be all but lost. The door creaks loudly, and every head in the room snaps in my direction.

Just perfect!

Schooling my features, I smile politely and tiptoe around the edge of the room, weaving between the stacks of books that line it in even rows. I'm comforted by their smell—libraries and bookstores are my happy place—that is, until a smug grin greets me from the one and only Sam O'Reilly. The tables that line the center of the room are mostly occupied. There are two open seats to choose from, one next to a woman with silver hair tied up into a bun, and one next to the unfairly attractive tattoo artist, whose blue eyes are practically burning a hole through me.

I start toward the seat by the woman, but she moves her purse to the chair. I take a steadying breath, cautiously tamping down the eye roll I want to give her, and spin on my heel to walk toward Sam. Sliding into the empty chair, I quietly dig my notepad out and face forward just in time for him to lean toward me and whisper, "You have a way of making entrances, don't you, princess?"

Four

Sam

A Tourist in Town

Olive slides delicately onto the chair, and it takes me a minute to get my bearings. Her strawberry scent tickles my nose and I can't help myself, leaning in to give her a hard time. She doesn't acknowledge my statement; instead, the woman who's driving me close to crazy pretends to take notes on the lined paper in front of her.

"There will be a large number of tourists in town starting this afternoon. As the town's event coordinator, I'd like to have a list of which businesses will remain open," Tony states, looking around the room.

A few people raise their hands, Howie nods, and Olive folds her arms across her lap, not saying a word. I clear my throat. "I'm open but by appointment only." Tony nods and looks to Beatrice Bushnell, who owns the flower shop and has for nearly thirty years. Beatrice isn't my biggest fan, but she did me a solid when she moved her bag onto the open chair next to her, forcing Olive in my direction.

"We already have extra bouquets put together and will be selling mums by the pair for porches." She shoots a pointed look at Olive. "If you didn't preorder, don't come asking for any favors." It seems like Beatrice doesn't appreciate the new girl's lack of porch decorations, or maybe it's just that she also can't understand what the new beauty is doing here.

Olive stares at her notepad, picking her fingernails nervously. I elbow her gently, and she glances at me from the side. "Don't worry about her, she's always moody," I whisper. She doesn't respond, instead writing a list of things I've never heard of like *museum wax*, *heavy-duty awl*, and the scariest of all, *bone scorers*.

Tony captures the attention of the room again, adjourning the meeting with a reminder to treat the tourists like guests and to have a good time at the festival. Chairs scrape the wood floor as business owners shuffle out. Olive tears her list off and, clutching the single sheet in her hand, carefully places the notepad back in her bag. "What's a bone scorer?" I ask as she stands. I want to learn more about her, to get her talking.

"Oh, uh, just a tool I use for work." She pushes her chair in—essentially shoving me off both physically and with that answer—and slinks around me toward the door. Her dress sways with each step she takes, and I pause for a beat, admiring her before moving to follow. Thankfully, Tony stops her short of leaving. Instead of standing next to her and blatantly listening, I eavesdrop from beside the door.

"Are you getting settled in okay?" he asks her.

She smiles and nods, answering politely, "The cottage is beautiful. Thank you so much for setting it up."

"It was nothing. You know, Cath had that green couch just waiting to be used. She was excited you were coming, we all were." Tony puts a hand on her shoulder and looks at her like she's one of his daughters. *Are they related?*

Olive laughs lightly. "Cath is a doll. She just knew I was admiring that velvet from afar. Honestly, I appreciate your support so much. I've been meaning to make it over to thank you both, and to drop off a bottle of wine."

"It's our pleasure." He pulls her into a hug, releasing her quickly. "Call me if you need anything, and remember to kick the trash bin before you open it in case there's a critter inside. Take care."

Olive bristles a little and then, smiling once again, turns toward me and the door I'm blocking. "Sam." She looks between my body and the door. "Have a good day." Her voice is like honey, the sound rolling out and over me.

"Actually"—I open the door for her and gesture for her to exit—"I was going to walk with you back to Black Kettle. I need to, uh, ask Beau . . . something."

Smooth, Sam.

"Oh, okay."

We step down to the cobbled sidewalk and walk side by side in silence as we pass not one, not two, but three buildings. It takes me a minute to get the nerve to say something. For some reason I think no matter what I say, it'll be wrong. "How do you know Tony?"

Olive looks at me from under her lashes before returning her gaze to the ground. "He's my best friend's father." She shifts her bag from one shoulder to the other, bringing her hand down to her side. "Tony and Cath are amazing."

I step just slightly closer to her as we walk, my hand nearly brushing hers. There's probably a centimeter between our pinkies, and I notice a flush race up her neck as the proximity must become obvious to her too. "Why did you come to Mage?" I ask.

She looks at me tentatively before replying, "For the job. To work with Beau. I went to school for historic preservation, and I guess that's not as popular of a career as I anticipated." Olive looks from me to the ground and then back to me. "But I really love it, being able to take something that is all but ruined and give it life again." The way her voice picks up, I can tell she's sincere and smart. I wouldn't even begin to know what goes into her work. Before Mom started cleaning out the attic and making us help Beau, I didn't even know book restoration was a thing.

"It must take some practice to do something so tedious. You said you studied that in school?"

"Yep. Got the master's degree to prove it. But it's not as delicate or glamorous as you might think. Most of the time it's pretty messy actually." She smiles at me softly, and I feel like I won the lottery. This girl is smarter than she lets on, six years of studying anything makes her brilliant as hell in my book.

"I know a little something about meticulous work that's messier than one would think." *Jesus, Sam.* That didn't sound thirsty at all—*get it together.* "You should come by—"

"Oh, no offense, but I could never get a tattoo." Her statement stings a little. I don't care if she doesn't have them but does she dislike them? I was trying to suggest she stop in, not let me give her one. Clearly it was a failed attempt at finding a way to talk to her, again.

"That's cool, but back to why you chose Mage." I have to change the subject before she says anything else that could confirm my suspicions (the completely made-up ones) about her hatred for my life's work. "Is there somewhere else you could do it? I mean, you don't seem like the type to live here."

I don't mean for my words to come off rude, but it's honest, and I'm trying to investigate my assumptions unlike her. Sure, our town is eclectic and interesting at times, but we aren't fancy. She seems too country club for a place this grounded, too beautiful and put together. It's like that movie *Overboard*, where the heiress learns to live amongst the regular working people.

A breath escapes her pouty lips. "You don't know anything about me," she retorts before pushing into Black Kettle Bindery and all but running to the back of the store.

Shit!

I just wanted to start a conversation, but apparently with this one, I can't do anything but say the wrong words at the right time. Instead of following her, I turn on my heel and head back toward Eerie Ink.

Five

Olive

I Can Buy My Own Drinks

Ugh! I groan and roll my shoulders back, shaking the tension from my limbs to force myself to stop reflecting on the day I've had. I cannot allow Ariella to sniff out my latest obsession. I don't even know why I'm so fixated on him. He seems sort of like a jerk, and I'm here to do one thing—work. Speaking of the she-devil, I spot Ariella across the room, sauntering toward me in a leather miniskirt, a white silk tank, and heels. She looks like a sex kitten on the prowl, rather than someone meeting her bestie for happy hour.

"Hi. Oh my God, I can't believe you're here and we finally get to do this," she says, greeting me cheerily with a hug.

"I mean, if you weren't a big hotshot marketing boss, we could've done this any day this week." I grin so she knows I'm joking and not at all sad that I've been left to settle in alone my first week in town.

"Uh, yeah. I wish that all jobs came with a summer break. Working is the worst." She lays her head on the table, emphasizing her exhaustion from what could only be too much adulting.

"New job's that good?"

A smile blossoms on her face. "Actually, it is. I am hopelessly in love with marketing. I'm having so much fun, I just feel like a bad friend. How's Beau?" She wiggles her eyebrows and giggles at her own question.

"Whatever do you mean? Beau is a peach. *So* easy to work for. Not grumbly at all." I laugh with her. Beau is pretty great in reality, but he's an old man. Very set in his ways with expectations for everything.

The server, an attractive man with red hair and adorable dimples, slides up to our table. "Hey, Ariella, how's it going? Haven't seen you in a while." His voice crackles with something suspiciously close to nerves as his cheeks turn just a smidge past rosy.

"Hi, Howard. It's so great to see you." Ari places her hand on top of his resting at the edge of the table. "Can we get three witches' brews and three shots of tequila?" She freaking *winks* as she glides her fingers deftly over his hand.

"Y-yes. Coming right up." He scurries away on a mission to secure our beverages.

"Umm, what was that?" I ask, raising an eyebrow at her. Ari has always had way more confidence than me when it comes to men. She doesn't get nervous and awkward like I do.

"Oh, that's just Howie. We went to high school together . . . and he always gives me free drinks. I think he used to have a crush on me back in the day." She shrugs me off like I can't see the pink tinge creeping up her neck.

"Mmmk. We will be exploring that at some point. Who's the third drink for?" I ask, curiosity getting the better of me.

"Oh. Sorry, I forgot to mention I invited Meg. I hope that's okay."

"Of course. I love your sister," I reply, meaning it. Meg is younger than us by two years, but she's a freaking blast. Always up to no good or scheming up a new plan, she makes Ari's wild look tame.

Howie delivers our drinks along with something that, if I'm not mistaken, looks like a zero-dollar tab. Part of me hopes he didn't comp our check just to get in Ari's good graces, but the other part of me isn't mad about not paying for them if it means I get to watch whatever's going on with them unfold. I'm too nosy and interested in her love life to stop. I'll leave him a big tip to compensate.

As I take my first refreshing sip of witches' brew, more commonly known during the months that don't end in *b-e-r* as sangria, a very casually dressed Meg slides into the booth next to Ari. With a mischievous grin adorning her face, she doesn't have to say a word before I know I'm in trouble.

"*So*, Olive. How has Mage been welcoming you so far?" she asks, a knowing smirk dancing on her lips.

"Fine. Uneventful," I respond, glaring at Ari since she so obviously told her sister about my new gig as the town stripper.

"Meet anyone interesting?"

"Not really, should I have?"

"Nope." She pops the *p* on the word emphatically.

"What's happening right now?" Ari chimes in, glancing between us suspiciously. *Okay, maybe she didn't tell her?*

I widen my eyes at Meg, trying to decipher what the play is here. I haven't done anything other than go to work, get coffee, and spend an irritating amount of time wondering about mystery man, Sam.

"Oh, nothing. A little bird told me that Olive has a new friend in town, and frankly, I was shocked to hear who Little Miss Sunshine has made an impression on." Mischief paints her face, illuminating just how much of a scoundrel she really is. Ari looks at me, clearly wondering what I've been withholding.

"Oh, please. I haven't made an impression on anyone. Other than working at the store and my normal morning run, I've barely left the cottage," I repudiate her claim.

"Not what I've heard. Rumor has it, a certain sexy tattoo artist has staked his claim on the new little lady in town." She's goading me, and I don't appreciate it one single bit.

"You've met Sam?" Ari asks, a hint of glee in her eyes.

"Uh, fine. Yes, I've run into him a few times. Once at work when he was picking up an order, once at the town business meeting that Beau conned me into, and once on my morning run when I literally ran into him. Other than that, he's mainly taken to glaring at me from across the street." Covering my face with my hands, I wait for the onslaught of questions. Instead, their cackles rapidly turn into outright hysterics. I wait for them to say something more, but my patience is waning. "What is so funny?"

"Sam is the one guy that every girl in this town is in love with, not counting us, obviously. It's hilarious that all it takes is one Southern belle strutting into town, and he's gone all caveman," Meg says between sucks of air as she continues to fall apart.

"Okay, let's not get carried away. The guy isn't even nice to me. He acts like I'm an idiot . . . He even left me a fluorescent running vest so that I don't make the mistake of accidentally bumping into him again. I'm positive your source has it wrong."

I'm not sure who I'm trying to convince at this point, them or me. He's nothing like the other guys I've dated, but then again, most of my dates have been with a bunch of sticks-in-the-mud who my parents insisted on setting me up with. They all either wanted me to ask my father to invest in their latest start up or enjoyed telling me all the ways I needed to transform myself to be a better fit for them. After years of trying to mold myself into the perfect package my mother expected me to be, the last thing I need is another person to remind me of my shortcomings.

"Sam is a catch, don't get me wrong. But the funny part is, he thinks he actually stands a chance," Meg says, once again wiggling her eyebrows at me.

"What is that supposed to mean?" I huff, downing the remainder of my drink.

"Oh, come on. We all know you're . . . How should I say this? Closed off? When it comes to dating, I mean." She shrugs as if she didn't just pinpoint one of my greatest insecurities. I'd love to be open to it, to wear my heart on my sleeve. I'm just not sure the thing thumping in my chest can withstand any more rejection before forgetting how to beat all together. I take back what I said about loving Meg.

"That's not true. He's just not my type," I say, defending myself before it's really necessary.

Ari shakes her head and sucks a healthy amount of sangria through her straw. "Do you have a type?"

"I, uh, yeah. Of course, I do." Not that I could tell anyone what it is. I try to keep my distance—I've spent most of my life working to meet expectations. In the past, the men I've dated haven't been any different than my parents, always trying to fit me into a perfect little box. And while most of the time that's my comfort zone, it's also exhausting to be stuck there. It's easier to avoid the whole dating thing in general, keep people at an arm's length so they never have a chance to be disappointed with me.

"Mmmk. We'll definitely be coming back to this." Ari throws my words from earlier back in my face as I inadvertently allow another groan to slip past my lips. Damn that beautiful man-child and his sexy-as-heck tattoos.

"Are you planning to go to this Hollow Hearts thing tomorrow?" I ask, desperately trying to steer this conversation away from Sam and my dating life in general.

In unison the sisters respond with a resounding, "Of course!"

It's the best event of the season besides Halloween itself," Meg adds.

"Tell me more. You know I'm a sucker for a good opportunity to people watch."

"I mean, the whole thing is kind of sad really. There was this witch Irina who escaped here from the trials . . ." Ari's referring to the famous Salem witch trials, Beau informed me of that much. "She was supposedly courting one of the judges, and he was supposed to escape with her to avoid the trials. But legend has it that something went wrong, and they didn't end up together. She died an old, lonely woman. No one really knows the whole story, but we celebrate her escape. It's sort of like the antithesis of Valentine's Day. Being single and lonely is the name of the game."

"That sounds . . . depressing?" I question their enthusiasm for what seems like a pretty dark event.

"No, it's a blast. There's a lot of cute crafts and seasonal decor to peruse, spiked cider, usually a kissing booth or risqué bobbing for apples. It'll be the perfect way to introduce you around, since you're definitely not interested in Sam," Meg chimes in while they both raise an eyebrow in my direction.

"Great! Maybe I'll visit the kissing booth more than once," I shoot back, not convincing anyone that I will be going within five feet of such a thing. I don't do casual, but I don't do committed either. Three dates is my sweet spot. No one can get hurt in such a brief period of time—and my mother can't get her hopes up.

They roll their eyes but thankfully go back to chatting about work and Meg's return to college. She's just home for the festival, which is better for me. I don't need the nosy Nellie tracking my whereabouts or who I have and haven't met yet.

After another drink, we're all yawning and ready to pack it in for the evening—adulthood. Meg and Ari stand from our booth, giving me gentle hugs and waves goodbye. I'm lingering a bit. I still need to get to Howie and either give him a large tip, or demand that he allows me to pay him for my bill. The guilt of drinking for free is eating at me.

Standing, I peer out across the dark tavern, searching for the adorable redhead. My eyes land on a set of unmistakably blue ones staring me down, yet again. He's sitting next to an attractive man that's chattering away while Sam isn't paying the slightest bit of attention. Instead, he's locked in on me, looking better than I've ever seen him in a backwards hat. *Did he have to wear the hat, I mean, really?* Choosing not to engage more than necessary, I nod at him in acknowledgment but head toward the opposite end of the hand-hewn bar. Howie saunters over, an apologetic look etched across his brow.

"Howie. I'm Olive. I need to pay you for my drinks." Direct and firm, not giving him a chance to deny I've been indulging for free.

"I-I c-can't let you do that, Miss Olive," he stutters, his nerves evident in how furiously he's wiping the already clean bar top.

"I won't tell Ari. I promise. I don't want you to get in trouble."

"Oh. I didn't. Ari drinks on her dad's tab, although now that you mention it, I probably shouldn't have told you that because she thinks I give her free drinks. And well, if she believes that, maybe . . . You know what? Nope. Never mind." He's talking in circles, and I can't help but smile at his innocence. I want to pinch his cheeks and put him in my pocket. He's so cute in a nervous and maybe a little nerdy kind of way.

"Okay, well please let me pay you. I can't let you put my drinks on Tony's tab."

"I didn't. Sam paid," he says, shrugging like it's not a big deal when in fact it's a huge deal—to me.

"Nope." I toss forty bucks on the bar. "Give him his money back or keep it. But please tell him that I do not take free drinks from strangers. If he's going to pay for things, he has to ask permission first." I wink, turning to make a quick exit before any arguing ensues. Howie might tell him or he might not. Either way, my conscience is clear. I don't owe anyone a thing.

Six

Sam

Sam's Sandwich Service

"Dude, quit staring at her. You're making it weird." Max smacks me on the shoulder, redirecting my focus from where Olive stands at the other end of the bar. I tip my beer to my lips, shrugging at his comment.

I've been playing this little game of cat and mouse with her for the past few days, and while I'm still not convinced there could be anything between us other than physical attraction, it's been a fun and educational new hobby. Like when she ran into me, I was shocked to see her outside and not in a gym. I didn't expect her to enjoy the great outdoors or be unafraid to run in the dark. It surprised me, in a good way, and I can't help but wonder if maybe there's more to her than meets the eye.

I'm pretty positive she doesn't find me equally as intriguing, but why would she? I'm not fancy like she is. I'm also thirty-two compared to her maybe twenty-four—but the biggest reason lies with how grumpy I've been toward her during each interaction. I can't name the reason for my mood, I think it's just her. Something about the way she snaps that mask right into place when we interact, it drives me crazy that I can't do a single thing to keep her walls down, even just for a second.

"You gonna tell me what this is all about, anyway?" Max nudges my shoulder again, sipping his beer. "Bridg said she thinks you have a little crush."

I scoff at him, motioning for the bartender to come over, when I spot Olive walking out the oversized front door. "It's nothing, she's just new in town. She needs someone to look out for her." Max coughs into his fist muffling the word *bullshit*, like we are teenagers again.

Howie approaches, laying two twenties on the dark wood bar in front of me. "She, uh, she said you can't buy her drinks without asking permission." I can tell by his body language that he doesn't want to be in the middle of whatever he *thinks* is going on. He's fidgeting with a bar rag and looking at his shoes instead of making eye contact.

I was trying to be nice, to buy her drinks to make up for being kind of an ass before. I guess I should have been more direct . . . Why am I so bad at this all of a sudden? I push the money back to him. "Take it. Consider it a consolation for trying." He nods at me, walking away to slip the bills into the tip jar that's teetering on the edge of the backlit shelf, opposite of where I'm sitting. "Can I get a turkey Reuben to-go with fries," I call over to him. He doesn't reply, just lifts his chin in acknowledgement.

"Where are you gonna put that?" Max asks, raising his brow at my order.

We just finished eating no less than fifteen minutes ago, so it probably does seem weird for me to request a second dinner. But he doesn't know that I noticed Olive's lack of a meal. That I saw and disliked the thought of her not, at the very least, leaving with a warm sandwich to eat when she gets home. I don't know why I feel compelled to look out for her, to take care of her. She carries herself around like she's got her shit together, but

I guess I've noticed, in the little moments when no one else is watching, how she picks her fingernails or glances at groups of people talking as if she wishes she was included. Like earlier today, when I stood outside of Black Kettle waiting for her to see the gift I left her, I thought it was going to be entertaining, that I'd get to watch her not play it cool for once. Instead, she clutched the vest tightly to her chest before tossing it aside and saying something to Beau. Maybe I'm being presumptuous, but it made me think—even if she would never admit it—that the gift meant something to her. She may be a debutant, a Southern belle on the outside, but there's more to her, and I want to find out what it is, even if I shouldn't.

Max elbows me, this time in the ribs, "Hello . . . are you going to answer me?" Pulling me back from staring at the TV that's airing some late-season baseball game I'm not actually paying attention to.

I chuckle a little, finishing the last swig of my lager. "It's for my fucking lunch tomorrow. Not everything is a big conspiracy."

My brother laughs, an outright bellow of a sound. "Now that's really bullshit. Mom's making tortellini tomorrow for the festival." He looks at me, his eyes trying to decipher what I'm up to. "It's for the girl, isn't it?"

"No, Max." I sigh heavily. "It's for tomorrow, between appointments. I have to eat something. I can't be running out to get an early meal from Mom, at least not if I intend to be done in time to help with set up." I'm overexplaining, lying through my teeth to my only brother.

I hate lying, and I've done it twice this week. But I don't need anyone meddling even more than my mother surely already is. And I haven't even decided if I'm actually going to drop the sandwich off. This whole thing could be true, I could lose my nerve and not put it on her porch. Thankfully, I don't have to keep up the ruse for long as Howie slides a paper bag across the bar to me. When I take my wallet out to pay, he holds a hand up and shakes his head no.

I shift to stand. "Thanks, Howie," I say, smiling at the man who just reduced his tip to give me this food. I place my hand on Max's shoulder. "Bye, bro. See ya tomorrow." I clap his back one time and walk out the door, hoping I can muster the courage to actually deliver this thing.

Pushing into the crisp early-fall air, I take a deep breath and head out of the square. I'm not being creepy by knowing where Olive is staying; I actually know the owner of the home she's renting, and it happened to naturally come up in conversation. It's also on the way to my place, so if it doesn't look like she's there or awake, I can just carry on. How the hell *am* I going to deliver this, though? That's the real question. Drop it on the porch and ring the doorbell? I don't have her number. Fuck, I didn't think past my ridiculous urge to feed her.

Rounding the corner, the faint sound of a porch swing swaying in the breeze tickles my ears. Olive's hair blows in the breeze with it, like fire dancing in the moonlight.

Shit!

I also didn't think about how I would handle actually seeing her. Dropping the bag via an old-school ding-dong ditch felt easier than talking to her. Don't get me wrong, I love the view, but we don't exactly have the best track record when it comes to even something as basic as talking. I take my steps slowly, trying to buy enough time to figure out what I'm going to do, but she spots me approaching when I'm about a house away.

"Sam?" Olive calls out.

I increase my pace, moving to stand at the end of the path leading to her porch. "Yeah, funny seeing you here." She's dressed down, almost like she's ready for bed.

"At my house?" she asks, standing to move to the porch steps, bringing her adorably relaxed face into my view. She's holding a book.

I run my free hand over my hair and down my neck, scratching lightly. "Uh, yeah. I, um, know the owner. I guess I heard someone had rented it recently." I don't admit to outright knowing this is where she's living. My stomach flops with the awkwardness of this whole thing.

She smiles sweetly, that same pageant-worthy, bless-your-heart look, "*Okay* . . . good night." Olive turns toward the door, but I stop her by stepping through the gate, causing a creaking sound as I do. She whips back around, a puzzled look on her face.

"I noticed that you didn't eat. At Union. I thought maybe you'd want this." I reach my hand out, showing off the to-go bag. "Consider it my apology for trying to buy your drinks."

She cocks one hip out to the side, placing her hand flat against it. "Is there something about me that screams, I want to eat your leftovers?" she asks, the line between her brows deepening at the same time the practiced smile slips into place. I have the sudden urge to run my thumb over it, to smooth out the confusion.

"It's not leftovers. I, uh, got it for my lunch tomorrow." Her face morphs from puzzled to frustrated, and I know I messed up. What I said doesn't make sense even to me. Why am I so rattled by her? This is why I keep acting like a pissed-off jerk around her. It's like I forgot how to be normal, and I'm frustrated with myself but I take it out on her.

Olive stares at me, her mouth opening and closing a few times before she abandons her stance and sits down on the top step of her porch. "I have to be honest." She lets out a chuckle quietly to herself, placing a hand over her mouth. "I don't really know how I'm supposed to respond here."

I take a few steps closer, stopping when I'm about a foot from the bottom of the three steps leading to her cottage. "Can I sit?" I try to convey with my eyes that I'm going to attempt to not be rude to her for once. "Just so I can explain." Olive nods, peering up at me with something suspiciously close to a grin.

I brush a few stray leaves from the bottom stair, cleaning a spot to take my seat. Once settled sideways so that I can see her while we talk, I sit the bag of food next to her. A few beats of silence pass as we take each other in, both of us vacillating between examining the other person and looking off into the distance.

"Are you going to explain, or are we just sitting here?" she asks, leaning toward me, saying it no louder than a whisper. It's almost like she's pretending we are sharing a secret, and it makes me laugh.

"Honesty time?" I raise an eyebrow, waiting for permission to proceed. When she nods, I continue, "Union Tavern makes the best turkey Reuben known to man. Eating it is a rite of passage in Mage Hollow."

Olive looks at the bag, then me, then the bag, and back to me. "And you thought that because I'm new you would bring me a sandwich at"—she checks the time on her phone—"9:45 on a Friday night? I've had it before, by the way."

"I was just being neighborly. Is that a crime, princess?" My words come out a little gruffer than intended, again. She has a right to think this is bizarre. I would. But at the same time, I had good intentions, and is it my fault that she turns me into a bumbling idiot in her presence? She seems to keep perceiving my attempts at flirting as being annoying or belittling . . . I swear, I used to be better at this.

Olive places her hand on her chest. "Well, isn't that sweet of you." The Southern accent in her voice comes out much thicker than normal. She's mocking me. I wouldn't say I don't deserve it, but it's still annoying. I already know she's brilliant and beautiful—I didn't know that I needed to add a sense of humor to the list of positives.

I move to stand, reaching for the bag next to her. "Well, I'll just take this back then, princess. Since you don't seem to like your neighbors." A grin lifts the corner of my mouth at the same time a red blush sweeps up her neck. Olive attempts to swat my hand away, but I grab the bag and shift it into the hand furthest from her.

"I, uh, I like my neighbors just fine." She stands and reaches across my body, brushing her chest against mine accidentally. I don't miss the heavy breath she sucks in through clenched teeth at the contact. In this close proximity, I can practically see her pulse racing at the side of her neck. "And I love turkey Reubens."

I let her snag the bag from my hand, not moving an inch away from her. "Maybe we could get—"

"I better get inside. It's late."

Olive takes a step back, replacing the distance we momentarily lost. I can't help but notice the slightly rosy appearance of her cheeks. "You're welcome, princess," I say, winking at her in hopes that the pretty red flush will creep up her neck one more time. Even if she did dodge my attempt to ask her out, I like knowing I affect her in some way.

Without a word, Olive turns on her heel and marches inside her house. When the door closes and the lock clicks into place, a "Thanks, Sam" cascades across the quiet night air, muffled only by the door between us.

Seven

Olive

The Hollow Hearts Festival

"Yes, Mother. I understand." I nod as if she can see me. Thank heavens she can't or I'd definitely be up a creek for the numerous eye rolls I've tossed her direction over the last . . . Ack! Thirty minutes.

"I just don't want you to think that anyone would judge you if you came home. I mean, we all know this is a phase and you will realize you need to settle down. I wouldn't want Theodore to be snatched up while you're up there gallivanting." Teddy is the esteemed son of an oil tycoon. In other words, the perfect husband for Anne Bowman's one and only daughter.

"Mother, it's not a phase. It's my career, and you know, I just looked at the time. Ari will be here any minute for the festival. You wouldn't want me to look disheveled now, would you?" I twist the knife, preying on what has to be her greatest fear. Someone could snap a photo of one of us looking average. The horror.

"Okay, make sure you wear Pillow Talk lipstick. It's your best shade, dear. And for God's sake, don't slouch."

Don't slouch? I'm walking around an outdoor festival, how would I even pull that off? "Okay, Mother. Pillow Talk lipstick and no slouching. Gotta run." I hang up, immediately slouching further into the couch just to spite her. You'd think after years of trying to fit the mold she crafted for me, I'd be used to it. But her words still sting every time just as much as the first.

A knock cuts my pettiness short. I hop up to greet Ari and Meg at the door.

"Hey, wow you look . . . Is that Pillow Talk?" Dang it, I can't help that it's truly the best shade.

"Yes, but don't tell my mom."

"Why would I tell your mom? She hates me," Ari says.

"Never mind. Is this okay to wear?" I spin slowly to show off my outfit. I opted for tight black jeans, Doc Martens, an oversized cream cable-knit sweater, and a bow in my half pulled-back hairstyle. The bow, a pale rust color with creamy lace, is my favorite part.

"You look perfect. Do you have a tank on in case you get hot from all the smooching?" Meg coos.

"Shut up, Meg." Turning to Ari, I ask jokingly, "When does she leave again?"

I grab my crossbody, and we head out. A quick lock of my door and I'm in the fresh air, heading toward the first of what I hope is many Mage Hollow events. As I step off of the porch, an image of Sam flashes in my mind.

I think he was trying to be sweet last night. He was endearing with the way he wanted to take care of me. No one's ever worried about me like that before. And a part of me wanted to keep talking to him, but when I started to feel the slightest bit of comfort, he called me princess and took me right back to all the ways I'll never live up to that title, not the real me anyway. I wish I could. I wish I was open and fun and . . . normal. But just like all the other times I've had a slight interest in someone, the thoughts of them seeing my flaws overwhelms me. With Sam, it's tenfold: He's handsome and funny, gruff and demanding. He makes my head feel like it's in one of those paint mixers, all shaken up and confused. I don't know how I could ever anticipate what he wants or needs in a relationship, how I could ever meet expectations.

As we turn the bend into Mage Square, I'm hit with a myriad of emotions, pulling me back into the moment. Shock. Awe. Insane wonder. If every resident brought three friends, there still wouldn't be this many people in the square. They're everywhere, pouring in and out of the Brewhouse, lined up to get in the tavern, hunkering down on the curb and stuffing a variety of seasonal delicacies in their faces. I love it.

Beau refusing to open the shop today suddenly makes so much sense. Far too many sticky fingers to be touching our precious gems of history. I honestly can't decide where to look first. Ari leads the way, and I'm thankful I don't have to choose.

We browse the craft section, chock-full of tables lined with hand-made gifts, decor, and the occasional home-cooked soap or lotion sprinkled in. Meg buys some fall-scented wax melts to stave off her roommate's "affinity for sweaty men." I pick up a string of pom-pom garland that's the perfect shades of pink and peach to match my hippie Halloween vibe.

"Are you hungry?" Ari asks us.

"I could eat," Meg replies.

"Sure," I say, my stomach rumbling at the suggestion.

"You have to try the pumpkin ricotta tortellini that Mrs. O'Reilly serves." Ari grabs our hands and leads the way.

"O'Reilly? As in Sam O'Reilly?" I ask, narrowing my eyes at her.

"Yeah, she's his mom. She only makes them once a year, and it's a must-have," Meg explains.

"Sounds weird but okay, if y'all insist." I'm helpless to resist. I don't want to admit it, but meeting the woman who made Sam is an opportunity I can't miss.

We link arms and walk toward the end of the square. I can't help but notice the way the trees lining the street get more vibrant every day. Fall is beautiful here, captivating in a way that even if there wasn't an event, it would still feel like Mother Nature was hosting her own party, with ribbons of scarlet and orange strung from each tree. At the other end of the cobblestone street, the tents and tables are spaced wider to accommodate the food section, allowing people to spread out. I spot Howie at the tavern's booth and give him a brief wave. He's become somewhat of a friend now that I frequent his work for lunch and am emotionally invested in the crush he shares with Ari—the one that neither of them will confirm but that I'm convinced needs to happen.

"Figures the line would be long," Meg complains.

She's not kidding. There are at least fifty people in front of us waiting. The tortellini must really be worth it.

"After we eat, we should check out some of the games." Ari wiggles her brows at me.

"I'm not kissing anyone," I spit out, putting my hands up in surrender. Inside, I'm frustrated. I wish that I could let go of worrying about what others might think or how I could be perceived. That I could open up and be carefree, just for one day.

"That tracks," a familiar voice growls out to me, in passing. I turn to look, and yep. As suspected, it's Sam. Except he's not alone. He's walking in the other direction with his arm draped around another woman. My heart flutters as heat and annoyance crawl up my neck.

"You okay?" Ari wraps her arm around my shoulders.

Desperate not to show the angst I feel, I respond, "Totally. Yeah. Why wouldn't I be?" My voice shakes with unease.

"I just . . . Look, we were just giving you a hard time the other night. I know you aren't with anyone because the right person hasn't come along, not because there's anything wrong with you," she reassures me.

"No, I know that. I told you. He's not my type. He's a . . ." I glance behind me, watching him retreat. "Um, he's a walking red flag." I don't know if I believe the words I'm saying, but he's so hot and cold, it's the only logical conclusion I can make.

"He's the furthest thing from a red flag." Meg presses her lips together, like she's thinking of a way to explain. "I know he looks like your everyday bad boy, but he's super kind, the type that would carry your grandma's groceries to the car, that kind of nice."

"I'm sorry, but that's not the version of himself he's shown me. He's so wishy-washy. First the flashing incident and rubbing my face in it. Then scolding me for running alone and giving me a vest to mock me. Not to mention trying to pay my tab last night, like I'm not a big girl who can take care of herself, and then showing up to my house with a sandwich." I'm rambling, the onslaught of encounters pouring from my lips.

"Hold the fuck up. Did you say the flashing incident?" Ari gasps, pulling both my arms so I'm facing her completely.

"Umm. Yep. There was one witness." I groan, shaking free from her grip and covering my face.

Laughter erupts from our small circle. Ari and Meg fall apart so loudly I can't help but join in. We cackle to the point of wheezing, the kind of laughing that's silent because it's coming from so deep.

An older gentleman behind us in line clears his throat, dramatically crossing his arms and nodding as if to say, *You're next, move it along*.

"Hello, girls. I assume you want the special?" a beautiful woman with chocolate-brown hair and soft features inquires. Ari and Meg nod emphatically. "Who is this darling little thing?" the woman asks.

"Hi. I'm Olive. It's nice to meet you, ma'am." The politeness drips from my words like honey.

"A Southern belle, oh boy. My sons are going to be like a pack of ravenous vultures when they see you. My name's Mabel O'Reilly. Please look me up if they give you any trouble." Her words are sweet but there's a sternness to her brows, like she actually expects me to find her and tattle if they are ever up to no good.

"Sam already has his eye on her, from what I'm told," Meg chimes in. When is this girl going to learn to quit airing my business? I might kill her before she goes back to college.

"That sounds right. He's always been a sucker for the cute ones. But Max might give him a run for his money this time. Wait, are you the new little thing working for Beau?" Mabel winks at Meg like they are conspiring to conjure up my dating dreams. She's asking, but it seems like she already knows the answer.

"Yes, that's me." I can feel the pink painting my cheeks.

"Oh good. I've been meaning to call you. I have this old book I found in our attic. I'd like to have it examined and restored, but it's too fragile to transport. I'm afraid I will ruin it if I touch it too much. Do you make house calls?" She's peering at me with hopeful eyes, but the truth is, if it's in that poor of condition I probably can't help her.

"Oh, um. I'm actually not sure. Beau hasn't said anything about that. Could you put on some gloves and bring it in that way?"

"Oh, sweet thing, you have to come see it. I can't do any of the remaining cleaning in the attic until it's moved, and I'm really on a deadline. You must come over tomorrow, say around four." It's a statement, she isn't asking. Ari and Meg shoot me looks that ask what the big deal is as I take my plate from a man who looks so similar to Sam, he's almost certainly his father.

"Okay, I'll come by and have a look, but I'm not sure if I can help. I'm excited to try this too by the way. Ari and Meg have been going on and on about it. It was nice to meet you." I exchange phone numbers with Mabel before offering a small smile and walking away. I couldn't stand there all day, even if I had too many questions to count about these O'Reilly brothers.

We take our time devouring Mabel's delicious delicacy. When Ari and Meg said I had to try it, I was skeptical. But I'm pleased to report that the tortellini are like soft, buttery pillows that sit weightlessly on your tongue. When I bit into the first one, an explosion of fall wrapped around me like a warm blanket. I'd consider dating any of her children for the opportunity to snag this recipe.

"Ready to check out the games?" Ari asks, moving a bit slower now that we are all stuffed to the gills.

"Yes, but maybe we should have done that first. I need a nap." Groaning, I pull her and Meg toward the trash bin to deposit our empty plates.

We walk toward the carnival section of the festival, stopping only to buy tickets so that we can play. I spot the balloon darts game first, then there's a pumpkin toss set up, apple bobbing, and the one and only kissing booth. Opting to steer clear of any potential lip locking, I lead us to the pumpkin toss. A few rounds in, it's safe to say we aren't any better than the seven-year-olds we are matched against, but I feel free. For once, I'm having fun, letting my hair down.

"I don't know about you, but I think I'll snag a smooch or two. The hockey team is stacked with hotties this year," Meg chirps.

Apparently the local AHL team hosts the booth every year. Meg wasn't joking when she said there's a few tall drinks of water over there. Ari and I follow, exchanging glances to communicate that we are absolutely not participating. That is, until I get about ten feet closer and see Sam laughing with that woman, his arm still draped over her shoulder.

I have no claim to him—heck, I don't even really like him. There's just something soul-shatteringly annoying about seeing the man show up on my doorstep with a meal one day as if he's hitting on me, and then being on a date with someone else the next. I have a hard enough time letting anyone in. It irks me that the one guy who's been able to overwhelm me even a little is turning out to be a player. This is why I don't even try anymore.

Deciding not to let him stir me up and to take back a little of my self-respect, I take a leap and step up to the booth, asking, "Who's the star player?"

"That would be me, beautiful. I always score," says a six-foot-something sex symbol with shaggy brown hair, stomach-turning dimples, and piercing green eyes.

"How much will these get me?" I hold up a string of tickets as long as my arm.

He winks and my stomach drops, not in a good way. "I'll kiss you for free." He's too eager, which means it won't be a great kiss. Probably all tongue, no subtlety. See, this is the problem. Even when I want to, I can't just let go and live a little. I glance slightly toward the man who's got me all hot and bothered—not the one in front of me. He's still draped over the other woman. *Screw it.*

"Alright, let's do it." I throw caution to the wind despite my internal protest.

He reaches out, gently caressing the side of my face. I close my eyes, leaning ever closer when "I don't fucking think so, Max" ricochets through my ears. A hard, calloused hand slides between mine and Max's faces, inadvertently grazing my lips. I don't have to open my eyes to know that voice.

Anger bubbles just under my skin. *Do not make a scene, do not make a scene . . .* My eyes snap open to stare down Sam.

"What do you think you're doing?" I ask, tone terse, jaw locked, sweet Southern charm nowhere to be found. Mom always said it wasn't often that I got my feathers ruffled, but when I did, I could get madder than a hornet in two seconds flat. She also always reminded me how unattractive that quality is.

"Saving you from the biggest mistake of your life, princess." He's calm, like it's every day that he saves strangers from random hockey players' kisses. Meanwhile, the team laughs, heckling Max.

"Hmm . . . last time I checked, who I kiss or don't kiss is none of your business." I cock my hip to the side, placing my fist on it to show I mean business.

"Well, last time I checked, I made it clear I wanted it to be."

"Did you now? How is that exactly? By teasing me, yelling at me for running alone, and trying to pay for my drinks? Or was it the awkward stare downs from across the street and the completely random dinner last night?"

"Actually, yes."

I roll my eyes, a small huff of laughter breaking free. He's insane. This isn't how you win a woman over.

"Well, I don't buy it."

"Well, you should."

"I don't."

"One date then."

I pause, my mouth open. A date? *Why do I not hate the sound of that?* I'm not sure what I'm more caught off guard from—his response or my feelings about it. I think maybe if I'm honest with myself, he was trying to ask me out last night. But I am not admitting that now.

I must freeze for longer than I think because he lets out a grumpy laugh and says, "I'm telling you now. I want a date. One date to prove myself."

"No," I say, emphatically.

"Why not?"

"Hmm, let's see." I tap my finger to my jaw as if I'm thinking deeply about this. "You are literally here on a date. You had your arm draped around her no less than five seconds ago." My eyes are ready to jump out of my skull as I point at the woman. Is he seriously doing this? I know I should be poised. My mother's voice practically shouts in my head, *Don't make a scene, Olive.* But, I can't.

He laughs. Not like a little chuckle, but a full belly-rolling laugh. "Oh, that? That's Bridget. She's my sister." The anxiety and clear effort to cover up being caught makes me let out an exasperated breath. It did not look brotherly when they were laughing together earlier.

"Mmmk. I think I'm good. No thanks." I shift on my back foot, turning to walk away and rejoin my friends who are undoubtedly watching this blowup.

"That was so hot!" Meg fans herself for emphasis.

"No, it wasn't," I quip back, continuing to walk.

"But actually, why won't you give him a chance?" Ari asks, linking arms with me as we hit the sidewalk.

"Are you serious?" I halt completely, turning to look at her.

"Yeah. I am. We told you he's a nice guy, and he clearly has an effect on you. Why not take him for a spin?"

"I just . . . There's something about him. I can't. He is literally on a date right now," I say in mock concern for the girl I don't even know. There was something about his denial that I believe. But the evidence all points to him being committed to someone else, and that's easier than admitting that I'm afraid of the way I feel around him.

"That's his sister, Bridget. He was telling the truth, and you're scared. You might actually feel something for the first time in . . . maybe ever, and you're running. I hate to say it, babe, but there's a chance those college guys were right." Remorse or pity, I can't be sure which, passes across her face. Even my best friend sees it. She can tell I'm not capable of taking a leap. And in my defense, all those "men" I dated in college wanted me for only two things—Daddy's bank account and my ability to look pretty at a party.

"Let's just go get some drinks," I plead, desperate to clear my mind of this whole thing.

"Okay, but we will be circling back to this," Ari concedes, for now.

Eight

Sam

The Hollow Hearts Festival (Sam's Version)

At seven in the morning, it's safe to say I'm not my best. Early Riser is a nickname I lost around the time my first tooth fell out. Since then, it's been more like Lucky to Be Up by Lunch. Lately, I've had more and more responsibilities piling on that require me to get up early, though—not to mention how I tossed and turned after my interaction with Olive on her porch.

Today's the Hollow Hearts Festival, which means I have to not only get in two clients before noon, but also check in on Mom's booth and convince my sister to be my date. The first two things are easy, the third not so much.

The door chimes, announcing Xavier's arrival.

"Hey, man, how's it going?" I ask, trying to drag myself out of my stupor.

"Too early for this shit," he grumbles, practically flopping face down on my table.

"You can go to sleep, bro. Let the buzzing take you away."

He won't, only a true masochist could sleep through what I'm about to do to his skin. We've been working on a back piece for the better part of six months. Today I'm adding the final touches of shading and fixing up a few spots that didn't heal perfectly.

Xavier's been one of my closest friends over the years. A while back, eighteen months give or take, he was in a motorcycle accident. While he was lucky to walk away from it, his back suffered some serious road rash and scarring. He hates it, so we're covering it up.

"Right. You get too much joy from torturing me," he groans before yawning. "Tell me something to wake me up."

"I got nothing, man. Business as usual around here." Shrugging, I turn to grab a paper towel and sanitizer for his skin.

"Momma O gonna make you serve food today?"

"Nah. I'm helping with set up but attending the event for fun. Are you planning to go?"

"You know I wouldn't miss it. Cami would kill me if I didn't take her to get a funnel cake. She's scary when she has a craving." He shudders at the thought of his very pregnant wife. I chuckle but deep in the farthest corners of my mind, I can't help but be a little jealous. Not of the baby part—I just want to have someone who I don't mind bossing me around. I thought by thirty-two I would.

"Happy wife, happy life. I guess," I say, as I finish wiping his skin, setting up my ink, and prepping my gun.

"Speaking of wives, how's the dating scene these days for Mage Hollow's most eligible bachelor?" Xavier turns his head to look me in the eyes, not allowing me to spew any bullshit.

"It's wicked boring. Same choices, different day." I school my features, so I don't give away the idiotic crush I'm harboring.

"Ahh. There it is." He points his finger at my face. "Is a certain new-in-town Southerner getting you down?"

I scoff, audibly. "I don't know who you're talking about."

"Is that why Max said you've been hauling boxes for Beau Brooks at six in the morning every day this week? There was something in there about her running in a sports bra . . . what was it?" He places his finger on his chin, pretending to be deep in thought. He waits longer than necessary, just asking for my anxiety to fill in the gaps.

"It's not my fault that she thinks it's necessary to run completely alone in the wee hours of the morning. Someone's gotta look out for her. That's all it is." My tone is defensive. Can't I just look out for the newest resident without everyone assuming it's more? *No, dumbass, you can't. Because it is more.*

His eyebrow raises. "So you're telling me you would be fine with Max making his move then? I heard she's wicked beautiful, everyone's talking about her." He's taunting me about my little brother moving in on my girl. Except, fuck. She isn't my girl. She ran back inside last night like her ass was on fire—though, to be fair, I probably did chase her off a little with my attitude.

"Not a problem." The words come out jagged, like sandpaper in my throat as I say them.

"So, who are you gonna bring to the festival then?"

I don't answer him right away, opting to start abusing his back instead. Normally, taking it easy on his fragile skin is top of mind, but right now I know I'm taking my frustration out on my best friend. Fifteen minutes pass in a blur before I decide to fess up.

"I'm going to con Bridget into coming along." A weird lump forms in my throat. Ever since Olive blew into my life, it's been like my insides are claiming her as mine, when she most definitely isn't. I wish I was taking her to the festival today, seeing her face light up the first time she experiences one of Mom's tortellini or wins a carnival game.

Since she flashed me on the sidewalk, images of her have been playing in my mind on an endless loop. It's weird, actually. I've dated many times before, but something is different with Olive. She has this air of grace about her, as if the inside of her may actually be more beautiful than the outside. Except, I have a feeling she doesn't let most people see all sides of her. For sure, not me. To everyone else in town, she is a sweet, quiet Southern belle. Yet, when I have interacted with her, she's always working double time to keep her guard up. I wouldn't even know how to begin to crack that arm's-length facade she displays.

"How's Bridget?" He's fishing for information. Xavier knows all of my siblings well. He worries about Bridget the most for some reason, I guess because she's only a year younger and used to follow us around.

"She's fine. She dumped Jessa. Again." I swallow hard. Xav has never liked Jessa. Not that I have either, but my sister insists on getting back together with her every single time they split up. Jessa is over-the-top dramatic, and she doesn't treat Bridget well. It irritates the hell out of me.

"Let me ask you something," he says, while sitting up slowly so I can wipe him down with sanitizer and put on his wrap. "If you thought you had a chance, would you go out with the new girl? Or is this just some game to say the bad boy got under the good girl's skirt?"

"What? Are you joking? You know I'm not actually a fuck boy, right?" My heart is pounding so hard it might beat out of my chest. Does my best friend really believe I'm the town player?

"I know you aren't deep down. But I can't help but wonder sometimes if the image you display of being this badass, tatted-up, doesn't-give-a-fuck guy is starting to sink in a little further than intended." His assessment floors me, like he took a sledge hammer and rammed it into my chest. Breathing is difficult. There is one thing I know for sure: I cannot allow this assessment of me to harbor even a sliver of truth. Time to fess up.

"Alright, fine. You got me. I want to go for the girl like nobody's business. I am practically a stalker at this point with how much I've been hovering. But I seem to put my foot in my mouth every time she's around." Resignation marks my face as I start applying his wrap.

"What do you mean? Why don't you just sack up and ask her out?" Xavier demands.

I rattle off the list of excuses I've built over the past week. "She's out-of-my-league gorgeous. She's younger than us, just getting started in her career, so who knows if she plans to stick around here. Besides, there's no way she'd want to be with someone like me. She comes from money, and I'm pretty sure she has a perfect IQ."

"You've lost your mind. Cami is going to love this." His shoulders shake with laughter at my expense.

"I bare my soul and you laugh. Why are we friends again?" I ask, huffing while I toss the scraps of my supplies into a trash can under my table.

A smirk pops the dimple in his right cheek. "It's just that it took you long enough. Did you really think I didn't already know? Lovesick puppy was written all over your ugly mug when I walked in. I had to make up a bullshit insult just to get you to crack." Damn it, I need new friends .

"Okay, wise one. Doesn't change that she probably believes I'm a bumbling fool."

"Oh, yes it does. You deserve to be happy. Stop being a dense, self-deprecating asshole, and go after what you want. The chase might be rough, but the reward will be worth it." With that, he stands, grabs his phone, and walks out. He doesn't pay, best friend discount and all, but still. Just walk away when I need support.

My second appointment went off without a hitch. An easy flash piece that took a quick forty-five from start to finish. My hands are grateful for the break they're getting today. Ten years of tattooing, the last six on a daily basis, has earned me a very frustrating case of carpal tunnel.

"You going to spread that tablecloth, or are we going to stand around all day?" Patrick O'Reilly doesn't allow anyone to slack on the job.

"Yeah, Dad. Is this the last one?" I ask, mumbling the words softly so my mom doesn't overhear. No one wants to piss off Momma Mabel.

"Yep. That should do it. Have you met anyone new recently?" he asks, a sheepish grin blooming on his face.

"I'm going to kill Max. That fucker spreads more gossip than old Mrs. Beasley." I guess it could have been Bridget, but Dad usually gets his gossip from my brother.

Dad chuckles and shrugs. "He just wants to see you happy. Between you and your sister, someone has to keep me informed."

"Bridget is going to figure it out. Just give her time. And I'm not looking to date," I reassure him, unconvincingly.

"Sure. I don't believe a word you just said, and I don't appreciate being lied to. Bridget did the same when I talked to her this morning." His face shifts into the all-too-well-known look of dad disapproval.

"How do you know Olive would even be interested, Dad? That's right, you don't. You're just listening to Max's bullshit." My voice is thick with frustration at his meddling and judgment.

"What bullshit?" Bridget asks. Her words come out sounding curious, not accusatory, letting me know she didn't hear the whole conversation. She wouldn't appreciate Dad and me talking about her love life, or lack thereof.

"Oh, we were just talking about what Xav and Cami are going to have. Who waits to find out the kid's gender these days?" The lie comes out too easily, turning my stomach at the effortlessness of it. If there's one thing I don't do, it's lie. I loathe it. Honesty is a virtue I live by and pursue relentlessly, but here I am again, with my third lie of the week. My dad has taken note of just how smoothly it trickled out, raising his eyebrow in marked disappointment.

Bridget shrugs nonchalantly. "It's so weird, right? I don't know what to buy for the baby shower."

"You don't need to get them anything. I already gave them a gift from all of us," I mutter, under my breath.

I haven't told my parents that I used the extra money I made this year to start a college fund for the little one. At my age, I don't need permission for how I spend my earnings, but since I bought property a few years ago, they would worry about my finances too much if they knew. And there are some things that just don't need to be public knowledge.

Shaking off the uneasy feeling in my gut, I ask, "Want to walk around"? The line is forming quickly, and if we stick around here, Momma Mabel will make us dawn hairnets and start serving.

"Yeah, let's go look at the games. Maybe you can win me a stuffed pumpkin pillow this year." Bridget tugs on my arm, pulling me away from my parents' booth and toward the carnival area.

I can't help but feel Olive's presence, even before I see her. My eyes search, damning me to notice her perfect figure, her long, flowy strawberry blonde hair, and that smile I can't get enough of. Her laughter bellows out like a smooth jazz tune, calming me and pissing me off in equal measure. I wish I was here with her, experiencing it all from her point-of-view.

Her silky voice is chattering along with the Marino sisters when I hear her say something about refusing to kiss anyone. I can't stop a mumbled quip from slipping out against my will as we pass. "That tracks."

She puts off the vibe that she would be too good to participate in a kissing booth—yet another reason why we probably aren't compatible. I used to work that booth, and something tells me she would despise it. I hate the way my perception of her dictates what I think she will and won't like. I'd much rather get to know her.

"What tracks?" Bridget looks at me like I've lost my mind, but after a quick shake of my head, she continues babbling about something Nora, our younger sister, told her. I'm not paying attention. Thoughts of Olive kissing someone other than me, ping-pong around my brain. She said she wasn't going to, if I heard her correctly. Did I hear her right?

We played a few games, and as Bridg hoped, I easily won her the pumpkin pillow she coveted so much. I'm considering it a feel-better gift after everything that went down with Jessa. Just as I'm thinking of the devil, I spot Jessa approaching with Crystal, another girl we went to high school with and one who happens to be quite skilled at breaking up relationships these days.

"Hey, let's step over here for a sec. We need to talk." Nudging my sister toward the side of the street, I wedge us strategically between two booths so she won't see her.

"What's wrong, Sam? I know that look," Bridget demands.

"I just thought we would get out of the way for a minute. How are things?" *I am not selling this at all.*

"Is it the new girl?" Her voice drops to a whisper as she asks the question.

"What?"

"Is that why we are hiding? Did you see her or something?" Bridget peers out like she's working an episode of *NCIS* and might spot the killer.

"No, I just wanted to tell you what Max did last week." I pull her back to my side and drape an arm around her shoulders, turning her so she can't see Jessa.

"Oh God. What did that idiot do now?" she asks, as we tumble into a fit of laughter. Max is always doing something a little reckless or stupid. I could say just about anything, and she would believe it.

When we get it together, Bridget says, "Sammy, I saw her. I know you are just trying to keep me from seeing her with someone else, but I'm fine. Seriously, I am."

I offer her a half smile, and she kisses my cheek, whispering in my ear, "If you want her, you probably shouldn't let her kiss Max."

The words stun me momentarily. I whip around toward the kissing booth, and sure enough, there's Olive. She's leaning in, hanging on every word my little brother spews. Tension boils beneath my skin. He knows I'm interested, even if I didn't admit it last night. Jealous rage isn't an emotion I've ever felt until this very moment.

Shaking out my arms, I take ten self-assured strides in their direction, arriving in the nick of time to intervene. Before I have time to think, my hand slides between their faces, lightly touching Olive's lips as I attempt to separate them. Watching the rage vibrate through her is a sight to behold. Something about pissing her off turns me on, just a little.

Words are exchanged, then to no one's surprise, she yells, stomps, and runs off with her lady gang. I didn't expect her to actually jump into my arms and run off into the sunset with me, but I needed to stop that kiss, consequences be damned.

"Thought you weren't interested, big brother," Max says, coolly.

"You fucking know I am." My finger jabs into his chest. Why the hell is his chest so built? I might break my finger from the damn concrete wall that is his muscles.

Max laughs. It starts as a slow chuckle but ends up as more of a bent-over hyena cackle. "I wasn't actually going to do it. I planned to kiss her cheek, you know."

"Well, even that is too close for my girl." As I spit the words out, the realization of what I just said spreads across my face. "Shit, too far. I don't know what she is, but she's off-limits," I backpedal, trying to reel the words back in.

I barely even know this person, and I don't prescribe to the whole thrill-of-the-chase thing, but it's like a switch was flipped within me the second I laid eyes on her. I could have been dating all these years, but instead I've spent my time mostly avoiding it and casually hooking up every once in a blue moon. No one has ever measured up to the picture of love my parents painted, and I've accepted it. Until now.

"Jesus. Let's grab a beer. Maddox, cover my spot," Max hoots toward his hockey teammate, tossing an arm over my shoulder and nudging me toward the beer tent while grabbing Bridget's hand to drag her along. *What was I thinking? I should've stayed home.*

Nine

Olive

Let's Talk Tarot

"Wait, so she was in love with him but she left?" I twist the bottle I'm holding in my hand, and the cool condensation coats my skin.

"I mean no one actually knows for sure. But we were always told that he knew she was a witch and he let her escape." Meg slurps her drink a little too aggressively. "It's kind of poetic I think, less about her leaving and more about what he sacrificed so she could be free."

"It's kind of sad though, she probably wanted him to come with her."

"I disagree, he was probably a douche. It's that whole, *if he wanted to he would*, thing. I bet the jerk off left her all alone and scared." There's Ari, always the one to call the man on his bullshit. "But none of it matters, let's talk about your dating life, Ollie."

And that's my cue to leave. "Actually, I'm pretty tired. I think I'm going to head home."

Ari and Meg begged me to stay, even offering to bring the party back to my place to keep the girls' day going. But I want to be alone. There's only so much sulking I can do in front of my friends before I turn the night into my own personal pity party. I don't have a reason to be sad—mad maybe, but not minutes from spiraling out.

I push my way out into the night air, letting its crispness wash over me. The fall sun begins to set, illuminating the festival in the glow of the streetlights, and casting eerie shadows over Mage Square. Voices echo all around with the chatter of families making their way to cars and the hoots and hollers of young people just starting to get rowdy.

I've never been afraid of the dark. Maybe it's the fact that the girls and I've been discussing a brokenhearted witch all evening, or maybe it's the general ambiance of Mage Hollow that's making the air crackle with anticipation. Either way, there's a buzzing, a shift in the feeling I normally get when walking home alone.

With each step I take, my mind drifts back to how much Sam confuses me. He says he wants a date, to pursue things with me, yet I know deep down it won't last. If he's as nice as everyone claims, he will inevitably get tired of my inability to open up. Once he gets to know me, he'll be like all the others. I wish I could just let someone in without the fear of disappointing them taking over. Or the knowledge that they want me for reasons that have nothing to do with me at all.

I've never been very trusting when it comes to love. My parents always made me feel like love was conditional.

Win this crown, Olive, and I'll buy you a pony.

Stand up straight, Olive. You're embarrassing us.

Marry a man with money, Olive. Don't you care about your children's future?

I guess their words just sit in my mind like a reminder that if I do give my heart away, it'll get stomped on and sent back to me in pieces. It's not that I don't love my parents dearly, but the pressure that comes with being their daughter is suffocating at times. I've only ever made one decision that was just for me—choosing to come here and pursue my career goals over my mother's wishes. While in some ways taking that first step has been freeing, it's also been uncomfortable. I don't know if I'm brave enough to disappoint them in any other ways.

"Festival getting you down, dear?" An unexpected voice breaks through my thoughts. I look around, setting my eyes on an elderly woman a few feet ahead. She's dressed in a beautiful, ornately designed plum skirt with swirls of gold streaked across it. Her top is a black thick-strapped tank top paired with a shawl that appears to be made from the same material as her skirt.

"Oh, just ready to call it a day," I respond politely, making my way past her.

"Olive, you can tell me what's bothering you. I've wanted to meet you since the minute you arrived in town." The woman's voice is sterner this time.

Turning around cautiously to face her, I ask, "H-how d-do you know my name?" Fear wraps around my belly like a fist.

Her face transforms into a calming smile. The kind that your grand-mother would give you when you finally come to visit. "My dear, I've been in this town for a long time. Everyone knows Beau's new beauty." I don't know what I was afraid of. This woman is beautiful. Rosy cheeks, long, flowing silver hair, bright eyes, and perfectly manicured fingers. *Gosh, I'm losing it.*

"Of course, I apologize. I'm not from such a small town, so sometimes I forget how obvious it is that I'm the new girl." I return her smile, hoping to cover my rudeness.

"It's okay, dear. But do tell me, what's bothering you?"

Why does she want to know so bad?

"I only ask because this is the best night of the whole year, and you look positively forlorn." *Did she read my mind? I need to lay off the true crime podcasts.*

"Well, I guess I could share . . . Maybe you have some advice for me." The words come out as if compelled from my lips. As if I have no choice in the matter, at all. Or maybe I'm just desperate for a bystander's opinion.

"Oh, yes. I would love that. Do come and join me in my shop for some tea." Her bony hand wraps around my bicep, pulling me toward what looks to be a basement apartment. I notice a purple flashing sign that reads *Tarot—Enter Here,* with a neon finger pointing down.

The shop is creepy with its haphazardly hung sign blinking at an inconsistent pace, like it can't decide on any one rhythm. Cobwebs line the cobbled steps. It feels like we're walking into one of those rooms you desperately hope the victim in a horror movie will avoid. It's bone-chilling, but I'd be lying if I said my heart didn't skip a beat a little at the thought of what she might tell me. How bad could it be?

The door comes ajar with a loud creaking noise, without her touching the knob. Soft light leaks out, like the room is welcoming her. She pushes into the dimly lit space as I follow closely behind. It's shockingly empty, with only a cream-and-purple Persian rug, a single standing lamp, an ornate black desk, and a cat.

"Welcome to my shop." She ushers me further into the room, encouraging me to sit . . . Wait, where did this stately armchair come from?

"Actually, I think I'm going to go," I say, the words nervously tumbling from my lips. My gut is commanding me to leave this place at once. There's an air about it that feels life altering, like if I don't leave now, I may never make it out.

"I will hear of no such thing, Olivia. Be a dear and sit." Her voice is strong, self-assured, not craggy as it was when she first spoke.

I muster my courage, taking my seat as instructed. With a snap of her fingers, a cauldron ignites in flames behind her as she digs in her desk and pulls out a stack of cards. The cat pounces on a mouse in the far corner, and still, she says nothing.

I watch intently as she shuffles her cards with an occasional *hmm* or *aha*. Seconds feel like minutes as the time passes in my anticipation of what may happen next. Just when I begin to think I've been roofied by the bartender and will wake up from this nightmare soon, she speaks.

"Tell me, Olive, what seems to be the problem?" she asks, her face bemused.

"I-I mean nothing really. I have a good job, great friends, it's just . . . I should go, you don't want to hear this," I stammer.

"Your heart has been locked away for far too long, my dear. If you want the life you deserve, you must claim it."

"I don't know how." Admitting this to anyone, let alone some old lady that reads tarot for kicks at the local carnival, is a first.

"Yes, you do, Olive. You know why you keep it locked away. Tell me, let me help you." Her words are demanding, almost angry at my inability to open up. *Welcome to the club, lady, you aren't the first.* I sit silently, staring at the wall behind her, searching for a lifeline in the flames beneath her bubbling pot.

"Olive, I can't help you if you don't ask for it," she persists.

"What's your name?" I ask, fervently.

Flipping her hair in annoyance, she pins me with a sharp glance. "Irina."

I gasp. "Irina? Like *the* Irina we've been celebrating all day?" This cannot be happening, there's no way.

Disbelief settles into my brow. Their names are the same. She's clearly a witch of some sort. Her house isn't one I've ever noticed before, not that I have been here long enough to make that argument. I tick the coincidences off in my head. "You're her, aren't you? Why'd you leave the judge? Why are you . . . How are you here?"

My questions go unanswered as the tension radiating off of her intensifies. "Olive, do I need to tell you why you can't open up, or are we going to keep doing this song and dance all night?"

I have to make a choice: I either tell her, or I try to escape, which probably won't work and I'll die like one of those dumb girls in all the horror movies. I mean, what was I thinking, coming to a strange old woman's shop?

I weigh my options in the awkward silence, finally deciding the odds are better if I start talking. "Okay, fine." I take a deep breath, gathering my thoughts. "I have lived my entire life trying to fit into boxes that other people have created for me. Even when I was near perfect, it wasn't ever seen as adequate. I guess that's translated into my love life . . . Putting myself out there has always seemed too risky, like true love is one more thing I'll give my all to, just to be told I have room for improvement. Or worse than that, it won't be true at all. It'll be another arrangement my mother made for me, another box to fit in."

She gently pats my shoulder, comforting me as an unexpected tear streaks down my face, plopping onto my lap.

"Sweet child, don't worry. Irina can fix it, but you must ask me to do so." The words sound lyrical coming from her lips, soothing me like a warm balm over my heart.

"Please, fix it. Help me allow myself to fall in love," I beg, losing the last bit of nerve I have.

"I can't."

Two words—matter-of-fact. I'm appalled. She lulled me in here and told me to open up and ask for help. I told her things that only Ari knows. And now she says she can't. *What the hell was the point of this?*

"B-but you said, you told me you would help." Shock seeps into my shivering skin.

"I will help, but I cannot dabble in love or fate. No one can do that but you, Olivia. Ask for something else," Irina urges.

"I-I don't know what else to ask for. I want to be, uh, I guess open to love?" I hesitate. Is it that I'm not open to love, or am I simply scared of what it means?

"Ahh, now we are getting somewhere. Be more specific," she says, encouraging me to continue.

"Uh, okay. Let me think." I close my eyes, trying to concentrate on all the things that I've been told in the past. Things I needed to change. The voices of my ex-boyfriends dance around in my head until the ask hits me like a train roaring down the tracks. "I want to wear my heart on my sleeve," I blurt out.

She hesitates, mumbling to herself so quietly that I can't make out what she's saying. Right when I think I hear her say, *I swore I'd never allow anyone to wear their heart on their sleeve again*, there's an echo in the room, *just do it, Irina. Let her learn the lesson.* This voice sounds different, higher pitched, more definitive. Panic resurfaces in my stomach, rolling it over and over like waves in a storm. "Done."

She snaps her fingers and the cauldron bubbles loudly, a rainbow of colorful liquids splashing over the side before turning black. Irina moves in a flash across the room, grabbing a ladle and scooping the liquid into a mug. With tentative steps, she carefully makes her way back to me.

"Drink this, my dear, and you shall wear your heart on your sleeve." She extends the mug out to my lips, and I rear back to avoid it.

"You must drink this, it is the only way."

"The only way for what? I don't even know what it is."

I know I'm the one that went along with this, that spilled my guts to a stranger, but is it smart to take a sip of whatever this is? She pushes it toward my mouth again, and I purse my lips like a child avoiding their first bite of baby food. My mother's voice echoes in my head. *Don't be rude, Olive*. Listening to her like I always do, I slurp at the liquid without another thought, going against my own judgment for what feels like the millionth time this week. The liquid is bitter, then sweet. Hot at first, but suddenly cold.

"Very good. Now I must tell you, if you change your mind, you must do so before the clock strikes midnight on Halloween. Once the night has passed, the change will be permanent," she says, like she's issuing a warning. Alarm bells sound in my mind. *What did I just do? What was that liquid?*

I say nothing. Instead, I stand, darting from my chair toward the door that is noticeably barred closed. The sound of her fingers snapping raises chills down my spine, and then there's a loud crack as the bar raises and the door flies open.

Racing up the stairs and back to the sidewalk, I feel dizzy, either from what I drank or from sheer panic. I suck in breaths so hard I fear there may never be enough oxygen in my lungs again. Looking from left to right, everything is exactly as it should be. As it was before. I turn toward my cottage, starting toward it in a jog but quickly picking up my pace to a full sprint. I have to get home.

Offensively bright light spills in through the paned windows of my bedroom at approximately 6:40 in the morning. It takes all my energy to restrain myself from shrieking in rage. My head feels like it's in a vice, bile stings the back of my throat, and my body aches like a swollen tick after a night of too much wine.

After leaving Irina last night, I sprinted back to my cottage, soaking in all the craziness of the evening. When I say I've never thought of going to a psychic before, I mean it. The fact that I so willingly went with her feels off. Almost like I'd been coerced. There are a few things a good Southern belle must never do, using witchcraft to alter your fate is definitely one. And thank goodness for that because I will never be doing it again.

It took me a few hours to come down from the whiplash of emotions, between Sam's intervention of my kiss and Irina. Restless and spooked were the general feelings of the night. The former because of Sam and his hauntingly beautiful face. He's a puzzle I can't quite figure out. Gorgeous but gruff, touchy but distant, confident but mysterious. Then there's the latter, I couldn't scrub my body hard enough to remove the feeling of aged fingers crawling on my skin.

I spent a solid hour searching around the cottage for anything that might be lurking in the shadows. Finding nothing out of place, I finally forced myself to lie down. That's when the anger made its home in my chest like an anvil weighing me down, making it hard to breathe.

This ferocity inside me wasn't new, it's a feeling I spent most of my life dealing with. Anger because your home is supposed to be somewhere you feel safe, seen, loved. Growing up, I wasn't ever in physical danger, but my yearning for acceptance ran deep. I spent most of my time wishing I could be more graceful, more poised, more perfect. But I never seemed to measure up. Despite my crowns and achievements, my brain was always too engaged for my mother's liking. I read too much and cared about things that should be a man's concern.

I know from being well-read that my mother is completely and utterly wrong in her assessment. But isn't it unfair that I couldn't have had a mother or father who liked my thirst for knowledge? A parent who would for one small beat put their own agenda second to the dealings of their daughter's heart? And maybe that's why I struggle so much with opening up; it seems pointless when the result is always the same.

My cottage last night didn't feel like the safe, euphoric place I've come to adore the past week. The cozy sage cabinets with ethereal sparkling white quartz counters morphed from decadent and homey into over the top, with too many places for a ghost to hide. The wide-plank pine floors creaked under my footsteps, alerting me to potential hidden compartments rather than the worn mystique of a well-used space. What I saw as character changed in an instant to something else. Something darker.

After losing hope that sleep would find me, I turned on reruns of *The Office* and drifted off to the voice of my favorite overzealous leading man, Michael Scott. His celebration over Holly's nonengagement rocked me gently away.

Ugh! I need water or an IV. Maybe both. I didn't drink that much yesterday, yet my mouth is drier than the Sahara. The tea . . . there had to be something wrong with that tea. Tossing the covers back, I settle my feet on the floor, but not before glancing to make sure it's free of traps. I make my way into the kitchen, filling a glass with water, chugging it down, and filling it again. Looking around, I see my humble abode is back to being warm and appealing. The velvety soft green sofa beckons me to lie down as I grab my phone and begin to scroll.

I shouldn't do it, but I find myself compelled to learn more about Sam. I open my social media app, searching for the one and only Sam

O'Reilly. Spoiler alert: There are 12,382 people with that name using the internet to document their lives. I attempt to narrow the search with filters, giving up after a ten-minute deep dive yielded little results. *I can look up his business.* I type in "Eerie Ink, Mage Hollow, Massachusetts"—it pops right up. *Holy shit.* He is super talented. Like *Ink Masters*–level work. (Yes, I spent a semester in college binge-watching every episode in an attempt to eliminate what Ari referred to as my "snooty" tendencies.)

To many people's surprise, I've never actually hated tattoo artwork itself, it's more a lack of exposure multiplied by an intense fear of my mother. There's also my insane fear of needles and my tendency to pass out. That's the biggest reason why I've never, nor would I ever, consider marking my own body.

Peeling myself off the couch, finishing yet another glass of water mixed with electrolyte powder, I throw on a sports bra, running shorts, and sneakers, avoiding the mirror and my appearance at all costs. I need to run, it will give me clarity. Selecting my Bad Bitch playlist, I'm pounding the pavement in under five minutes.

Thirty minutes flashes by as I'm lost in thought. I can't help but wonder what Irina meant when she said it was done. What was done? I don't feel any different.

Logically, I can't be changed, right? Like, what would that even mean? Am I going to be more open to possibilities? Yes, but that's because I'm choosing to be. It had to all be fake, a hoax to get the new girl acclimated to town. Ari and Meg undoubtedly put the woman up to it. They wouldn't drop the Sam thing all night. This is probably just their attempt at forcing my hand. I figure I'll just swing by and let them have their big laugh. Ari knows I'll be running, I can picture her standing there with "Irina" coffee in hand, giggling.

I turn the corner, taking my usual route into Mage without a thought. I pass by Union Tavern and glance up ahead toward Eerie, but something's not right. Last night, the psychic's shop was in between the two. I wasn't drunk enough to have forgotten where it was—except it's not there. Slowing to a walk, I spin carefully, eyeing every shop lining the street. My eyes are desperate to find that glowing purple sign, not so I can revisit the shop, but so I know where my enemies lie, and that I haven't absolutely lost it.

It's gone. How can it be gone? Surely someone has seen it. I must've been worse off than I remember. Maybe I made a turn somewhere or went around back? It must have looked different with all the festival tents. I'm too chicken to go searching alone right now. Ignoring the unsettling ache churning low in my belly, I turn around and what do you know, there's Ari heading into the Brewhouse.

Swiftly making my way down the block, I grab the door and hightail it to where she's waiting in line.

"What are you doing?" I shout, grabbing her arm tightly.

"Getting coffee. What the hell's wrong with you?" Her face transforms from pissed off to confused faster than I can get the words out. I have never in our entire friendship been this rough with her. But it's coming out of left field for good reason.

"You can tell me the truth. How much did you pay the old bat?" My words are laced with anger, fear taking over again.

"I don't know what you're talking about, but you're making a scene. Take it down a notch," she whisper-shouts as her eyes shift toward the onlookers. They might be more afraid of the way I look than the words coming out of my mouth. A mirror purposefully wasn't one of my stops this morning.

Guilt over making things awkward seeps in and I relent. "Fine. Get me a PSL, I'll find a table." I walk away, spotting a pair of comfortable high-back chairs next to the picture window.

Ari grabs our drinks and makes her way over to me cautiously. She's looking at me funny, like I have something on my face. *Shit, is there something on my face?*

"When did you get that?" Ari points a finger at my shoulder. My hand shifts to the spot where my collarbone ends at the front of my shoulder.

"G-get what?" I ask, my eyes moving to the bare spot that's . . . that's not bare at all. A small black outline of a heart is inked into my porcelain skin. *Oh my gosh! This can't be happening.*

Abandoning my chair, I race toward the bathroom with Ari nipping at my heels. Flinging open the door to the one-room stall, I all but trip over my own feet clawing to get to the mirror. The heart is small and jagged, as if the old woman drew it herself. Not unsightly, but definitely out of character for me.

"Are you going to tell me what's going on, or are we going to stand here and pretend you didn't just accuse me of something whilst forgetting you got a tattoo last night?" Ari's words come out laced with annoyance.

"I-I don't know." I cover my face with my hands, hoping if I don't look it'll disappear.

"How do you not know? Tattoos hurt like a bitch. Don't tell me you don't remember getting it." She slurps her coffee while clutching mine so tightly the top is almost popping off.

"I didn't get a tattoo. I mean . . . it looks like I have one, but I didn't get it. I swear. This has to be Irina." My confession tumbles from my mouth before I can rein it in.

"What the fuck? Did you hit your head or something? Drink this coffee." She pushes my drink to my lips as if this problem can be solved with caffeine. I oblige because . . . well, because it's pumpkin spice and that has to be nice.

"We need to talk."

Four words that always come before something bad. It's all I can muster to get her moving. We exit the bathroom, then the coffee shop, turning to walk toward my cottage. My steps quicken, my stomach twists and turns, rioting at this—I don't know. This situation. We make it to the porch before I empty my stomach's contents onto a bush at the edge of the wraparound.

"Jesus, you're freaking me out. Let's get inside." Ari gently steadies me as we unlock the door and make our way to the couch. She grabs a glass of water then sits down, silently waiting.

"Okay, this is going to sound crazy." She raises an eyebrow as if to say what about this morning hasn't been weird. "When I left you and Meg last night, I met a tarot card reader." I can't bring myself to say *witch,* even though I know in my soul that's what she was. "She seemed kind, like a grandma of sorts, and she wouldn't take no for an answer when she asked me to tell her what was wrong. I know it sounds bizarre, but at the time I just couldn't refuse her. I went into her shop, and she knew things. She told me my heart was locked away. I told her why I don't open up, and well . . . she told me she could help."

Ari's eyes are about to pop out of her head. "How? How did she say she could help?"

"She told me to ask her for something. She said she couldn't deal in love or fate but that she could do something." I glance at Ari from beneath my eyelashes. I know I'm going to admit what I wished for, but it doesn't make it less embarrassing. "I said I wished I could wear my heart on my sleeve."

The silence hangs between us. There's no laughing or saying gotcha. I don't need to ask her to know Ari wasn't behind this. Her face is stark white, as if she saw a ghost.

"Say something," I whisper.

"I—okay, so you went with a witch, asked to wear your heart on your sleeve, and today you wake up with an actual heart tattoo. There has to be an explanation. Are you sure it's not henna? Maybe she roofied you. Did you eat or drink anything when you were there?" Logic, there it is.

"Yes! Actually, yes. She made tea, and I drank some. I did feel dizzy afterward. Maybe she drugged me." The thought of it shouldn't excite me, but it's better than believing that I was actually cursed by a witch.

"Okay . . . you drank tea. I bet it's fake. Let's go scrub it off." We make our way to the bathroom, turning the faucet on high and slathering a rag with soap. As I sit on the porcelain throne, Ari mercilessly rubs my skin to remove the tattoo. After twenty minutes, ten of which were spent thoroughly covering every detail of my interaction with Irina, we succumb to the fact that this isn't going away.

After giving up, we curl up on the couch to make a game plan. "So, all we need to do is keep it hidden until we can go back and see her. All the shops open at noon on Sundays. We won't leave this house until right before, and you can wear a sweater when we do." Ari's confidence in the plan is reassuring, except I haven't told her yet that the shop isn't there anymore.

"About that . . . I was running this morning, before I saw you, and the shop was gone. Like nowhere to be seen." I squeeze my eyes tightly shut. I can't watch her reaction.

"Excuse me, what?" she shouts.

"I said it's gone."

"I heard you. B-but what are we going to do? It can't just be gone. We have to find it." My heart fills with warmth at her use of the word *we*. At least I'm not alone in this. I mean, aside from the fact that it's happening to my body.

"Go shower and get dressed. We've got a witch to find." She snaps her fingers, the sound reminding me of Irina and inducing another tremor through my body. But instead of hesitating, I move. Off to the shower and to find the damn witch.

Ten

Sam

A Surprise Dinner Guest

I should have let Olive kiss Max. Not because I want her to end up with him, but because it isn't cool to take her choices away from her. I've never been a fan of telling any woman what to do or when to do it. I value the women in my life as equals, and how I behaved yesterday was borderline caveman. But that's what she does to me, and it's not the first time I've invoked my wishes or opinions on her. *What the fuck is wrong with me?*

One look at that milky skin covered in white cotton panties and I was hooked. It's not logical the way I'm drawn to her. She's irritatingly beautiful, to the point that she makes underwear suited for a grandma sexy, but even more than that, she's smart as a whip and downright funny when she uses her Southern charm as a vessel for sarcasm. A saccharine package that sucked me in, then repeatedly knocks me over the head with a mixture of lust, amusement, and downright annoyance.

"What-ah-ya lookin' at today, Samuel?" Mrs. Beasley asks, her thick Boston-accent voice releasing me from my ever-present thoughts of Olive.

"I'll take two loaves of sourdough and some pumpkin cinnamon rolls, please." After placing my usual order, I look around waiting for her to bag it up.

With the tourists still lingering from the festival, there are more people milling about the market than usual. This is my Sunday standard—well, this and Mom's dinner.

Taking the bag gingerly from Mrs. Beasley, I offer her a nod before checking my shopping list. I need to find a pie to bring to dinner and restock on the grass-fed beef I've come to love. I wonder what kind of pie Olive prefers. Is she a cherry lover? Or perhaps she prefers a peach cobbler with her Southern background. As if my barrage of thoughts, which never stray far from her, conjured the one and only, I spot her examining some apples a few tables down. I approach slowly, tapping her on the shoulder lightly and leaning in to whisper in her ear, "Hey, princess. See something you like?"

Olive spins abruptly, nearly knocking into me, her strawberry-scented hair wafting as it whips past my face. Her eyes are wide, like she's more than startled from simply bumping into me.

"Uh, hi." She shifts on her feet nervously, looking around like she's searching for someone. "It, um . . . seems like you're stocking up," she says, settling on examining my purchases. Dragging my eyes from the tips of her black Chuck Taylors up to her freckle-dotted face, I drink her in.

"This is nothing, princess. Cooking for one, unless you want to come for dinner sometime." It's more of a statement than a question; I'm counting on her turning me down.

"Oh, I-I wasn't looking for an invitation. I just wondered where you put two loaves of bread. Must have a secret workout routine you're hiding. Maybe at one of those fancy places with green drinks." Is she? No . . . She couldn't have just paid me a compliment and mocked me all in one breath.

"Are you flirting with me, princess?" I ask, coming right out with it.

"I, oh . . . I'm not sure. But maybe not if you don't stop calling me princess." Her cheeks turn a slight shade of pink with her sheepish reply.

"Look, I know we didn't get off on the best foot, but I am serious about what I said last night. I want to take you out." My words come out a little more growly than intended. But I feel like I might die if I don't get her to agree to one date, to give me one shot.

"I don't know, Sam. I know you believe that's what you want, but you don't really know me." Her shoelaces seem to have suddenly become very interesting, as if she can't bear to look at me when she turns me down. My stomach drops then jumps like a pole vaulter, launching into my throat. I know in my bones she isn't saying no because she doesn't want to. It's something deeper, a past hurt.

Compelled to do anything in this moment to soothe whatever insecurity she's failing to mask, I reach out, placing my index finger gently under her chin, lifting. When her eyes meet mine, it's electric. She can hide or run or whatever it is she's doing, but I'm locked in. Hell, I was a goner when I called her mine not even twenty-four hours ago. Not that I'd admit that to her.

I run my knuckle over her soft cheek. "Olive, listen to me. I mean, really pay attention." I search her eyes to make sure she's following my command before continuing. "You're right. I don't know you well at all. But from what I can tell, you're a good friend, kind to others, you work hard according to Beau, and you're gorgeous as all hell. You may be a little fancier than I am"—a small breath escapes her lips, and that mask she usually holds firmly in place slips just a smidge—"but I'm nicer than I probably seem, and I do know what I want. It's pretty simple, princess. A chance. Just give me one chance to take you out." The pulse in her neck picks up, her eyes turning from light green to a deep emerald. I know she wants this, but will she admit it?

"Olive, we gotta go. Get a move on," Ariella Marino shouts from across the street outside Union Tavern, breaking the moment I think we were about to have.

Olive's lips morph into that perfect smile, and it's almost like I once again can see her wall building itself back up, brick by brick. "I should go." She throws her thumb over her shoulder toward Ariella, turning to leave without a response.

"Wait." I grab her hand, grasping for just a second more as I run my thumb over the inside of her wrist. "Let me have your phone," I demand.

"Why?" she asks, confusion written like poetry across her face, but she hands it to me anyway. I type in my number and call myself. "Now you have my number. Think about what I said."

She smiles softly, briefly flashing her pearly whites before taking her phone back, and starting to walk away, again. I can't help calling out, "Olive, I'm serious. Call me." With that, I turn toward my mother's favorite blackberry pie and away from my girl.

"Ma, I'm here," I call out, pie in hand, walking into my childhood home as I do every Sunday.

"We're out back. Set the pie on the counter and come on out," Mom shouts.

The state of the driveway indicates I'm the last of my siblings to arrive. Thankfully, I'm the favorite, the eldest son, fixer of things that break, and ruler of Mabel O'Reilly's heart. It's okay to admit it, we all know the truth.

Pushing into the swinging door that separates the kitchen from the main hallway of my parents' historic home, I'm greeted by my sisters, Nora and Bridget. They're hovering over a bottle of wine, whispering as if they hold the key to state secrets.

"Ladies, how's it going?" I ask, tentatively. For all I know, they could be gossiping about me.

"Oh Sammy, so glad you're here," Nora squeaks, her voice laced with something I can't quite pinpoint. The way her voice lifts with my childhood nickname, means it must be bad.

Looking at Bridget with my eyebrow slightly raised, I ask, "What's her deal? Why are you two hiding in here whispering?"

"Oh, you'll see. Mom has a surprise for you, Sammy." Bridget pats me on the shoulder, sliding off her stool and undoubtedly heading to the backyard. I have no idea what she is talking about. Mabel O'Reilly is a straight shooter—she meddles out loud, not in secret.

"Don't try to sort it out in that pretty little head of yours. Even I didn't see this one coming," Nora chirps, following after Bridget. I hate having sisters. Okay, I don't really. I actually adore them, but their ability to say things without actually saying anything is unparalleled.

I shuffle to the fridge, desperate to shake off whatever the hell that was. Pulling on the door, I bend to find room, sliding the pie into the only available spot, wedged between a jug of apple cider and an orange Tupperware straight out of the seventies.

"Well, I'll say, that's a view a girl could get used to." Olive's honey voice reverberates off the walls of the fridge like a sound bath washing over me. I pull my head out too quickly, banging it on the edge that separates the freezer.

"Olive? Ouch. What're you doing here?" I rub at the knot that's quickly forming, completely at a loss. I asked her to have dinner with me, but I didn't imagine it being a family affair.

"No, you're right. What *am* I doing here? Um, your mom asked me to come by and look at a book she found in the attic. I tried to say no, but she insisted and then, what do you know, when I got here, there weren't any books . . ." She eyes me suspiciously, as if I may have had something to do with this. "When your mom couldn't find the book, I went to leave, but Max showed up, followed by your sisters, and then Mrs. Mabel just wouldn't let me go. I told her I couldn't stay, but she insisted. And well, I didn't want to be rude, so I just thought, why not?" She paces back and forth, a nervous look and hesitant smile gracing her lips.

"I'm glad you're here." Walking toward her, I tentatively grasp her arms, attempting uselessly not to get lost in her sweet scent.

"Are you sure? It's weird, I'm making it weird. I just, I-I want her to like me." Her cheeks are flushed with an adorable pink glow. She's embarrassed that she crashed a family dinner, when all I can focus on is the fact that she wants my mom to like her. She cares enough to not disappoint my parents, and we aren't even dating, yet. She's perfect, I knew it the minute I saw her.

"I promise it's okay. I was just a little surprised we skipped texting and went straight to meeting the parents. Let's get out there though." I gesture for the door.

"Okay but, uh, Sam, this is just dinner. Please don't get the wrong impression, I wasn't trying to invite myself. I would never do that. I didn't even bring a bottle of wine, and I feel awful about it." There's the charming girl I'm finding myself entirely too fond of.

"Sure, princess. It's okay if you find me irresistible." I wink, walking toward the door. "But you could have just used the number I gave you if you wanted to see me." I leave her standing in the kitchen doorway, mouth agape as I mentally fist pump with glee.

As I walk out onto the sprawling cedar deck, Nora, the baby of the family, is perched on the arm of the chair her boyfriend, Tom, is occupying. Bridget is slouched into a two-seater wicker couch, and Max is sitting in between my parents, comfortably sprawled out in an Adirondack chair with the fire pit serving as his footrest.

"What kind of pie did you bring me, darling?" My mom looks guilty, and her scrunched up eyebrows tell me she's desperate to avoid the obvious setup she's responsible for.

"Blackberry today. I was looking for grape but it isn't out yet." I offer her a small smile and a look that says we will be discussing the meddling later.

In other families, a new love interest would never be invited to a family dinner so soon. Not so in this pack of nosy Nellies. They can't help but sink their teeth into the naive Southern belle. I can tell by the way my mom looks at Olive, she's got some plan cooked up.

"Sammy, how was the market today?" Bridget bellows, intentionally attempting to maintain my status as the center of attention.

"Busier than usual, I guess. There were lots of out-of-towners from the festival." I shrug, conveying ambivalence.

"What about you, Olive? What did you do today?" Nora asks, smiling into her wine glass. Neither of my sisters are willing to let this awkward tension die.

"Oh, um. Not much." Her nonanswer causes me to glance her way. Clearly she went to the market, but for some reason she doesn't want them to know that. It seems a certain beauty might be in over her head.

"Well, you went to the market. Remember we talked?" I add. Mom's face practically glows in delight. I shouldn't give her ammunition, but it's impossible not to goad Olive, even just a little.

"I, uh, yes. How could I forget? You were reminding me that you'd like to go out sometime, right?" Her eyebrow rises in a challenge. *Game on, sweetheart.*

Max's face morphs into a shit-eating grin, Mom blows out an overexaggerated breath, and the girls giggle in delight.

"Well, it looks like you have your work cut out for you, big brother." Bridget chuckles as she stands, slapping me on the shoulder.

"Nah, she's already at the family dinner. Looks like she couldn't resist me after all." I take a long pull of my beer before clinking bottles with Max.

"Come on, kids, time to eat." Mom stands, sweeping her arm for us to follow. When Mabel issues an order, we fulfill it every time.

Dinner consists of an array of Irish delicacies. Shepherd's pie that's bubbling around the edges, colcannon mash, and soda bread. It's heaven, and much to my surprise, Olive isn't timid about digging in with the rest of us. She could have been reluctant—eating with Max has that effect when you have to fight for even a small portion—but she grabbed a plate and seemingly enjoyed everything. We are stuffed to the gills now, but Mom insists on breaking out dessert.

"Max, when's the first game?" Dad asks, ready to make small talk after a mostly silent meal.

"Coming up, a couple of weeks," he says around a bite of blackberry pie, bits of crumbs tumbling from his lips.

"Where are the games?" Olive asks, dabbing her perfect mouth with one of Mom's cream cloth napkins.

"At the arena over on Crow. Not too far from your place, actually."

"That's not on my usual running route, but now that I know the hockey team practices there, I might need to switch it up. I've never watched a game in person, I would love to see one." Olive smiles politely at Max but refuses to make eye contact with me. I can't tell if she's being nice or trying to drive me nuts. Either way, it's working. Feeling bold, I reach under the table and run my fingers lightly over her arm, taking satisfaction in the way a flush of red creeps up her neck.

"Yeah, for sure. Come by anytime. Happy to give you a tour."

"What number do you wear?" She spies me out of the corner of her eye. Is she trying to trick me into reacting? By sheer force of will, I don't.

"Twenty-two. It's always been my favorite. It's also the number of goals I scored last season."

Max is eating up the attention. The rest of us quit asking about his professional hockey dreams about four concussions ago. At this point, I'm concerned about the number of brain cells he will have left if he doesn't give the sport up soon. Don't get me wrong, he's good, but I don't love not being able to be out there to protect him.

"Can I buy your jersey somewhere? I'd like to dress the part if I'm going to come to your games. Be a real Max O'Reilly groupie." A devilish grin splits her lips. I haven't quite seen this side of her before, but I have a sneaking suspicion that she's not going to stop until I give her some sort of reaction.

"Didn't take you for a puck bunny, princess. But if that's what you're into, you can borrow my jersey when we go together." I growl the words just enough to let her know she's won, careful to throw in that the only way I'd like to see her supporting my baby brother is with me by her side, even if it makes me look like an ass, again.

"That's very sweet of you to offer, but I think I'll decide who I attend with," she whips back.

"Alright, kids. That's enough. Thank you all for coming, but it's getting late and Dad has an early morning helping Beau with restock. Sammy, be a sweetheart and get Olive home safe. She walked here, and it's far too late to go it alone."

Mom once again issues our marching orders. There's zero point in resisting. Plus, I want to take Olive home anyway. But I'd love it if I could offer without it being because my mother told me to. I swear, it doesn't matter how old I am, the woman will always tell me what to do and when to do it.

We all scurry about grabbing our belongings, carrying empty bowls and trays to the kitchen, exchanging hugs, and heading toward the door. In the shuffle of helping clean up and snagging my leftovers, I don't notice Olive sneak out. When I step onto the porch, she's nowhere to be seen.

My heart races as I think of her walking home alone. She doesn't take her own safety seriously enough—not that we live in a dangerous place, far from it. But anything could happen. She could trip and hurt herself, get lost or take a wrong turn. I slide my helmet on as quickly as possible and rev the engine, determined to find her.

It doesn't take long for me to cross town, it's maybe ten blocks in total, but looking for her feels like it takes hours. My eyes scan the dark and abandoned sidewalks, searching until finally, I spot her sashaying through the white picket fence gate in front of her cottage. There's no denying she hears me hovering. My bike does little to disguise my approach as the engine hums and rattles.

She doesn't turn around to look, she simply raises one hand moving it side to side in a perfect pageant wave while unlocking her door with the other. *Ugh!* This woman is going to be the death of me.

Eleven

Olive

A Sort of Pumpkin Patch

I should not have gone to the O'Reillys' house last night. Something told me Mabel was up to no good, but I take my work seriously and didn't want to disappoint Beau if word got back that I was turning down jobs. I knew from the minute I walked in that there wasn't ever any book to examine, and when Max and the girls waltzed in, the jig was up.

But I also couldn't be rude and just leave, and it was a little fun to mess with Sam. If I'm being honest, though, it was also a little awkward. I'm not practiced in letting loose or showing off my more playful side. But it felt nice, oddly like part of me was more open to putting myself out there. What is it about this man that intrigues me so much? He was growly and possessive about the hockey thing, but also sweet to his mom and funny with his siblings. I should be questioning if I can trust him, but for some reason, I'm not. I know deep in my belly that he's one of the good ones, if for no other reason than the love he has for his family.

My alarm chimes for the second time since I've hit snooze. I skipped my run altogether this morning, which is completely unlike me, but I think I needed the rest. I toss the covers back and step onto the cool wood floor, making my way to the bathroom. I pull the door shut, locking myself in, just in case. I'm still a little spooked from the whole Irina situation. Stepping toward the shower, I reach beyond the glass doors to turn on the spray when I see it.

There's no way. There must be something wrong with the reflection. The tattoo could not possibly be bigger than it was yesterday. I spin toward the mirror hanging above the vanity counter, rubbing the sleep from my eyes to be sure I'm really awake. Sure enough, extending from the scraggly heart are green pumpkin vines, varying in lengths from an inch to maybe four at the longest. Hanging off one of the vines is a small red book that appears to be vintage with tiny, almost imperceptible words where the title should be.

I clammer through the drawers in search of my contacts—I have to put them in to get a better look. My heart is racing as I fumble through the task, sacrificing two dailies to the drain before I'm fitted with a full set. Inching closer to the mirror, jamming my stomach into the vanity ledge, I make out the words *Beguiling Books*. What the heck?

Darting from the bathroom, I run to grab my phone, returning to snap a picture and send it to Ari.

It's growing . . . What am I going to do?

Ari

What the hell? What does the book say? I can't make it out.

Beguiling Books

Ari

What does that mean?

I don't know, but I'm freaking the fuck out. We need to find that witch.

Ari

First off, did you just type the F word? I'm working on it, I promise. I researched all night and came up with almost nothing online other than the old legends we already know. Did you find anything?

It was called for, this is nuts. And no! I was at Mabel's most of the evening.

Ari

Oh, how was the book? Beguiling?

That's not funny! There was no book, it was a setup to get me to their family dinner.

Ari

WHAT? You're joking.

Nope

Ari

Wow. I knew Mabel was a meddler but damn . . . How was it?

This conversation deserves more than a text, so I hit send on her name and the phone barely rings before she picks up. "I know we need to discuss the whole, you're cursed thing. And we will, but tell me you and Sam are dating, first."

"No, we're not. But I did have fun teasing him about going to Max's games."

"You didn't. I'm telling you, this man does not fall for anyone, and yet, he's smitten in fewer days than I can count on my fingers. Actually, are we sure you didn't ask Irina to put a spell on him specifically?"

"Rude," I burst in. "Maybe he just finds my personality endearing, or I'm just new and it's all a game."

"*Or*, and hear me out, he has a fetish for giant white period panties, and you happen to be the only woman to uncover his secret." I can hear her snickering to herself as she says it.

"Hilarious. They aren't that big, thank you very much. Seriously though, we're getting off topic. What are we going to do?"

"Well, I didn't find much online. Maybe there's something at Black Kettle . . . an old spooky book of spells or something historical. You need to see what you can dig up. I'm coming over tonight to formulate a plan. I'll meet you at the Brewhouse after work. We can grab coffee and go to the cottage to brainstorm." Ari must be getting ready to head out for work. I can hear the click of her heels as she walks around and the not-so-subtle clang of her door closing.

"Okay, I'll see what I can find. See you later. Oh, and Ari . . . Thanks. I'm glad I don't have to do this alone."

"It's not every day that your goody-two-shoes bestie shows up with a random, and might I add, not that well done, tattoo. Don't mention it." I scoff at her statement but she isn't wrong. This is not top-quality work, although the vines are much better than the heart itself.

We hang up, and I step into the steaming hot shower spray, avoiding my reflection like the plague. Even though I know it won't work, I spend extra time scrubbing at the tattoo as if by some chance this really is all a big joke. After ten minutes of wasted effort and my skin begging for relief, I jump out and ready myself for the day. It's not cool enough for long sleeves in the shop yet, but long sleeves are a must if I intend to keep this tattoo from Beau, and everyone else for that matter.

Slinking into tights and a bell-sleeved emerald dress, I put my hair up into a long, flowy ponytail with a matching bow, slick on some sheer makeup including mascara and eyeliner, and slide my toes into my brown Mary Janes. A quick stop for coffee first, and then it's just me and my mission to find out anything and everything about Irina.

"Ugh," I harrumph a pile of dusty, old books onto my desk. This is the fifth pile of the day, and my eyes are nearing a state of permanent strain from too much staring at the pages.

"Olive, you have a visitor," Beau bellows from the front of the store.

I slide my hands down the front of my dress and smooth the flyaways that have escaped to dangle around my face while I make my way to the front.

"Oh, hi." A whirring breath releases from my chest when I see Sam. Not that I'm comforted to see him, but I'm glad after my search has yielded almost no results that I don't need to discuss how to magically transform any books found in someone's attic at this very moment.

"Can I steal you for a minute to talk?" He wears a sheepish grin, and those sparkling blue eyes tell me he's up to something.

I glance at him sideways for a brief moment before agreeing, "Um, sure. Come back to my desk." I turn and head in the direction. It's not completely private, but Beau is listening to smooth jazz and I've seen him nod off a time or two since he returned from lunch. Sam will be able to speak freely without interruption. I round my desk and plop into my rolling chair, desperate to get off my feet while I listen to whatever he needs to say.

"Comfortable?"

"Actually, no. I'll be better when I can take these shoes off for the day, among other things." I dare him with a look to ask me to expand. He won't though, I know it.

"No one expects you to get this fancied up, you know. The lady who had this job before you wore mostly jeans and romance book T-shirts. Carol was very casual." He raises an eyebrow, then shakes his head as if he's trying to get the picture out of his mind. I think what he described sounds rather delightful.

"Thanks? But this is just who I am. My momma taught me to dress to impress no matter the occasion." I cross my arms. This couldn't be what he came to talk to me about. "What can I help you with? I'm, um, a little bit busy." I nod toward the pile of unopened legends strewn across my desk.

"I wanted to see if you had given any thought to going on a date. You left in a hurry last night, and I didn't get to ask you properly." Sam looks at his shoes, and there's a shyness to his question.

"I'm sorry, Sam—" His face drops even more, and I immediately realize that wasn't the right way to start. Trying to course correct and not hurt his feelings, I explain, "It's just that I've been trying to settle in, dealing with work research and stuff, you know. I haven't even had a second to decorate for fall, and that's one of my favorite things to do. I have the perfect porch for it, and instead it looks like the anti-autumn scrooge lives there." I ramble as he leans in, hovering over me and hitting me with a burst of his warm cinnamon scent. He's close, like really up in my space.

Sam lifts my chin with two fingers. "I get it, but I'm determined. When I set my mind to something, I don't give up easily." The words ghost over the shell of my ear as his lips graze my cheek, sending a shiver down my spine. "Prepare yourself to be wooed."

"I-I will think about it . . . I promise." I'm breathless from our proximity, my face still tingling from his touch.

Sam smiles the most drool-worthy smile as he takes a step out of my space. I know he can see how he affects me, and I don't like it at all. A part of me does want to try for a date, and that in itself says something about him. There's just the other part of me that is scared to let him in. He already makes me feel off kilter. If I gave him a chance, he'd have the power to wreck me, and with so much up in the air (and painted on my skin), it's a little overwhelming.

"Good. What time do you get off tonight?" *Whatever time you want me to. Oh my gosh, where did that come from? Stop it, Olivia. Get your head in the game, he means work.*

"Oh uh, six but I . . . I have plans with Ari," I quickly stumble through my nonavailability before he has a chance to show up again later and think he's going to bully me into a date. My stomach flip-flops at the thought, in a good way.

"Same time that I'm helping Mom finish the attic clean out. Text me, if you feel like it." With that he turns on his heel and saunters toward the front of the store. I hear him say a quick goodbye to Beau and then the door chimes and he's gone. I guess if I learned anything it's that Sam's still determined and his mother is not a complete liar about her cleaning efforts.

I right myself and dive into another book about the legends of Mage Hollow, scanning for anything that might be associated with Irina, but the problem is almost everything is about her. I could probably recite her entire life history at this point, or at least what's documented, and I'm still not any closer to finding the old bat. My eyes are heavy with fatigue and dust. Am I just going to be destined to live with this tattoo? Where did that other voice come from when Irina was going on about not letting people wear their hearts on their sleeves? And what lesson did the unknown voice want me to learn? What did she say again about making a decision before Halloween? Every day that passes, the clock is ticking down.

Her words echo in my brain. *If you change your mind, you must do so before the clock strikes midnight on Halloween. Once the night has passed, the change will be permanent.*

. . . the change will be permanent.

"Ollie, wake up." I'm jolted from my slumber as Ari shakes my shoulders and works to peel me off the desk. Glancing down, I notice a puddle of drool has seeped all over the book I was entranced in. *Great, I'll have to fix that.*

"W-what are you doing here? I must have drifted off." I rub my face, trying to wake from whatever I was dreaming about.

"I came at six, and Beau said you'd been out for a while. You seemed so peaceful, so I took my time looking through some of these. But it's getting late, and we need all the time we can get. Move it, toots." I can see Ari is trying to hide her grin.

I look at my watch, and shoot, it's already approaching eight. "Was Beau mad? I mean, he could have slammed a book or something to wake me up. Lord knows I've done it to him multiple times over the past week." I scan the store, waiting to locate him and see his disdain.

"Not at all. He said it comes with the job and something about old legends being better than melatonin. He left at six. He locked up but told me to remind you to make sure you double-check the doors when we leave." She crosses her arms and widens her stance. "So, are we going to leave or . . . are we drinking on the job?"

"Definitely leaving." I stand and shuffle around the desk, grabbing my stuff and making sure the back door is locked before we head out the front.

Mage Square is practically dead at this time of night. Aside from Union Tavern and the Brewhouse, nearly everything closes at four on the dot. We walk leisurely down the cobblestone sidewalk toward the infamous corner where I performed my greatest flashing event. A calm silence reverberates between us, neither wanting to discuss our findings or lack thereof where someone may overhear.

I notice Ari start to bounce with a bit more pep in her step as we approach my street. "What has gotten into you? Don't tell me you're excited about this." I stop to turn and look at her directly. I don't have it in me to be joyous about my predicament. I'm always grumpy about it when I wake up.

"Nope, nothing to do with that, babe. But you should, um, you should turn around and look at your house." Her eyes gleam in delight. *What the heck?*

"You're being weird. Don't try to scare me out of my house. I'll end up in your bed, and you know it's true." I glare at her, crossing my arms for emphasis.

"Shut up. The last place you're ending up is sharing a bed with me. You kick and talk in your sleep. But I'm not saying you won't end up in someone else's bed." She chuckles to herself before grabbing my arm to spin me around so I'm facing my cottage.

I can't believe the sight of it. There are pumpkins of every color mounded on the porch, and mums in brilliant shades of yellow, orange, and purple cascading down the steps. The porch swing has a fresh coat of paint with a blanket thrown over the back and what appears to be pink and orange pillows situated in the corners. There are candles strategically placed all around, glowing with a perfect amber hue. It's stunningly beautiful, more picturesque than even Pinterest could have imagined. My mouth is gaping as I take it in. "Ari, you shouldn't have. This must have cost a fortune." It's everything I've ever wanted when it comes to fall decor. I'm overwhelmed with the kindness of it.

"I didn't." She hops up and down clapping her hands.

"Wait, what?" I whip my head around to look at her. "What do you mean you didn't? Who did and how do you know about it?"

"I walked past here on my way to Black Kettle. A certain someone with big muscles and tattoos was hard at work, with the help of his dad I might add, which just . . . it was so cute." She grasps at her heart like she's holding it in from bursting. "He saw me and asked me to distract you for a bit while he finished up. I thankfully didn't have to try very hard because you were already out like a light." She grabs my hand and pulls me toward the cottage for an up-close look. I'm speechless. No one has ever done anything even remotely close to this for me, and it means he listened when I told him I didn't have time to decorate.

We take the stairs leading up to the porch one at a time, and the scene is even more magnificent up close. My head is spinning. I sit slowly on the swing after pressing my fingers to the paint and ensuring it was dry. I burrow into the pillows and grab the cream chenille blanket to wrap over my legs. As I do, my arm tingles—it's not painful but definitely noticeable. I rub at it, a brief thought of the tattoo passing through my mind, but Ari captures my attention.

"You sit tight. I'm going to grab some wine inside." She takes the keys out of my hand and spins toward the door. "Oh, and you better text him, like right now." Ari winks as she unlocks the door, heads inside, and closes it tightly behind her.

I swipe my phone and open a new message, not even sure what to say. Tears fall down my face, happy ones. My heart bursts that someone, anyone, cares this much. I wouldn't say I'm normally a happy crier, but with everything going on, the new job, the tattoo, it's just nice to feel heard. Like for once, something I said mattered.

Instead of sending a simple thank-you, I pop open the camera app and take a selfie. I snap a few, one with my tongue out, one smiling, and one laughing at the over-the-topness of this whole thing. Sending them is way outside of my comfort zone, but he went the extra mile, and at this moment, it feels right. I hit send followed by a quick note.

> You win! I'll go to dinner if you have any money left.

Before I can even set my phone down beside me it dings with an alert.

Sam

> Why are you crying?

> They are happy tears . . . Did you not see the YOU WIN part?

Sam

> I didn't mean to make you cry, happy or not. But I did see it, and I might be doing a celebratory dance right now.

> Please send proof or it didn't happen.

A minute later, a video pops up of Sam dancing around his house shirtless in low-slung, gray sweatpants. My mouth goes dry, and my eyes practically pop out of my head. I knew the man affected me, but this is another level. I think I'm having a hot flash.

"Um, am I interrupting something?" Ari approaches with a shit-eating grin on her face.

"No, nope. It's nothing." I tuck my phone under my leg, hiding it from her view.

"Nope is right. We are not keeping whatever just made you lose your mind to ourselves. You are sharing whatever glorious thing just happened or I am going home and pretending that you don't need saving from some crazy witch." She raises an eyebrow in challenge.

"Fine, but you can't tell anyone you saw this or I swear I will disown you. He sent it just for me," I warn her as I pull up the video and hit play.

"Holy mother of pearl. You have no idea how much you could sell this for at the dollar auction. The ladies of Mage would line up to see this eye candy." Ari fans herself, then hits play to watch it again.

"Alright, that's enough mooning over my man." I swat at her, taking the wine from her hand and gulping it straight from the bottle.

"Excuse me. Did you just refer to someone as *your* man?" She swipes the wine back, taking a glug. I guess we aren't using glasses tonight.

"I—you know what I meant. Don't make this a thing," I plead.

"Fine, but I could never forget a thing like this. I will remind you if and when it's necessary. Now tell me what you found today before you took a little nappy poo."

"Okay, but first, I need to go look at my arm. It's burning." I hop up and race inside to my room. When I strip out of my dress, sure enough, there are three small pumpkins surrounded by candles hanging off one of the vines.

Shit!

Twelve

Sam

A Princess That Turns into a Pumpkin

"Do I go casual or what?" The phone crackles on the other end with the occasional slam of a microwave door or cabinet.

"What now? I gotta be honest, I'm a little busy getting things together around here, man." I know Xav is hustling around his house, trying to prep essentials for when the baby comes, and I can hear Cami yelling things in the background, adding to his mounting list.

"What should I wear on a first date?" I repeat the question, annoyed that I'm nervous enough to seek fashion advice from my friend.

"You got it bad, bro. Hey, Cami, what should Sam wear on his first date?" I hear her shout something in response but it's muffled by Xavier's laughter. "She said . . ." He wheezes. "Wear jeans and a nice flannel. She also told me to make sure I put this in my best man speech." His chuckles hit the line again, and I can't help but laugh along with him.

"Very funny. When you call me to help fend off your daughter's prom date, I'm going to laugh in your face."

"It still could be a boy, and if not, she will never date," he quips back.

"Nah, it's a girl. It's what you deserve after this phone call." I smile into the phone, picturing him with an adorable baby girl bouncing around. He's going to be a fantastic dad. "I'm going to let you go. Call me if Cami goes into labor."

"Not for a few more weeks, bro. Good luck. And, Sam? Be yourself." He hangs up, and a small pang of jealousy burrows into my belly. I want what he has.

I shake off the thought and sift through my closet, searching for the blue-and-black flannel my mom got me for Christmas last year. Spotting it, I quickly grab it, give it a spritz of cologne, and toss it over my arm as I head into the bathroom for one final beard and hair check. I brush my teeth, put on my shirt, grab my wallet, and head out the door.

I'm rounding my old blue Chevy when the nerves hit their peak. What if I mess this up or she realizes I'm too different from her? My palms start to sweat as I open the door to jump in behind the wheel. I should've gotten flowers or something to give her, but I planned to buy her something where we were headed. I turn the key in the ignition, firing my truck up, the smooth rumble mimicking the tension coiling through me. Looking behind me and slowly backing up, I slam on the brakes. What the hell is my mom doing here?

I throw it in park and roll down the window as she approaches. "Hey, Ma, what-ah-ya doing? I'm headed out." She approaches with a smile on her lips, eyes twinkling.

"I know. Your father told me it's your first date." Her eyes glisten with joy, or maybe anticipation. "I brought you something to share with Olive. I think it might help you win her over." She hands me a plate of brown butter pumpkin cookies and steps back from the window.

"Mom, let's not get ahead of ourselves. Shouldn't you want her to win *me* over?" I remind her who her child actually is, even though the thought of earning anything with Olive makes my heart skip a beat. I shouldn't feel this way about someone I barely know.

"I said what I said, Samuel. A mother always knows what's best. Now don't mess it up," she warns me off with a finger pointed directly at my chest.

"Yes, ma'am. Now can I go, or did you want me to be late?" I sigh heavily, widening my eyes at her.

"Go, don't keep her waiting." She shoos me out of the driveway like she isn't the one who caused this delay. A part of me could be annoyed that she's so invested in my life, but the wafting scent of freshly baked cookies quickly evaporates the thought. *Okay, Ma, I'm going to get our girl.*

I don't live far from Olive, just a few blocks, and I'm pulling up to the curb in front of her cottage in no time. The decor Dad and I put out still looks fantastic, even though it's been a couple of days. Walking up to the door, I take in the view, picturing her sitting on the porch swing, reading a book or drinking her coffee.

I rap on the door twice, waiting for her to answer. After a minute or two, I lift my hand to knock again, but the door opens, sending a wave of her strawberry scent rolling onto the porch, nearly flattening me.

"Hi, I just need, like, two minutes to finish getting ready. I'm so sorry." Olive rushes off toward what I assume is her bedroom. "Make yourself at home," she shouts before closing the door after her.

I step inside, clicking the door closed behind me, and take in the space. It's nice here, an upgraded kitchen opens to where I'm standing in the living room. A green velvet couch is placed in the center with a cozy stone fireplace across from it, and the coffee table is scattered with colorful books. I approach, taking a seat and lifting a few of them to see what they are. Scanning the backs tells me Olive has an affinity for romance novels. I don't recognize any of the authors immediately, not that I spend much time in that section of Black Kettle. Names like Margaret Rose, Cassandra Moll, Lainey Lawson, and Mallory Meyers lay claim to the novels. Their covers are works of art with vivid scenes; I could tattoo these, and they would turn out stunning.

"See anything you're interested in?" Olive's voice is curious. Does she believe I've read any of these?

"No. But you have quite the collection." I stand, turning toward her, the couch positioned between us. "You look gorgeous." A slow breath leaks out as I take her in. My mouth goes dry. Her hair is down in long cascading waves, and her lips are painted the perfect shade of pink. But the best part is her glowing smile.

"Thank you, blue looks good on you." Her cheeks blush as she pays me the compliment.

I can't help but reach for her hand. "Come here." I tug her around the couch and wrap her in a hug, tucking my nose into her hair. Strawberries and cream float through me with every breath I take. It's intoxicating.

"Are you, um, ready to get going?" She looks up at me, melting me with her smile and giving me one last hard squeeze.

"Yeah, I am."

We head out, and I help her into the truck before rounding it to get in.

"Where are we going?" she asks, settling in and buckling her seat belt.

"Ah, if I tell you, then what would the surprise be?" I grin at her, then reach out to take her hand in mine, giving it a gentle squeeze. "It'll be fun, promise."

A short and relatively silent drive leads us to Baxter's Pumpkin Palace, a Mage Hollow staple where you can do everything from getting lost in a corn maze to shopping for seasonal decor and picking your own pumpkins. It's one of my favorite places and holds so many memories from my childhood.

"This is so cute. I can't wait to see everything. Where should we start?" Olive asks, bouncing slightly with obvious excitement. I think it's the first time I've seen her look completely comfortable, and I like it.

"Corn maze?" I suggest, unbuckling before once again rounding the truck to open her door.

"You know, I really am not trying to be rude, but you could have asked for a map like a sane person." Olive stares at me before spinning in circles searching for a way out.

"Scared, princess?" I smirk at her, raising an eyebrow.

"No, I am most certainly not scared, but if we get stuck out here all night, I will never let you live it down. And quit calling me princess," she huffs and crosses her arms, jutting a hip out. I chuckle to myself, grabbing her hand and leading her out of the corn maze.

"You know we weren't ever really lost, right?"

"No, I think you got lucky." She stifles a laugh and pats my arm lightly. "I'm not saying that I'm great at directions, but I do think if I hadn't made that left turn fifteen minutes ago, we would have just kept going deeper and deeper until we were stuck for life."

She's playing defiant, but we have been having the time of our lives. Since the minute we left the house, it's been quiet, stolen glances, non-stop laughter, and lighthearted jokes. This might be the best first date I've ever been on, and it's magnified by the fact that it's the first time she hasn't immediately snapped her walls into place. I feel like we are getting somewhere, making progress.

"Want some warm apple cider?" I link our hands, noticing how soft and delicate hers are compared to mine.

"I would love that, thank you." Olive hip checks me as we swing our arms back and forth walking toward the small food truck set up every year at the pumpkin patch.

We step up to order, and Olive practically drools over the cookies and pastries on the menu. "Should we get some dessert to share?" She gives me puppy dog eyes, but she doesn't know I have that special treat from Mom hidden away under the seat in the truck.

"Nah, I've got something else in mind." I wink at her, stepping closer to order two ciders to go.

"Sam, it's a first date. What kind of woman do you take me for?" She eyes me wearily, like I might try something.

"Just come with me. You'll see." I grab our drinks, handing one to her, and lead us to my truck. Popping open the tailgate and patting it so she knows to sit, I open my door and pull out the plate of cookies. "Close your eyes, princess."

"Okay, but seriously, you have to knock it off with that nickname. I promise I'm trying to be nice, but it's driving me nuts." She squeezes her eyes shut, and I plop the plate in her lap. "What's this?" She peers down at the mound of cookies. "Di-did you bake for me?"

"Nope, must've been magic." I slide onto the tailgate, sitting down next to her.

"What? You . . . You believe in magic?" Her question comes out breathy, almost like she's shocked that I would say the word magic.

"Nope, not even a little. I know that's not what someone from Mage Hollow is supposed to say. But I'll never understand the obsession over something that is so clearly fictitious." Olive doesn't say anything; she stares at her shoes and swallows hard, instead. Does she believe in magic?

"Who, uh, who baked these then?"

"My mom did," I admit, hoping it doesn't scream, *He's a momma's boy*, and send her running for the hills.

Olive peels back the plastic wrap, grabbing a cookie and thrusting it into her mouth. "Ermaghad, tha womah is a wizah," she mumbles around a mouthful, carefully chewing. "She bakes and cooks. She's kind of amazing," Olive clarifies after swallowing.

"I'll make sure to tell her you said that. I almost ran her over on my way out of the driveway." I shake my head thinking about my meddling mother, even if I'm a tad grateful for the assist here.

"What's she normally like? I mean, when she isn't trying to set you up on dates?" She takes a sip of her cider, gently wiping away a small drop that escaped on her lip with her thumb.

Shaking myself out of being mesmerized, I say, "Oh, um, she's my mom. She's funny, a great cook, and a supportive wife. What you see is what you get with her. She loves her family and works hard, but she's a straight shooter."

"I bet you and Max gave her a run for her money when you were growing up." It's not really a question, more of a known fact.

"Nah, I think the girls made it rougher on her than we ever did. They always had some drama going on. Max and I just did dumb stuff but nothing too terrible. What about your mom? What's she like?"

"Oh boy . . . how does one sum up Anne Bowman?" She looks off into the distance, swinging her feet just enough to make the truck wobble. "My mom is the perfect Southern belle. Gets up with the sun, never caught without lipstick on, and always planning the next party. She had very high expectations, still does, and I rarely meet them," she says with a twinge of sadness.

"That can't be true. From where I'm sitting, you're damn near perfect, princess." I run my hand softly down her arm, linking fingers with her and giving a gentle squeeze. She bristles a little, like a chill has taken over.

"Why do you do that?" She looks directly in my eyes.

"Do what? Are you cold?"

"No, continue to call me princess when I asked you not to." She releases our hands and grasps her cup with both of hers, waiting for my answer. What should I say? I thought it was our thing, trading barbs and Southern-coated sarcasm.

"Well . . . to be honest, I thought you secretly liked it." Her eyes bug out of her head. Okay, nope, she doesn't. "When I saw you have your Marilyn Monroe moment, I stopped not because I'm a total creep, although I didn't mind the view, but because you looked like a damsel in distress. But then you righted yourself and walked across the street like nothing had ever happened. I guess it made me think for a second, there's a real princess, someone who straightened their crown and kept the show going. It also helps that you're beautiful, like my very own Cinderella waltzing about." I look at my boots, afraid of gauging her reaction.

Her hand slides across mine as she pulls herself closer. "Sam, that's sweet. I thought that you did it because you thought I acted like a princess, you know, in a bad way. I'm sorry."

"I mean, you do have tendencies." She swats me on the arm, but I grab her wrist before she finishes making contact.

"Not nice. Let me think. There has to be something I could call you that would drive you nuts. Maybe I'll ask Max." She winks at me, then goes back to sipping her cider.

"That's cold. Maybe I'll change it to Ice Princess from now on." I smirk so she knows I'm joking, or at least I hope she does.

"Can I tell you something?" Olive looks at me with doubt in her eyes. I reach out, wrapping an arm around her and pulling her close.

"You can tell me anything."

"I don't even know why I'm telling you this. I never tell anyone. But the reason it bothers me is because my mom always called me that. I was always her little princess . . . until I wasn't anymore." Her voice shakes as she says it. I use my first two fingers to tip her face up toward mine.

"What do you mean? How could you ever not be her little princess?" I search her eyes for an explanation.

"Never mind, it's nothing. Just, I'm sorry, we were having a good time and now I ruined it." She shakes her head and takes a deep breath in through her nose, out through her mouth.

"How you feel is not nothing. I want to know. I want to be here for you, and I hate that whatever's happening is hurting you." I brush her hair off her face tenderly.

"I'm fine, I promise. But please, let's lose the nickname." She hops off the truck, grabbing the plate of cookies and placing them on the bench seat inside my door.

"Done, no more nicknames." I smile at her sincerely. If she doesn't like something, then I won't do it. It's as simple as that. "Do you want to go walk around inside the barn and look at the crafts they have for sale?"

"Sure, but have you ever seen a Southern woman shop?" She chuckles to herself, shaking her head, then links her arm through mine as we walk toward the barn. Each time she touches me it's like electricity jolting through my body. I'm becoming addicted to the high I get from the buzzing.

Once inside, we stroll through each carefully curated booth, looking at everything from creepy voodoo dolls to classic fall decor. There's garland, pumpkins, and enough cinnamon brooms to make a person's eyes water. Olive picks out a pink ghost that looks a little like a stuffed tissue made out of glass, holding a sign that says, "Welcome to my humBOOle abode." To me it's a little cheesy, but she adores it, so I insist on buying it for her. She stomps her foot in protest until I take a risk and tickle her side, making her giggle and succumb to my will.

Afterward, we walk around the pumpkin patch, looking at the different shades and varieties when one strikes her eye. "Look at this one! It's so ugly it's perfect."

"Don't you have enough pumpkins already?" I challenge her with a look. I know for a fact there are already seventeen strewn across her porch because I put them there.

"Is there such a thing as too many pumpkins?" She winks, spinning toward the register, daring me to beat her there. I take off sprinting, hurdling a hay bale to get to the desk before she does.

"You can't buy me everything. I have a job, you know." She places her free hand on her hip, pouting out her perfect bottom lip.

"I'll buy you anything you want. It's a date, and I happen to be a gentleman." I grin at her and take the pumpkin, which is really more of a gourd, from her hands to place it on the scale.

"That'll be six dollars, Sam. Aren't you two just adorable," Mrs. Baxter says, looking back and forth between Olive and me. "My husband used to bring me here after hours to pick out my favorite pumpkin. It seemed silly at the time—we own the place. But I lost him last year and have missed him and his goofy ideas every day since." I hand her a ten and push the change back to her as I grab the pumpkin to head out. "He sounds like my kind of guy. I'm sorry to hear that we lost another good one."

Olive takes a step around the table toward Mrs. Baxter. "Can I give you a hug?" she asks.

"Oh dear, I would like that very much." Olive wraps her arms around the elderly woman, whispering something in her ear that makes her giggle. "It was nice to meet you, Olive. Please come back anytime." Mrs. Baxter grabs Olive's face and leans in, touching their noses, and then releases her with a wink.

We walk back to the truck in silence. Butterflies dance in my belly as our night comes to a close. I place the pumpkin safely on the floor and help Olive into her seat, reaching around to buckle her in, not failing to notice how her breath hitches when my hand grazes her belly accidentally. I stroll around to my side and hop in, but before turning the ignition, I ask, "What secrets did you share with Mrs. Baxter?"

"Oh, nothing, except that I promised to let you buy me pumpkins without a hassle from now on. You know, since it's the right thing to do." She winks at me then faces forward.

The drive to her cottage has me reflecting on what a truly amazing date this has been. This woman is everything I've ever wanted. She's sassy and smart, and she's beautiful beyond words, but most importantly, she's kind in a way that not very many people are. She started to open up to me a little bit but then quickly closed herself off again. I want her to trust me, but I admittedly don't have a ton of experience in the getting-deep-emotionally department. With her, though, I don't care what it takes. I want to see her smile as much as I want to keep breathing, and if that means talking through whatever she's keeping locked away, I'm willing to do it.

We pull up to the curb, and she reaches to unbuckle her seat belt. "Don't open that door," I warn as I hop out and quickly circle the truck.

"Sam, I'm capable of opening my own door." She crosses her arms and refuses my hand as she leaps from the truck.

"I know. But that doesn't mean you should have to." I reach for her sides, tickling her the tiniest bit as we walk up the porch steps, stopping at her door.

"Stop tickling me or I'm going to drop Boo," she squeaks as she carefully sets the ghost and pumpkin down on the porch swing. "Thank you for an amazing first date."

I grab her hand and pull her into a hug. "The pleasure was all mine." I slowly drag my finger across her freckles. "Thank you for agreeing to come with me." She peers into my eyes as our breaths mingle and our lips draw closer together. We are a whisper away from kissing when the door flies open, smacking the wall with a crack.

"Shit, oops, sorry. I thought it was just Olive. Didn't see you, Sam." Ariella Marino stands in the doorway in Snoopy pajamas with green goop dripping down her face.

Olive jumps back. "Ari, what are you doing here?"

"I'll just give you two a minute. I needed to talk to you." She slams the door in our faces, and I can't suppress the chuckle that bursts from my lips.

"That was, uh, that was not where I thought this was going." I run a hand through my beard, still fighting off the laughter.

"So sorry about that. She's never been very good with boundaries. But I should go see what she needs. Thank you again." She reaches out to squeeze my hand, and I take the moment to pull her in for one more quick hug.

I place a brief kiss on her forehead. "Thanks for a spectacular date. Please text me later."

Smiling, she lifts her hand to the spot I kissed. "I will. I promise." Olive opens the door and disappears inside, leaving me to head back to my truck and drive home.

Thirteen

Olive

Some Roads are Dead Ends

"What in the heck was so important you needed to crash my date?" I scoff, stepping out of my boots and untying my shirt on the way to my bedroom.

"Hmm, let's see. The fact that you have a tattoo that is clearly growing, by the minute I might add, and we still haven't found Irina." Ari crosses her arms.

"It's not growing by the minute!" I shout from my bedroom while rifling through my drawer for a nightshirt and sleep shorts.

"You sure about that?" Ari leans against the doorframe looking me up and down suspiciously as if she chased me in here to prove a point.

"Wha . . ." I start to ask what she's talking about, but a quick glance tells me she's not wrong. Not only do I have pumpkins, candles, and a heart, but now there's a cute little Boo added on, and the vines are longer, perfectly woven amongst the items. "No, how is this possible?" I didn't feel it this time, maybe because I was distracted by the best first date I've ever had. My heart skips a beat as I'm thinking of how easy it was to be with Sam. He was completely different today, not grumpy at all.

Abandoning my mission to change, I throw the nightshirt over my shoulder and flop onto my bed, covering my face with my hands. What am I going to do if the tattoo keeps growing at this rate? I won't be able to hide it forever.

I glare at her. "I can't answer how it's possible, I honestly can't even believe it is. I grew up hearing about witches and magic and all the things you're living, but I guess I always thought it was a load of crap." Ari settles herself next to me on the bed and stares at the ceiling, careful not to get any of her face mask on my comforter.

"For me it's even weirder. I mean, obviously because it's on my body. But also, I didn't grow up with any of this. I wasn't even allowed to trick-or-treat." I huff a little, not ready to face the mirror or the truth. I asked for this. It's exactly what I wanted, except I don't know how a book, a few pumpkins, some candles, and a ghost represent my heart.

"Are you going to ask me about my plan?" Ari shifts, bumping my arm with her face, green goop plastering itself to me.

"Ew! Go wash that off and then you can tell me." I stand, walking to the kitchen to rinse my arm when my phone dings.

Sam

I had fun tonight. Thanks for going, I hope I can see you again soon.

I respond right away, part of me wishing our night wouldn't have ended already and the other part glad that Ari intervened. I don't know how I would've explained my arm and what's happening to Sam. He made it clear he doesn't believe in magic—it doesn't get more enchanting than a potion induced tattoo that grows and changes.

You are so sweet. I had the best time, and I'm looking forward to doing it again.

Sam

How about Friday?

Sounds like a date.

Sam

It is!

"Who are you texting? Lover boy?" Ari waltzes into the kitchen, fresh faced and looking for trouble.

"Actually, yes. We had a nice time tonight but—"

"But what?"

"I . . . well, what am I going to do if things, you know"—I swoosh my hand in the air—"heat up between us?" I can feel the blush creeping up my neck, and I reach for a glass of water to cool down my throat.

"Um, I actually don't know other than telling him the truth or making sure you never undress. That's why you need to call in sick tomorrow." Ari grabs a bag of salt-and-vinegar chips from the cupboard and moves into the living room. I follow, ready to eat my feelings.

"I can't call in sick. What would Beau think?" I plop down on the couch, stealing a handful of the salty bits of heaven that I adore so much.

"He would think that you're sick. You may not want to go, but we have somewhere to be."

"Where are we going?" I can't just be expected to risk a brand-new job. She better have an actual plan.

"Salem. To catch a witch." Ari raises an eyebrow in challenge. She knows I'm going; getting rid of this tattoo has to be the priority, even if I'm risking pissing Beau off.

"Fine, I'll call in sick, but we have to actually find something there." I crunch a few more chips, and she fills me in on the plan. After a draining rundown of all we haven't found and what could possibly happen tomorrow, I feel myself drifting off to thoughts of Sam and Irina.

I'm startled awake by what sounds like someone beating down my door. Who the heck has the audacity? I roll off the couch, a half-eaten chip falling to the floor as I slink my way to the door, trying my best not to disturb Ari, who's conveniently passed out on the floor. I grasp the door handle, not thinking about my appearance or attire before opening it.

"Wow . . . that's not what I expected you to look like at"—Sam glances at his watch—"8:53 in the morning." He takes me in, looking me over thoroughly, probably assessing if he wants to run for the hills. I swipe a hand at my hair, trying to tame whatever it is surely doing, and toss him an awkward smile.

"I, uh, yeah. I usually don't, but I guess I slept in." I shrug in an attempt to play it cool, even though my stomach is rioting as a reminder that it is wholly unacceptable to be seen in such a state of disarray. I have no clue what he's doing here.

"I heard. I brought you this and came to see if you were okay." He hands me a steaming cup of pumpkin spice latte from the Brewhouse. I grasp it greedily, sucking down a sip as quickly as possible.

"Ahh. Shi-oot, it's hot." I wipe my mouth with the back of my hand, my face twisting in discomfort from the scalding liquid as I set the cup down on the entry table.

"Sorry. I thought you'd want it fresh." He reaches out, running his fingers through my hair, removing a potato chip and handing it to me. "Looks like you were maybe saving this for later." There's that million-dollar smile.

"Oh, um, yeah actually." I toss the chip in my mouth like a lunatic and crunch it down.

"Oh my God. Why did you eat that? It was a joke." He looks horrified. *I am really selling myself here.*

"I-I don't know. I think I'm still asleep." I laugh at the ridiculousness of this interaction and how I must look before realization settles in that I'm wearing only a thin layer of panties and my long-sleeved sleep shirt. I casually tug the bottom hem down and then my sleeve as mortification settles in. The tattoo shouldn't peek out, but I also can't be sure it didn't grow again while I was sleeping.

"Clearly. I just came by to see if you needed anything." He eyes me suspiciously. "You don't look sick, so what is it? A case of the brown bottle flu?"

"Well, I don't look good." I peer down at myself, wincing at just how disheveled I really am.

Sam grabs my face, his rough palms scraping the sides of it gently as he pulls me closer to him. We are a very bad morning breath away from kissing. Is this seriously how our first kiss is going to go? He looks deep into my eyes. I can't fight the way I'm staring back into his. There's something about him that's so disarming, it's like every interaction makes me want to open up to him more even, though opening up to anyone is about as foreign to me as it gets.

"You are every bit as gorgeous right now as you were the first time I met you at the store." He presses a tender kiss to my forehead and then releases me.

"There's no way that's true." I practically purr the words out. He has me all hot and bothered from one little touch. Maybe it's the leftover tension between us that Ari so rudely interrupted last night.

"It is, Olive. Now, I don't know what you're up to, but I do know that you called out of work, which doesn't seem like something you would do. If you're not sick, which we both know you aren't, can you at least tell me what's going on?"

"It's my fault," Ari yells from her spot on the floor.

Sam and I both look to where she's lying. We can't see her body since the couch is obscuring the view, but her hand is up as she wiggles her fingers in greeting.

"I see. That makes sense." Sam nods toward Ari, and I slink out the door and onto the porch, closing the door behind us.

"She's, um . . . She needs my help with some girl stuff today. I didn't want to call out, but she really needed me and I didn't know what else to do." I'm trying to reassure him that we're okay without giving him any details.

Sam runs his finger down my cheek. "It's absolutely okay. You're a good friend, I admire that. Just don't let Beau catch you out and about. That old man can be a little grumpy when he doesn't have someone to cover his lunch break. Oh, and if you ever are actually sick, please let me know." He's so close, my body is responding in a visceral way. My stomach does a flip, warning me that maybe it's too fast for my feelings to be more than just physical. Maybe this is the lesson the strange voice wanted me to learn; if I'm vulnerable, I'll learn the hard way.

Sam must notice that I'm lost in thought. He lifts my chin between two fingers so that I can't avoid looking him in the eyes. "Hey, where'd you go?"

"Sorry." I bristle at myself, shaking off the negative energy that comes with thinking about Irina and the mystery voice. "I will, I promise. But, um, I should probably get back in there before anyone sees me and calls the landlord on me for indecent exposure." Sam chuckles, raising an eyebrow in challenge.

"Wouldn't be the first time you've exposed yourself in public around here. But I'm inclined to agree with not wanting you out here on display. Come here and give me a hug before I leave you to it." He stretches his arms out wide for me to walk into. I take two steps forward, enveloping myself in his warm, strong, cinnamon-scented embrace. Sam lifts me up as I wrap my legs around his waist and bury my face in his neck. I don't know what has gotten into me, but something about him caring where I was or even thinking to bring me coffee has me ready to throw all caution to the wind.

"Can I kiss you?" he whispers.

"Are you serious? Like this?"

"I've never been more serious about anything." He looks me square in the eyes, heat and something else reflecting back at me.

"Yes, plea—" Before I can finish the word, his lips crash down on mine. They are soft yet firm, and I can hear a slight groan release in his throat. He breaks away, but I dive right back in, not ready to be done so fast. I slide my tongue over the seam of his lips, asking for entry. He opens, deepening the kiss as our mouths mingle, desperate to gain even an inch of purchase. I feel my back hit the side of the house as his hands wrap around under my butt to hold me up. He lightly kneads and massages as we lose ourselves for who knows how long. The sparks between us are undeniable, but suddenly reality sets in that we are in public and I'm supposed to be sick. I break away, sucking in the air he has stolen from my lungs.

Sam is still holding me up, his erection pressed perfectly to my center, my arms around his neck. I bury my face in it so I don't dive back in for round two—or would this be three? Who knows.

"That was . . . I think I need to know the brand of chips you buy." He smirks, as I look up at him in horror.

"Oh my God. I'm so sorry. I—put me down so I can go die of embarrassment." I swat at him trying to wriggle free.

"I'm joking, babe. That was the best kiss I've ever had in my entire life." He peppers my cheek and neck with kisses, reassuring me before blowing a raspberry near my collarbone. "Can't you tell?" He leans forward, pressing himself into me a little harder. I can't help the squeak that tumbles from my lips as sparks ignite through my core, and my vagina turns slick. My mind is still stuck on the word *babe*. I thought I'd hate it, but weirdly I don't.

"Um, yeah . . . yes." I wiggle free this time, Sam setting me down gently on my feet. "It was for me too." I can feel the pink blush racing up my neck and onto my cheeks.

"Be careful, with whatever you're doing today." Sam places one more kiss on my cheek, adjusts himself downstairs, and turns to walk back to his bike. I watch him put his helmet on, my stomach churning with the flaps of a thousand butterflies. He lifts his hand to wave when I shout, "Thanks, Sam. Text me." With a quick nod, he mounts the bike and races off down the road.

I lean back against the side of the house, my fingers touching my swollen lips, and close my eyes. This man is going to be the death of me, especially if we don't find Irina. And soon. Every time I start to feel like maybe I could actually let myself fall for him, I get a weird tingly sensation in my arm and am ripped from dreamland back to the cold reality that I'm literally cursed. Getting myself together, I shake off the exchange and go back inside.

"How is your lover boy this morning?" Ari asks, leaning against the kitchen counter, clothed and sipping my drink.

"Was I out there that long? Give me that." I dart across the room, grabbing my drink and taking the final glug of it. I pull the sleeve of my shirt up to my elbow, and sure enough, there's a bag of salt-and-vinegar chips hanging out next to Boo. *Oh, my hell!*

Ari notices but instead of bringing it up, she responds to my question. "Nope, only maybe ten minutes, but we overslept. Howie has been waiting for us at my place for thirty minutes, so you need to move it, sister. Go rinse off from whatever just happened out there." She shoots me a knowing look, but all I can do is smile as I skip into my bathroom to shower and change.

A quick twenty minutes later, we are out the door, rushing into Howie's vintage Bronco idling in front of my cottage. Ari had texted him to tell him where we were so we didn't lose any additional time. I still haven't figured out why he's escorting us, but I'm going with it in hopes of playing matchmaker if nothing else comes out of this day.

"Hey, Howie. How are you?" I ask, sliding into the backseat.

"Hi, Olive. I'm good." He smiles at me in the rearview mirror, pink dusting his cheeks as Ari slides into the front passenger seat. "Where am I taking you ladies?"

"Hi, Howard. Thanks for coming with us." Ari fastens her seat belt before patting his hand on the gear shift in gratitude. "We need to go to Salem, to the historical society to be exact."

"Learning about witches?" His gaze meets mine in the rearview again, and I realize she didn't tell him what we are going for, just that we needed to go somewhere and he jumped at the opportunity to drive us like the sweet golden retriever he is.

"Oh, sort of," I say. Ari spins in her seat to look me in the eyes and nods. "I have a little something going on, and we are trying to get to the bottom of it." Howie pulls away from the curb, making his way down my street and toward the edge of town.

"What's going on that you need to go to Salem?" When he asks, he seems genuinely curious, not nosy.

"Can I trust you?" I ask, attempting to assess his response via the single small mirror in the center of the truck.

"I think so?" This sweet man doesn't know what's about to happen.

"So, I met Irina during the Hollow Hearts Festival, and she put a spell on me, and now I have a tattoo."

"I'm sorry. What the fuck did you just say?" Howie's tires squeal as he slams on the brakes and slowly pulls to the side of the road.

"You heard her, Howard." Ari nods, as if to put him at ease. "She met the real Irina, the one from all the legends, and she cast a spell on her."

"I thought I was the only one."

"Excuse me, what?" I shout, unbuckling and clambering forward onto the center console to look at him.

"I met her once. I thought I was crazy for years," he explains, putting his hands over his face in what I think is shock.

"You've met her? Why? What did she say?" Ari asks, pushing me back so she can also see his expression.

"Look, it was a long time ago. Remember Brian Danfield?" He shifts in his seat, turning fully toward Ari.

"Yes, I remember him, the only kid in tenth grade that could grow a full beard. What does he have to do with this?" Ari asks, unbuckling her seat belt and tucking her leg up under her.

"You never thought it was weird? The beard, I mean?" he asks, a slight wrinkle in his brow.

"I guess, but that beard paid off for him big time. We went to senior prom together." Ari's face turns a fluorescent shade of red at the reminder of that particular facial hair. There's a story I've never heard. Howie's face twists in pain for a split second before returning to normal.

"Brian and I saw her at Hollow Hearts that year. She took us to this creepy room, I guess it was her shop. I had a bad feeling about it, so I bolted, but Brian stayed. A week later he had a full beard. I never asked, but I always thought something weird had happened there. I mean, there was no way that guy was just suddenly able to grow a beard like that. Or at least that's what I told myself," he mumbles the last bit as Ari and I exchange glances.

"Okay, Howie. I've been there, in the shop I mean. That's where she took me, but I can't find it to get her to undo this." I pull at the neckline of my shirt, revealing my shoulder and the top of the tattoo.

"The shop is not there. It's nowhere." Howie's eyes glisten. He's resigned himself already, I can tell, that we aren't going to find Irina.

"Did Brian ever find her again?" Ari asks, reaching out to pat my knee.

"Not that I know of, but once he had the beard and the popularity, we didn't talk much." He sinks back into his seat, closing his eyes.

"It's okay, Howie. Thank you for telling me. I just need to find answers, and you have to promise not to tell anyone." I pat his shoulder, reassuring him that I'm not upset.

"I won't tell anyone, but I do want to help you. You won't find anything in Salem. They all but banished every trace of her and her sisters when they escaped. But I know a few people in town who might know something about the old legend. I could ask around if you're okay with it." Her sisters? How have I not come across anything about her siblings? Is it one of them that spoke to her—the mystery voice?

Ari and I nod simultaneously. "Please help me, Howie. But don't give anything away."

"Yeah, she doesn't want lover boy to know," Ari chirps.

"Sam? I won't tell anyone, I promise."

"Yeah, Sam. It's new and a magical tattoo is really unexplainable." I shudder thinking about what he would say if he knew. Not only is it embarrassing that I even needed her help opening up in the first place, but he would think I'd completely lost my mind.

Howie nods in understanding, puts the car back into gear, and pulls away from the curb. "You ladies up for lunch at Union instead of a road trip? I want to get there before old Mr. Weiss gets in. He might know something."

"That would be great," I say. I'll have to sneak in the back so Beau doesn't catch me, but if there's a chance someone knows something, I'm not missing it.

Fourteen

Sam

A Few Questions and a Dare

I didn't expect my first kiss with Olive to be on her porch the morning after our first *official* date, but I'm glad it happened. I knew from the minute I saw her there was something special between us. An uncanny attraction, a pull like nothing I'd ever felt before. Even my mother sees it, and she has never once liked anyone I've dated. Mabel O'Reilly is hard to please, but a few hours with Olive and she's practically placing an announcement in the *Mage Hollow Herald* that her eldest child has a girlfriend.

Is it just that it's finally my turn to find my person? Or is there something unique about her that I might actually get over my fear of not having what my parents have? It's too early to know, and we've gone from zero to a hundred quickly. My normal response would be to pull back, rein it in, break it off. But with Olive, it's different. I feel a sense of responsibility for her happiness. Almost like if I take care of her everything else will fall into place as it should. Not to mention, I miss her and it's only been less than a week. That alone makes this whole thing different.

"So where are you taking her this time?" Max brings me back to the conversation, snapping his fingers in my face across the table.

"I'm thinking of going for a drive up the coast. Take her to the cabin for a movie." I shrug before tucking into another bite of the Reuben I ordered.

"Romantic. You must be serious about this girl." Max takes a glug of his Coke, waiting for my response.

"I think I am. I mean, it's so new, but there's something about her that feels different than everyone else I've ever dated."

"She's your Mabel?" His face lights up as he asks the question. He already knows the answer.

"Maybe. Mom thinks so. But what if it's all just the allure of something new? What if it blows up in my face?" I'm caught in this weird place between trusting my heart and wondering logically about how fast you can find your soulmate. I know it happened quickly for my parents, but I also know that's rare.

"Nah, man. I can see it, and Mom clearly does. Olive is special. I wish I found her first." He looks down at his half-eaten sandwich, and there's a hint of longing on his face. It's not a surprise. We all grew up dreaming about that once-in-a-lifetime kind of love. We saw the ultimate example of it daily. But it doesn't mean it's guaranteed to happen for us.

"You'll find the one. Maybe if you stop spending all your time getting beat to hell on the ice, she'll pop up out of nowhere." I shouldn't give him shit about his hockey career, but the big brother in me is worried about him. He's killing himself with training, and if he has another concussion this year, he might never be the same.

"Don't you start giving me shit for following my dreams. I get enough of that from Mom." Max shifts uncomfortably in the booth. He doesn't like being confronted with what we all know is a very real fear of his that he chooses to stuff way down deep and ignore.

"Alright." I shrug and put on a sympathetic smile. "I won't berate you, but at some point, we will have to face it together. I always have your back, you know. I'd hate for that pretty face to get messed up in some brutal fight and never recover."

He grins at me knowing that I'm serious but also never far from trading jabs with him.

"Thanks, Sammy. Even if you're an asshole, I love you."

"Love you too. Now am I paying or is it your turn? I have a date to plan." I wave Howie over to our booth to grab the check, extracting my card before Max has time to answer my rhetorical question. I'm the big brother, I own my own business, I'm paying.

"I'm not sure if I dressed appropriately. You didn't exactly tell me where we're going." Olive shifts nervously on the steps of her cottage as we prepare to head to my truck.

"You look beautiful just the way you are. I don't give a shit what you wear." I smile at her. It's true. I made out with her for the first time after extracting a day-old chip from her hair.

"Okay, but I still would like to know, just in case." She bats her eyelashes at me, tugging at the hem of the beige-and-white flannel coat she has on. I'm not sure if it's just a cultural difference with her being from the South, but I've noticed she spends quite a bit of time worrying about her appearance and if she's saying the right thing. I just want her to be comfortable and relaxed with me.

"It's nowhere fancy, I promise. We're going for a drive up the coast. I'm the only person you're going to see, and I'm already here." I kiss her forehead before tugging at her hand to pull her toward my truck.

"Okay, but if we run into anyone, my mother might curse me all the way from Alabama." Her mother sounds like a piece of work. Olive reluctantly makes her way to the passenger door, allowing me to open it and help her inside. I shut her door and round the truck to get in.

"What's this about your mom?" Curiosity is getting the better of me. I get the feeling Olive's mom had a tendency to regularly make her feel less than amazing.

"Nothing, it's fine. So, a drive up the coast. That sounds . . . scenic?" Olive blows off my question, but I let it go. For now.

"I figured you haven't been outside of Mage Hollow much since coming up here. There are miles of coastline and lots of cool lookout spots." I turn the ignition and rev the truck for our journey. She doesn't know I packed all the essentials to set up our very own drive-in movie complete with snacks. Or that I'm taking her somewhere special to me.

"That sounds amazing." She looks out the window as we make our way out of town toward Route 1. As I take the turn onto the two-lane highway, her breath hitches at the sight of the changing fall leaves. It's my favorite spot in town, where the trees cover the road with their vibrant burnt-orange and red leaves. The starkness of the black pavement and the sound of waves crashing on the coast create an almost eerie but quintessential fall experience.

Olive unbuckles her seat belt and scoots to the middle of the bench, grabbing my free hand and placing it on her thigh while intertwining our fingers. I nod toward her seat belt and she pulls the middle one across her, fastening it.

"Tell me something about this road. It's so beautiful, but it feels like it has stories to tell." Her eyes light up as she takes it all in.

A chuckle rumbles deep in my belly. "Oh, I'm sure there are plenty of stories etched in the history of these trees. It's a good thing they can't talk, or Max and I would probably still be grounded."

"Oooh, do tell. What did little Sam get into back in the day?" She bounces softly with excitement.

"Hmm . . . let's see. Up here there is a bend in the road, you'll see it in three, two, one." I point at the curve as we take it slowly. "Max thought he was a Formula One driver for the first six months he had his license. I pulled his car out of that ditch at least three times without ever telling Mabel."

"What? She didn't notice the scratches?" She leans into me like if she's closer she will know the story faster. I don't hate it.

"No, I'm pretty sure that woman knows everything we've ever done in our entire lives. She just never called us out for it. I think she liked knowing that we were looking out for each other." I shrug as I turn on my signal, preparing to make a left onto an unmarked road.

"Oh my gosh. She totally does. She told me to call her and tattle on you the first time I met her." Olive can't control the giggle that bursts out of her. It's like sunshine, her laugh, and the sound of it melts something inside of me that's been cold for far too long.

"She what now?" I side-eye her, careful not to take my eyes off the bumpy gravel road we're traversing.

"When I met her at the festival, she literally told me to call her if you or Max gave me a hard time. I couldn't believe it, but then she conned me into coming over to look at that book that never existed, so now it kind of makes sense." Olive leans forward trying to get a better look out the windshield at where we are going.

"She means well. She just meddles a little when she thinks she knows what's best for us." I pull the truck into the clearing that overlooks the stone beach, parking in our own personal little cove, the forest all around us.

"What is this place? It's stunning. We aren't going to be arrested for trespassing, right?" Olive unbuckles her seat belt and slides toward the passenger door. I hop out and sprint around to open the door for her.

"Does it make you nervous to be here?" I grin at her, raising an eyebrow, wondering how much of a risk-taker she is.

"I'm not scared, but please don't call my parents to bail me out if we do." She hops out of the truck, not taking my hand, and walks toward the edge of the ten-foot cliff to look down at the water.

I laugh following closely behind, wrapping my arms around her waist as we stand together to look out. "I own this land. There's a small cabin tucked into the trees over there." I point to the right, and the structure comes into her view as she spins to face me.

"Why? I mean, do you live here?" Olive peers up into my eyes, confusion etched in her brow. I run my thumb along the crease, smoothing it out.

"Nope. I just loved this place as a kid. My dad would rent it once or twice a year from the old man who lived here, and we would come out to camp. My parents always stayed in the cabin but us kids would put up tents and have bonfires out here. When the owner was selling, I had just had a good year at the shop, so I bought it thinking one day I would build a house on the land. I haven't yet."

"Sam, that's amazing. It's so gorgeous, I can see why you would want to live here." She presses up onto the balls of her feet, placing a soft, chaste kiss to my lips. I feel like my heart could explode from her proximity, the feel of her in my arms, and her love of my favorite place in the whole world.

"Are you ready to see what else I have in store for our date?" I ask, knowing I need a few minutes to set everything up.

"Let's do it." She tugs my hand, and we walk back to the truck.

I grab the essentials needed to set up the projector screen and head toward the trees after giving Olive instructions to pull the truck to the center of the clearing and spread out the blankets and pillows in the back. Rigging this screen up is something I'm nearly a professional at, seeing that I've been doing it for years for our family outings out here. I have it up and ready to go in a matter of minutes. Olive works hard to create a cozy setup, complete with flannel sheets and a huge fluffy comforter that I threw in so she wouldn't be cold.

From inside the truck, I pull out the basket of snacks and the actual projector to sit on the roof of the truck and play the movie.

"Did you look in my cupboards when I wasn't home?" she asks as she rifles through the snack bag.

"Huh?" I turn around, seeing her sitting with her legs tucked up underneath her and snacks strewn all around.

"How did you know these were my favorite chips?" Olive holds up a bag of the same wavy salty crisps she had in her hair the other day. They are hard to find here. I had to drive three towns over to get a bag.

"I remembered from the taste of them." I wink at her before a laugh breaks free.

"Oh my gosh, stop. I can't believe I did that. Clearly there is something wrong with me." She covers her face with her hands, hiding her embarrassment. I climb into the truck bed and crawl over to her pulling them away.

"I'm teasing you, babe. I asked Ariella," I say, pressing a gentle kiss to her lips. Her breath hitches slightly.

"Okay, but seriously, I promise I'm not usually so . . ." She waves her hand around in the air. "Nuts, disheveled, unhinged?"

"I liked it. It led to the best kiss I've ever had. I will always buy these chips from now on." Olive's cheeks turn an adorable shade of pink as she scoots back into the pillows and tears open the chips.

"Well, now that I know, I will just eat these instead of popping a breath mint." She winks before popping a chip in and crunching it down. The sight of her so relaxed and casual stirs something in me, and I have to adjust myself before I let my guy downstairs get away from me.

"What are we watching?"

I grab the two discs from my bag and hold them behind my back. "Left or right?" I ask.

"Mmmm . . ." She licks the salt off her thumb and index finger, sucking tenderly while she eyes me. *Fuck, I wish I was one of those fingers. Stop it! You need to woo her, not jump her.*

"Left."

"Good choice." I pull the movies from behind me, revealing that she selected *Practical Magic*. It's a classic and one that I've watched numerous times with my sisters and mom. I insert the disc in the player, hit start, and settle in next to her, stealing a chip as I wrap my arm around her, pulling her close.

"You really are a nice guy, aren't you?" The question makes me laugh before I can respond.

"What? I think so?"

"Well, it wasn't obvious when we first met, and I was completely convinced you hated me for some unknown reason. Ari and Meg swore you were nice, but I just hadn't seen that side of you yet, not until the porch decorations." She looks at me like she's shocked that this could be the real me. Almost like she doesn't trust it or that it could be too good to be true.

"I didn't hate you. I hated that I thought I would never have a chance with you. And some people might say I'm anything but nice. That's usually just them judging me on how I look, though."

Olive shifts slightly. "Yeah, I know how that feels."

I kiss her lightly on the cheek, brushing a few strands of hair out of the way first. "I hope you don't just think I'm nice, but that you believe it."

"How are you so calm about this?"

"Calm about what?"

"About this." She gestures between us.

"I'm not. Believe me, I'm scared out of my mind that I'm going to fuck it up. I wish every day I had some sort of cheat code so that I'd always make you happy and never mess it up. But I'm not going to let the first person I've ever felt this connection with slip through my fingers without a fight. I've worked hard for everything I have. This is no different, other than it being more important." I slide my hand up and down her arm gently, enjoying the feel of holding her. Olive shivers a bit as I do it. "Are you cold? Let's get this blanket on you." I pull the comforter up over our legs, snuggling her in closer.

"No, I'm just . . . never mind. Why is it more important?"

Christ! She's not going to let me get away without sharing some of how I'm feeling.

"Because it's you. I've waited a long time to meet someone who I had this kind of connection with. I don't want to fuck it up."

"Oh, Sam. You won't, but I hate to break it to you, I'm not that special. I'm just a girl who flashes the town her oversized underwear from time to time." Olive laughs at her own joke.

"I mean, you said it, not me." I hold my hands up in surrender. "But you are so much more than that."

"How could you know that?" She's turned serious, shifting her body to face me fully.

"I just do. Like when you came to my mom's house to help her with a book. How you started to open up to me at the corn maze, and when you gave Mrs. Baxter a hug. You have a kind heart. You're a good egg." Her cheeks turn a deep crimson as she looks away. "Hey, don't hide from me." I touch her chin softly while turning her back to look me in the eyes. She bristles slightly, shaking off whatever she was feeling.

"Let's play a game."

"So, we aren't actually watching the movie then?" I hit the clicker to pause it.

"I've seen it a million times. I want to know you better. Let's play twenty questions." She grabs the strawberry licorice I packed and tears into one.

"Okay, haven't played that one since middle school, but I'll give it a go. What are the rules?" Her eyes bug out at my question.

"Um? It's pretty simple, we ask each other questions and answer them."

"I know that, but shouldn't we make it more interesting?" I grin at her as she shifts, clearly thinking about my proposition.

"Okay . . . what do you propose?"

"How about if one of us refuses to answer, they have to do a dare instead?"

Her mouth drops open as a sound that's half laugh, half scoff bounces out. "That's literally just truth or dare then."

"And?"

"Okay, fine. I'm going first though. How old are you?"

"Thirty-two. How old are you?"

"Twenty-four."

Jesus, I knew she was younger than me, but eight years . . . I'm surprised by how intelligent and poised she is. At twenty-four I was a fucking nightmare.

"What's your middle name?"

"Dare. I choose dare." I cross my arms waiting for her to come up with something.

"Seriously? It's that bad?" She looks around the truck and then the clearing we are in. "Okay, I dare you to show me your most embarrassing tattoo."

I shift up onto my knees and start unbuckling my belt. Her face morphs into what I think is shock as she covers her mouth with her hand. "Don't be shy now. You asked for it."

"Wait—oh my gosh. Wait." Her hand is up in the universal sign for stop. I can't help my roaring laughter.

"I'm kidding." I sit back down and pull my arm out of my flannel button-down. "This one," I say, pointing at some very poorly done barbed wire that is mostly covered but can still be seen on the inner part of my bicep.

"What even is that?"

"It was barbed wire when I was seventeen. But I grew up and realized it was a mistake, so this is all that's left." She takes a minute looking over my arm, tracing the lines of ink that outline the different pieces.

"These are beautiful." Her words come out soft and breathless.

"Thanks. What's your middle name?"

"Anne. After my mother. What's your next tattoo?"

"Olive Anne, that's—"

"It's actually, Olivia. I just go by Olive."

I put two fingers under her chin and lean in to kiss her. "I don't have one planned. Would you ever get a tattoo, Olivia?" I'm curious if she would, not that it's a deal breaker either way. She made it pretty clear after the town hall meeting that she wasn't interested. But I have to ask again, now that things are different between us.

She looks around rapidly, avoiding my question. A sinking feeling lodges itself in the pit of my stomach. I've been worried the tattoos would be a problem for her. I ask again, and still no answer. I'm about to ask what's wrong when she blurts, "Is there a bathroom out here?"

"Oh, uh, yeah. In the cottage. Let me get the keys."

We scoot out of the truck bed, and I pull them from the seat inside. Olive and I walk toward the cabin, avoiding the branches that have fallen since I last cleared the path.

"You going to answer my question? Or do I need to give you a dare?" I ask, while unlocking the door and flicking on the lights.

"I'll answer, just, um . . . let me use the bathroom first."

Why is this such a big deal? I would think it's a simple yes or no. This feels exactly like the day I walked her back to work. Something is off, but I don't know what it could be. Unless she doesn't want to hurt my feelings by saying no. Does she think I want her to say yes just because it's my job?

Olive heads into the bathroom I've directed her toward, and I step back onto the porch to give her privacy. It's not a big place, and you can hear everything. I don't want her to feel awkward even more so than she apparently already does. I sit down on the front step and wait.

Fifteen

Olive

A Lie and a Revelation

"Shit, shit, shit." I peer down at my phone, willing it to have even one bar of service in this small bathroom that's plopped directly in the middle of nowhere. Ari would know what to say, how to answer the question without outright lying, more than I already am.

When Sam asked me about the tattoo, it was like I could feel Irina's fingers carefully etching in another. There's a tingle I've noticed from time to time, and I'm beginning to associate it with new images appearing on my skin. I had to get somewhere alone, and quick—before the bile rising in my throat became an all-out shit show. I never should have suggested playing a game where this had even a smidgen of a chance of coming up.

I stow my phone and wash my hands for the third time, deciding that it's unlikely my cell service is miraculously going to change at this point. Sam probably thinks I'm having tummy issues, I've been taking so long. I know I shouldn't look at my arm, it's going to shake me up more if there is something new. But also, I need to know if I'm overthinking this. Before grabbing the door handle to head out, I slip my arm out of my jacket and squeeze my eyes shut. Taking three deep breaths, I open them and . . . What the hell?

Not only do I have new additions on my arm—a truck bed stuffed with blankets and pillows, a film reel, and a few hearts stemming off one of the vines—but also, they are moving. Almost like they are dancing and shifting with my feelings. This is bad, so very, very bad. A sharp pain sears through my bicep. As I look at the source of my discomfort a thick black angry-looking cloud appears. Is it an omen? Is it about to rain?

I don't have time for this. I've got to get home and figure out what's happening. I shove my arm back into my sleeve and fly toward the exit of this adorable cabin. I don't take a spare moment to soak in the carefully appointed decor or the plush sofa.

"Whoa. You okay?" Sam stands, moving quickly out of my way as I barrel off the porch.

"Yes. Yep. This is embarrassing, but I think you need to take me home. Something isn't agreeing with me." I don't want to insinuate that my lunch is thinking of making an unholy appearance as the third wheel to our date, but it's better than admitting that I'm cursed.

"Oh, okay. Of course. Let's go." Sam grabs my hand and eyes me thoughtfully.

We make our way back to the truck in awkward silence. Sam immediately opens the door for me and ushers me inside while he picks everything up. He hops into the cab to drive me home, leaving the screen up.

"Don't you need to take that down?" I feel guilty for lying and making him rush out of here. But this is a new development. I don't know what it means, and I don't intend to figure it out with him. What would I even say? He doesn't believe any of this is possible. He's told me magic isn't real.

"Nope, it's more important that I get you home. I can come back to take it down later." He shifts the truck into gear and starts our trek toward my house. The whole time I can feel my arm tingling and throbbing. I know it's blossoming with either new or changing tattoos, and my stomach flips at the mere thought of it.

We ride in amicable silence as I peer out the window. This isn't who I am. I'm not a liar. I don't open up or make myself vulnerable when it counts, but I also don't hide. I was taught to address problems head on and with a smile. Guilt is bubbling so thick in my tummy that my lie might not turn out to be one after all.

"Can I stop and get you anything before we get to your house?" Sam asks, a sad, perhaps disappointed, look donning his face.

"No, thank you. I'm so sorry I ruined our night. I was having fun." I try to give him some solace that this has nothing to do with him. I reach out and give his hand a tight squeeze. Deep in my heart I know he is probably regretting ever taking a chance on me in the first place.

"Olive, stop." Sam pulls up to park in front of my cottage. "You do not ever need to apologize for not feeling good. Whatever the reason, you do not need to say sorry to me." He presses a gentle kiss to my cheek, then hops to open the door for me.

"Thanks again. I'm sor—"

I start to apologize again, but he stops me by pressing a kiss to my lips. I guess he isn't concerned about getting sick. Waves of comfort wash over me for the briefest of seconds. I wish I could just let go and enjoy the date he had planned—I wish I didn't have this stupid tattoo.

"I told you, no more saying sorry. Now get in there and please feel better. If you need anything, let me know. I will call you in the morning."

With that, I walk toward my porch, climbing the stairs slowly as my anxiety settles in. I unlock my door, slip inside, toe off my boots, then collapse to the floor. I prop myself against the door, hanging my head in my hands over the embarrassment and guilt of leaving. Suddenly there's a knock followed by Ari yelling, "Olive, let me in."

I peel myself up off the floor and shake out my shoulders, trying to release the tension that's built up. Opening the door, I ask, "How did you know to come?"

"I got like a hundred SOS texts from you. I figured it was important, so I ditched my Witches' Brew and literally ran here." She's huffing and puffing, short of breath.

"Sorry, I was with Sam and things started getting weird. I didn't have service, and I just kept trying to send the message. I didn't know it would come through a million times."

"What do you mean weird? Did he do something?" She pushes past me, kicking the door closed on her way to the couch.

"No, no, no, of course not. He was sweet and perfect. He asked me if I would ever get a tattoo—" I sink down into the couch beside her, tucking my feet up under me.

"Wait, why is that weird?" she interrupts before I can finish.

"It's not that . . . I just didn't know what to say, so I said I needed to use the bathroom. He took me to his cabin, which by the way I think is adorable. When I was in the bathroom, I took a peek at my arm, and the tattoo wasn't just growing. It was moving, dancing almost, and when I freaked out, a dark storm cloud appeared. I didn't know what that meant, so I just said my stomach hurt, and we hauled ass back here."

"Okay?" She eyes me suspiciously, like this couldn't possibly be a big enough deal to end a date.

"Ari, this is nuts. How am I supposed to live a normal life with this . . . this thing on me always causing problems? How can I have a normal relationship when a simple question sends me spiraling because I'm afraid he's going to find out I'm nothing more than a liar?"

Ari shifts toward me, grabbing both of my hands and looking directly in my eyes. "You are not a liar. You have something going on, something that is magical, and frankly, as much as you hate it, kind of cool. There is a simple solution to all of this. You could just tell him."

I stand abruptly, making my way to the kitchen for water as a lump forms in my throat out of frustration. She doesn't get it. I could never tell him. It's not even believable, in the first place, he would think I'm insane. I down a full glass before searching the cupboard for comfort cookies. As I bite into the first bit of chocolate-creme-filled goodness, Ari approaches.

"Look, I know it wouldn't be easy to tell him, but if you're actually thinking of giving him a real chance, you should. Howie and I don't think you're crazy. Hell, Howie can corroborate your story, and even if Sam doesn't believe you, he just needs to see the tattoo change once and he'll know it's true. I feel like it's my duty as your best friend to tell you that I think he's the real deal. I've never seen you happy like this, and lying, even if it's by omission, is clearly tearing you up." She wraps me in a hug, and I know she means well, but still, she does not understand.

"I'll think about it. I'm sorry for making you come over. It's not really an emergency. I think I just want to go to bed." I need space, time to think.

"Okay, I'll head out. My day starts early tomorrow anyway. I'm helping with an event up in Salem for the agency." She hugs me once more then heads toward the door. "Call me if you need me," she shouts as she exits.

"I will," I whisper before heading to my bedroom. I only have a little more than three weeks to figure this out until I'm stuck with this thing permanently.

As I lie in bed, my mind keeps racing between what Ari said and what happened with Irina. She's not wrong. I could show him. But then again, he told me earlier this evening that he wished he had a cheat code to make dating easier—fool proof. Wouldn't telling him be the same as giving him exactly that? And is this what Irina and the mystery voice meant? Did they want to let me learn the hard way that allowing people to see all parts of you never ends well?

"Wake up, sweetheart. Your father is waiting in the living room." I toss and turn as the sound of my mother's voice hangs in the air. Groaning, I shove a pillow over my face. I must be dreaming—my mother is a thousand miles away—but I still don't want to wake up and take on the day.

The door to my bedroom creaks open, and I swiftly grasp for the covers to pull them over my head. If I'm covered, then the boogeyman can't see me, right?

"Olivia Bowman, do not hide from me." My mother's voice is louder now, demanding. I peer out from under the covers and *shoot*. She's here, in my room, and I'm sleeping in a tank top. What in the world is she doing here? Who let her in my home? My mother cannot see my arm under any circumstances.

"Mom?" I shift my head out, careful not to expose another inch of skin.

"Yes, hunny. Your father had a meeting in Boston, and I thought it would be fun if we popped in to surprise you."

"That's . . . that's great, Mom. Thank you." I blink, not fully believing what I'm seeing. Full hair and makeup done, my mother is dressed primly, in a sleek red shift dress and heels. "Are you going somewhere special?" I ask, eyeing her attire.

"Olivia, you know it's important to put your best foot forward at all times. This is a very normal, casual outfit." My mother scoffs, then takes in the heap of clothes piled on the chair in the corner of my room.

"You should be ashamed of this mess. Get up and get dressed. We would like to see the town you've chosen over Theodore," she says, her nose in the air as she exits my room.

Damn it! I have to get dolled up just to walk around Mage with the world's snobbiest couple. I love them, in my own way, but parading around town wasn't on my agenda today. Also, I'm supposed to be working. Saturdays are busy.

I slip out of bed and put a robe on before grabbing a long-sleeved burgundy velvet dress, tights, undies, and a bra. I head for the bathroom without glancing at the living room or acknowledging either of my parents. It's rude, I know, but so is showing up unannounced when your daughter is in the middle of an existential crisis.

After a quick shower, blowout, a full face of makeup, and dressing, I make my way to face them, dreading every judgment that's bound to come my way. "Good morning, Dad." I give him a gentle kiss on the cheek, bending over the tufted chair he's sitting in reading the newspaper.

"Good morning, Olivia. I take it you didn't know we were coming?" He raises an eyebrow at me conspiratorially, as if to say silently that he also finds my mother relentless.

"No, but it's a wonderful surprise. Mom, you look radiant." I give her a side hug as I plop down beside her on the couch.

"No flopping or slouching, Olivia. You will wear out this fabric in no time." I straighten my spine and move to perch on the edge of the sofa as she is doing.

"Yes, Mother. Where would you like to go today?" I peer at them both, moving my head back and forth, waiting for the agenda to be set.

"Well, dear. We have already seen your place of work. We stopped in on our way here so that your father could ensure you had the day off." I groan inwardly. Beau is going to want to murder me for leaving him all alone on the busiest day of the week. I hate that my parents feel like they can just show up and demand the day off from my boss on my behalf. "We would like you to show us the rest of the uptown area, and then, I have arranged for our car service to take us to the city for a nice dinner and a show this evening."

"Okay, let's get going. There isn't much to see, but it's all within walking distance." I stand and head to my shoe rack to grab my black wedge booties. Bending to zip them up, I notice my father reluctantly placing the paper down as he makes his way to grab his peacoat. It's really not that chilly here, but compared to Alabama it does feel brisk.

As we head out, my mother comments on the porch decor. "This is stunning, Olivia. I don't know how you found the time to do all of this. Did you hire someone?"

"I, um, yes, someone did it for me." It's not a complete lie. I didn't actually do it myself, but I also didn't pay anyone. If I admit that I'm seeing someone, she will lose her mind. No one except Theodore, the man my mom insists is the one for me, is good enough for her daughter.

"Well, I hope you tipped well. It's captivating." She shivers a bit, tightening her scarf as we head down the sidewalk.

We make it about two blocks before her heel catches in the cobblestones while we cross the street. "This is ridiculous. The city manager should be ashamed of himself. A woman should be able to cross a street without nearly killing herself." She whines and crosses her arms as my father dutifully drops to a squat and works to unstick her heel.

"Wedges." I point to my shoes. "You have to wear these here." I don't acknowledge her attitude or the air of pure superiority she exudes. It's honestly hilarious how Anne Bowman, a once poor farm girl, could be so uppity. My father is from old money, and she behaves like she was born into it too, not like someone who is only one divorce away from having nothing again. It makes me a little sick how much I have aimed to please her throughout my life. Even living in the most gorgeous place on earth isn't good enough.

We make our way into the square—yes, I warn her about the crosswind so she doesn't flash anyone—and we head into the Brewhouse for a warm pick-me-up.

"This is adorable. I love the aesthetic. Richard, take a few pictures so we can have Tabitha mimic this in the sitting room." She orders my father around, and, like the good lackey he is, he does what she says while I place the order for two black coffees for them and a pumpkin spiced latte for me. Once we have coffees in hand, we mosey next door to a cute little decor and gift shop. It smells like heaven as the scents of fall waft through the store and the cozy could-be-on-HGTV vibe envelops us.

"I haven't had a ton of time to explore all the shops just yet. But this is one of my favorites. There are so many cute items. Once I earn a bit more, I'm planning to get all of my home decor from here," I whisper quietly to my parents as we look around.

"You do still have the card we gave you, don't you?" My dad's face is marked with concern as he worries that I don't have access to their unlimited coffers.

"Yes, but I'm trying to make it without your money. No offense." I run my hand over a knotted rug, feeling the rough yet smooth texture against my palm.

"That's nonsense, Olivia. What would you like here? We can buy one of everything." My father starts his trek to the checkout counter prepared to do just that, but my mother stops him by putting a hand across his chest.

"No, Richard. She walked away from the life we worked so hard to give her. If she wants to live this life on her own, she's going to have to do it the hard way." With the gauntlet dropped, she exits the shop, the door's small bell ringing in my ears.

After a few more stops and judgments, we make our way back to the cottage to relax—in other words, my mother makes herself at home, reorganizing my cupboards, commenting on my scandalous choice in books, and perusing my closet. My father reads his newspaper and stays silent. We spend an hour doing this awkward song and dance before my phone rings and my mom notices someone named Sam is trying to get ahold of me.

I silence the phone and tuck it into the pocket of my dress. I haven't responded to him once today, despite his attempts to check on me. I'm not avoiding him, but I also don't know what to say. I can't keep lying to him, and I can't tell him the truth. Not to mention, I wouldn't dare introduce him to my parents. They are nothing like his. They are not warm and inviting. He would hate them, and they would judge him.

"Who was that?" my mom asks, raising an eyebrow at me.

"No one." I cross my arms and lean against the kitchen counter.

"If it was no one, then why didn't you answer?" She's on the scent like a bloodhound searching for its next kill.

"I can call him back later. It's not a big deal." I turn and grab a glass from the cabinet before attempting to fill it with water.

"*Him?* What would poor Teddy think?" she hisses in a breath.

"Teddy? Is that what we are calling him now?" I set my glass on the counter, spinning to face her.

"Yes, he is going to be my son-in-law. Of course I have a nickname for him." She feigns innocence.

"No, Mother, he isn't. Unless you have another daughter, there is zero chance that Theodore is ever going to be your son-in-law." I've had enough. Enough of the meddling, enough of the demanding way she tries to dictate my life, and enough of the showing up unannounced. It's too much, and frankly I don't even understand why she wants to be around me. When she is, nothing I do is ever good enough.

"You will come around. Once you come to your senses and realize you're done living in this squalor. I just hope he waits that long." She shifts on her feet and crosses her arms in defiance.

"Out!" I shout at her, my voice shaking. I point toward the door as my stomach lurches to my throat. I've never once in my life stood up to her. But for some reason, today I feel like I can. It strikes me as odd, but it's freeing at the same time.

"Excuse me? Do not yell at your mother, young lady." Richard has decided to enter the conversation.

"This is my home. Which I pay for completely on my own. I love you both very much and appreciate all you have done for me, but enough is enough. You show up unannounced, judge me and this beautiful town, and now you are trying to dictate who I spend my life with. Nope." I pop the *p* in the word for effect. "Get out and do not come back without calling first, ready to apologize." They look stricken, as if I have just laid out the most despicable behavior they have ever seen. To be fair, I've never once raised my voice to either of them. My mother grabs her coat, scarf, and purse and scurries onto the porch, slamming the door behind her so hard the walls rattle.

My father approaches, kissing my forehead and whispering that he loves me before following her and shutting the door softly behind him. It's at this moment, for the first time ever, that I truly see him as spineless. He allows her to run his life, and he follows along with her ideas even when they're wrong. I grab a bottle of wine and an opener from the cabinet, then go to draw a bath.

Pouring bubbles into the tub as the warm water splashes and fills it, I undress and uncork the wine. It isn't until I'm soaking and a few glugs into the bottle of red that I realize my tattoo is changing again. It's been one week and the tattoo covers most of my upper arm now, a few of the pieces are permanent, like the book, the truck, the pumpkins, and Boo. But woven in between are pictures that change with every thought or feeling that pops into my head. It hits me that this is a reflection of my life, like a live action reel depicting it as it unfolds. The red streaks mimic my rage, the bubbles blossoming represent the soothing bath I'm taking, and there's even a bottle of wine continuously pouring red liquid that drips down my arm only to fall into nothingness. It's weird having my internal war that's raging visible in technicolor before my very eyes. At the same time, where my usual inner monologue is muddy and full of self-doubt, this makes it easier to unscramble my emotions, and I'm not sure what that says about me.

Sixteen

Sam

Something Isn't Right

"I understand, thanks for calling and letting me know. I will see you next week on Thursday at three." I hang up, shaking my head at how my day has completely fallen apart. I was supposed to do two large tattoos today, but both clients had to reschedule. One for the stomach flu, thank you for not sharing the love. The other because his in-laws decided to come into town, and now he is playing "entertainment committee." (His words not mine.)

It's not unusual to see cancellations in this business, tattoos are a big commitment. But it is weird to have blocked my whole day for these two, only to have both of them unable to make it. Walk-ins do happen. I suppose I'll be hanging out and waiting around most of the day.

My phone buzzes with an incoming message. I'm hoping it's from Olive. She hasn't responded to my attempts at checking in, and I'm starting to worry she really is sick. I've already consulted with my mom and Max. Both told me to wait it out and if I haven't heard anything by the end of the day, they would check in with her themselves so I don't scare her off.

I glance at my phone, a small flutter in my stomach, until I see the name Beau Brooks in my notifications.

Beau

> **Are you busy today?**

I shoot back a reply.

> No, my day completely fell apart.

Beau

> **Olive called out. I need help at the shop if you can swing it.**

It's not the first time I've given Beau a hand. Whenever he is short-staffed and I don't have appointments, I come over and relieve him for his lunch break.

> Sure. I'll be there at eleven.

Beau sends me back a thumbs-up, and I scan my shop thinking of what I can do to kill time for the next hour. The books are up to date and everything has been cleaned. I guess I'll burn time by sorting old files and clearing out drawings I don't ever plan to use.

At ten till eleven, I lock up and walk over to Black Kettle Bindery. The door chimes as I enter, there's not a customer in sight.

"Hey, Beau." I spot him nodding off reading a book behind the front counter.

"Oh, Sam. I'm so glad you're here. Olive couldn't make it in for the second time this week. I need to go home to make sure Mr. Pickles is fed."

"I hope she's okay. Did she say why she wasn't coming in today?" I pretend like I don't know she's sick, or at least that she was last night.

"She didn't. Her father pranced in here like he owns the place and demanded the day off for her." Beau huffs and pushes his glasses up his nose.

"Wait, what? Her dad came in?" Her parents don't live close by. Did she know they were coming?

"He sure did. Mr. High and Mighty waltzed in here and introduced himself like I should have already known who he was. He must be a big deal where he comes from, but he isn't one here," Beau says while shuffling papers around on the counter.

"And you just agreed?"

"What was I supposed to do? Olive and I will be discussing her attendance at work when she returns. If she doesn't want this job, I will find a replacement." He grabs his hat, keys, and wallet to head out.

"Beau, she loves this job. I'm sure there's an explanation." He doesn't stay to listen to me try to convince him she's perfect for Black Kettle. Instead, he whips open the door and saunters out.

I know I shouldn't do it, but I can't help sending her another text. It's the third of the day, which I realize is bordering on too many. I'm a fucking grown man who has apparently lost all chill. She's an adult, and she will respond when she can. I hope.

> Hey, again. Helping Beau out, and he said your parents are in town. Let me know if you need anything.

As suspected, my text goes unanswered, and after five minutes of double-checking and re-reading it, I decide to grab a book that details the history of tattooing to pass the time. Two hours flies by, and the next thing I know, the door is chiming once again with Beau's return.

"How is Mr. Pickles?"

"Well fed, no thanks to Olivia." Beau sets his hat on the coatrack and shoos me out of his seat behind the counter.

"She's good at what she does, just hear her out." I can't help but remind him that he needs someone like her, someone with the very specific set of skills that are the backbone of his business. My advice might be selfishly motivated, but that doesn't mean it's untrue.

"Well, she did look miserable. Maybe you're right." He opens the book he left behind earlier and glances at the pages.

"You saw her?"

"Yes, on my way out earlier. She was walking out of the Brewhouse with two of the wealthiest looking people I may have ever seen." Something about Beau pointing out their financial status makes me nauseous. I'm not a yacht club kind of guy and likely never will be.

"Why did she look miserable?" I'm genuinely worried. She hasn't said much about her parents, but the little glimpses I've had have not been great.

"Her mother was barking orders at her. Beautiful woman, but a total witch." I've never heard Beau speak this negatively. It must be bad. Tension vibrates at the base of my skull, causing a dull ache to take root. I'm not sure why I'm so protective of her, but the thought of her being subjected to criticism on any level irritates the hell out of me.

"Do you need anything else from me?" I'm curt as I grab my stuff, ready to head out.

"Nope, thanks." He nods at me, returning to the pages that will likely have him back to sleep before I cross the street. "Oh, and Sam—" He calls out as my hand wraps around the doorknob. "I know you like her, anyone would. Just tell her to come to work. There's a pile of restorations stacking up, and my eyes aren't what they used to be."

I glance back at him over my shoulder and give him a friendly wave. Beau's a good man, he knows Olive's a keeper as much as I do.

As I step onto the sidewalk into the crisp fall air, the austere charm of Mage hits me. I've lived here my whole life, and I don't like to think I take it for granted, but sometimes I do fail to notice the appeal. Thinking about Olive showing her parents around, I can't help but wonder if they noticed all the little things. Did they appreciate the nod to our history in each hand-hewn sign? Did they see the way each shop has a carefully curated aesthetic that both separates it from the next and maintains enough cohesiveness to tie the town together? Each step I take over the cobblestone sidewalk pulls me down a rabbit hole of Mage's history.

"Hey, Sam," Howie shouts and waves from up ahead at Union. He's sitting at one of the wrought-iron bistro tables that line the restaurant's wrap-around patio.

"Howie, how's it going? You on break?"

"Nope. Just nowhere else to be." He seems sad or maybe lonely. There's something on his mind.

"Mind if I join you then? I also have nowhere else to be." He perks up at the question. We haven't really hung out one-on-one, but he seems to be a nice guy. He's a few years younger than I am, but he can pour a mean drink and occasionally comes up with something so funny and unexpected it knocks your socks off.

"Yeah, uh . . . that would be cool." Howie scoots the chair across from him out with the toe of his Chuck Taylors, making room for me.

"Not working today?" I ask as I plop into the seat and peruse the menu that he pushed across the table. I don't know why either of us pretends we need to look at it. I could probably recite the damn thing.

"It's my day off." Howie leans forward. "Can I ask you something?"

"Sure, shoot." I fold the menu and place it back on the table knowing I'm ordering the usual.

"What's so special about you? Is it the tattoos?" His question isn't accusatory, more curious. Does he have a thing for Olive?

"I'm going to need more to go on here . . . I'm not special."

"You don't even try, and the women they just, well, I've seen it at the bar so many times. They just gravitate toward you. What's your secret?"

His question makes me laugh so hard there are tears leaking from the corners of my eyes. Howie's face instantly deflates.

"I'm sorry. I know from your perspective it might seem that way. I'm only laughing because it couldn't be further from the truth. Sure, the ones I'm not interested in might think I'd be fun to take for a spin, but that's all it is. The ones—and let me say there have been very few, maybe one—that I've actually seen a future with, don't even text me back." I slump down in my chair. I didn't really plan on telling anyone outside the family how much this Olive thing is getting me down.

"Are you talking about Olive?" Howie asks, a mixture of relief and pity on his face.

Sabrina, the server working the patio, approaches to take our order. We both go with the Reuben and Harvest Moon drafts. When she walks away, Howie turns his hand over at me as if to say out with it.

"Yeah, man. She's different, and I'm falling hard for her. It's too fast, and I know it's probably destined to blow up in my face, but I don't know. Wait—you guys are friends. Forget what I said." I shake my head and look out across the square.

"Sam, I know we aren't really friends, but I'd like to be. And this is Vegas. What happens on the patio stays on the patio."

Sabrina returns with our beers, placing them down and confirming the rules of Union. "He's right, Sam. What happens on the patio stays on the patio, and Howie is the most trustworthy man I know. You're in good hands." She leaves as quickly as she came, her sentiment hanging in the air.

"Okay, fine. Vegas rules. Olive won't text me back. I took her out last night, but she said she was sick and bailed early, and now she's ghosting me and I'm a fuckin' wreck."

His eyes practically pop out of their sockets when he looks at me. "She's not ghosting you. The she-devil is in town."

"The what?"

"The she-devil. I don't actually know her mom, but from what Ariella has said, and seeing her strut up and down the square most of the day with her nose in the air, I'd wager it's a pretty accurate name." He shrugs and takes a long, slow pull of his drink. "Besides, Olive's just got a lot going on. At least you have someone to ghost you. By the way, what is ghosting exactly?"

"Hold up. You're younger than me. How do you not know?" I check his expression to see if he's fucking with me, but it's clear he isn't. "Ghosting is when you're talking to someone and then they just stop responding. Like radio silence, no communication. Like a ghost disappearing into the night."

"Oh, so what every girl I've ever liked has done to me. Good to know I can call it something now." More beer disappears from his glass as he sinks lower into his seat.

"Alright, as much as I want to unpack everything you said about Olive, it appears we have bigger fish to fry today. What's going on, and who do I need to be mad at?"

"W-w-what? Mad? There's no one to be mad at." His denial only makes me more curious. This is a good distraction. It's nice to not be alone in my misery.

"Is it Sabrina? I saw her eyeing you. Is there something going on there?"

"Ew, no. She's my cousin."

"Okay . . . hmm. Is it Allie Walker? I saw her chatting you up at the Hollow Hearts Festival."

"She wasn't chatting me up. Whatever that means. Why would a girl like that be into a guy like me?" He motions from his hair down to his shoes.

"Howie, is that short for Howard?"

"Yes?"

"Howard, listen up. It's time for you to get one of my world-famous pep talks—"

"What are we giving poor Howie a pep talk for?" Xav slaps me on the shoulder from behind. He slings a white paper bag overflowing with to-go containers onto our table and sits backward in a chair while leaning his chin in his hands in intrigue. He must have spotted us on his way home with carryout.

"It's fine, I do not need a pep talk." Howie finishes his beer and waves at Sabrina to bring another. I'm starting to like him more and more by the minute. Did I see my day ending up with me and Howie drinking our feelings together? No. Am I mad about it? Also, no.

"As I was saying, you need a pep talk, and Xav here is in the circle of trust since I've had to give him damn near a thousand of these over the years."

"Scout's honor, it's the bro code. What happens in a pep talk is sacred." Xav holds three fingers up for proof.

"Howard, you have everything to offer someone. You're handsome. I know you hide it, but I have a feeling there're muscles under those concert tees you wear, and you're on track to take over your uncle's business. You're a walking panty dropper, or briefs, whatever you're into is good with us."

"It's women. Well, one woman," Howie interrupts.

"Either way, you're smart, you're funny as hell, and anyone would be lucky to have you."

"I'm funny?" There's doubt in his eyes, almost like he's trying to think of a time when he made someone laugh.

"Of course you're funny. Like when you come out of nowhere with a classic one-liner. Or when you talk shit to the drunkards on Friday nights thinking no one can hear you." I'm not great at coming up with specific examples, but Xav and I have spent countless hours laughing over something Howie's said. Xav nods in agreement.

"Okay, that still doesn't answer the question of how you *get* the girls." He shakes his head in disbelief.

"I don't. That's what I've been trying to tell you. You could walk in there right now and pick someone up, no questions asked. But it doesn't matter if it's not the right one." Howie harrumphs at this revelation.

"Are you going to tell us who she is?" Xav leans in a little closer, clearly eager to learn about his crush.

"No." Howie crosses his arms and leans back in his chair.

"No? I told you about Olive ghosting me, and all I get is no?" I avoid looking at Xav. He doesn't know about the latest development, and I don't want to recount it right now. I chug the remaining quarter of my beer instead.

"Not forever, just for right now. She doesn't know, and this is a new friendship. I have to keep you coming back for more, right?" Howie shrugs, and Xav and I erupt in laughter. See, he's funny. He's maintaining an air of mystery to keep us on the hook.

"Okay, fine. But I was going to stay in this friendship either way."

"Me too, but I gotta run or I won't be staying in my marriage. Cami takes her food seriously these days." Xavier stands from his seat, grabs his bag, and heads out with a wave.

Howie and I continue our back-and-forth, putting away a few more beers and our food before calling it a day. I didn't expect to hang with him this afternoon, but it was nice. It got my mind off Olive and sort of filled that hole from where Xav has been somewhat absent lately. His life is changing with the baby coming, I get it.

As I exit Union, I give Olive a call. It goes straight to voicemail, and I decide to walk home. It's the responsible thing to do, and fresh air will clear my head. Crunching leaves under my feet, each step is heavy. I wish she would just let me know she's okay. I don't like that everyone seems to have had a less-than-stellar experience with her parents.

She deserves better, and I can't help but wonder if her parents are the reason it always seems like she's holding something back. Like the tattoo question she never answered. Is she afraid to tell me she can't get a tattoo because they wouldn't approve? Does she think if I knew they would judge me, it would change what we are building?

I walk up the steep stairs to my small porch. It's not sprawling like Olive's, more of a landing at the top of the steps. My house is old, a starter-home that I thought would be a good flip one day. Turning the key in the lock, I push inside.

The hardwood floors have been refinished, and the kitchen has been remodeled with white cabinets, marble counters, and a subway-tile backsplash. I have a Victorian rug in the living room, but my furniture is mismatched, and the focal point is the large TV hung over the fireplace.

Sloughing off my shoes, I walk to the laundry room that's at the end of the open-concept living space and strip off my clothes, tossing them in the washing machine. I strut in my birthday suit back to the front of the house to take the stairs up to the second floor, where there are three bedrooms, including the primary. The two spares haven't been touched aside from making one my workspace.

Attached to my primary is a small bathroom. I walk in and turn on the shower as hot as it will go when my phone dings from where I placed it on the dresser. Hurrying, I turn off the water and make my way back to the bedroom to pick it up.

Olive

> I'm sorry I didn't respond earlier. My parents showed up as a surprise.

> I heard. I'm glad you're okay.

Olive

> About that, I'm sorry I had to ditch you last night.

> I already told you not to apologize.

The phone rings, and I immediately answer.

"Don't tell me you're calling to protest the no apologizing rule."

"I'm well . . . Okay, I was, but I won't. How was your day?" There's a shakiness to her voice.

"Uh, it was fine actually. I covered your shift at BKB for Beau's lunch, then hung out with Howie at Union." I crawl into bed.

"Now I really am going to say sorry. How mad was he?"

"Who? Beau? He wasn't mad, but I think your dad might not be on his list of favorite people." This makes her laugh. It's throaty and full until I hear her let out a deep sigh. "Olivia, what's wrong?"

"You called me Olivia." Her words are soft, almost a whisper.

"I did. You are not okay. I can tell, and this is serious. I need you to tell me what's going on. Howie mentioned you have a lot on your plate. Let me help you," I say, pleading with her to let me in.

"What did Howie say?" Her voice goes up an octave, and my heart thumps in my chest. What does he know that I don't, and why didn't my new friend tell me?

"He didn't say anything. Just that you have a lot going on and that you aren't ghosting me. What does he know that I don't? Because I'm trying here, babe. But I can't force you to open up to me."

"He doesn't know anything, not really anyway. It's just that, well, it's embarrassing." She pauses, and I hear her moving around like she's sinking under her blankets. I can practically hear the gears turning in her head.

"You never have to be embarrassed to tell me anything. I'm on your side here. Please just let me in," I say, trying to convince her, again.

She sucks in a breath before saying, "Okay, fine. My parents aren't like yours. They aren't warm and inviting. They think my being here is throwing away everything they've ever done for me."

"Why would they think that?"

"Because I'm supposed to get married." *What the hell did she just say?*

"Um, excuse me, what? You're engaged?"

She bursts out laughing. A full-blown wheezing-for-air laugh that would be hilariously delightful if I didn't feel like I made out with someone else's fiancé a few days ago. "No. No, no, no. I'm not engaged, nor have I ever been engaged. But they think I should be, to Theodore Wilson the Third, heir to the Wilson Oil Empire and esteemed member of the Mobile Country Club." Her voice gets very high-pitched as the words tumble from her lips. "But it's never going to happen. I refuse to be put into a little box where I have no purpose, and that's exactly what I'd be settling for."

"A couple things. First, I'm glad you aren't settling because you deserve the world and it would be a fucking shame for anyone to give you less than that. Second, I'm glad you're not engaged, I mean, that would totally suck for me. But I have to ask, was there anything between you and Ted?" She laughs again, a bright melodic sound.

"No, *Ted* has always been a no-fly zone. There's only one person I'm even remotely interested in, but I'm fairly certain he's going to get sick of me soon." Olive is nervous, I can tell by the way her words trail off.

"Olivia, I need you to listen to me. If you're talking about me, and I hope you are, there is zero chance of me getting sick of you. You've captivated my every thought since the second I saw you." I do my best to reassure her. I know it's too early to be making promises, but I can sense that she needs the stability right now. I also know in my heart that even if she decided she didn't want me, I'd still ask how high if she told me to jump. Women like her don't fall for men like me. I'm lucky to be in her presence at all.

"Sam . . . you're too good to me." She sighs heavily, or maybe it was a yawn. "Tell me more about Howie. I didn't know you guys hung out."

"I mean, there's not much to tell. I ran into him, and we drank our sorrows away. Me worrying about you—do not apologize—and him over some girl he's in love with. He wouldn't tell me who." She squeals, and a delighted, robust sound vibrates through the phone. "I take it that means you know who it is."

"I have a hunch, but I'm not sure. I hope it's Ari."

"Actually, I could see that. There's a weird vibe between those two. Do I need to let you get back to your parents?" I don't want to cut this off, but if they are waiting, I don't want to be the reason she's being rude.

"No. When can I see you again?" She changes the subject flawlessly, and I'm left with more questions. I can't imagine her leaving them to sit in the living room alone, but they couldn't have just come for one day, not a thousand miles, right? Something is up.

"Well, I'm free tomorrow night, if you're not entertaining your guests." I try bringing it up in a different way.

"I'm free. How about if I plan a date this time. Text me your address, and I'll pick you up at seven."

"Alright. I'll see you at seven." She clearly yawns this time. "Go to sleep, and I'll see you tomorrow, sweet girl."

"Good night, Sam."

"Good night, Olive."

We hang up, and I abandon my plan to shower, instead drifting off to thoughts of Olive. She's hiding something. It's not a fiancé, but there's more to the story. I don't know how I know, but I feel there's something just out of reach every time we talk.

Seventeen

Olive

Ghosts in the Graveyard

The door jingles as I walk into Black Kettle. It's early, and the shop is closed, but I have plenty to catch up on after missing a couple days this week. I'm hoping I can make headway on this local legends book so that when Beau gets in, he's less mad at me and more thrilled with my progress.

Flipping the light switches and locking the door behind me, I make my way toward the back of the shop, passing dusty shelves as I approach my worn but sturdy desk to set down my bag and get busy.

"Hello, Olive." Beau is perched at my desk, arms folded, sitting in the dark as if he was waiting for me.

"Beau, I didn't realize you'd be in yet. I'm so sorry about this week. I never would have wanted to put you out, it's just my parents can be a bit—"

"Relentless? Arrogant? Demanding?"

"Yes. All of those things and so much more. They don't take kindly to me saying no, and I didn't know they were coming so I couldn't schedule around it. But I love this job, and I plan to spend all day catching up so I can be ready to take on the week."

"We can't choose our parents, but we can choose who we surround ourselves with, Olivia. I'm glad you're making up for lost time, but please do not put me in this situation again." His brow is furrowed, his tone stern.

"I promise." I smile at him as he extricates himself from my workspace, allowing me to slide into my seat. His joints crack audibly, and I'm reminded how this isn't just his store, it's his life's work.

"I'm going to get out of here. Mr. Pickles doesn't like to be left alone for very long. But let me know if you need anything before I'm back." With that he's off to spend quality time with his cat, and I'm left with a mountain of work.

I'm grateful he's a forgiving man. Losing this job would not be ideal, especially in my current predicament. When I woke up this morning the tattoo had grown again, the permanent pieces still intact but the vines wrapping nearly to my elbow now. There were hearts popping up as I thought of Sam and dark, stormy creatures that looked like Death Eaters from that one movie about witches and wizards. I'm assuming those are my parents.

Seeing those ghastly figures made me wonder, at what point did I start resenting them for who they are? I was loved as a child, I certainly had everything I physically needed. I just can't pinpoint when exactly their push to be perfect changed from something I wanted to attain to something I loathed. It was probably around the time my mother started trying to find me a husband.

I want to say it was a singular moment that made the difference, but it was really more of a slow trickle. A crack that festered and grew over time into this momentous divide. I wonder if maybe I had let them see the sides of me that they hated a little sooner or if I had exposed them in small doses, if things would be different. My mom had to have had these same aspirations at one point; she wasn't raised with a silver spoon in her mouth. As I wrestle with the thoughts the Death Eaters gobble up the artwork on my arm, almost like they are eating away my soul.

My phone pings, alerting me to a new text. It's a voice message from Sam.

"Hey. I hope you slept well and enjoyed your run this morning. I promise I'm not a creep, but you ran by my house while I was drinking my coffee and you're distracting, I couldn't help but watch. I can't wait to see you tonight."

He's funny. I ran by his house on purpose, but I don't know if I want to admit that. What if he thinks *I'm* the creep? Like a zap of electricity, my arm explodes with butterflies, their cornflower-blue wings flapping about. I guess there's no denying how I feel. It's exciting and nauseating at the same time. There's freedom in not having to say it out loud, in knowing my feelings manifest on my sleeve. But there's also terror in knowing that someone else might see it, they might know my inner workings. I'm closed off for a reason. There's always a chance that whoever knows the truth won't like what they see. My parents didn't, even when I had straight A's, was crowned Miss Alabama, and got voted the kindest person on campus in college.

I decide to send Sam a voice message back. I find it to be a superior form of communication. My thumbs don't go numb from all the typing, and I don't have to volley the conversation as much as I would during a standard phone call. Tapping the microphone on my text app, I hold it down.

"Morning, Sam. I ran by your house on purpose. I'm also not a creeper." I laugh at myself before continuing. "I wanted to make sure I knew where it was before our date tonight. Want to play a game while I'm at work?"

Not even ten seconds pass before I receive a response.

"Always, but wouldn't I be distracting you? Don't you have work to do?" he asks, scolding me playfully.

"Listen up, buttercup. I'll determine when I'm too busy for you," I chide him back.

"Oh, I see. She's sassy today. I have a client coming soon, but I'll play until then."

After fixing my cardigan so none of my arm is showing, I send him a video of me rolling my eyes. Another quick response comes in.

"Do I need to show you what happens to naughty girls who roll their eyes?"

Heat tickles below my panty line. I take a leap out of my comfort zone. "I dare you to try. Now, come on, let's play a game. We never finished our twenty questions, so I propose that we continue that, and if there's something that one of us doesn't want to answer, we owe each other a dare on our date. I'll go first. I can't get a tattoo. That's the answer from the other night. Now, what's your favorite food?"

While I wait for his reply, I open the book I've been working to restore and get started. Light is beginning to trickle in through the front window, and casting a warm glow across the bookshelves up front. It's beautiful, but the wait for his reply does weird things to my belly. On one hand I don't want to get too attached when experience tells me it likely won't work out. On the other hand, there's something about him that's so soothing, it's like a part of me knows I can trust him even if it's hard to. A few minutes pass, and I'm starting to think he doesn't want to play when a message comes in.

"I would have to say the pumpkin ricotta tortellini you tried at the festival, but that will be changing very soon, I hope."

I snap a photo of my face with one eyebrow tilted up and my finger on my lips in confusion and send it his way along with a text that says:

Huh?

Maybe I'm naive but I have no clue what he's talking about. I hope he doesn't think I'm cooking him dinner tonight.

"Babe, I have a feeling you are going to be my favorite thing to eat very soon." His message rings out, and I start to fan my face. Holy moly, I've never had a man be so sweet yet so forward in my life. My insides are melting and the space between my thighs is slick.

"Hoo boy, was there a question in there somewhere?" My voice shakes as I reply, and little sparks fly all over my arm. It's actually pretty amazing to watch as I pull my cardigan sleeve up a bit higher to look.

An incoming message pings on my phone.

Sam

As much as I want to play this game, my appointment just walked in. See you at seven.

The kiss emoji makes me smile as the sparks on my arm fizzle into ashes falling toward my wrist. I guess my emotions are fizzling out at the loss of our game. Back to work.

With the crisp fall air and earlier sunsets, the light is waning as I make my way down my steps toward Sam's. My leather tote bag is slung over my shoulder, chock-full of candy and DVDs for a date night at his place. I figured it was casual enough, and it's not like we watched even a few minutes of our movie the other night. I'm calling this a redo. I pull my peacoat a little tighter as the wind picks up.

Looking back at my cottage, I can't help but feel overcome with the beauty of fall and all the decor Sam carefully placed. I pick up the pace after checking my watch, hoping to get there right on time.

I spent the remainder of my day reading and carefully treating each page of a book on old Mage Hollow legends. There were plenty of details on Irina's life, along with her sisters, but nothing that would lead me down the path of finding her. The book mostly covered the trials that took place and detailed how this little town became a safe haven for the magically inclined.

The only semi-helpful fact was that Irina lived out her days here. There weren't details as to where she lived exactly, but there are plenty of homes around town that date back far enough. It's possible that hers is still standing and could potentially lead to a clue.

As I step over fallen leaves and carefully navigate the uneven terrain, I find myself looking around each tree or corner waiting for something to pop out. A black cat, a goblin, a ghost . . . it could be anything. My skin prickles and the air feels a tad thicker as I approach the cemetery. I chuckle to myself as I think of holding my breath as I pass.

I remember my friends saying that when we were kids. Whenever we would drive past a cemetery, you had to hold your breath the entire time or you were destined to be haunted. Maybe I slipped once or sucked in air a little too quickly. Is that why I'm in this situation? No, but it makes me feel a little less crazy to consider the possibility of it even for a second.

"Olivvviiiaaaa," a whimsical voice calls out like an echo reverberating against the walls of a cave.

I stop still in my tracks, turning furiously to find the source of the noise. It's dark enough out that there could be someone hiding just about anywhere.

"Olivvviiiaaaa." Again, the voice rings out. Speeding up my pace in case this is some sort of sick joke or setup, I make it halfway to the cemetery when I spot her. Under the arched metal gate leading in, Irina stands with her hands on her hips. Her hair is flowing in the breeze, a thick cackle echoing across the distance. She waves at me then turns toward the cemetery, seemingly floating inside across the grassy path.

I run, full speed, with everything I have. I need to catch her. This is the chance I've been waiting for, and I refuse to miss it. As I round my way through the gate and onto the brown dying grass, her voice rings out with my name again. She's taunting me. I pick up the pace even more when I spot her leaning on a tree halfway across the expansive plot of land.

As she floats to the left, leaves whoosh into the air like fall-themed confetti, raining down on the gravestones below. I dodge one of the marble grave markers, dropping my bag so that I can dart after her. A few more paces, and I've almost made it when she lifts up into the air and flies right over my head. Astonished, I stand looking up at her, sucking in breaths with my hands on my head.

"Please, Irina. Just make it stop. I don't want to do this anymore."

A wicked cackle rips through me as my arm screams out in pain. I claw my coat off, ditching it while my fingers work furiously to undo the button at my wrist and roll up my sleeve. My skin is on fire, and I need to see what is happening. This feels different than the sensations I usually have; it hurts more.

It's too dark for me to see anything. *Shoot.* I pull my phone out of my back pocket and flip on the flashlight to reveal the image. In bold red letters are the words **Yes, you can. Open up, Olivia, or be miserable alone.** There's an hourglass with sand trickling out and numbers scribbled below it counting down: **22 days and 10 hours**. My hands are shaking. I accidentally drop my phone. This has to stop.

"This is what you wanted, Olivia. The clock is ticking. Make your decision on Halloween." Irina's shrill voice rings out in my ears, and pain shoots up my neck. I lunge toward her once more, desperate to grab hold of her. I don't need to wait to decide. I already know that I want this gone. That I don't want to be so vulnerable that every thought I have is shown to the world. Even if I *can* cover it with clothing, I can't hide it forever—at least not from Sam. It's too much. I'm too exposed.

My fingertips are inches from reaching the bottom of her skirt when my toe catches on the edge of a flat gravestone. I'm tumbling forward, unable to stop the inevitable impact with the ground. As my body connects with the soft grass, my head hits last, striking the edge of another headstone with a loud crack.

I groan from the searing pain in my skull. Reaching up to my temple, hot sticky blood drips down my cheek. I pat my pockets for my phone, I need to call Ari. *Shoot, I dropped it.*

Willing myself to move, I take a deep breath before pushing up onto my knees. I attempt to crawl back to where I came from, but my vision is blurry and the throbbing in my head intensifies. Each time I pick up my knees to move forward, I get a bit woozier.

Blood is mixing with fresh tears as they stream down my face. This is it. This is how I die. Anne will be so disappointed at the utter lack of grace that I'm exhibiting in my final moments.

Sam! He's going to think I stood him up, that I ditched him once again. It was one thing to forgive what he believed to be bathroom troubles—not showing at all is a completely different story. An unexpected sob rips out of me.

"Irina, help me. Please," I beg, pleading for assistance from the very individual who got me in this mess. Instead of swooping in to save the day like she did the first time, I'm met with deafening silence. She's gone . . . I know it in my bones. Forcing myself to push forward, each shift of my body aches. How hard did I fall?

It feels like it's been an hour, and I haven't made it more than a few feet. I give up, lying down for a second, praying that the pain will subside. If I can just rest for a minute, think in peace, I can come up with a plan. But as soon as I'm flat on my tummy, the world goes black.

Eighteen

Sam

The Mysterious Disappearance of Olive Bowman

Checking the time on my phone, seven forty-five, I pace the small front stoop searching the street for signs of Olive. She said she would be here, and while I know she could have gotten tied up at work or maybe she was taking longer to get ready, something feels off. I have a sinking feeling that she's not coming.

I could go check on her, make sure nothing bad has happened. But what if she shows up here and thinks I stood her up? Leaving now is risky. But so is waiting and not being there if something terrible has happened. *Think, think.* Where could she be? Ariella!

Unlocking my phone, I navigate to my contacts, hovering over her name for a second before hitting the call button. I hope I don't live to regret involving Olive's friend, but what choice do I have. I wait impatiently while the phone rings not once, not twice, but three times.

"Sam? Is this a butt dial?" The confusion is clear in Ariella's tone.

"Nope. Are you with Olive?" Straight to the point, if she is, then I know I've been stood up. My heart races. The sound beats in my ears. I sit down on the top step so I don't keel over from my nerves.

"No? I thought you had a date at"—there's a pause on the other end—"seven. She's never late, Sam. Where is she?" Why is Ariella asking me? If I knew, I wouldn't have called her.

"That's what I'm trying to figure out. She hasn't shown. And look, if she's standing me up, just tell me. But I'm actually worried here."

"She's not!"

"Okay, well that's good, but where is she? Can you track her phone?" It's invasive and I hate asking her to do it, but isn't this the exact reason that location feature exists?

"Yeah, I can. But, Sam . . . if she's at home, I think I should be the one to go talk to her. I don't want you showing up in case she had a change of heart," she says, her tone full of warning.

"Yeah, okay. That makes sense," I relent.

"Good. I'm pulling up the app now. Give me just a second . . . What the fuck?" She swears and my body erupts in nervous goose bumps.

"Where is she? What's wrong? Why are you cussing?" I'm terrified and annoyed all at the same time. *Just tell me already, put me out of my misery.*

"Olive's phone is at the cemetery. It's showing she's there and I just . . . Why would she be there?"

"I don't know, but I'll meet you."

I hang up and race down the stairs and off my porch, nearly tripping twice on the way down. What if someone took her? What if she is hurt? Why would she even go into the cemetery? I knew I should have picked her up!

The Mage Hollow Cemetery is only a few blocks from my house, and I find myself crossing under the metal arch in record time. It's dark, and

I don't know what the situation is, so I slow my pace. As I take a few tentative steps forward, shining my phone's flashlight back and forth down the rows of final resting spots, Ariella steps up beside me, heaving breaths.

"Jesus, I haven't run that fast in, maybe ever?" She puts her hands on her hips. "Anything yet?"

"I just got here. Can you pull up her location and see how close we are?"

Ariella looks at her phone then points toward the center of the cemetery. We don't run. I want to with every fiber of my being, but I don't know what's happened, and I don't want to sneak up on anyone. As we get about halfway to where Olive is, or at least her phone is, we spot her bag. Abandoned on the ground, movies and snacks spilling out.

Ariella sucks in a breath beside me. "Shit."

"What?" I snap at her.

"That's a thousand-dollar custom bag. No way she dropped that or even dared to set it on the ground unless she was forced." Her voice shakes. I can tell she's getting worried.

"Let's stay calm." I'm trying to keep it together, to ignore the voice in my head telling me this is very, very bad.

We keep walking until Ariella says, "We should be right on top of it."

I shine my light back and forth on the ground beneath us, searching for her phone.

"Oh my God, Sam." Ariella takes off running to the left. I can't make out where she's going until she crumbles to the ground, letting out a thick wail.

I sprint after her, Olive's slight body splayed on the ground in front of me. I don't even realize I'm calling the emergency line until an operator's voice sounds aloud on speaker. "Mage Hollow 9-1-1, what's your emergency?"

I shove the phone at Ariella, dropping to my knees and running my hand down Olives' face. She's out cold. I lean closer to assess if she has any injuries. Carefully brushing hair out of her face, I see it. She hit her head—or maybe someone hit her? I'm not sure, but there is sticky red blood smeared across her face and a small, maybe two-inch gash on her forehead.

Ariella tells the operator that we need an ambulance, explaining exactly where we are. She's shouting responses to an endless slew of questions, demanding someone get here as fast as possible.

I lie flat on my belly, cautiously putting my lips to Olive's ear. "I'm here, Olive. Ari and I are getting you help. Please be okay, baby. I need you to be okay."

The logical side of me knows that she is probably okay since the cut is no longer gushing; I can see it's more of an ooze. But I don't know how long she's been out or if she has other injuries. The whirring sound of an ambulance brings me a sense of relief and dread.

"What's the situation here?" a paramedic asks Ariella.

"We, uh, we don't know. She was supposed to be going on a date with Sam but didn't show. We tracked her phone and this is . . ."

"Sam O'Reilly, sir." I stand up to introduce myself. "We found her like this. It looks like she hit her head." He eyes me suspiciously but moves closer to Olive, kneeling beside her and checking her pulse.

"She's got a strong pulse. Probably knocked herself out, but we'll do a full workup on our way to MH Memorial. Tina, get the backboard and stretcher," the paramedic barks at his partner.

"Can we ride with you?" I ask him.

"Only one of you can come in the rig. Name's Johns, by the way. John Johns." He extends his gloved hand to me while he waits for Tina to cart everything he needs over from the ambulance.

"Uh, nice to meet you, John. Please take care of her." My mind is stuck on his name. Whose parents would do such a thing? Ariella and I make eye contact. I can tell from her smirk she's thinking the same thing.

John Johns and Tina (last name unknown) carefully place a neck brace on Olive before turning her over onto the backboard and hoisting her up onto the stretcher. I keep thinking she's going to wake up with all the jostling, but nothing. Olive is out, completely lifeless, and my stomach is officially lodged in my throat.

Turning to Ariella, I say, "You go with them. I'll grab my truck and meet you over there."

"No, Sam. You should go. She's going to need things from home, and I'm not sure she would forgive me if I let you rifle through her panty drawer in search of pajamas."

"We can worry about that later. I can run faster than you. Just go, I'll be there as quickly as I can."

With a nod, Ariella races to the ambulance and disappears inside. As soon as she's gone from view, I run. I have to get to the hospital as quickly as humanly possible. I don't want Olive to wake up and wonder where I am. Then again, maybe she wouldn't expect me to be there? I'm hooked on her, but this thing between us is still new.

Shaking off the thoughts as my feet hit the uneven sidewalk, I focus on what I do know: I care for her, more deeply than I should. The paramedic didn't seem overly panicked about her condition. She's in good hands.

I reach my truck in no time, hop in, fire up the ignition, and peel out of my driveway.

Hospitals all have the same smell. It's a mixture of bodily fluids and bleach. The scent tickles my nostrils as I approach the circular desk in the emergency room and step up to the counter. A nurse with silver hair tied in a topknot with a pen says, "Do you need to be seen?" She eyes me suspiciously. Most people her age do, given my tattoos.

"No, ma'am. I'm looking for Olivia Bowman. She came by ambulance." I turn to search the waiting room for Ariella but don't spot her.

"Are you family?"

"I'm her boyfriend." It's a bold statement. Certainly not one we have discussed, but this situation calls for a little exaggeration. I think.

"You'll have to take a seat. Her family is with her. I'll need to check if she is accepting visitors." Her family? What? How?

As I'm wondering what the nurse means, an automatic door opens into the ER and Ariella calls out, "Sam, over here."

I don't wait for the nurse to confirm I can go. Instead, I walk swiftly over to Ariella and slide into the hallway before the door closes again. I can faintly hear the nurse yelling for me to wait.

"Where is she?" I ask, plopping down in a tattered leather chair next to Ariella.

She points into the room straight ahead. The curtains are drawn. All I can make out is six pairs of feet crowded around the wheels of a hospital bed.

"Did they tell you—"

"No. They haven't said anything. She came to for a few minutes on the ride here. But nothing she said made any sense. Did you two have a fight?" Ariella crosses her arms and sits back, slouching against the leather chair.

"What? No? Why would you ask that?" I stand and begin to pace, but she stops me, coming over and leading me back into the chair with a shove.

"She was begging you to forgive her. And you know, it doesn't really all add up. You were supposed to be with her. What would she need to apologize for?" Ariella asks, tension radiating off of her. It warms my heart to see her being protective. My girl needs good friends in her corner, and Ariella seems to be the best.

"She doesn't have anything to apologize for. The last time we spoke was this morning. I can show you the text messages." I hold out my phone for her to look. I don't have anything to hide.

"No, I don't need to." She wraps her arms around herself tighter, giving herself a hug it seems. "I just want her to be okay. I'm sorry I questioned you. This is all just so unlike her. She's predictable, cautious. Always where she needs to be, early and overdressed." She sighs, appearing to let some of the tension go as she unclasps her arms.

The door to Olive's room opens with a distinct swooshing sound as a physician waltzes out. "Are you Olivia's family?" *Time to lie. Again.*

"I'm her sister. This is her boyfriend, Sam," Ariella answers.

"Okay. She is going to be fine. We gave her a few sutures to ensure minimal scarring from the cut, but overall, it wasn't that bad of an injury. Foreheads and noses are bleeders." The physician flips through his chart. "She doesn't have a concussion, so I'm assuming she passed out from exhaustion or the sight of her own blood. We have administered some pain medication for the headache, and she's getting IV fluids. Once that is finished, she will be good to go home. Can one of you keep an eye on her for the night?"

"Yes, thank you, sir," I say, reaching out to shake his hand.

"You're welcome. You can go in and see her now. Her clothing is in a bag at the foot of her bed. We needed to check her for other injuries." He walks away, down the hall and into another patient's room. I head toward the door, but Ariella places a hand on my arm, stopping me.

"Sam, should I go in first? Just to make sure she's okay to see you?" Her voice trembles like she's nervous about something. My skin starts to buzz with suspicion. Why would she not want to see me? What's the big secret?

"Nope. If she doesn't want me here, then she will need to tell me that herself. I care about her, Ariella. I'm not waiting another minute," I say as I slide the door open and push past the curtain. Ariella follows me in.

Olive is lying in the bed, monitors beeping and tubing coming out of her hand. Her head has a small bandage, and she's covered up by a white cotton hospital blanket. At first, she looks like she's sleeping, but a slight flutter of her eyelashes gives me the go-ahead to speak.

"Hey, baby." I sit down in the chair closest to her bed, scooching it up so I can rub my fingers gently down her cheek. "I'm glad you are okay."

"S-sam. I'm so sorry." A single tear falls down her face, and I swipe it away.

"No. Please don't apologize. What happened? Do you remember?"

"Hi, Ollie. I was so scared. I'm glad you are okay." Ariella stands on the other side of the bed, squeezing Olive's hand through the thin blanket.

"Ari? How did you know?" Confusion paints Olive's brow, the strain of frowning causing her to wince in pain and lift her left hand to her head. Ariella's eyes widen, and her brows shoot into her forehead as I see a very interesting mix of tattoos adorning Olive's arm. *Wait, what? She told me she couldn't ever get one. Why would she lie? It's not like I would have cared, it's literally my job.*

"Ollie," Ariella gasps, grabbing at the sheet to cover her up while Olive's face turns an almost comical shade of pale.

"Uh, tattoos? Thought you didn't have any of those?" I have to ask. Why are they making this such a big deal?

"Sam, I . . . It's not, uh, it's not what it looks like," Olive spits out, her voice shaking.

"It looks like you have tattoos. Which by itself is really not a big deal." I glance at my own to make my point. "I just don't know why you wouldn't tell me."

"There's more to the story. It's hard to explain." Olive won't look me in the eyes, instead she's fiddling with the blanket.

"Can you give us a minute?" I ask Ariella, hoping that maybe a moment alone will give me some clarity. This seems like one of those things that shouldn't be causing this much turmoil.

"No, I'm not leaving her alone for this." Ariella crosses her arms and juts a hip out in a power stance.

"For what? What do you think I'm going to do to her? I tattoo other people for a living for fuck's sake. You are constantly showing up or interrupting us. Then you accuse me of causing a fight with her. And now you won't let me talk to my girlfriend alone?" They noticeably exchange looks, and I start to lose it. Between Olive constantly putting up a wall and Ariella always interrupting us, it's all a little much. I didn't think anything of it before now, but it's adding up—something's not right here, and I refuse to be in the dark any longer.

"Lower your voice. This is a hospital," Ariella scolds me.

"No. He's right. Give us a minute, Ari. I'll be fine, promise." Olive looks at Ariella meaningfully before shifting her gaze in my direction. Ariella huffs but does as she's told and slides out of the room. "You're right. I have been keeping something from you," Olive says, turning toward me.

I swallow hard, her words echoing in my head. *I have been keeping something from you.* Sweat beads on my forehead and nausea bubbles in my belly.

"What is it? You can tell me anything." I reach out, grabbing the hand closest to me and pulling it to my lips. I place a small kiss on her knuckles before setting her hand back down on the bed and leaning forward to stare into her eyes.

I can't fathom what she's going to say. The whole thing seems really dramatic for a few tattoos. But then again, I know better than anyone how misjudged a person can be from having them. For only being two weeks into this thing, I care about her so deeply. I mean it when I say she can tell me anything. "I-I, uh. You're not going to believe me."

"Just tell me," I say, nerves churning in my stomach.

"Well, I was cursed by a witch at the Hollow Hearts Festival." It's like an explosion in my head when she says it. *What? What does that have to do with anything? I just wanted to know why she lied about having tattoos, and now she's telling me she's cursed.*

"Sam, say something, please. I'm telling you the truth. Ever since that night . . ." She swallows hard, slowly swiping her tongue out to lick her lips. "I have had these, uh, these tattoos. I never went and got tattooed. They just started showing up."

"You hit your head, that's all this is." I stand and pace. I grew up hearing stories about magic and ties to witches. The lore runs deep in Mage Hollow. But this is nuts, there's no way what she's saying is true. I know the mechanics of tattooing. It can't be possible.

"Sam, stop pacing. I wouldn't lie about this. I swear this is real."

There's no chance that what she is saying is true. But why is she trying to make something up? Why when she starts to let me see the real version of her does she always have to snap this facade back into place and shut me out? What she's saying is ludicrous.

The door slides open and Ariella walks back in. "She's telling the truth, Sam. I didn't believe it at first either, but I've seen them change," she chimes in.

"Nope. No. This is too much." I run a hand down my face, a useless attempt at wiping away my disbelief. "Olive, I care about you, and I thought we had something special starting here. But this isn't going to work if you're going to lie. Magic isn't real, and I can't even believe you would try to pretend it is." I start to exit the room, but she calls out to me.

"Sam, please." Tears flow down her cheeks as I turn to look at her again. "I promise I'm not lying. I want what we have too. I care about you." Her voice strains as she says it.

"If that's the case, then come tell me the truth, when you're ready. But for now, I don't know if you hit your head too hard or if you just need to work up the courage to be honest. Either way, I'm going home." I walk back over and place a gentle goodbye kiss on her cheek.

As much as it's ripping out my insides to leave, I feel things for her I've never felt for anyone, and being lied to is more than I can handle right now. I leave the room with the sound of Olive's sobs shredding my heart as Ariella whispers soothing words to her. I don't believe in magic, unless it's the kind I feel between the two of us.

Nineteen

Olive

It's an Ambush

18 Days Until Halloween

"All set here, Beau. I'm going to wrap up and head out for the night, if that's okay." I grab the last of this week's restorations and place them in a neat stack on my desk for tomorrow. This is the first day since the incident with Irina that I haven't had a headache. It's also the fourth day that I haven't seen Sam. Since he stormed out of the hospital, he hasn't been completely silent—he answers my good-morning text and my good-night text each day, but there's nothing in between. I've tried explaining, thinking that sending messages would be easier to swallow than processing it all in person. But with little response, frankly, I've had it. I know he doesn't believe in magic, but he must believe in something if he actually thought there was magic between us, right?

"That's fine, Olive. Thanks for working hard these past few days. I know it couldn't have been easy with the spill you took. How did you say you fell again?" Beau narrows his eyes at me. He hasn't believed my story about the ladder from the second I told it. But he isn't getting the truth; I already have one person convinced I've lost it. I won't add another to that list.

"Thanks. I fell off my ladder trying to hang a new light in the kitchen. Busted my head on the edge of the countertop." I squeeze past him on my way toward the door.

"Mmmk, well don't be climbing on anything else, young lady. I'll see you tomorrow," he says as he plops down in the chair behind the cash register.

"Bye, Beau." I wave at him before grabbing the doorknob and pushing my way out onto the street. The air is getting chillier by the day, wind picking up as it comes off the bay. Leaves fall to the ground with each shake and shimmy of the branches. It's almost magical in its own right the way they coast and land so effortlessly in beautiful mosaic patterns on the sidewalk.

I don't have time to admire them as much as I normally would. I had Ariella scope out Sam's work schedule using a fake client name, and I know this is the only night he doesn't have any appointments this week. I pick up my pace, power walking toward his house, crunching those same mosaics on the ground without reservation. I'm ambushing him. I've missed him these past few days, and that's not something I've ever felt or said about anyone. I'm on a mission to make him understand—it's a last-ditch effort, but one that my heart needs to move on. Not to mention, the clock is winding ever closer to Halloween. I have a little more than two weeks until this tattoo becomes permanent.

Speaking of it, my arm has been a flurry of unsightly new additions recently. I gained a tombstone for the event in the cemetery that says *Don't Forget* where the name should be. *Thanks, Irina.* There's also a broken heart that I attribute to Sam leaving the hospital. The vines are wrapped in swirling patterns down my arm now, hovering about an inch above my wrist. The only time this week that any of it resembled happiness was when I walked into the Brewhouse. I'd peeked when the burning sensation started, and sure enough . . . little pumpkins and lattes danced on my arm. I guess coffee does make me happy after all.

As I approach Sam's house for the first time, I can't help my nerves. *What if he turns me away? What if he doesn't want to listen?* Acid creeps up my throat, and I slow my pace, hesitating briefly at the bottom of the steps. I place my right foot on the first stair when the door flies open, landing with a crack against the house. My eyes dart up immediately to a grinning Sam standing in the doorway.

"Four days is a long time to wait. Are you ready to tell me what's really going on?" Sam moves to lean against the doorjamb, crossing his arms.

"I-I, uh. Huh? I didn't think you wanted to see me, and I had this whole speech prepared to make you let me in." I walk up the remaining steps, stopping on the top one confused.

"I was telling the truth." I don't wait for him to argue. I push past him, ascending the final step and waltzing right into his home.

It's beautiful. Freshly stained hardwood floors and an open-concept kitchen, dining, and living room area. The furniture is a bit manly for my taste, but this place is very homey. I kick off my shoes and unzip my coat, hanging it on a coat rack in the entryway like I own the place. I set my bag on the hall table and walk to the large tan leather couch. Sam follows, sitting down on the opposite end of the sofa.

"Sure, Olive. Why don't you come in so we can talk," he says, his grumpy attitude from our early interactions clicking firmly back in place before he scooches deeper into his spot and presses play on some music he had cued up on the TV.

"Listen up, Sam." I snap my fingers to get him to look at me. I said this was an ambush, and I meant it. I've never wanted to hang on to someone like I do him. I'm here to play hardball if that's what it takes. "I told you the truth. I met a witch named Irina at the Hollow Hearts Festival. I didn't know it at the time, that she was a witch I mean. But she was. She asked me some stuff, I told her I wasn't the best at sharing my feelings. Bada bing, bada boom. Tattoo on my arm." I start to unbutton my cardigan so that I can show him.

"Olive, you don't need to do that," he says as he holds up his hand to halt my undressing. "I told you, I care about you. But this is wild. You know this sounds crazy, right?"

"Of course, I know it's unusual. It's happening to me." I point a finger at my chest before continuing to undo my sweater. "But I can prove it to you. I've spent the last four days trying to come up with just about anything that I could tell you to continue keeping you in the dark, but that's not fair. To you or to me. This is who I am, for now at least. And I want to keep seeing where things go between us, which is scary enough, so just let me show you." I shuck my cardigan off, revealing my black silk tank top and completely exposing my arm.

Sam scoots closer to me. Our thighs touch as we sit next to each other on the couch, and he looks curiously at my arm. "You can touch it," I whisper, the words stuck in my throat as my body buzzes from the sheer proximity of him.

His fingers glide gently over each tattoo. "There's no raised lines. It's like this is deeper than a normal tattoo." I can tell he's trying to find the lie with how hard he is concentrating. My body shivers as he touches me, a warmth slipping down my belly between my legs.

"Kiss me," I blurt out.

"What?" he asks, looking at me like I've lost it.

"Kiss me and watch what happens. Look at it now, remember what it looks like. Ready?" I ask, checking his face for confirmation.

I reach my hand behind his neck, turning him into me as I press my lips against his softly. His mouth is like a pillow beckoning me home. I can't help but to lick the seam of it, begging him to open and let me in. He complies and we get lost in the fervor of our make out. I slide up and over his lap so I'm straddling him, my skirt hitching up around my waist. Holding his face in both my hands, I dive deeper into the kiss. It's like we are making up for lost time, both taking what we need and infusing it with passion, frustration, and something else. After a few minutes, we split, gasping for air. He smiles at me, a shy, adorable grin that's made even cuter by his swollen lips.

"I'm not sure what was supposed to happen, but God, babe. I could do that for a very long time." He presses another soft kiss to my lips.

"Me too, but look." I put my arm in front of his face so he can see it. Where everything was in stark black before, the tattoos are in vivid color now. There are lips dancing on my arm and even Boo is making a smoochy face.

"H-how? This can't be real," he says, scraping a hand down his face in denial.

"I told you. It's magic."

"Magic isn't real."

"Clearly, it is." I widen my eyes at him. There's literally no other explanation for why this could be happening. He doesn't need to understand it, Lord knows I don't.

"I just, uh, I've never believed in magic. But I *am* sorry I didn't believe in you," he says, looking up to the ceiling and taking a deep breath.

"I know it's weird. Believe me, I feel it and see it change every day. But it's here, and you'll get used to it." He won't, I haven't. But what am

I supposed to say? The hunt for Irina has been futile at best. Unless I embrace the tattoo, she won't help me get rid of it.

He kisses me again, a deep open-mouthed kiss. He slides his hand over my backside, under my skirt, but then pulls away, biting my lip slightly on the retreat. Sam glances at my arm like he's testing a theory, and fireworks erupt in little blazes of glory among the vines. It usually tingles or burns when the pictures change, but for some reason right now, it's like each little shift on the movie reel sends a zap down my spine and into my center. I want him, maybe more than I've ever wanted anything. This is what we've been building toward. There's an undeniable chemistry between us, and each time we have kissed, I get a little closer to not being able to control it.

I reach for his pants, trying to unbutton them, but he places a hand on top of my fingers to stop me. "Olive, if we are doing this, I need to know something first."

"What is it?" My words come out a little exasperated, and he chuckles before wrapping me tightly in his arms and kissing my neck.

"I need to know you will be honest with me. I know why you kept this a secret, or at least, I think I do. I would have. But there can't be anything else. I'm already feeling things for you that scare me. I don't want to get my heart broken," he says. My heart melts. I don't want to get hurt either, and while I'm scared to open up to him, right now I can't find it in me to care.

"I promise, if any more witches approach me, you will be the first to know," I say, shifting so I can look him in those deep blue eyes.

"Wait, she approached you?"

"Yes."

"Where?"

"When I was walking home from the festival."

"Jesus, Olive. You walked home alone? In the dark? With a thousand strangers around?" Sam bristles and shakes his head.

"I, uh . . . yeah. I promise I will be more careful. But I am an adult, I run alone all the time in the dark."

"I guess that's good enough for me, just be more careful." Sam stands, hoisting me with him and carrying me upstairs. We pass by two doors, probably spare bedrooms, and bump into the wall a few times when we get distracted and start kissing again. We can't help it. It's like now that the burden of my secret has been eliminated, I'm powerless to stop my desire to rip his clothes off. Finally, he pushes the door to his bedroom open, walks in, kicks the door closed with his foot, and plops me on the bed.

I reach out, grabbing the waistband of his jeans, and return to work on unbuttoning them.

"Olivia Bowman, stop it right there," Sam says in a growly command.

I pout and cross my arms.

"I'm a gentleman. You are not going to do anything to me until I've worshiped every part of your beautiful body. Pout all you want, baby. But you won't be sorry when you're screaming my name." Goosebumps race over my skin, popping up faster than my brain synapses can fire. He trails a finger across the sparks igniting on my arm. "Look at that, my good girl likes it when I talk dirty. This is insane, but I think it might be useful." Sam grins as he playfully reaches the hem of my top to lift it over my head. I glance at my arm. Little flames are burning red-hot all over it. *Damn it, this thing is already giving everything away.*

Sam kisses my neck, sucking on that tender spot right above my collarbone then moving lower to my lace bra. He licks my nipple through the fabric before saying, "You are stunning. Are you sure you want to do this?"

I don't have to say a thing. A single look at my arm reveals tiny blinking signs that read yes, yes, yes. Sam reaches behind me with one hand to unfasten my bra. As quickly as it falls down my chest to the floor, he leans over me, laving on each breast until they form tight peaks. A moan sneaks out of me from the attention. Sam shows his appreciation by returning to kiss my lips in a slow, gentle press.

"Can I have my way with you, sweet Olive?" he asks, peering deep into my soul.

"Yes, but only if I get to have fun too." I shove him up so he's standing in front of me beside the bed. I grab his shirt's hem and lift, revealing an unfair amount of muscle. This must be a twelve-pack, but the best part is the swirling pattern of tattoos adorning his chest. There's a family crest and some other smaller tattoos along with a smattering of chest hair. It's neatly trimmed but a reminder that he is all male. I kiss his chiseled stomach, and a growl rumbles deep from his throat.

"I can't let you have your way with me until I've tasted you. I've been dreaming about what it would be like since the first time I saw you," Sam says, leaning in to kiss me once more.

He slides his hands under my arms to lift me gently from the bed. I reach around to unzip my skirt, watching it skate down my legs. When I look up, there's heat in his eyes. His pupils are dilated in what I assume is arousal.

Sam reaches out, snapping the black garter that attaches to my knee-high stockings. "Christ, baby. You weren't wearing these the first time I laid eyes on you." His voice sounds gravely at best, the words thickly laced with desire.

"I thought, uh, hoped that I'd get to show these off today." I wink at him before perching on the edge of the bed, running a hand up under my panties and through my center, then around my clit. The ache for him has become so intense I almost can't help it. My arm tingles as technicolor swirls dance across it.

Sam grabs my hand, removing it from my aching core and pulling it to his mouth, sucking each finger tenderly. The tension between us is so hot I almost lose control at the sight of him.

"So sweet. But not nearly enough." He pushes me back while dropping to his knees and spreading my thighs wide. "Can I taste you?" he asks, while peppering the inside of my knee with kisses.

A chuckle roars out of him as I whisper, "y-yes." My arm tingles as my answer appears in script scrolling across it.

He pulls my lace thong to the side, burying his face in my core. With a long, slow lick, followed by suction on my clit, my back is arching off the bed. He hums a little as he makes slow circles around it, and I catch him grinning when my tattoo reveals just how much I like the roughness of his beard scraping against my tender parts.

"I wondered if I'd need to shave the beard, but I'm happy to learn you like it." He's enjoying this, learning what works and what doesn't.

"Sam, please," I beg.

"Oh no, baby. You're soaked for me. I'm going to make this last, take all the time I need to learn what you like." He dives back in, this time moving quickly. His tongue flattens against me and skates back and forth until my thighs shake, and he once again breaks contact.

"You know how I knew when to stop?" I raise my head to look him in the eyes questioningly. "Because you told me you were close. Tiny little embers were growing, almost ready to explode into roaring flames . . ."

"Sam, please. I'm begging you," I plead, throwing my head back against the soft comforter.

"This won't do." He stands and grabs the pillows from the top of the bed, pulling me up to prop them beneath my back. "I want you to watch me. Look into my eyes while I make you come."

I nod in agreement as little hearts slide down the vines on my arms and snap like sparklers when they hit the ends. Sam goes back to work, rotating between fast and slow, licks and suction. My orgasm is building like a fire being stoked within me, a tidal wave about to crash.

"I'm close, so close." Our eyes meet, and he grins.

"I know. Let go for me." As the words leave his lips, I do as he commands.

"Sam. Oh God!" I scream, closing my eyes while letting euphoria take me away. I didn't know it was possible for it to be that good. Maybe it was the way he teased me, or maybe it's just him. Either way, I'm completely sated and wrung out when he climbs up on the bed, still half clothed, to pull me into his arms.

Twenty

Sam

Mother Always Knows Best

I could lie here with her in my arms for the rest of my life. The thought scares me but at the same time, brings a sense of peace. The witch, the tattoo—that stuff is weird. I've spent days trying to reconcile why she would make up such an insane lie. But it's not one, I've seen it now. I don't know how it's possible, it freaks me out, but my feelings for her are stronger than my fears about the mysterious tattoo. My feelings will outlast this spell, I'm sure of it.

Olive shifts beside me, pushing the arm I have draped over her aside and sliding off the bed.

I sit up, prepared to follow her and drag her back to bed. "Where do you think you're going?"

"Bathroom." She eyes me before strutting off to handle her business. I lean back into the bed, adjusting the painful erection I've had since she kissed me downstairs. I'm not going to do anything to resolve it, at least not until she goes home, as difficult as that may be. We need time to figure out whatever this is between us before going all the way.

Olive comes out of the bathroom and leans against the doorjamb, looking at me. Her eyes are hooded, and she's still wearing those sexier-than-sin garters. The thought occurs to me that she's sort of a sexy librarian. Prim and proper on the outside, but a secret vixen underneath. My cock stiffens further. I didn't think it was possible.

"See something you like?" I ask, scraping a hand down my face and into my beard with a grin.

"Mm-hmm." She nods before walking over to the bed and climbing on top of me. Her nimble fingers are unbuttoning my jeans before I can blink—the breathing room feels incredible.

"Lift up," she commands. I move my hips so she can pull my pants and boxer briefs down. My dick springs free, hitting my belly. Olive's eyes turn round and appreciative as she looks me over. I can't help the smile that sneaks onto my lips.

"You, uh, you don't need to worry about me. I can deal with it later," I say. I don't want her to feel pressured into anything. I know it's a delayed response, but with her on top of me, words are hard.

"Nope, you might be a gentleman, but I also know how to serve." Olive leans forward and swiftly takes me between her lips, sucking me from root to tip. *Fuck!* Her mouth is hot and wet, the suction is incredible.

"Shit. That feels so good."

"Mmmm . . ." She moans around me, the vibration buzzing in a delicious form of torture.

She licks up the underside, swirling her tongue around the tip of my cock. My hips bounce a little, and she opens wide, taking me to the back of her throat. I've never been with someone who's able to take all of me so perfectly. She's enjoying it too, I can tell.

"Fuck, you're doing amazing, baby."

Olive smiles, using her hands to work me over while she watches my face like she's studying. When a small moan sneaks out of my throat from the pressure her small hands are applying, she takes me back in her mouth. Olive is taking me so thoroughly, hollowing her cheeks out on each pass while cupping my balls and applying the perfect amount of pressure.

"I'm going to come. You have to stop." I look down at her, making eye contact as she shakes her head no. I guess if this is what my girl wants, then who am I to deny her.

I buck my hips a few more times, pumping in and out of her mouth at a steady pace. Her eyes water slightly at the corners, but each time I pull back, she leans in, pushing me further. It's so fucking hot, I'm losing it. I can't hold it in anymore—I explode in her mouth, hot jets spurting down her throat. She doesn't move a muscle, she simply swallows and proceeds to lap up every last drop. If I wasn't already falling for her, I would be now. Olive swipes her mouth on the back of her hand and curls up beside me.

"That was . . . I don't have words." I pull her on top of me and kiss her like my life depends on it. I can taste myself, but I don't even care. After a few minutes, she breaks away, laying her head on my chest while tracing my tattoos with her fingers.

"How did you, um, decide that you liked something enough to keep it on your body permanently?" she asks, her voice a soft whisper.

"I'm not sure. I guess in the beginning it was more for the thrill of it than anything. But then I fell in love with the history of the art, and it became more about honoring the beauty of it." I pull her in closer, grazing my lips on her temple.

"I never considered getting one, before Irina's spell I mean. My mother would kill me." Olive shifts so her leg is over mine like she's a koala bear wrapped around me.

"She didn't let you get away with much, did she?" I ask, patiently waiting to see if she will open up.

"No. She's not a bad mother. She just has high standards and expectations. Having a tattoo would not go over well at the country club." Olive burrows into my side a little closer. There's a hint of her holding back, but I won't push her to say more. I can sense this is something she needs to tell me in her own time.

"I see. Well, Mabel wasn't pleased with the first one, if it makes you feel better," I say, closing my eyes briefly, remembering how my mother reacted. She'd lost it, crying about how the body she made was ruined for all time.

"What? No way. Mabel doesn't seem like the type, she's so loving." Olive sits up, gently placing a hand on my chest and positioning herself to look into my eyes.

"She's loving, for sure, but she is fiercely protective. Once she realized how much I loved it, she got on board." I pull her into my arms, hugging her to my chest and kissing her forehead.

"It must be nice to know you always have a safe place to land," Olive says softly before blowing out a long, slow breath.

"Hey, look at me." I use my hand to prop her head up, so she can see my face clearly. "You have a safe place to land, with me."

"That's sweet, Sam. But you can't say things like that. You don't know enough about me to form a full opinion, yet." Olive scooches so her bottom is perched on the edge of the bed and she's facing my dresser.

"I know plenty, Olivia Bowman. Whether you want me to or not, I see you. You're kind and compassionate, funny and a little sassy"—I sit up next to her and wrap my arm around her middle, pulling her close—"stubborn, but also easy to take care of. You are the real deal, and I'm not sure what ideas you have in this beautiful brain of yours, but I am not going anywhere."

She doesn't say anything in response, she simply closes her eyes and breathes deeply, almost like she's afraid to accept my words. It's okay if she doesn't believe me yet. I plan on showing her that I'm the kind of guy that sticks around.

"Ma, I'm here. Can someone give me a hand?" I shout, struggling to juggle three very large pumpkins as I make my way through the front door of my childhood home.

"Be right there," my mom shouts back.

I make my way into the dining room, since it's the first place to set anything down, as Mabel sashays in, wiping her hands on her fall-themed apron.

"Sam, you didn't need to carry three at a time. Dad and I can help you," she scolds me.

"I know, but there's a lot of them, and I have an appointment to get to in an hour." I shrug and check the time on my phone.

"And you thought it would take an hour for the three of us to carry in seven pumpkins?" My mom raises an eyebrow at me. She can read my every thought and feeling. She knows something is up.

"No, uh . . . there's something I wanted to ask you." I look at the floor and am instantly eleven years old again, afraid of what she's going to say.

"Come with me," she says as she grabs my arm and leads me into the kitchen, motioning for me to sit on one of the barstools. I do what I'm told and get rewarded with a freshly baked pumpkin cookie and a glass of warm apple cider. My dad just shakes his head and swipes a cookie off the tray, waiting to watch whatever is about to unfold.

"Do you believe in magic?" I blurt out, bits of the cookie tumbling from my lips.

"What kind of magic?" Mabel asks.

"Any kind?" I shrug before taking a slow sip of my drink.

"Yes."

"Yes? What do you mean, yes?" I ask.

"I wouldn't say that I believe in magic in that a witch walks around casting spells on people, but I do believe that magical things can happen, especially when it comes to matters of the heart." My mom shifts her gaze to my dad for a brief second before looking me in the eyes. It's like she's trying to decipher where this is coming from. I'm not going to tell her about Olive. I just want to know if she thinks that what we have is real. Don't get me wrong, I like having the cheat code to her every emotion at my disposal, but it also makes me wonder if she's really in this for me or if it's just a result of whatever spell she's under.

Last night, she didn't respond to my declaration about knowing her well enough to know I care for her. She just sat there silently working through her emotions, refusing to let me in. I could see what she was thinking on her arm, but I didn't acknowledge it because seeing it isn't the same thing as her opening up and actually telling me. Instead, I snuggled her until we got hungry, took her to get some food, and dropped her at home.

"Is there a particular reason you are asking me this, Sammy?" My mom runs her hand down my cheek and pats my shoulder.

"I think, uh, this is hard. I think that things with Olive could be really serious, but I also know it's fast. I really care about her, it's like there is this magical connection between us and we are just meant to be." I don't make eye contact. I'm a thirty-two-year-old man going to his mom for dating advice. It's pathetic.

"She's the one," Mom confirms. "I knew it the moment I saw her. There are some things that are just written in the stars, and she's it for you. It was like that for Dad and me, you know. We met and it was—oh, what do the kids call it . . . instalove. I couldn't go another minute without him in my life." My mom clutches her heart thinking about it as her eyes tear up.

"Yeah, I think that's what this is, and I'm scared."

"What are you afraid of?" Mom asks.

"Messing it up. Not being what she wants me to be."

"Samuel O'Reilly, stop it right now. You are a catch, and I'm not just saying that because I'm your mother. That girl would be lucky to be with you and to have my grandchildren. I have great genes, she should be so fortunate." Mom throws her towel on the counter in a tizzy.

I can't help the laugh that bubbles up from deep in my chest. There's nothing like watching her get worked up over the thought that one of her children would do something wrong or somehow be inadequate. She wears "mom goggles," meaning we are always perfect angels in her eyes.

"Okay, but how do I win her over?" I ask, trying to bring her back to the world where we aren't mad at Olive for fictitiously saying I'm not good enough.

"Well, with how nervous you are, I'm having second thoughts about whether we should win her over." She places both hands on her hips, thinking. "Actually, no I'm not. That girl is a doll. She's absolutely perfect in every way."

"There is one thing I'm not sure about," my dad interjects.

"Let's hear it," I say, scrubbing a hand down my face.

"How would she handle the pumpkin guts?" he asks.

"I'm not sure that's the best way to win her over." I shake my head in disbelief that he's suggesting that splattering pumpkin all over Olive could be the key to making her mine.

"Sure, it is. If she is going to be my daughter-in-law one day, hopefully soon, she needs to be able to make a mess of things. You need to invite her. Saturday at six sharp," Mom quips, turning and walking out of the kitchen, out the front door, and straight to my truck to grab two pumpkins.

"We'll need to get another one of these," I say, trailing after her and grabbing the final two.

"Bring one from her porch, I think she can spare one. Which, by the way, you did a beautiful job on even if it is clearly over the top."

"Noted. Thanks, Ma. I do have to run, but I'll see you Saturday." I sit the pumpkins on the top porch step and lean in to kiss her forehead before turning back to my truck.

"Sammy, don't tell her about it. Let it be a surprise so we can gauge her reaction," Mom shouts, toeing the front door open.

"Will do." I slide into the front seat of my truck, wondering if surprising Olive with the famous pumpkin smear is a good idea. I guess we will find out.

Busy Saturday?

Olive

I don't know, depends on if a certain guy wants to take me out or not.

What's his name? I'll kick his ass.

Olive

Some guy named Sam. Jury's still out on whether I like him or not.

Oh, that guy. Well, the whole town heard you scream his name the other night while he tasted you. That has to mean something, right?

Olive

SAM!

See, still screaming it.

Olive

Okay, mister. What's on Saturday?

Pumpkin carving with my family. We usually have a bonfire too. Want to come?

Olive

I would love to, but can we make it more than once this time?

Now whose mind is in the gutter? Pick you up at five thirty, babe.

Olive

Sounds like a date.

Olive

Twenty-One

Olive

An Indecent Pumpkin Seed

14 Days Until Halloween

"Not again. I swear this woman is relentless," I whine to Ariella while my phone rings again on the dresser. Part of me does miss my mom, but I also don't want to deal with what she will undoubtedly say if I pick up.

"She's still calling?" Ariella looks unamused by my mother's attempts to get in touch with me.

"She probably just wants to scold me for throwing her out of my house or tell me how Ted is moving on." I toss the third shirt I've tried into the growing heap on the chair in my room.

"Who's Ted?" *Of course that makes her perk up.*

"Theodore, but Sam sarcastically called him that and it feels kind of fitting," I say, explaining the new nickname for the one person my mother has always seen as my future husband. Theodore and I grew up together. Anne has always had her heart set on a lavish wedding with me in a poofy dress and my bank account with an extra four zeroes. But Ted is gross. He thinks he's a gift to women everywhere with his slicked-back hair and grabby fingers.

"Ugh, that guy. Yuck. Ted is a perfect name for him. Can you pick a shirt already? I need to get out of here or Sam is going to accuse me of cock-blocking him again."

"No, he won't. But what do you wear to carve pumpkins? I don't know what's expected."

"Just wear the cream sweater. It covers your arm. Wait . . . how are you going to scoop the guts?"

"What do you mean?" I ask her, honestly not picking up what she's getting at.

"You have to stick your arm inside the pumpkin. Most people would roll up their sleeves." Her eyebrows shoot into her hairline like she can't believe she's having to explain this to me.

"How far? Maybe I can go like this deep?" I point to just above my wrist where the pumpkin vines stop. Not much has changed on my arm since the other night with Sam. There's a small firework bursting off of the vine just below the crease of my elbow, but other than that, it's stayed consistent. Well, except for the eye rolls that appear when Beau is driving me nuts or the dancing coffee cups when I drink my daily cup.

"Maybe just have Sam do it for you?" Ari asks as she grabs her phone and jacket to head out of my room. "I'm gonna go, but text me later to tell me how it goes."

"Okay, bye. Thanks for not helping even a little," I chide her. But in reality, I'm glad she came over.

After Ari leaves my house, I slump onto the bed. I'm tired of having to hide, but also scared that this is giving too much away. Sam made a comment about wanting a cheat code, and he actually has it. I sit wondering if I'll ever be able to trust that what's between us is real. It feels real in my heart, but my stupid head always has to come to the party with logic.

The sound of the door being rapped echoes through the cottage. Without thinking, I hurry to open it and am greeted with a very handsome and a slightly mischievous-looking Sam.

"I'm sure Max would be happy if you show up like that, but Mabel won't be when I hit him for ogling you," he says, a grin ghosting his full lips as he drinks me in.

"Huh . . . ?" I start to ask, but then remember I only have on a pair of fitted jeans and a bra. "Oh, yeah. I'm sorry, I can't find anything to wear." I grab his hand and pull him inside, closing the door behind him.

Sam pulls me into a hug and presses a tender kiss to my neck. Being in his arms is incredible. It's like being tucked into a big, strong, safe cocoon where nothing in the world can hurt me. I peer up into his eyes, standing on my tiptoes to sneak a kiss. It was meant to be quick, but a single flick of his tongue and the next thing I know, my back is hitting the door as I wrap my legs around his waist. We taste and explore each other while his fingers press into my thighs and I grind against him.

After who knows how long, Sam breaks the kiss, opting to nuzzle my neck. "God, you're so beautiful. I could stay here all day, but my mom will actually hunt us both down if we don't get a move on."

"Right, okay. Yeah. What should I wear? I can't . . . I can't show my arm, but long sleeves will get ruined from the guts, *I think*." I know there's hesitation in my voice.

Sam glances at my arm at the exact same time I do. Pumpkins roll down the vines with giant red X's through them. "You think? Have you ever carved a pumpkin?" Sam asks, leveling me with a look of curiosity.

"Uh, yeah, sure I have. I mean, who hasn't? Of course, it's just that—"

"You haven't. I can tell, remember?" Sam interrupts me, pointing to my arm. The traitorous little thing has cartoon Pinocchios slipping down the vines. *I hate this stupid curse.*

"Okay, fine. I've never carved a pumpkin. My mother always said it was too messy. I begged but she wouldn't ever let me do it." I wiggle out of his grip and walk toward my bedroom, needing some space for my embarrassment.

Instead of giving it to me, Sam walks up behind me and wraps me in a bear hug. "It's a little sad, but I'm actually kind of glad you're a virgin," he whispers in my ear.

"What? I'm not," I say, spinning in his arms to face him.

"You're a pumpkin virgin. I get to show you the ropes." Sam chuckles, kisses the top of my head, then smacks my ass. "Now get a move on. I'll pull the guts out for you, so just wear whatever."

I do as he commands and grab a green cable-knit sweater, pulling it over my head. "Okay, I'm ready."

We head out as I slide into a pair of flats near the door. I grab a pumpkin from the porch that won't be noticeably missing and hop into Sam's truck. On the ride to Mabel's, Sam fills me in on his clients from the week, and I tell him the latest reason Beau got mad at me. Spoiler alert: I referred to his feline friend as Pickles instead of Mr. Pickles when he brought him in for a visit. There's something strange about that cat. I can tell he's an old soul, or maybe otherworldly. What kind of cat prefers eating radishes and cucumbers over tuna? I asked Beau that very question, and I swear the cat gave me a judgmental look—I was eating a greasy slice of pizza at the time.

Gravel crunches under the tires a few minutes later as we pull into the driveway. A wave of nerves hits my belly unexpectedly. I've been here before—heck, I've already been to family dinner. But things were different then. For starters, Sam had never given me an orgasm. *Ugh, why am I thinking about Sam's . . . thing, when I'm about to walk into his mother's house?*

"Everything okay over there?" Sam eyes me suspiciously.

"Yep, fine. I'm good," I say, attempting to cool the redness in my face through sheer force of determination.

"You're blushing. What are you thinking about?" He pokes my side, tickling me just a little.

"You don't want to know."

"I think I do." Sam unbuckles and slides across the bench seat, placing small kisses on my neck.

"Nope, I have to face your mother. If she's spying out the window, which we both know she is, I will never be able to go in after she sees us kissing." I shove him off gently, unbuckle my seat belt, and hop out of the truck. It doesn't take long for Sam to exit the vehicle, grab my pumpkin from the bed, then give me a stern look as he stalks toward me.

"I always open the door for you, babe," he growls quietly in my ear.

"Not necessary, as I've told you, many times." I wave him off and begin making my way to the porch. As I take the top step, Sam is nipping at my heels. He places his free hand around my waist, halting my trek.

"Do you want to give Mabel a reason to meddle?" he asks, lips grazing the shell of my ear.

"N-no, thank you," I whisper, breathlessly. My body is heating up from his closeness. If we don't get in this house soon, we'll never make it inside.

"Then please just let me be a gentleman. I like opening doors for you. Chivalry and all." Sam moves around me, grasping the door handle and pushing his way inside, only to glance back at me and wink. *Holy hell! I'm pretty sure my panties just melted off.*

"Ma! We're here," Sam shouts.

"In the kitchen, come on in," Mabel replies.

It smells amazing in his parents' home. Scents of cinnamon and nutmeg waft in the air mixed with something a bit more rustic. Maybe cedar or spruce. The house itself is pretty large, but the small cozy rooms of the historic place warm my heart. I can picture Sam and his siblings dawdling down the halls as babies.

Sam and I walk into the kitchen where Nora, her boyfriend Charlie, and Max are hanging out with Sam's parents. They each have an apple cider in their hands, and the rosiness of their cheeks clues me in that maybe it's paired with something stronger.

"Would you two like some cider?" Mabel asks, already ladling two mugs full.

"Yes, please. It's nice to see you again," I say, reaching out to give her a small hug and handing her the bottle of cabernet Sam said she loves most.

"Oh, you too, Olive. This is so kind. I'm so glad you came to carve pumpkins with us. Although I should warn you, it gets a little competitive." Mabel hands me a mug of steamy cider as I glare at Sam. How could he not have warned me? I'm not experienced at this. I'm definitely going to make a fool of myself.

"Actually, Ma . . . It's Olive's first time. I thought we'd maybe dial down the competition this year," Sam says. I know he's not doing it to embarrass me, but I am embarrassed anyway.

"Oh, uh, okay. Well, Olive, how would you feel about being the judge?" Mabel looks at me, a hint of curiosity and pity mixed in her expression.

"Yes! Let me do that. Oh, and congratulations all, Sam is going to lose this year," I remark, while elbowing him in the ribs lightly.

"He loses every year, that's not really saying much," Max chimes in before stealing a pumpkin cookie off of a cooling rack and promptly getting his hand smacked by Mabel.

"Olive, don't listen to them. I'm the winner every year, and I expect it won't be changing anytime soon," Sam's dad whispers conspiratorially as he walks past me to refill his cider.

"I guess we'll have to see . . ." I start to tell them that I'm a tough judge and they won't be able to sway me, but then Bridget rolls in with a tray of biscuits that smell like heaven and rightfully distracts the group.

"Sorry, I was waiting for these to finish baking. What did I miss?" she asks, setting the pan on the counter and sloughing off her coat.

"Nothing. Olive is judging this year because she's never carved a pumpkin before," Nora announces nonchalantly as my stomach drops. They must think I'm so ridiculous.

"Oh, cool. Wait . . . why not?" Bridget asks, turning to look at me.

"Uh, it's just not something I was ever—"

"It's none of your business." Sam jumps in to save me from having to answer. "Should we get started before we lose all daylight, or does someone want to lose a finger?" I'm grateful that I don't have to explain my mother to his perfectly normal family.

"Yes, let's do that." Mabel takes off her apron and makes her way out back, the rest of us filing out after her.

Everyone takes their place at their respective pumpkins and begins the process of removing the stems and scooping guts. Peering into the backyard, I see what every family I've ever dreamed up looks like.

"Come on, Olive. Don't you want to learn?" Sam asks, winking at me.

I approach him and look into the hole he's made. It's a web of orange slime mixed with seeds. My arm tingles, and I can only imagine what's being displayed. Sam grabs my hand and sticks it inside, gooey wet mush coats my fingers. I sort of love it. We take turns scooping. Sam takes over once I reach the point of needing to roll up my sweater, which we both know I can't do.

"You're carving this one, just for fun." He hands me a small serrated knife with a fluorescent orange handle. I glance between the knife and the pumpkin, unsure what to do. When he notices he wraps his hand around mine and helps me jam the knife into the gourd.

"What now?"

"Just seesaw it back and forth to make whatever shape you want for the eyes."

I do as I'm instructed and minutes later have a fairly decent pair of ovals staring back at me. I move lower, attempting to make the mouth when Mabel approaches.

"You're doing great, hunny," she says, patting my shoulder and observing my work.

"It's not award winning, but I think it's cute," I respond, smiling slightly. It's actually hideous, with two lopsided eyes and a jagged mouth, but it's my first.

I take a minute to notice everyone finishing up. Some of their pumpkins have beautifully carved faces while others are etched with words. How did they all get so good at this?

"Want to see mine?" Sam whispers in my ear.

I nod at him, waiting for the big reveal, when a giant glob of pumpkin guts lands directly on top of my head. "What the fud—" I begin to shout *fudge*, when the next wave smacks the front of my sweater and the sound of Nora cackling rings in my ear. I look up, making eye contact with all of them for a brief second. Seven smiling faces greet me before all hell breaks loose.

Like a frenzied food fight, pumpkin innards begin to fly. Everyone is being pelted with the gooey substance, and all they can do is laugh. Realizing I better get in on the action and quick, I grab a handful and throw it with all my might at Sam. Unfortunately, he dodges it and it lands with a loud wet smack against Mabel's cheek. Shoot!

"I'm so sorry," I say quickly, but instead of being mad, she doubles over laughing and then launches a handful in my direction.

After several minutes of flying pumpkin guts and precarious hits on Sam's family, his dad announces that the annual pumpkin smear has come to a close. Each of us is covered in an array of pumpkin flesh and seeds. My sweater is matted so thick with it, I think the best course of action will be tossing it straight in the trash.

"Okay, everyone, time to get changed for dinner," Mabel says.

I look at Sam, my eyes practically popping out of my head.

He gives me a reassuring look then says, "Ma, since we were surprising Olive, she didn't bring a change of clothes. I'm going to run her home to get cleaned up." Sam nods toward the gate in the fence, signaling where we exit.

"Oh, Sammy, I'm sure we can find something for her to wear," Mabel puts her hands on her hips.

"No really, Ma. It's okay. I'll take her home to get cleaned up." Something transpires between the two of them, an unspoken understanding.

"Fine, if you insist. But you two are not leaving until I've packed you up some stew and biscuits. I'll be right back," Mabel says, already starting toward the kitchen to get our food.

"Mom doesn't let anyone leave hungry. It'll just take a minute." Sam looks at me reverently, and my heart melts even more. This man and his amazing family are so kind, almost too nice. I feel like I'm waiting for the other shoe to drop.

Mabel rushes out with a huge container of beef stew, a foil-covered plate of biscuits, and a sack filled with cookies. We couldn't eat this all in one sitting even if we hadn't consumed food in a week. We make our way to the truck, and I slide in gingerly in an attempt to not muck up the interior too badly.

It's a short drive, filled with far too much laughter over my initial reaction to being pelted with pumpkin guts. Sam explained it's a yearly tradition, and one that is never shared with new significant others until it happens. Reflecting on it, I have to say it was one of the most freeing experiences of my life. The ability to throw caution to the wind and just let loose isn't a privilege I've had often.

We arrive at my house and make our way inside, undressing in the entryway so that I don't have to peel dried pumpkin off the floor for weeks to come. Conveniently, Sam had a bag with a change of clothes with him. I guess he knew to come prepared. Down to our final layers, we walk to the bathroom, Sam's lips on my neck and his hands wrapped around my belly.

"Do you, uh, do you want to go first?" I ask, turning to face him after I set the shower to hot. He presses a kiss to my lips, and I feel it all the way to my toes.

"How about together? I mean, if you want to." I can see the trepidation take over his expression as he asks me. Of course I want to. He's like a walking underwear model with his ripped muscles and beautiful tattoos. I kiss him again, stretching on my tiptoes to meet his pillow-soft lips.

"Is that a yes?" He peeks at my arm briefly, and my stomach bottoms out. I know it's a natural reaction, one I'd probably do too, if the roles were reversed. But it also gives me pause—is this how it's going to be now?

His face sinks when he notices that I caught him. "Hey, I'm good with whatever you want. I just want to make you happy." My heart skips a beat. I'm massively overthinking this. I need to live in the moment—let go and have fun.

I tentatively bring my hand to the elastic at his waist, deciding to seize the moment instead of running scared. I tug his boxer briefs down slowly, admiring his impressive length as it springs up toward his abs. Standing and carefully reaching around, I unclasp my bra, letting it coast to the floor. A myriad of pumpkin seeds fall with it, causing us both to laugh.

"I guess I was saving those for later," I manage in between wheezing.

"Come on, baby." He leads me into the shower and under the spray. Hot water cascades over my skin in direct contradiction to the cool air of my cottage. My nipples pebble and goose bumps breakout across my skin. Sam runs his hands up and down my arms before leaning in and kissing the tender spot behind my ear, then down my neck and onto my breasts. Any chill I had evaporates instantaneously as my center becomes slick with need.

"You are the most gorgeous thing I've ever seen," Sam growls out quietly as he steps back to drink me in.

I take a second to squirt some body wash in my hands and rub them together, creating a lather. Stepping forward so the spray is hitting my back, I run my hands from his neck, down his arms, and across his abs, landing on his impressive cock. I take my time feeling the hard planes of his body under my fingertips, careful to get all remains of pumpkin off his skin. Sam hisses out a slow breath when I wrap my hand around him and tug slightly.

Quickly, he peels my fingers off of him and says, "My turn."

He turns me around, so the water is splashing my front, and grabs the bodywash, putting a generous amount in his palm. Sam steps up close behind me, his cock pressing into my backside as he wraps his arms around me and covers me in suds. I can't help but grind back against him just slightly.

"You better stop or I might not be able to avoid taking you in this shower," he grounds out in my ear.

I press back harder, rocking my hips gently in a circular motion. "I dare you," I challenge him, feeling brave and oddly comfortable in my own skin from how he looks at me.

He spins me around forcefully, and my back hits the shower wall. Our tongues tangle in a sexier-than-sin kiss, and I wrap a leg around him, desperate for friction between my legs.

"Nope, I haven't tasted you yet," Sam grumbles before quickly dropping to his knees and placing one of my legs on his shoulder. He looks up at me with hooded eyes. I think I might lose it right here and now just from his need reflecting back at me.

Sam wastes zero time diving in, flattening his tongue against me and moving it back and forth in purposeful flicks. He swirls it deep into my core, dipping inside me as a growl catches in his throat. The sight of him buried between my legs is enough to do me in, but when he moves higher and lightly nips my clit, I almost lose it. The momentary pain followed by the soothing sweep of his tongue makes sparks wink behind my eyes. I bite down on my lip, drawing blood. It feels so good, I know I'm losing control as my legs start to shake. "Oh my God," I mumble as he suctions my clit, focusing all his attention exactly where I need it. A scream rips out of me. "Sam, holy hell, Sam!" And then I float into another world.

Sam stands, wiping his mouth on the back of his hand, and leans in to kiss me. I just came harder than I think I ever have, but with his mouth on mine, I'm ready to do it again.

"I-I need you, Sam," I say, wrapping my leg around his waist again and grinding into him.

"Are you sure? I'm clean, I got tested a few months ago and there hasn't been anyone since."

"I'm sure, and me too. A year ago, no one since." My stomach riots at the confession, but if there's a time for transparency, it's now. Sam doesn't acknowledge the admission. He simply kisses me again before pulling away.

"Fuck! I don't have anything with me," he says, shaking his head and running a hand down his face.

"The pill, I'm on the pill, and I take it religiously. We're good," I rush out, kissing him with all I have, hoping he doesn't turn me away.

Sam spins, turns off the shower, steps out, and reaches over to grab each of us a towel.

"Is that a no?" I inquire, nervous that somehow he's going to walk away right now. The thought is always lingering in my mind: When is he going to realize I'm bound to disappoint him?

"Not a no. I'm just not going to bury myself in you for the first time while attempting not to slip in the shower. We're going to bed." He says it matter-of-factly, like he knows exactly what he wants and how he wants it. My skin ignites in tiny vibrations. The thought of being with him in this way turns me into an inferno.

I step out of the shower and onto the mat as Sam wraps me in a towel. Before I know it, he's wrapped his arms around me and hoisted me over his shoulder like I weigh nothing at all, carrying me into the bedroom.

Twenty-Two

Sam

An Address and a New Lead

I set Olive down on the bed gently, astounded by how beautiful she looks with wet hair and water dripping down her body. She's everything I've ever wanted physically, but what's on the inside far outweighs that. The subtle ways in which she second-guesses herself breaks my heart. Olive is kind, intelligent, thoughtful, and absolutely not deserving of ever feeling less than perfect.

I hover over her, pressing gentle kisses to her lips and face. "I've wanted you since the first day I saw you, baby. This probably isn't going to last long," I say, trying to be upfront that I will not be able to go the distance, so to speak.

"I'm not worried about that, I just want to feel you inside of me," she mewls out, grasping to pull me closer.

Olive kisses me, flicking her tongue out and deepening our connection. She's running her fingers up and down my back, and I can feel the precum beading before I'm even inside of her. Reaching between us, I grab my cock and give it a calm-down squeeze, just enough to buy myself time to get inside of her. I rub myself from her clit down into her soaking center and then I push in. *Fuck! She's so tight.*

"I, um, I don't want to hurt you, so I'm going to do this slowly," I manage to say, breathing deeply through my nose.

"You won't hurt me, Sam. Just, well, you know already."

At her command, I drive my hips forward, seating myself fully. Olive is so snug around me I'm worried I've hurt her, but she doesn't wince.

"I'm going to move, are you okay?"

"Yes, Sam. Oh my gosh, you're so big. It feels so good." Her center goes slick all around me, the heat and moisture almost make me lose it. I pull out and then grind in again. Stars wink behind my eyes.

"Harder, Sam," she commands.

I pull out, slamming into her harder as I lift her legs onto my shoulders. I'm moving so quickly and forcefully, I'm a little afraid I'm going to break her. But her eyes are fixed on mine, and I can tell she's enjoying it from the waves of fire erupting on her arm.

I pull out, grabbing a pillow and lifting her up so that she's propped at the right angle. Leaning forward with my hands on either side of her, I push back into her again. Olive meets me each time, grinding onto the base of my cock when I bottom out deep inside her. I slow my pace, pulling out and using my fingers to rub circles on her clit. She's so wet and tasted so sweet in the shower, I can't stop myself from dipping lower and sucking on her clit again.

"Sam, I need you . . . please," she begs, and I move to hover over her again.

"You're so sweet, baby. I'll never get tired of tasting you." I swirl my fingers on her pussy again, dipping one inside and bringing it to her lips. She sucks my finger, tasting herself. "See, delicious isn't it, good girl?"

Her arm flares with the word yes, followed by kiss faces and fireworks. I'd be lying if I said that the tattoo wasn't incredibly helpful when it comes to knowing what she likes.

I flip Olive onto her stomach and lift her hips into the air as I sink back into her. She's always gorgeous, but with her hair fanning out all around her and her face pressed against the mattress, this might be my new favorite vantage point. After a few more hard pumps, we both scream each other's names as we float into oblivion.

Olive rolls over when I finally pull out, and I lie on top of her, holding my weight by propping my elbows underneath me. "Baby, that was . . . It was . . ." I can't form words.

Olive leans up, kissing my mouth softly. "It was amazing," she utters, breathlessly.

"I've never been with anyone like this," I admit. I'm not sure if I should tell her that she's my first without a condom, but it feels special. I like knowing this thing between us is somewhat of a first for me.

"Me either. It never felt like a good idea." My heart grows three sizes knowing we are finally sharing something that feels deeper. Olive has been tentative in telling me just about anything. Most of the time I'm prying information out of her or gauging her reactions based on her arm. This is progress.

"I should go clean up. I think I still have pumpkin in my hair." Olive pushes me off of her with a light shove.

"I'll come with you. I can wash your hair," I reply, knowing it's probably a bad idea as it will surely lead to more. But I don't want any distance when we just had what I think is a breakthrough.

"That's okay. I'll just be ten minutes." She leans in to kiss me, then saunters off to the bathroom. I hear the door click close, and I know that, for whatever reason, she needs space to process what we just did.

I want to be sad or maybe a little annoyed, but I can't. I know I'm probably overthinking it, she's told me in many direct and indirect ways that she doesn't let people in. I know as much as I want to hold her right now, she needs the time to think through things, and pushing her would be a mistake. I sink back into the bed, closing my eyes and replaying everything that just transpired, wondering if I took it too far or did anything to make her uncomfortable.

"Sam, wake up." Olive presses a kiss to my lips, causing me to stir awake.

"Too early, need sleep," I mumble in return.

"Nice try, I'm leaving for my run, and I'm pretty sure you have a local business owners' brunch. Beau told me about it. I assume you go to those too?" She ruffles my hair then strokes her dainty fingers down my beard.

"Shit! I spent the night?" I sit up, rubbing the sleep from my eyes. Olive giggles then shoves me back lightly.

"Don't act like it's a bad thing. When I came back from showering, you were passed out. I have to say, I didn't take you for a snuggler, but you make a pretty great little spoon," she says, blushing a bit when I turn to look at her.

"What time is it?" I ask.

"Seven-fifteen."

"Way too early for a run. My meeting's not till nine-thirty. Come snuggle with me instead." I turn wrapping my arms around her and pulling her to the bed. I can't help but tickle her a bit just to hear that melodic laugh.

"I have to run. I've skipped too many lately," Olive explains, peppering me with little kisses. "Take as much time as you need, just lock up with the key under the mat when you leave if I'm not back."

"Uh, fine. I guess duty calls. Can't stay hidden away in bed with me all day." I shrug then promptly toss the covers back to stand. I'm still in my birthday suit, and I can't help but notice the way her breath hitches at the sight of me.

"I-I'm leaving now, call me later." Olive practically lunges for the door.

"Will do. Oh, and Olive? Thanks for last night," I say, grinning at her. Instead of saying anything, she walks back over and kisses me. Just a simple, chaste kiss, but one that I feel all the way from the ends of my hair to the tips of my toes. We're going to be okay. I know just from that small gesture that she doesn't regret last night.

I dig around in my bag and throw on the sweats I packed before collecting my pumpkin-covered clothing from the front door. Exiting, I retrieve the key and lock the door before returning the key under the entryway mat. She should find a better hiding spot. Anyone looking could easily find the key and let themselves in. Shaking my head, I walk to my truck and dart across town to change for the business brunch I have to attend before my first client.

"Here we go again. Mrs. Beasley will never get over the one time that she lost half a loaf of bread to the seagulls. What does she expect the council to do? Block all birds from flying near the farmers' market?"

Beau grumbles under his breath to me. I take another bite of eggs, opting not to get involved.

"We have a new update from Stan Overby. Improvements are coming to the historical society that I think are going to delight all of you," Tony Marino bellows.

"Good morning and thank you, Tony. I'm not sure how excited any of you will be about this news, but I am ecstatic to share that after years of searching, we've finally identified the home of our favorite witch, Irina Hallowell." My breath hitches and my skin turns clammy. Did he say they know where she *lived* or *lives*? I lean forward in my chair to listen intently. While the whole tattoo thing is still super bizarre, I don't understand why Olive is so hell bent on getting rid of it. I wouldn't want to go anywhere near that witch again, but this could be the clue Olive has been waiting for. "We received an anonymously donated article that indicates that the old cottage on Crow may have belonged to her. It's pretty run-down, but plans to survey the property and catalog anything found inside are underway, with work slated to begin mid next week."

Shit! Once they get started, no one will be allowed to go near the place. If we want to check it out, we're going to have to get in and out prior to them roping it off. Stan continues droning on about enhancements to the tourist experience in Mage and how the historical society is the "real" attraction. I'm not about to disagree with him, but I think there's something to be said about the appeal of our town and the plethora of fun seasonal events that actually provide the real pull.

"I can only imagine the business this whole Irina thing is going to drum up. Olive and I will need to spend extra time digging through backstock in case interest peaks. Is she available today?" Beau asks quietly.

"No, she's busy today. Maybe tomorrow?" I respond as if I don't know that tomorrow is a standard workday. I can't wait to get out of here to call her. Beau just rolls his eyes and huffs under his breath about that being obvious.

"That's all for today. Please drop suggestion cards in the basket by the door on your way out, and don't forget about the upcoming Christmas Walk. I will need engagement from everyone in town to pull it off," Tony says, adjourning the meeting.

I stand, scooching my chair back with a squeak across the tile floor. In a matter of seconds, I'm pacing on the sidewalk, willing Olive to answer her phone.

"Miss me already, Sam?"

"Always. Are you busy today?"

"Nope, unless Beau needs me for something. Although I have girls' night tonight, so I'll need to be back by five to get ready."

"Okay, I have a lead on Irina. Stan gave everyone the address to her assumed home after receiving an anonymous tip. The society is going to start their survey and restoration next week. I think we should check it out, and if we're going, we need to do it tonight or tomorrow," I explain.

"Oh, uh, okay . . . It has to be tonight. We'll get caught snooping if we go during the day." Olive comes through with logic, thank God.

"Okay, can you cancel girls' night?" I ask, hoping she's on board.

"No, but I can bring Ari with me. Why don't you bring Howard? Double date!" Olive's voice goes up three octaves on the last statement. I can't help but chuckle at her enthusiasm. A part of me hopes she's that excited about us, too.

"I'll ask him. But does he know? You know, about your arm . . ."

"Yeah! He's known for weeks. It's all good," Olive chatters out. The knowledge that everyone, or what feels like everyone, but me has known hits me in the gut. I need to have a conversation with her, tell her how I feel, because it's killing me holding back.

"Oh, um, alright. I'll stop by Union after my last client and see if he's in," I respond, stopping myself from saying too much.

Seeming to sense my inner turmoil, she says, "I'm sorry, Sam. I just didn't know how to tell you. It's this crazy out of my control thing, and I thought it would be just one more reason for you to leave, you know." I can hear her sigh on the other end of the line. I get why she didn't tell me sooner, and we have made progress—she's even started to tell me about her mom. But I want more, I want everything she has to offer.

"Baby, let me make something clear. I'm not going anywhere. You keep saying I'll leave, but from where I'm sitting, it feels like maybe you're the one afraid of this. I'm all in, I promise." My voice cracks as the emotion of last night and now today starts to bubble up. I think I'm in love with Olivia Bowman.

"Thanks, Sam. I'll see you tonight."

Twenty-Three

Olive

At Home with Irina

13 Days Until Halloween

"Ollie, I got the eye black as requested," Ari shouts, barreling through the front door with three grocery bags and an overnight tote.

"Looks like more than just eye black. What is all this?" I ask, grabbing the groceries from her and placing them on the counter.

"Oh, just a few things to make this more fun. I figured if we could potentially end the night in jail for trespassing, or worse, cursed by Irina, we better do it on a full belly." I gawk at her. She did not just compare my predicament to jail.

"Um, thanks? I guess." I rifle through the bags, pulling out a couple bottles of wine, two kinds of chips, crackers and cheese, and a package of Oreos. It's quite an impressive spread if we were kindergartners, minus the wine.

I reach in a drawer and pull out a wine key. "Hey, the wine is for after. Wait, actually, maybe it's for both. I'm nervous, are you nervous?" Ari placed her tote in my room and is now pacing the living room.

"Yeah, the last time I saw her I ended up in the hospital. Of course I'm scared. But this time we are going as a group." I try to reassure her as bile nips the back of my throat.

"A group? I thought it was just us and your lover boy. Which, by the way, your bedroom has a vibe. I'm going to need clean sheets if you want me to stay here." Ari waves her arm around like she's wafting the air.

"The sheets have been changed, and I don't kiss and tell." I place both hands on my hips as a sign that I'm serious. Instead, she doubles over in laughter.

"Yes, you do! I literally could describe every peen you've ever seen from memory. Don't act all high and mighty now. Spill it!" she shrieks between laughs.

"Well . . . fine. I guess I do. It was amazing. He's got an impressive, uh, man part. I don't think I've ever seen one so big, and honestly, those tattoos, they do something to me," I admit, joining in on her laughter.

"I knew it. I could tell you were walking funny." She claps her hands together and smiles from ear to ear.

"No, I'm not!" I defend.

"I know, I was kidding, but seriously, you are glowing. How are things going outside of the bedroom?"

"Good . . . great, actually. I just wonder when he'll realize that I'm not this amazing person he's built me up to be. He acts like I'm the shiniest penny, the special toy everyone wants, and that's just not true. I'm just a regular person, and I'm afraid when he figures it out, I'll be in too deep." I try to push down the knot forming in my throat.

He's everything I've ever wanted, but then again, he could just be trying to win me over. I've noticed him judging my feelings and moods by my arm from that first night I showed it to him. It was cute for twenty minutes, but then it started to make me wonder if the reason he's so perfect is because he has the cheat code. Am I getting the real version of him or the one that's like Mel Gibson in *What Women Want*?

"Okay, babe, here's the thing. I've always known you were special and hoped that one day you'd see it too. But . . . since it seems like you're not getting it, I'll tell you. You're not all the horrible things that woman convinced you that you are. You're a true friend, a kind and loving person. You are good for so much more than being a trophy wife. I could go on for days, but none of it matters if you don't embrace it. I mean, isn't that how we got into this mess? You asked to be open, to expose your heart. This is what you wanted," Ari says, obviously frustrated with me.

"Yeah, I did. I guess I just didn't think it would be this hard. I worry every second if I'm saying the right thing, doing the right stuff. For heaven's sake, we had sex and afterward I locked myself in the bathroom to shower alone and overanalyze every second of it. I'm a mess, Ari. A tattoo isn't going to change it." I pop open the Oreos and shove one in my mouth.

"You're not a mess, you're the most put-together person on the planet. You're scared, and that's normal. But can you honestly say that you haven't enjoyed opening up with him, not even a little?" she asks, challenging me to deny it.

"No, I can't. It's been nice to have someone to talk to. Other than you, of course. And he's so understanding about everything. Ugh! Okay, we have to stop. They are going to be here, and I don't want him to worry. We have enough on our plate tonight." With that, I head into the bedroom to get my sneakers.

The door sounds with a couple of loud knocks.

"Come in!" I shout, as I walk back to the kitchen.

Sam and Howie let themselves in, taking their shoes off at the door and walking into the kitchen. Sam's eyes meet mine, and I know he senses something is off.

"Howard, I didn't expect to see you this evening," Ariella quips before popping the cork on a bottle of wine and taking a long glug.

"I wouldn't have missed a chance to help Olive. Besides, it would be cool to expose the beard story, you know, if Irina keeps records or something." Howie shrugs, reaching out to grab the bottle from Ari and taking his own pull. I can't help but notice the T-shirt he's wearing is just a smidge tighter than normal—I see you, Howie, showing off the goods to get the girl.

"Hey, can I talk to you for a second? Alone?" Sam whispers in my ear as he sneaks up beside me.

"Yeah, uh. Ari, please play nice with Howie. We'll be right back," I explain, pulling Sam by the hand to my bedroom. I close the door behind us, and he wraps me in a tight but comforting hug, nuzzling his nose in my neck.

"I missed you today," Sam says. I pull back and look in his eyes. There's a genuineness reflecting back at me. I stretch up on my toes to press a kiss on his lips.

"I, uh, I missed you too," I manage.

"Everything okay?" He's concerned, I can feel it. But he doesn't need to be, not about me leaving him. I'm the one who's afraid he'll be the one to walk away. It's my insecurity.

"Yep. I'm just nervous, I guess. The last time, well, you know what happened."

"Olive, I would never let anything happen to you. I'm with you this time, I promise. And I'll help you find whatever answers you need, even if I'm starting to think this arm of yours is pretty cool." Acid hits my throat, and my body starts to buzz. He thought I was a liar at first, but now it's cool?

"It's not cool, Sam. I know you like being able to see what I'm feeling and thinking, but it's horrible for me. I can't even walk into the Brewhouse without coffee cups swirling around my forearm. I can't fight with my mother without a Death Eater flying across my arm," I groan, pushing out of his arms fully and crossing mine. She's continued calling and I keep ignoring her, but the reminder is always there on my arm in vivid depiction.

"Whoa. That's not what I meant at all. I lo—like you either way. I just meant it's crazy cool that something like that is even possible. Please, babe, don't fight with me." His eyes shift to the floor and his face falls. Did he almost tell me he loves me? No, he couldn't.

"I-I'm sorry, I'm just on edge. It's not your fault," I backpedal. We have stuff to do, and he's right, fighting is not going to help anyone. This is a me problem and not his responsibility to work out.

"Come here," Sam says, pulling me back into his arms, pressing kisses on my face. "I care so much. Let's just go and see what we find. No expectations. I've got you." I melt into him, kissing him deeply.

There's a knock at the door, "Um, sorry . . . We need to go, and uh, Ari said she couldn't interrupt you guys anymore?" Howie's hesitant voice comes through the door muffled.

Sam and I break apart trying not to laugh at the notion of Ari sending Howie to do her dirty work. We exit the room, and I promptly apply eye black on each of our faces. Between the all-black outfits, beanies, and under-eye makeup, we look like a bunch of cat burglars ready to launch a full assault. Let's hope we don't get busted because there's zero chance of playing this off like we aren't up to no good.

"Okay, so what's the plan when we get there?" Howie asks, as we step onto the porch.

"We get in, see if she's there or if there's a clue of where to find her, and we get out," Ari explains.

"Right, but how are we getting in?" Howie pushes back.

"The door, I presume." Ari lets out an exasperated sigh and rolls her eyes like the answer is so obvious.

"I have a lock-picking kit if we need it," Sam chimes in, breaking the tension.

"Why?" I ask, my eyes bugging out of my head.

"Because I've locked myself out of my business more than once, and locksmiths are expensive. I'm not a thief." He holds up his hands in the universal sign of surrender.

"That's exactly what a thief would say, don't ya think?" Ari snips out.

"Alright, before we end up taking each other out with what is clearly too much nervous energy, let's move." I take off at a slow jog, hoping they follow. Driving would have been too obvious to anyone passing by, and the exercise will help us all, I hope.

It's about four blocks of Ari complaining as she trudges through piles of leaves that have collected on the sidewalk, Howie trying not to comment on her clear lack of physical prowess, and Sam staying glued to my side. We slow to a walk as we turn the corner onto Crow, spotting the downtrodden cottage in the distance. It sits back from the road more than the others. At one time it probably would've been surrounded by trees. There's a buzzing in the air. A strange sensation overwhelms me, and I stop.

"I don't know if we should go any closer," I say under my breath. My chest feels heavy as my arm turns tender with what feels like scratches clawing their way from my wrist to my shoulder.

Sam places an arm around me, pulling me into his side. "We don't have to go in if you don't want to, but I promise you're safe with me. The decision is yours."

"Yeah, Ollie. We're doing this to help you. If it doesn't feel right, we can figure something else out," Ariella reassures me.

Taking a few slow, deep breaths, I shake my shoulders and walk forward once again. I have less than two weeks at this point to figure it out, I can't stop now. As we get closer, the cottage comes into view. It's what you would imagine any witch's lair to look like: a small black house with ivy clinging to the sides sporadically. The windows appear to be cloudy with age and neglect. The roof is covered in moss. I'd bet there are all kinds of creatures lurking inside.

"Well, it looks like no one's been here in a long time. Maybe we can get in and out unnoticed after all," Ari chirps. She has no clue what we are dealing with, and frankly, the positivity annoys me.

"Should we just try the door?" Howie asks, shrugging.

Sam walks up the small step leading onto the front porch, and the door creaks open with a screech. My stomach flips. It reminds me of the door popping open when I entered Irina's shop. I glance at Howie. He's the only other one of us who's met her, and his face has turned as pale as a ghost.

Sam clicks on his flashlight, peering inside slowly before pushing the half-rotted door completely open. He motions with his arm for us to follow, and I clutch for Ari's hand as we take the step up.

We walk in, cautiously pushing cobwebs out of the way, and my body erupts in chills. My teeth chatter so loudly that Sam immediately backtracks asking, "Are you okay?"

"Yeah, uh. Just cold," I lie. I'm not okay. She warned me, she told me in the cemetery I needed to embrace it before making my decision. But I have, haven't I? I came clean to Sam. I've tried opening up on my own.

Howie and Ariella head upstairs with flashlights, leaving Sam and me in the main room. Looking around, I notice a rocking chair made of wood branches placed by a stone fireplace. A cobweb-covered cauldron lies on its side on a pile of ash. There's a small table centered in the room, and what I assume was a kitchen on the left. It's basically some shelves and a prep island made of wood, but she wouldn't have had a stove or modern appliances back then.

Sam nods at me and we walk toward the shelves. I run my fingers across a collection of books, sending dust swirling into the air—they must be first editions. Beau would lose his mind. I'm careful as I extract them, trying to make out the worn titles in only the glow of a flashlight.

"Olive, look, there's something here," Sam says from the other side of the kitchen.

I take the ten steps toward him tentatively, stepping over a pile of orange and red leaves that must have blown in when the door opened. Unease settles low in my belly. It's a book. Sam moves to pick it up. "Stop, try not to touch it," I snip out. Leave it to my restoration training to kick in at the worst possible time.

"I, uh, okay?"

"It's fragile. If the society is going to claim this place, there's a chance that Beau could get these. I don't want to ruin them." I try to justify my outburst with logic. The real reason settling into my bones is more that I don't want him to be the next one carrying a curse.

I shine my light on the book, carefully dusting it off with a featherlight touch. "Oh my gosh, this is incredible. How did it survive in these conditions?" I lean in, careful not to get too close.

"What is it?" Sam asks, rubbing his hand up and down my back.

"It's Eleonara. She's so beautiful." I hurriedly move it over as a spider crawls across the cover, making me gasp.

"Who's Eleonara?" Ari inquires as she descends from upstairs and crosses the room.

"It's a book, one of the first of what would today be considered romance. John Dryden was an English poet, and supposedly he wrote stories about falling in love. Not that anyone has ever seen an actual complete copy." I try my best to explain. There's a real chance I'm the only person aside from Beau who would even care.

"Did you find anything upstairs?" Sam looks at Ariella and Howie.

"Nothing, she didn't leave much behind," Howie explains.

"Or someone cleaned house." Ari props her hands on her hips.

"Wait, what's that?" Sam points to a carving in the center of the table.

"Looks like it's just their names," I whisper, afraid to draw too much attention to the script. The wood has been chipped away to spell out: **Josephine, Beth, and Irina**. But below the names it notes: **Never again will we wear our hearts on our sleeves.** If Sam or anyone else sees it, they will know this is all some sort of trick—that Irina isn't helping me, she's playing a game.

Out of nowhere, a loud rumble sounds as the cauldron pops up into place and a fire ignites below it. A rat scurries across the floor, bumping into Ari's boot and beckoning a shrill shriek from her lips. We all take off in a sprint, desperate to get out of the cottage while we still can, or at least that's why I'm running. In a matter of seconds, we fly out the door and across the crunchy, dying grass.

"Holy fucking shit! What in the actual fuck just happened?" Ari yells, hands on her head trying to catch her breath.

"Magic, that's what happened." Howie shrugs then begins to walk back in the direction of my house as if we didn't all just receive the fright of our lives. Sam, Ariella, and I exchange skeptical looks before following after him.

In the last hour and a half, we have gone from running for our lives to passing a bottle of wine in my living room. Ari is perched on the armchair in the corner, Howie is propped up on the floor against the edge of the fireplace, and Sam and I share the couch.

"Okay, but seriously, that was some freaky-ass shit." Ari takes a long sip from the bottle of cabernet she's clutching. "I can't believe you both went into her shop with her. Are you nuts?"

"I, uh, well, I didn't feel like I really had a choice. She kind of forced me in her own witchy way, and I didn't know who she was," I explain.

"Yeah, it's not that easy to say no to her. She's very convincing. The only difference between Olive and me is that I wasn't alone. And I got the hell out of dodge." Howie reaches out and grabs the bottle from Ari's hand. I can't help but nudge Sam when I see his cheeks turn the slightest shade of pink after his fingers graze hers.

"You could have had a beard, Howard. Shoulda stayed," Ariella quips at him.

"Don't remind me," he grumbles.

"Alright, you two. Are you sure you didn't find anything upstairs?" Sam looks at them like they must have come up with something. They both shake their heads no.

I can feel the tears bubbling up. You know, when you get that knot in your throat and it's only a matter of time before the pressure builds and the wet droplets streak down your face. This whole thing has been a lot, and tonight I was genuinely scared—it felt like the cemetery again, but different.

"Ollie? Are you okay?" Ari asks, a look of concern etched in her brow.

"Um, yeah. I just really wanted to find something that would lead me to her. Instead, I found an early seventeenth-century romance novel. If that's not ironic, then I don't know what is," I say without thinking. I haven't explained the whole purpose behind this tattoo to Sam. Not really, anyway. I'm sure it's not hard to figure out what I asked for, but he doesn't know the details. He isn't aware that if I remove it, I'll be destined to be alone and closed off forever. He also doesn't know that the very thing that will likely happen to me was Irina's whole point. The cauldron tipped before anyone else read the inscription on the table.

"Why is it ironic?" Sam asks, thoughtfully.

"Well, just because, uh, because it's my emotions on my arm. My heart is on my sleeve, you know."

"Speaking of your arm, what's it look like right now?" Howie inquires, shifting to his feet to come closer to me.

I shrug off my black zip-up hoodie as their audible gasps ring out. Across my arm in giant red letters, it reads: **GET OUT: 10/31**. Along with the message Irina clearly sent me are cauldrons bubbling, my standard items that never leave, and little doors slamming shut. I'm not convinced the doors are representative of her cottage. I think those are symbolic of my heart shutting out the possibility of things working out with Sam, not that I'm going to voice that aloud. A single tear slips down my cheek followed by a cascade of waterworks I'm powerless to stop.

"Hey, it's okay. Come here," Sam shushes me gently while wrapping his arms around me. I melt into him. I wish I could just believe that this is real between us. But between my fear of him using my arm as a cheat code and my inability to share what I'm feeling on my own, I know it can't be. I think this is all a sick game of chess for Irina, so to speak—and I'm destined to lose.

"It's all going to be okay, Olive. I'm going to head out, but you know where to find me if you need me." Howie runs his hand across my hair, ruffling it just a tad before slipping on his shoes and walking out.

"Yeah, we can do our girls' sleepover night another time. I'm going to let you guys hang." Ari reaches across Sam, hugging me around his arms and pressing a kiss to my temple. I love her so much—why can't I be open with Sam the way I am with her? I close my eyes and take a few deep breaths while she makes her exit.

"Baby, I feel like you're not telling me something," Sam whispers, his tone tentative.

"No, it's not that. I just, I don't know if . . ." Another round of tears make their appearance and my voice cracks.

"You don't know what?" His eyes are pleading for an answer. I take a deep breath, chug down a large gulp of wine, and wipe my eyes with the backs of my hands.

"I don't know if this is going to work out between us," I utter, choking on the words as I say them.

His face falls and he runs a hand through his hair nervously. His voice cracks when he asks, "Are you, um, are you dumping me?"

I know he can see my arm, so I almost don't have to explain. But I know I need to, for me. "No, but I'm scared. You keep saying things about how much you care and how important I am. It's just that you don't know enough about me. I'm bound to let you down, and I'm afraid if we keep this up, then I'll be heartbroken when you figure it out." I cover my face with my hands. I know it sounds so childish. I keep pushing him away even though he's everything I've ever wanted.

"I told you earlier, I really, really like you. Not just the good parts, but the sad and grumpy ones too. I just need you to hold on long enough for me to convince you. Can you do that? Can you just give me a chance to prove it to you?" Sam doubles down.

"I'll try, I promise I'll try." I pull him tight against me and press a kiss to his lips. The thing is, I'm not lying when I say I want to try. I think I'm falling in love with him, but there's something inside of me that refuses to believe that it's the right thing. Is it that I can't tell if he's being genuine or just relying on my arm to tell him what I want? Maybe. Is there a way to find out? Only on Halloween—less than two weeks to go.

Twenty-Four

Sam

Chopping Wood and Walls

Gravel crunches under the tires of my truck as I pull into the clearing on my property. I haven't been out here since the last time I brought Olive—well, only to pick up the movie screen anyway. I was thinking of something that she and I could do to get her mind off all of this curse business and it occurred to me that maybe the best way to do that is to get away from the world. It's an escape, even if it's only for a night. I enlisted some reinforcements to help me get the place ready for an overnight stay; the cabin was not really ready the last time she went in. I want it to shine.

Hopping out and walking over to the edge of the drop-off, I can't stop thinking about how much it bothers me that she is so determined to get rid of the tattoo. Not because I need it to see how she's feeling or because I need to be with someone who shares my love of tattoos, but because she seems to believe that it's just another way in which she isn't absolutely perfect. She's mentioned a few times that I'm going to wake up one day and realize she's not the one for me. I've known from the minute I laid eyes on her that she was special, and the more time we spend together, the more I know I'm right.

I can see my future with her so clearly. It hurts to even think she might not feel the same, or at least not as strongly, as I do. I'm putting my fears aside, though, because I meant it when I said I would convince her. She needs time to sort it out, more than the few weeks we've been doing this, and I plan to be here while she does.

My sister's beat-up red Honda pulls into the clearing, bringing me back to reality.

"Hey, I got the stuff you asked for," Bridget shouts across the clearing after slamming her car door.

I walk from the edge of the drop-off toward her vehicle. "You good? You didn't have to come if you didn't want to." I can tell from her body language she's keyed up today. Something has her upset, and I don't need her stomping around here all day.

"I just, shit—I didn't want to talk about it. I promised myself I was coming to help and I wasn't going to bring it up," Bridget rambles, fiddling with the hem of her shirt and staring at the ground.

"What happened, Bridg?"

"I saw Jessa with her new girlfriend. They were picking out bath towels when I was getting the comforter set. I tried to get out of there quickly, but I couldn't help myself. I crept into the aisle next to theirs and I heard her say . . . she said she loves her." My sister's eyes are watery.

"Hey, none of that." I wipe under her eyes and pull her into a hug. "It's her loss. She will wake up one day and realize what she's missing. I know it doesn't feel like it right now, but the love of your life is out there waiting for you. I promise."

"Thanks, Sammy. I know it's stupid. I don't even know why I care," she says, shaking the tension from her shoulders and pushing out of my embrace.

"You care because you have a big heart and you loved her. Sometimes things aren't meant to last forever, but it doesn't mean the love you shared was any less real. It just means that you will carry the lessons you learned with you into your next relationship. You'll be more prepared for the one."

"Don't tell anyone I said this, but you're pretty smart, Sammy." My sister slugs me in the arm, then pops the trunk of her car and begins unloading the new bedding and decor she picked up for me.

Bridget and I carry the bags to the cabin and place everything inside.

"What are we going for here?" she asks, looking at the freshly cleaned interior.

"Well, I did a deep clean already, but I want it to feel homey. And I'm trying to eradicate Mom and Dad from the vibe," I respond, bristling a little at the thought of this once being their love shack.

"Okay, I think I have everything I need to manage that. If not, you'll be going to the store this time." It's not like her ex will be there all day long, but I understand the sentiment.

"I'm going to head back out there. Max and Howard should be here shortly to help with the outdoor stuff," I say, pulling the door handle to leave.

"Sounds good."

I mosey back to the open space, taking time to pick up sticks on the pathway to ensure it's clear. I have big plans for this walkway, and it's going to take all day to get it done. Approaching the end, where the trees kiss the open grass, I stop to look back. I hope my plan works. If it does, it will be magical. And not in the Irina kind of way.

"Where do you want this thing?" Max yells from the driver's side window of his truck. He's pulling in a trailer with a backhoe and enough flagstones to cover the path. When I see the size of the machinery and rocks, I'm actually impressed he made it into the property with all the bumps. I had sand delivered earlier today, so we should have everything we need to get this done.

"Just back it up as close as you can," I yell back as Howie pulls into the clearing and jumps out of his Bronco.

"This is remote. How long have you had this place?" Howie asks, rounding his truck and coming up to stand beside me as we watch Max struggle to turn the truck and trailer around.

"A couple of years. Been coming here my whole life though. We've never given it the face lift it needs." I walk to the truck, holding my hand up, and Max brakes. "Max, just leave it here. We can drive what we need over with the backhoe."

"Yeah, bro. Have you ever tried to back one of these up? It's fucking impossible." He puts the truck in park and hops out. "Hey, Howie, good to see ya," Max says.

"So, what's the plan, Sam?" Howie asks, looking around.

"I want to make this an actual walking path. If we use the backhoe to level the ground, we can lay sand, then place the stones. Or at least that's what YouTube told me." I lead them to the pathway and point at the cleared area.

"Where do you want the dirt we remove?" Howie inquires thoughtfully. I hadn't thought about that.

"Uh, maybe we just start a pile over there?" I point to a spot in the clearing that isn't too dense with trees but where the dirt won't be an eyesore.

"That should work." Howie nods in agreement, then heads back to the trailer and begins unhooking the chains on the machine. I asked Howie to help because I've seen him operate this kind of equipment before when we all pitched in to renovate the park in Mage Square. I know he knows what he's doing, and I definitely don't. In a matter of minutes, he's inside the backhoe and driving toward where the walkway meets the cabin porch while Max and I watch.

"This seems like a lot of work for a date, big brother." Max slaps me on the shoulder.

"It's not just for one date. It needed to be done, and now I have an excuse. I plan on her sticking around, and she deserves something nice," I rattle out. Frankly, I'm glad I finally have a reason to use the place.

"You love her?" Max asks, reaching in the cooler I filled to grab two beers and plopping into a camping chair.

I sit down next to him and take the beer he offers, popping the tab and sucking down the amber liquid. "I think so, yeah."

"You're not sure?" he pries.

"I've never been so sure of anything in my life. She's the one who's hesitant." I take another sip, hoping to wash down the acid that stings my throat when I think about her not being my person.

"Nah, she's the real deal. She's just scared," Max says confidently.

"How do you know what she is?"

"Have you seen the way she looks at you? It's like you hung the moon for her. It's kinda gross actually." Max laughs and shakes his head.

"No, she doesn't. I mean, our chemistry is off the charts, I know that. But she holds back emotionally. She's not sure about me," I push back.

"Who's not sure about who?" Bridget asks, walking up to where we're sitting and helping herself to a drink.

"Sam doesn't think Olive's that into him. But as someone who knows how scary it is to love something that you have the potential to lose, you just need to give her time," Max answers her and explains where he's coming from with his hockey career on the line, all with a smug look on his face.

"You're kidding, right? The girl looks at you like you literally hung the moon. It's kind of gross." Bridget bristles a little, and Max busts out laughing.

"Did you plan that?" I ask.

"Plan what?" Bridget glances between Max and me.

"You literally just said the same thing he did, almost word for word." I point my beer bottle at her accusingly.

"Nope, it's just the truth, big brother. Calling it like we see it." She shrugs.

"Almost all cleared, fellas. We need to bring the sand in. I'll dump it, and you can spread it," Howie shouts at us over the rumble of the backhoe.

"Time to work." Max and I stand, abandoning our drinks and grabbing some rakes and work gloves.

Bridget heads back inside and we work mostly in silence while Howie continues to drop loads of sand on the two-hundred-foot-long path. We spread it evenly, leveling the sand out between the steel edges we placed. The project is going a lot quicker than I expected. The three of us working together helps.

When we finish spreading the sand, we check to make sure it's level before beginning to lay the flagstones. They are heavier than they look, and by the time we've managed to lay half of them, we're all exhausted.

"I know you didn't have to help do this on a random Wednesday, but I appreciate it. I couldn't have done any of this without you two," I say, sitting down on a log that's lying near the path.

"Not a problem, Sam. Feels good to be doing something other than tapping kegs," Howie says as he places another stone.

"Yeah, Coach will count this as at least two days' worth of weight time. It's nice to be in the fresh air," Max chimes in, finding a spot a few feet down from me.

"She's going to love it," Howie adds, grabbing another stone. I had no idea how hard of a worker he is. He hasn't stopped once. "That is, if we finish." He gives Max and me a pointed look. I guess there's no break time when Howard is around.

A while later, we lay the last stone on the walkway, and Howie dumps the remaining sand over the top. Max and I use large brushes to fill the cracks and tamp everything down. Bridget comes out on the porch to take in the view.

"This looks amazing. I didn't think you'd finish today, but it's incredible. Now the only thing you need is a swing overlooking the water and some lights strung from the trees to light the path. Want to see inside?"

Max, Howie, and I exchange looks. Did she really just suggest great ideas that require more work? We head over to where she's standing on the porch and peek in. From what I can tell, it looks amazing. She's decorated every inch of the place, turning it from an old, dusty cabin into a cozy home. I'm so appreciative to have great friends and family. I couldn't have done it without them. My heart is overflowing with gratitude.

"You did a great job, Bridg. Thank you . . . thanks to all of you for the work today. You're better friends than I deserve," I say, meaning it.

"It was fun. Great practice for my portfolio," my sister replies. She's working on becoming a certified interior designer. There isn't anyone in the world with her eye for style or knack for decor. I was happy to be the first to hire her.

"I think I'm going to head out," Max says, the others nodding their agreement.

I walk with them back to the clearing to say goodbye before returning to the cabin. I ditch my clothes at the door and head straight for the bathroom to shower. Once cleaned up, I take a minute to observe my sister's work. The L-shaped couch has a new cream cover, and there are too many throw pillows to count. She's placed picture frames on the fireplace, hung artwork on the walls, and there are even new rugs in all the right spots. The bathroom has a new shower curtain, and soap, and toothbrush holders. Bridget went all out.

I head into the kitchen to grab water from the fridge and power up the Wi-Fi. The cell service is terrible out here, but the wireless internet makes things manageable. I climb the ladder to the loft and sink into the bed. I thought Bridget was over the top when she suggested a down comforter and mattress topper, but I stand corrected as I sink into the cushy bedding. I send her a message:

This bed feels like heaven. Thank you again!

Bridget

I told you so. You're welcome.

Instead of texting Olive like I normally do, I press call on the FaceTime app. It rings a few times before her face pops up on the screen.

"Hey, Sam?"

"Hey. What're you up to?"

"Um, nothing. Just a little baking. Why are you FaceTiming me?" Her question makes me laugh. It's not like it's that weird of a thing to do, or at least I don't think it is?

"Just wanted to see you. It's been a couple days, I missed your smile."

"Oh, okay. I missed you too. Where are you, and where's your shirt?" She looks closer at the screen like she's trying to decipher where I could be.

"Well, my shirt was dirty so it's outside with the rest of my clothes," I explain, taking pleasure in the way her cheeks instantly turn a bright pink. "And I'm at the cabin. You know, out on my property."

"Oh cool, that's cool." Olive fans her blushing face before continuing, "I didn't know there was a bed, although I guess that makes sense if your parents used to stay in there."

"Yep, see." I shift from under the covers to sit up so she can see more of the loft bedroom. She also can see more of my upper body, and I don't hate the way it makes her suck in a breath.

"Alright, you can cover back up now. It's not nice to show off when I'm not with you," Olive scolds me, and I laugh.

"Noted. Speaking of that, the seeing-me part, not the naked-me part, can I take you away on Friday?"

"Where to? I have to work on Saturday at ten."

"Here, to my cabin. I made some changes I want to show you," I explain, hoping she doesn't turn me down.

"Hmmm, that depends." Olive presses a finger to her lips. "Will there be food, and will you be wearing clothes?"

"Yes to food, I plan to cook you dinner. Optional to clothing." I smirk when her eyebrows shoot up. "Are you surprised by my cooking, or is it the clothing comment?" I ask.

"Cooking, I was . . . um, I was hoping clothes were optional," Olive stammers as she swipes her finger through what looks like some sort of batter and pushes it between her lips, sucking tenderly. My mouth goes dry and my body buzzes.

"Now who's being unfair?" I choke out.

"What? I'm not doing anything. Just making sure the muffin batter tastes okay." She bats her eyelashes.

"Mmmk. You're a naughty girl."

"Says the man with the dirty mouth," she quips back.

"You guys are disgusting," Ariella pops into the screen, making a face like she's pretending to vomit.

"Hi, Ariella, nice to see you again." This makes Olive laugh, and Ariella waves. That girl has a way of showing up when I least expect her to. I swear it's a skill, like she was born to ensure Olive and I always get interrupted when things take a turn.

"Okay, I should go though," Olive says. "We are baking and drinking wine. If you're lucky I'll save some muffins for Friday." Olive winks at me, then flashes me a megawatt smile before blowing me a kiss.

"There's only one muffin I'm interested in, just so you know." I blow her a kiss back and wink.

"Gross! She's hanging up now." I see Ariella's disgusted face before the call disconnects.

I sink back into the bed, laughing to myself. There isn't a doubt in my mind: I'm in love with Olivia Bowman. I just really hope she loves me back.

Olive

Hidden Magic

8 Days Until Halloween

"Why is it you don't have a car again?" Bridget asks as we turn onto the main highway leading toward Sam's cabin. I shift in my seat, trying to come up with the best way to explain this without divulging too much information.

"I don't have the money to buy one," I offer, shrugging when her eyes bulge at my confession.

"Don't you come from a rich family?"

"I, uh, well my parents are well-off, yes. But I decided to take a different path for my life, and that also meant walking away from their money," I explain. I didn't really want to get into this, especially not when I should be getting excited for my date. But I'm not a great liar, and Bridget seems like the kind of no-bullshit girl that could handle my truth. Also, she's driving me to the date, so she deserves a good reason.

"Whoa. I gotta give you props, I don't know if I could have done that." Bridget shakes her shoulders a bit, shaking off what I assume is shock.

"You could if you'd met Ted," I quip, looking out the window, trying desperately not to picture his smug face sipping whiskey at the country club and smoking a cigar.

"Who the hell is Ted?" she asks.

"The man my mother wanted me to marry," I reply casually.

"Wait, what? Girl, your life is weird." Her simple assessment makes us both laugh. She has no idea just how bizarre it truly is.

"Was that not obvious enough when you had to drive me to a date with your brother?" I ask.

"Well, yeah. I mean this is definitely a first. But Sammy is really into you, and when he called me in a panic about the meal he's trying to make, I really didn't have the heart to say no." Bridget claps a hand over her mouth. "Shit, shit, shit. Do not tell him I said that. He made me promise to not make things weird or to out him for being less experienced in the kitchen."

"I won't tell him, but if I'm about to get food poisoning, blink twice so I can be prepared," I say, hesitancy and humor equal in my reply.

"I promise you won't. I'm like ninety-percent sure he's been on video chat with Mom all day, making sure he doesn't screw anything up."

"I feel bad. He really didn't need to go to all this trouble." I shift again, readjusting the tin of muffins in my lap. I made a fresh batch for him after our phone call a couple days ago. We could survive on these, and worst case scenario, we can get some pizza.

"He cares about you, a lot." Bridget reaches over to squeeze my hand gently before making the turn onto Sam's private road.

As the gravel crunches under the tires, I can't help but feel a little uneasy. I care about him, too, I just don't know if what we have is real enough to go the distance. It seems like there's more weight to what we are doing here, like it could be long-term when nothing else has ever been like that for me. But there's also the question of how much of this is based on him having too much insight, how much of his patience with me opening up slowly is enabled by his ability to judge my emotions by my arm. I watch the fall foliage pass as we continue down the driveway, willing myself to stop worrying about things I can't control.

As we pull into the clearing, I can tell things are different immediately. The last time I was here there wasn't a set of hammock chairs hanging near the edge of the drop-off, overlooking the ocean. There wasn't a clearly defined path to get to the cabin. *When did he have time to do all of this?*

Catching my stunned gaze, Bridget says, "He put a ton of effort into this night. I hope you love it."

"Everything looks incredible. Am I supposed to go to the cabin? Or what's the plan?" I ask, hand hesitating on the door handle.

"Yes, I swear to God. The two of you are like a pack of toddlers wandering around. Get your stuff and go get your man. I gotta boogie." Bridget waves me out of the car in a hurry and promptly leaves once I step out with my things.

I start my trek, overnight bag slung on my shoulder and muffin tin clasped tightly in my hands, toward the . . . *stone pathway*? When we walked to the cabin just a few weeks ago, there was nothing more than dirt and branches to trip over. Now there is a beautifully laid flagstone walkway with string lights overhead. It's magical and breathtaking. I feel like a fairy floating to her secret little garden getaway. I'm sure he didn't do this just for me, but my heart skips a beat at the thoughtfulness. Someone who puts care and attention to detail into their home must be a decent human being.

"What do you think?" Sam asks, leaning against the railing of the porch steps.

"I'm speechless. This is gorgeous. When did you have this put in?" I reply as I walk toward the porch, sure that there's no chance he did this himself.

"Wednesday. Max, Howie, and I worked on it. I'm glad you like it." He grins from ear to ear.

"Wait, you did this?" I stop and point at the pathway.

"Yeah, well, mostly Howie did it while he bossed Max and me around." Sam shrugs like it isn't a big deal.

"Wow. This is incredible. I don't even know what to say." I walk faster, desperate to hug him. Sam meets me at the bottom of the steps, enveloping me in his cinnamon scent and wrapping me tightly in his arms before pressing a kiss to my lips.

"Wait till I show you the inside," he says, that panty-melting grin shifting back onto his face. Gah! He makes my body melt with a single look.

We walk up the steps and into the cabin, where the aroma of freshly grilled steaks and homemade rolls wafts to my nose. I toe off my shoes and carefully set my bag down before Sam helps me out of my coat. He takes the muffin tin from me gently and places it on the entry table.

"It's so homey in here. I didn't get to look around much the last time," I note, soaking in the chic aesthetic. The couch is plush and inviting, the kitchen smells heavenly, and the artwork is stunning. "Did you do the decorating?"

"No, that's all Bridget. She did an amazing job, didn't she?" Sam is standing beside me, glancing around like he's also in awe of how great the place looks.

"Incredible, I might need to hire her to do some decorating at my place." I grab his hand and walk into the kitchen, curious about dinner.

I carefully peek under the foil covering a sheet pan, spying steak, then I look under the kitchen towel covering a basket filled with buttery rolls. My stomach growls silently. I'm so hungry and touched that he worked so hard.

"Hey, no peeking. I'm just waiting for the baked potatoes to finish in the oven, and I have to make a salad. Do you want a glass of wine while I finish?" Sam asks, grabbing me by the waist and hoisting me up on the counter.

"Sure, that sounds good. I can help though, I don't need to just sit here." I wave my arm to the counter I'm perched on.

"Yes, you do. I'm cooking for you." Sam steps between my legs and presses a tender kiss to my lips.

I can't help wrapping my hands around the back of his neck and sliding my tongue across the seam of his lips. We take time exploring each other for a few minutes until the oven timer beeps loudly. Sam looks at me and then my arm, before shaking his head and turning to remove our side dish. My stomach drops at his small glance at my tattoo.

"You're distracting me. If you want to eat dinner, I have to finish making it first," he chides.

"Well, if you'd let me help, it would go faster." I hop off the counter and retrieve the muffin tin I brought along. Sliding up next to Sam as he pulls salad ingredients from the fridge, I pop the tin open and wave it in his face, slightly distracting myself from my own anxiety with a little banter.

"I brought you the muffins you were so desperate to eat the other night," I say, giggling a little when his face goes slack.

"Those smell incredible, but that's not what I was referring to, and you know it." He smacks my ass with a head of romaine and scooches me out of the way so he can finish prepping our meal.

It's wild to me that my body is so responsive to Sam. All it takes is one look from him and I'm ready to drop to my knees. I've never had this feeling with anyone, but then there's the niggling in my mind that maybe that's not a good thing. Maybe I'm caught up in the grandeur of it all, the way he makes my heart race and my center go slick. Does he really know me outside of the basics? Do I know him? And is he really this sweet, or is he just judging what I like from the obvious signs painted on my skin?

Bristling a little, I make my way to my bag and pull out a thick mossy-green cardigan. I need to see if things feel the same when my most vulnerable inner self isn't on display in a simple T-shirt. I planned ahead for this. I meant to cover up before getting here, but the awe of the work he's done distracted me.

"Cold?" he asks, looking up from chopping lettuce.

"A little, not bad though," I lie.

"I can put more logs on the fire, let me just get this in the bowl." Sam tosses everything in a rustic wooden container and pours on what looks to be homemade dressing. He mixes the salad a few times with his hands, quickly rinses off in the sink, and makes his way to tend the fire.

I watch him, chastising myself for not being all in. He's gorgeous and kind. He's got a stable job and two homes. He loves his family, and they're quickly becoming some of my favorite people too. I excuse myself to the restroom.

Clicking the door closed behind me, I start to pace. Even the bathroom has been transformed with new decor and details. He went to all this trouble to make this night special, and I'm freaking out over nothing.

Grabbing my phone from my back pocket, I quickly type out a message to Ariella.

> Freaking out, please tell me he actually likes me and it's not just because I'm the easiest woman in the world to read thanks to Irina.

I sit on the edge of the bathtub for a couple of minutes before remembering I don't have service. Then I give myself a pep talk. I know he cares for me, that's clear. And I care for him. I need to just stick to the plan and be present with him while also covered. I flush the toilet for effect and wash my hands before I pull the door open and come face-to-face with Sam.

"Hey, you okay?" he asks, concern etched in his brow.

"I'm great," I say, reaching up on my tiptoes to give him a kiss before sliding past him. He set the table while I was in there and everything looks delicious. "This looks so good. Let's eat." I slide into one of the chairs at the table.

"I hope it's good. I'm, uh, not much of a cook when it comes to fancy meals." He's adorably shy. I shouldn't give him a hard time, but I want to. I carefully cut a slice of steak and pop it into my mouth. A burst of flavor hits my tongue and a small moan sneaks out.

"Heaven. This is heaven. It's easily the best steak I've ever had. Please tell Mabel thank you for me." I grab the wine glass he placed at my seat and take a small sip while watching his face move from questioning, to mad, to two-can-play-this-game in an instant.

"Two things: Very funny and I'm going to kill Bridget," Sam says, pushing his own bite of steak between his lips. I can't stop the laughter that rolls out of me.

"Aw, come on. It's cute actually. Your sister didn't mean to tell me, but it's really good that she did. I might've expected meals like this on a regular basis if she hadn't. I think you should thank her."

"I would get lessons from my mom every day if it meant seeing the look you just had on your face over a bite of steak. That's a promise," Sam says, pointing his fork at me.

"Well, in that case, can you get the pumpkin tortellini recipe because there's nothing else like it, and I shouldn't admit how many times I've woken up dreaming about it."

"If it means you'll dream of me instead, I'll find a way to get it." Sam winks then tucks back into his meal.

We continue eating in amicable silence. This food is too good to not eat it while it's warm, and I appreciate the ease with which we can share a meal and not have to fill the void with conversation. It feels natural, like I could picture us doing this regularly, and the thought scares me.

"I'm so full right now," I say, tossing my napkin on my plate and pushing back from the table.

"Me too. I think I impressed myself," Sam says, reaching to grab the leg of the chair I'm sitting in and pulling me closer to him.

"You did good, Sam." I press a kiss to his cheek when I'm saddled up next to him.

"Want to watch a movie or snuggle? Which sounds better?" he asks.

"Well . . . I have been dying to see that bed you were in earlier this week. It looked so cozy, I think I could crawl in and go right to sleep."

"I'll let you in my bed, but I am not planning on letting you sleep." Sam kisses me softly before pulling on my bottom lip with his teeth. A slew of goose bumps pebble my skin as heat zaps up my spine.

"Easy, killer. I'll go change real quick." I stand and grab my bag, heading toward the bathroom.

Sam stops me with a hand on my arm. "I was thinking that clothes were optional."

"Trust me, you will like what I brought," I quip before heading into the small restroom to change. I brought something special that I think he's going to love. Something that also fits my own agenda.

Once inside, I dig through my bag and pull out the black lace lingerie I bought for this. It's almost like a bodysuit, with cutouts on the back and nether regions. It's long sleeved, so my arm will be concealed behind the black floral pattern. I also brought an oversized fluffy pink robe, just to tease him a bit. I undress quickly, fitting myself into the number and donning the robe. I fluff my hair a bit and slide on a hint of red lipstick.

When I open the door, Sam is nowhere to be found, our dinner abandoned on the table. I walk to the front door and drop my bag back down by my shoes, turning to see if I can spot him. The muffin tin is noticeably missing from the kitchen counter. Where did he go?

"Up here," Sam says, peering down at me from the loft I didn't know he had.

"How do I get up there?" I ask, looking for a set of stairs.

"The ladder." He points to a hidden wooden-rung ladder that's tucked just off the kitchen. I never would have noticed it, but now that I see it, I'm not sure how I missed it.

I climb each rung carefully, reaching the top and sliding my legs over to stand in the loft. Sam eyes me from the bed. He's lying with his hands behind his head and his shirt off. His biceps are huge. His chest and abdomen look like granite, bulging and dipping across the expanse of his body. His tattoos are beautiful in swirling patterns across his skin. My cheeks heat just looking at him.

"You gonna eye fuck me all night, or are we snuggling?" he asks, grinning at me.

"Snuggling, sorry. Uh, actually, I'm not sorry." I take back the apology. He's hot as hell, and he knows it. There's no point in me denying it.

I cross the room and slide onto the bed in my fluffy robe. Sam pulls me into him and nuzzles his nose into my neck, kissing between my ear and collarbone gently. I can't stop the way my body reacts to him. Tingles race up my spine and my jaw goes slack. Sam arches back into the pillows, burrowing us in while pulling me even closer against his hardened body.

"This robe is super soft, I see why you picked it." He runs his hand along the sleeve feeling the texture of it.

"I knew you'd like it," I say jokingly, laughing as he begins to tickle me.

Escaping his grasp, I move to stand beside the bed, slowly untying the belt. The shoulders of the robe drop first, then the remainder as I slowly release it to the floor. There's a second of nerves as I stand before him in nothing but the lace bodysuit, but that tension quickly diminishes when I see the lust that blooms on his face.

"Holy shit. I didn't think you could get more beautiful, but you look like a present, all wrapped up just for me," he says, climbing to the edge of the bed to pull me against him.

Sam grasps behind my neck, forcing me to bend into his kiss. Before I know it, I'm straddling him on the bed, our tongues twisting and exploring each other's mouths like we will never get enough. I grind my center against his cock, and a moan slips out of me.

Breaking the kiss, Sam says, "We have all night. I plan to spoil you, but I think I want dessert first." I'm confused by his statement for a second. Does he really plan to stop what we're doing to eat something?

Sam reaches over to the nightstand and grabs one of the muffins I made from the tin. He takes a small lick of the cream cheese frosting. "Mmmm . . . I love that you made these. Frosting is my favorite." Sam uses his free hand to motion for me to lie down on the bed.

I do as he commands and sink into the bed with my head landing among the pillows. He crawls on his knees until he's positioned over top of me, one leg on each side of my body. Sam takes the frosting-topped muffin and runs it along my neck, leaving a sticky trail of whipped sugar down my throat. Next, he skates the muffin across each nipple, then slowly over my aching center.

Abandoning the muffin to the bedside table, he leans down to whisper in my ear, "You're covered in sugar. I guess I'll have to eat you, good girl."

Sam licks the sugar off my neck, switching between getting it on his tongue and kissing me so I can taste it. Each time his mouth dips to mine I anticipate the sweet taste mixed with the pure unadulterated need that courses through my veins. My arm is covered, but I can tell from the sensation that many very dirty thoughts are being displayed across it.

He moves lower to my breasts, spending equal time sucking and laving on my swollen nipples through the lace material. He nips at them a little, and I arch my back, moaning at the sensation. He's careful to remove every bit of the frosting, and I find myself wanting to add more when he's not looking.

"Do you like that?" he asks, grinning at me while he shifts yet again lower and begins to flick his tongue against my center.

"Sam, it feels so . . . holy—"

He smiles, making eye contact with me as he sucks on my clit. Sam's fingers split me apart as he dips his tongue inside, humming in pleasure. Sparks wink behind my eyes, and tears threaten to leak out. The sensation is too much, it feels so good. I feel like I'm losing it. Quickly, he flattens his tongue and lashes side to side right where I need him while dipping two fingers deep inside me and crooking them at the perfect angle.

He reaches up with his free hand and twists my nipple into a tightly formed peak. It's almost like I'm being consumed by him, like he owns every part of my body. Sam begins to work me harder with his fingers while putting his full focus on my clit. My heart hammers in my chest, and I fall apart, floating willingly into oblivion.

Twenty-Six

Sam

Falling Alone

"You alive up there?" I ask, still positioned between Olive's legs.

"I think so?" she whispers.

"Are you asking me or telling me?" I laugh, licking up her center once more. Olive squeezes her legs together with a yelp.

"Need a minute, Sam." She swats at me, her hand landing on my arm to pull me up beside her. I can't help but feel like the king of the world. She's everything I've ever wanted, and call it macho, but I know she just had the best orgasm of her life. If I were a caveman, I would beat my chest in pride.

I wrap my arms around her, pulling her close against my body. I need to hold her, to show her how much she means to me. I spent all day preparing this date and I want it to last forever. I'm falling in love with her, there's no question. When I think about her, I think about the little ordinary things, like waking up to share coffee in bed, brushing her hair back from her face when she's sick, holding her hand when we walk down the street. Don't get me wrong, I want the big things too, but that's how I know this is different.

Olive rolls onto her side, sliding her hand through my hair. She's staring into my eyes, and I can't help but get lost in her. I wish I knew all the secrets behind those green pools of hers.

"That was something else. I want to repay the favor," she says, sliding her hand down my beard and chest, moving lower and lower until she dips her fingers below my boxer briefs. I suck in a breath trying to keep my cool.

"It wasn't a favor, baby. It was just as good for me, I promise." I kiss her lightly, but it quickly deepens.

Olive pushes my shoulder so I'm lying flat on my back with her straddling me. She kisses and sucks my neck before moving down to tug at my boxers. Before I can catch my breath, she takes me in her mouth, the crown of my cock bouncing effortlessly against the back of her throat. She hums as she glances at me, and I watch each time her cheeks hollow just before her lips release me. I push my hips down into the bed, effectively pulling out of her mouth.

"What are you doing?"

"Just watching you take my cock like there's nothing else you'd rather be doing." She blushes at my statement but runs her tongue up from the base, swirling it around the crown like it's a lollipop. Before I sink back into her, she places her hand flat on the mattress and scooches forward so she's directly over me. This time, when I hit the back of her throat, she swallows and takes me deeper than I knew was possible. Her eyes water, tears falling down her cheeks, and she gags slightly.

I pull out, concern marking my brows. "Jesus, are you okay?"

She smiles at me softly, my cock still sitting on her pillow-soft lips. "You're not exactly small. I, uh, couldn't help the tears."

"Not small? That the best you can do?" I joke, but I'm comforted to know she's fine. I'm clearly too protective.

"Sam, it's huge, and beautiful, and I have dreams about it regularly. Anything else, or can I get back to what I was doing?" Olive asks, a playful annoyance in her tone.

"By all means, but I'm not going to get off. I plan to do that buried deep inside of you." I smirk and wave at her to continue before placing my hands behind my head.

Olive licks around the crown, then takes me between her lips once more. She's working hard to get me to break my word, and between the suction and adorable noises she makes, I almost do. When I'm just about to lose it, I lift her up and kiss her like my life depends on it. She's rubbing herself against my cock, and with each pass, I'm desperate to slip inside.

"Ride me, baby," I command.

She reaches between us and lines me up perfectly. Inch by glorious inch, she sinks onto me, gripping me like a fist. It takes her a minute to get situated, but once she is, Olive leans back, placing her hands on my shins while she bounces in a flawless rhythm. Her breasts lift and fall each time I move my hips, driving me wild with desire.

I'm coated in her, drenched by her pussy, and all I can focus on is not blurting out how much I love her. I do—I mean, it's kind of sorted in my brain at this point. Yet each time she sinks down on my dick or grinds her pussy against its base, I fall a little harder. I buck up into her, meeting her with punishing thrusts just to take my mind off the three little words that aren't little at all.

"I need you to get there, I can't last much longer," I manage to say while reaching between us to rub her sweet spot.

"Oh my gosh, Sam. That feels so good."

I bite my lip so hard I taste blood as my orgasm rips through me. Olive screams as she falls apart with me. She falls to my chest, resting her head over my heart. *I wonder if she can tell it's beating for her and only her.*

My phone alarm blares in my ear with a loud repetitive beeping.

"Make it stop, please make it stop," Olive begs, pulling the pillow over her face.

"No can do, babe. We have to work, remember," I say, removing the pillow from her hands and pressing a kiss to her lips. I feel her smile, and I can't help but grin.

Last night was magical for so many reasons. There was the amazing sex, which we had more than once. Actually, four times if you count the quickie that happened with her bent over the kitchen table when we came down for snacks around midnight. I'm absolutely counting it, I'll never look at that table the same way again.

Aside from that, we laughed so hard swapping stories from our childhood, and Olive started to open up a bit more about her family. I feel like we are closer than ever, and I couldn't be more pleased to be waking up with her in my bed. The only thing that could make everything better is if we didn't have to leave, and didn't have to go back to regular life.

"What time is it?" she asks, rubbing the sleep from her eyes.

"Eight. I wasn't sure if you'd want to go home or straight to work."

"I brought everything I need to get ready here, if that's okay," she says, slinging the covers off and moving to stand.

"Of course, whatever makes you happy makes me happy." I capture her hand as she rounds the bed and pull her into me, hugging her around the waist as I sit on the edge of the bed, kissing her belly button through her oversized long-sleeve T-shirt. I'm not sure why she insisted on putting anything on last night; it's not like I'm not intimately familiar with every single part of her. She was adamant about it though, and if it makes her more comfortable, it's not a big deal to me. I would have had fun watching her arm reflect her feelings last night, but I knew them anyway.

"I'll go shower. Give me, like, forty-five minutes to get ready," she says, smiling at me before turning to climb down the ladder.

While she's doing her thing, I lie in bed for a while before deciding to make breakfast. Coffee, of course, and scrambled eggs with avocado toast. I mix the eggs with a little milk and put a pat of butter in the pan so they don't stick. As I'm swirling the eggs around, perfecting their light, fluffy texture, Olive approaches from behind and wraps her arms around my waist.

"I get dinner and eggs? You really shouldn't spoil me this way."

"I'll spoil you forever if you'll let me." I turn in her arms and touch my lips to her forehead. Her perfume wafts into my nose, the perfect strawberry scent. Her hair is tied up in a curled but flowy ponytail with a cream bow. She's wearing a black long-sleeve shirt with a skirt that juts out at her hips and lands below her knees. I notice everything about her, from the black stockings to the pale pink lipstick. She's the most beautiful person I've ever laid eyes on.

"Sam, you can't make those kind of promises," she scolds, her eyes boring into mine.

"I can make whatever promises I want. I don't say things I don't mean, you should know that by now." I boop her nose before returning to the eggs.

Grabbing a couple of plates, I slide a portion of eggs and a slice of toast on each, sprinkling on a little everything-bagel seasoning as I go. I set the plates down at the table, slide onto my chair, and notice Olive looks lost in deep thought.

"Hey, it's just eggs. It's not a promise I can't keep. Even if you end up saying this isn't working for you, I make them every morning and would be happy to throw a couple extra on." I'm trying to lighten the mood. It's not like I was proposing, although with the way she makes my heart explode, I very well could without reservation. I didn't mean to scare her off.

"I know that. I just . . . I usually don't let things get this far, and if I'm being honest, things are different with you, and that scares me." She worries her bottom lip between her teeth and stares out the front window from across the table.

I stand, sliding my chair next to hers and bending to turn hers so we are facing each other. Sitting again, I grab her hands and look in her eyes.

"Listen, it was just a saying, a nice gesture. I hate that we had an amazing night and now you are sitting here feeling scared. I know this may seem like it's all going really fast and that I'm coming on too strong, but I'm not the kind of guy who keeps secrets or lies about things. From the moment I saw you, it was like a veil was lifted, and I could suddenly see the world in full color. You are sweet and kind. Funny as hell and tough as nails. I've never had much luck in relationships before, and I always thought that meant something was wrong with me. But I realize now that it was because I hadn't met you. I don't expect you to reciprocate this, at least not right now, but I do need to tell you that I'm falling in love with you. The kind of love I'm not sure I'll ever recover from. And that scares me, too, so all I ask is that if you decide you don't want that or can't get there with me at some point, please let me down quickly." I don't stick around for a response, knowing she will need time to process what I said and that she isn't ready to say it back. Instead, I stand, push in my chair, and head to the shower to prepare for my day.

When I come out of the bathroom fifteen minutes later, Olive has cleaned the kitchen and is waiting with her bag on the couch. I quickly put my socks and shoes on, check that everything is turned off, and grab my bag to head out the door.

"Ready, Freddie?" I say, grabbing the handle of her bag to take it from her.

"Yeah. Sam, you don't have to do that," she says, resisting my pull on her bag.

"I want to," I say, peering in her eyes.

She places a hand on my arm, effectively stopping me from walking any further. I turn to look at her, but before I can register what she's doing, she kisses me. It's not an everyday, regular kind of kiss. There's emotion in it. All the things I believe she wants to say and feel are infused in this simple touch of our lips. It's life-changing and yet, there's a sinking feeling in my gut that we're at a crossroads and she's about to choose the wrong path.

After breaking apart, we walk to my truck in silence, and we ride to Mage Hollow in silence. We are in so much silence it's deafening. I want to throw up, to scream, to cry, to fight for her to stay in this with me. But I can't do any of that because, even if she doesn't believe it, I know her. She needs to retreat inward and process everything before she can deal with this head-on. I'm willing to wait and give her that space. What choice do I have otherwise?

I pull into my parking spot behind Eerie and turn off the ignition. Placing my hand on the door handle, I start to pull it when she finally speaks.

"Sam, wait."

I spin to face her.

"I-I can't say it. I can't tell you that I love you or that I'm falling in love with you. But it's not that I don't want to. I want to be where you are and to be sure. You're amazing in every way, and you're everything I've ever dreamed of. Please be patient with me."

I smile at her, the biggest smile I may have ever delivered in my life. My heart feels renewed. Even if there's a slim chance, I'm willing to go for it.

"I would wait forever, Olivia." I lean forward and pull her into a hug before pressing a kiss to her temple. Her shoulders shake with what feels like tears. "Why are you crying?" I ask, lifting her chin so I can look in her eyes.

"I just, I don't know. I don't deserve you, but I'm so grateful that you're in my life."

I swipe the tears from her cheeks and kiss her gently. "I'm not going anywhere. Well, except to work because Terry is standing at the front door waiting on me." I wink at her and grin.

"Oh, shoot, I'm sor—"

I press a finger to her lips, stopping her from finishing her apology. "Nothing to be sorry for. Go have a great day at work, and I'll call you tonight." I hop out of the truck and round the front to open her door. It warms my soul that she's finally resigned herself to letting me do it. I press one more kiss to her lips and watch her walk toward Black Kettle.

She's the love of my life, there's no doubt about it. I may have to watch her walk away from me for good at some point, but right now, I'm going to hold on for as long as I possibly can.

"You going to sit and moon over that girl all day, or am I going to get this thing finished up?" Terry interrupts my thoughts.

"Yeah, sorry, boss. I'm coming." I walk as quickly as I can to the shop door, unlock it, flick the open sign on, and begin setting up my station. Terry browses the wall pieces, then makes his way to me when I'm ready.

"How've you been? Looks like things were a little tense with Beau's beauty earlier," Terry says, sliding onto the table and taking his shirt off so I can finish adding color to a collection of birds on his chest representing his granddaughters.

"Is that what people are calling her?" I ask, raising an eyebrow. I'm not a fan of the nickname.

"Ah, you know how it is, new girl, works for him and all. Don't get your panties in a wad," Terry scolds.

"Yeah. I do know." I shrug and dip my tattoo gun into a bright blue ink.

"Is it serious?" he asks, wincing a little at the first strike of the needle into his skin.

"I think I'm falling in love with her, but I'm not sure if she'll ever be in love with me, if that answers the question," I say, proceeding to fill in the gaps between his bird tattoos.

"The women in this town, I swear to Christ." He shakes his head.

"What about them?"

"Well, you know, it's like they're all infected by that damn witch's prophecy. I just had this talk with my granddaughter the other day. Cynthia won't settle down with her longtime boyfriend because she doesn't know how to tell if it's real love. She wouldn't know love if it smacked her in the face, that girl," Terry huffs, forcing me to put my hand on his chest to hold him steady.

"What prophecy?" I ask, my stomach rioting at the thought of Irina.

"I mean, it's not actually a prophecy, but legend has it that Irina was in love with one of the judges during the Salem witch trials. When he wouldn't commit and run away with her, Irina and her sisters vowed to never again wear their hearts on their sleeves. It's not like these women today would be cursed or that any of it is even real, but sometimes I wonder. Their ability to be so dense is astounding," Terry explains.

I feel like I might throw up. Is Olive unable to commit to our relationship because Irina put a spell on her? Did she curse her to wear her heart on her sleeve as a sick joke, one in which Irina would never actually allow Olive to be vulnerable and open to love? Or is her hesitancy simply because she isn't sure she's in love with me specifically? I've never asked her what exactly Irina told her the first time they met, but she was mad at me that night over the kissing booth situation. I can't help but wonder if this is suddenly some sort of game. I think what we have is real, but is it? Does she care for me?

I finish Terry's tattoo in record time. I'm proud of the piece, and he is pleased with it. I clean him up and wrap him so the tattoo stays protected. After he checks out, I shoot Olive a text.

> Hey, can you talk later?

A few minutes go by before my phone dings with a response.

Olive

> Sure, everything okay?

> I'm not sure. Call me when you get done at work.

I clean up the mess from working on Terry, wipe down my table, and take out the trash. My feet feel like they weigh a thousand pounds as I approach the large bin. Why did I have to fall for the one girl who won't open up? I mean, the more I think about it, she covered herself all night last night so I couldn't even get a visual of how she was feeling. At the time, I thought it didn't matter, but now, I'm not sure of anything.

Terry was my only scheduled appointment today, but occasionally I'll get a walk-in or two. I head toward my office at the back of the shop and round the corner. "Jesus, you scared the shit out of me," I shout at Olive, who's perched in my office chair.

"Sorry, I just, you weren't out front, and I, uh, well after the text, I just wanted to make sure everything was okay." Olive's chewing on her lip, concern evident in her brow.

"Um, yeah. I just wanted to ask you about Irina." I thought I'd have more time to prepare for this conversation. Although, I guess it's a good sign she ran right over. "Aren't you supposed to be at work?" I ask.

"I told Beau I needed to talk to you for a minute. He grumbled but said it was fine. What do you want to know?" She stands from the chair and takes a few steps toward me.

"What did you say to her that night at her shop? Why did she do this to you specifically?" I gesture to her arm. It's hidden under her shirt, but we both know what I'm referring to.

"Sam, I . . . It's complicated," Olive says, reaching to grab my hand.

"What about this isn't complicated? I told you I needed honesty, and I opened up to you. It sorta feels like you're still holding back while I'm barreling straight toward heartbreak city." I pull out of her grasp and walk to my chair, flopping down haphazardly.

"Sam, I *have* been honest. Irina caught me in a weak moment, and I sorta just blurted out my feelings. It all happened so fast, I don't know what you want me to say." Her eyes are filled with tears.

"I want you to tell me that you didn't ask her to trick me. To make me fall in love with you just so you could break my heart, because it feels like I've got a lot on the line here and you're holding all the cards." I let out a long, frustrated breath.

Olive rushes over, sitting on my lap and kissing me with everything she has. When we break apart, she sighs heavily and then says, "No, I did not ask her to make you fall in love with me. I asked her to fix me because I've never been able to let go and allow myself to be vulnerable. After years, my whole life really, of not being enough . . . I didn't want to risk the rejection. It had nothing to do with you at all. I'm sorry that I'm not ready to say that I'm in love with you. Truly, I want to be brave enough to do that, but I'm not. Not yet anyway."

"So, this is just something you need to work through, and we are solid?" I ask, a small bit of doubt turning my stomach.

"Yes, we're good. I promise. I've never known anyone like you, and I've never felt like this before. There's just a lot going on in my life right now, and I need time to sort it all out," she reassures me.

"Okay, thank you for coming here. Thank you for being you and putting everything aside to rush over." I smile at her tentatively. There's a pit in my stomach. A part of me can sense she's simply telling me what I want to hear and not the whole truth of the matter.

"Always, Sam. You're important to me. Please, if you don't know anything else, know that."

Olive kisses me again, a simple, chaste kiss, before standing and leaving to go back to work. I do feel somewhat better about things. I've waited for what feels like a very long time for the right person. There's so much she's still not saying, I can feel it in my bones. But instead of focusing on that, I'm going to focus on being the man she thinks I am. The brave one who sticks with her, even if I'm destined to break.

Twenty-Seven

Olive

Am I in Love?

6 Days Until Halloween

Am I in love with Sam O'Reilly? That's the question plaguing my every waking moment since I left him in the shop yesterday. It's showing up in my dreams too. I think it's just a general state of being for me at this point. A simple question that I wish had a simple answer.

If I wasn't walking around with my every thought and feeling displayed for all to see, I believe the answer would be a resounding and easy yes. I'm indeed falling for him, head over heels. But that's not reality. The version that is true includes so many mixed-up feelings, between not knowing if I'm putting myself out there enough or too much. Wondering if he likes the real me or the cooked-up version of me who's brave and wears her heart on her sleeve. The insecure side of me thinks maybe I don't know him well enough to feel this strongly or that he only seems perfect for me because he can anticipate my needs with a quick glance at my arm. Or maybe even that I was an easy target for Irina, that this is a fun experiment for her.

"Ugh!" I yell, throwing a pillow from across my bedroom as hard as I can. A cup of water tumbles from my dresser to the floor as the fluffy projectile accidentally knocks it over. *Damn it!*

I jump up from my position lounging on my bed and grab a towel from the clean laundry basket settled in the corner of my room. Mopping up my mess feels strangely on par with what needs to happen in my real life. I need to talk this out with someone who can help, someone unbiased.

My phone pings.

Sam

Mabel would like to know if you will be attending family dinner tonight?

Olive would like to know if Mabel's son wants her there or if this is a pity invite.

Sam

Mabel said that her son is the one who insisted she invite you, and he doesn't like talking in third person this way.

You started it.

Sam

There's my girl. But seriously, will you come with me?

I have plans with Howie, but I would love to come. What time should I be ready?

Sam

What are you guys up to? Six.

Just having lunch. I'm hoping to discuss his love life. I'm thinking couples' costumes could be a good tactic to push him and Ari together. Thoughts?

Sam

Well, since I know you won't listen to a "don't meddle" speech, go for it. What are we going as?

Yet to be determined. Was planning to ask you to go shopping on Wednesday so we could find something.

Sam

I'd follow you to the moon. See you at six, and be careful.

He's such a sweetheart. *I'd follow you to the moon.* No one says that. The guys I dated in college would groan at the thought of going shopping with me. The ones at the country club would simply hand me a credit card and tell me to make sure I dressed to impress. No one has actually ever cared for my wellbeing like Sam does. But there's no way it's that simple, that he just wants to spend time with me however he can.

Checking the clock, I realize Howie will be here to pick me up in fifteen minutes. I scurry about my room, selecting a cropped pair of denim pants, an army-green long-sleeve bodysuit, and gold jewelry. It's casual enough for lunch but acceptable enough to go to a family dinner. I fluff my hair and grab my crossbody purse, coat, and boots while I wait by the front door.

Howie's Bronco pulls up to the curb, and I don't wait for him to get out. I cross the threshold, locking the door behind me, and skate down the porch steps to get in.

"Howie, how's it going?" I ask, smiling at him as I slink into the front seat and buckle up.

"Eh, it's okay for a Sunday. I had to break up a bar fight last night. It went super well." He gestures to a freshly painted black eye blooming on his face.

"Oh no. Are you okay? Does Ariella know? Did they get arrested? Who was it?" I spit out a slew of questions.

"I'm fine, and why would she know or care?" he asks, putting the truck in drive and pulling away from the curb.

"Howie . . . come on. I'm not blind. I know there's something going on between you two." I turn in my seat so I'm facing him slightly.

"Olivia Bowman, you need glasses. There isn't anything going on with us," Howie adamantly denies.

"Ugh, fine. But does it help knowing I'm on your side, and I want there to be something going on?" I'm prying, but we need to get this out in the open.

Howie laughs but doesn't answer me. I know I'm not the only person who can see the way they interact. It can't be my imagination, but then again, I don't have the best judgment right now.

"Where are you taking me? I don't recognize this part of town." I look out the windshield, noticing we took a turn onto a new road and appear to be traveling toward the ocean.

"My uncle doesn't just own Union. He has a small seafood joint down in Bishop. I thought it would be a good change of pace, and I had a sense you wanted to talk to me about something you might not want people in town overhearing." He gives me a lopsided grin and shrugs.

"Oh, what gave me away? Was it the text this morning that said 'I desperately need advice,' or was it the part where I said 'no one else can know'?" I quip.

"Both."

We laugh in unison before settling into a comfortable silence. This is why I like Howie so much. He doesn't push me to always fill the voids. He's okay with me sharing only what I'm comfortable with. Ariella would never be that way, she needs every minute detail. That's precisely why I chose Howie and not my lovable bestie for this conversation.

Howie pulls the car into a small parking lot that ends at the edge of the beach. We get out and shuffle into the restaurant. It's quaint with wood-paneled walls and nautical decor. The windows are shaped like portholes, and after a few glasses of wine, I'm sure I'd believe I was inside an actual boat. It smells like the ocean with fresh, whole fish displayed alongside a lobster tank at the host stand.

"I made a reservation for Howie," he says to a cute girl with blonde hair and a bright orange BoatHouse T-shirt.

"Hi, Howie, come with me," she coos. I can see the interest in her eyes, and my heart tumbles for Ariella. Howie is adorable. He has a secret hot body hidden under his clothes, and she is going to miss her chance if she doesn't get on it soon.

"Is this table okay?" she asks, sizing me up as if to decide whether this is a date or not.

"It's perfect. Thanks," I reply, sliding into a wooden booth that has a compass etched into the table under a thin layer of polyurethane.

Howie slides into his side and pulls the menus from where they are tucked behind a condiment caddy, handing me one.

"That girl was into you, Howard," I say before grasping the menu and opening it to browse.

"No, she wasn't. I'm not the type that gets girls by walking into a restaurant. That would be Sam." He shrugs and pulls open his menu for a second before closing it and laying it on the table.

"Well, that's just what I wanted to hear today," I groan.

"It's the truth. Sorry, Ollie." He shrugs again.

"We need to come up with another nickname. Ollie is what Ari calls me, and I hate it. How about just Olive?" I suggest.

"Nah, I like Ollie. It fits. But actually, don't look at the menu. I'm ordering us sushi, it's the best around. You do like sushi, right?" Howie asks.

"I love it, that sounds perfect." I close my menu, and he places them back where they belong.

"Can I get you two something to drink?" a server whose name tag reads Harper asks.

"I'll just have a Diet Coke, please," I respond, while Howie orders a water and tells her we want the sushi platter. Harper jots our order down in her notebook and walks away.

"Okay, so what is the big thing you wanted to discuss?" He eyes me suspiciously, like he thinks I'm here to talk about my arm. I'm not. Well, not completely.

"I think I might be in love with Sam, but also I think what is going on with us might be completely fake given the circumstances," I blurt out, covering my face with my hands. Harper delivers our drinks and quickly scurries away.

"And you thought I was the right person to discuss this with?" he questions.

"Well, I mean, yeah. You know us both, and you're the only other person who's met Irina. I thought maybe you could give me some advice or something to help me figure it out."

"Look, Ollie, I'm not really qualified in the love department. But I think Sam really cares for you. The day your parents came to town, he was an absolute mess wondering if you were ghosting him, and that was before he even knew they were visiting. I get why you feel like you can't trust anything right now. I felt that way for a long time after meeting her, and I didn't even get cursed. You have to trust your instincts though. You need to find a way to decipher what's real from what's not." Our server places down a gorgeous platter of sushi, briefly halting our conversation.

"How do I do that, though? I have spent so much time thinking about it, and I feel like the only way I will ever know fully is if I don't have this thing on my arm. I mean, I'm questioning everything. Each time I share something with him about myself, I have a tiny voice inside my head asking if I'm sharing it because I feel safe with him or because he can clearly see it anyway," I explain. I need someone to understand my hesitation here. Without that understanding, I just look like a big scaredy-cat.

"Ollie, I don't think you need me to tell you what to do. I think your mind is already made up. The only problem now is that we don't have a plan of how to find Irina so we can get rid of this thing." Howie brings some much-needed logic to the situation as he pops a piece of spicy tuna roll in his mouth.

I point my chopsticks at him and chew my own mouthful of raw fish thoughtfully. "I know that, but she said if I don't embrace it, then I'll never be able to open up. I'll be just like her, Howard. An old witchy woman who dies alone."

"Ollie, come on. You know that's not true. You are going to be whoever you decide to be, magic be damned. Just like with your mom. She wanted you to be one thing, but here you are, working and living your life." He is so matter-of-fact about it, confident that this decision is mine.

But it doesn't feel like it is at all. It feels like the moment I turned around and uttered those very first words to Irina, everything changed for good.

"I saw something at the house." Howie's eyebrows shoot up as he nods for me to continue. "On the table, under their names . . . it said never again will we wear our hearts on our sleeves."

"What does that mean? What are you saying?"

"I'm saying, what if this is a trick? What if she purposefully did this to mess with me, to hurt me."

"Why would she do that?"

"I don't know, but Sam looks at my arm all the time to gauge my reaction to things. Maybe she was trying to show me that real love isn't *real* at all. That no matter how good the guy is, he'll always take the easy road."

"I understand why you'd say that, I do." Howie runs a hand down his face. "But if you really believe that about Sam then you couldn't be more wrong. He's a good guy, Ollie."

I sip my drink, thinking about what he said. "Howie, I know that. He's the kindest person I've ever met. It's just, well, I'm torn because how will I ever know it's real if I keep the curse? But then again, if I get rid of it, I might lose him altogether."

"I can't answer that. All I know is that you will never regret betting on yourself, believing that you can be open and find love, that what you have with Sam is real. If you keep the tattoo, well, you probably will regret that. The unknowns would eat at you, for sure. But the good news is, you don't have to decide today."

After we finished lunch, Howie and I didn't talk about it again. There wasn't much else to say. He thinks I can choose, and I think I'm essentially screwed for life. I thought a lot about it on the ride home, and I do think I'm in love with Sam. But I also worry that, in this case, love isn't enough. If I've learned anything over the years, it's that love, no matter what we read or are told, is conditional. I think that Sam loves me because it's easy to do so with a constant guidebook at his disposal. Without it, I would just be like every other female, frustrating him with my inability to tell him what I need.

And that's just the kicker. That's what I was taught from a young age: Sit down. Be quiet. Know your place. Don't ruffle feathers. Don't gossip too much, but don't be a stick-in-the-mud. Be adventurous, but don't try to attempt things that are a man's responsibility. If we are too emotional, then we are moody. If we aren't emotional enough, we are heartless bitches.

"Deep in thought? Trying to find a way to get Daddy's money back?" Bridget interrupts my turmoil, whispering in my ear as she places both hands on my shoulders from behind.

"Hilarious, but no. Just thinking." I turn, smiling at her. I know she was joking.

"Too much thinking will give you wrinkles. Didn't you know that?" Bridget slides onto the stool next to me at Mabel's kitchen island.

"Now you sound like my mother," I quip, sending us both into a fit of giggles.

"I love that sound," Mabel singsongs from her place at the stove, stirring a pot of soup.

"What sound?" Sam asks, coming in from helping his dad chop wood, wiping his face on the bottom of his T-shirt and making my mouth water at the peek of his abdomen.

"The sound of my girls laughing in the kitchen. It makes my heart feel so full." Mabel turns, smiling at Bridget and me.

"This one is my girl, don't go claiming her." Sam wraps his arm around my stomach and drops a kiss to my forehead.

"That could be true, big brother, if she didn't like us more than she likes you," Bridget says, laughing at her own joke.

"I'm wounded. Olive, can you help me with something real quick? Upstairs," Sam whispers the last part, and Mabel winks at us both. This woman is actually endorsing me making out with her son under her roof. I think I love her and am terrified of her at the same time.

I pop up from my stool and follow Sam into the hallway and up the stairs as Bridget yells from the kitchen, "You guys are gross!" Sam and I both chuckle but dip into his old bedroom.

"This is cute." I take in his childhood room. It appears like not a thing has changed from when he left high school. *Sports Illustrated* swimsuit-edition pages still plaster the ceiling as if he had to fall asleep to them each night, and a prom picture of him in a suit and a girl in a silver dress is perched on his dresser.

"I, uh, yeah, I should probably help my mom clear this stuff out. I sorta forgot all this was in here when I felt the urge to kiss you."

"It's okay. It's not the type of bedroom I had growing up, but I could learn a lot about you in here," I reply, running a finger along the edge of his bed.

"Can the thing you learn be that you love to make out with me against the door?" he asks, a devilish grin on his lips.

I grab his hand and pull him to the door, sandwiching myself between it and him before snaking my arm around his neck and pulling his mouth to mine. His breath is minty, and his skin has a slight musk from working up a sweat. It's intoxicating to the point I don't notice myself being lifted.

I wrap my arms around him, and he grinds into me. After exploring each other thoroughly, we break apart, heaving for air.

"Maybe this wasn't a good idea. Now I want you and I can't have you," Sam says, running a hand over my hair to smooth it from our make-out session.

"I think it was a great idea. Keeps you wanting more." I wink at him and drop my legs, slinking out of our position.

"Is that so?" he asks, gripping the bottom of his T-shirt and pulling it up over his head so I can very clearly see his ripped torso. My mouth waters, and a squeak sneaks past my lips. *Traitorous body, I chastise myself, turned on by him even though my heart is constantly pleading with me to pull back.*

"Okay, so maybe the feeling is mutual." I cross my arms and pout my bottom lip out.

"It's okay, we have plenty of time. The rest of our lives maybe." Sam leans in and sucks my bottom lip into his mouth before biting it slightly. My body reacts in a visceral way while my heart races at the statement.

"Alright. I'm, uh, I'm going to go downstairs before anyone gets too suspicious. I'll leave you to get changed, since you clearly need a minute." I grab his hardened cock through his jeans and squeeze before turning to leave. Sam smacks my ass as I make my way out the door, and I laugh the whole way downstairs.

As I take the final step and round the corner to head back into the kitchen, Max stops me with a look and a pointed finger, telling me to come with him. I follow him into the dimly lit dining room.

"What?" I whisper.

"Are you serious about my brother?" Max asks, not wasting any time before diving right in.

"I, uh, yes. I'm serious about getting to know him better." Max looks at me with concern and disappointment.

"My brother really cares about you. I know this is fun and all"—Max sweeps his arm around to gesture at his home, his family, I assume—"but don't drag him along if you aren't all in. I'm pretty sure it would kill him if you broke his heart."

"Max, I'm not planning to hurt him. I care about him a lot too," I sputter quietly.

"Okay, but just, please. I want to believe you, but I've never seen him like this before, and he's kind of the glue that keeps us all together. I don't know what any of us would do if he falls apart." My heart warms at the sentiment. Sam is the big brother, the protector. Max wants to make sure Sam is safe with me emotionally, and it's really sweet. The only problem is, I can't and won't make any promises. I've made it clear to Sam that I need time to figure things out. I don't need to share that with Max, but I feel guilty for not being able to reassure him completely.

"What are you guys doing in here in the dark?" Nora asks, sneaking into the dining room with us.

"Nothing, I was just telling Olive not to break Sam's heart," Max explains.

"That's usually the talk you'd give to my boyfriend. I'm pretty sure Sam can handle himself. Come on, Olive," Nora scolds Max and then grabs my hand, dragging me into the hallway and then to the kitchen.

Sam is waiting, sitting on a stool and eyeing me suspiciously. Nora notices and approaches him while depositing me at the stool next to him. "Sorry, I just stole her for some girl talk real quick." Sam doesn't look convinced but takes my hand and presses a kiss to my cheek as I scooch onto the stool.

"You, okay? You look like you've seen a ghost," he whispers in my ear.

"Yes, I'm great. Someone got me hot and bothered upstairs. Just needed a minute," I lie, not wanting to tell him about his brother's speech.

Sam chuckles softly and kisses my neck discreetly before Mabel pulls a loaf of bread from the oven and shoos us to the dining table.

Twenty-Eight

Sam

Paper-Thin Costumes

I can see from the large glass windows that Olive is approaching. We're meeting after my last appointment of the day to go look for costumes, and she's about ten minutes early. There's a woman splayed across my table, and right as I'm leaning over her and tattooing something on her chest, Olive pushes on the door handle and waltzes in, pageant smile firmly on her face. I know she understands this is my job, but we've never really discussed the sometimes-awkward positions I end up in.

"Hey, babe. I'll be done in just a few. Do you want to hang out here or wait in the back? Either is fine."

"I'll wait here," she replies, taking a seat on a plush velvet couch in the front sitting area, eyeing a few books of my artwork on display in front of her.

I continue working for a few minutes, putting the final touches on, while Olive browses through one of the books. I know from the cover it's the one labeled *Magical Musings*, which is only a tiny bit ironic given her predicament. Instead of focusing more of my attention on Olive, I wipe down my client, show her to the mirror, and then place a plastic wrap over her skin. She seems happy, from what I can tell. Moving quickly, I clean my station and ring her up. As the woman makes her way to exit, she side-eyes Olive, and my stomach flips. It's evident that my girl was an unwelcome guest to whatever agenda this client was hoping to push, and that puts me on edge because everything is already so up in the air between us.

"Hey." I walk up and wrap my arms around Olive's middle for a hug, an attempt at calming any nerves she may have over that interaction.

"Hi," Olive says, smiling at me before reaching on her tiptoes to give me a peck.

A grin tilts my lips up. "Are you ready to become someone else with me?"

"Always. But actually, who are we going to be?" Olive asks as I let go of her and walk toward the back to grab my things. She follows behind me, I think hoping for an answer.

"I have no clue. I thought maybe Raggedy Anne and Andy, but then Bridg told me she thinks they are siblings, so that won't work. Do you have any ideas?"

"Ariella and Howie won't reveal their costumes, but Ari assured me we'd never think of it. Maybe something funny? Like salt and pepper or hot sauce and eggs?"

"Olive, I already told you I'm falling in love with you, and this does not change that, but neither of those things are funny," I quip, grabbing her hand and leading her outside and into the cold.

I lock the door after turning the open sign off, and we head down the sidewalk toward the costume shop, Sally's Specialties.

"Okay, fair. But sometimes the most obvious costumes are ironically funny. At least to me," she justifies.

"You're not wrong. Let's see what we find. We still have a few days if nothing seems right." I kiss her temple and then thread her fingers through mine. I want to show her that no matter what, we will figure it out. While Halloween costumes may not be the biggest challenge our relationship faces, they still demonstrate the ability to adapt to what we're given and make it work.

The door chime rings, bringing me out of my head and into Sally's Specialties. This place has a distinct scent, like mildew or old books. I have to assume it's from decades-old costumes sitting abandoned on the shelves. A friendly older woman with bubble-gum pink hair welcomes us. "Take a look around. Fitting rooms are in the corner. If you need something you don't see, I might have it in the back."

Olive and I nod and thank her before making our way to the first row of costumes. There's a wide variety of outfits, ranging from Morticia Addams to Barbie and Ken. Nothing that feels like a perfect fit though. Olive is running her fingers over a long green velvet dress from *Shrek* when I startle her from behind.

"How do I look?" I ask, laughing to myself.

I'd put on a long curly blonde wig that I think is supposed to be like David Lee Roth. It looks ridiculous with my dark brown beard. Olive can't help the laugh that bursts out of her.

"I think maybe you weren't meant to be a blond," she says, still wheezing.

"Oh, come on. You know it's doing things for you." I grin, then admit, "Okay, so I think we aren't going to find something prepackaged that works for us. Let's go look at the racks back there and see if we can piece something together." Looking at three circular racks with mismatched merchandise, it seems like previous customers have come in and disassembled the prepackaged costumes, leaving behind bits and pieces.

"You lead the way. I'll try anything at least once," Olive says, winking at me like she's up to no good. I know she's teasing me, but she better be careful if she doesn't want me to make a move in the fitting room.

We grab several items off the racks and pile our clothes into the dressing area. My fingers are working to unbutton my shirt when Sally (or at least that's the name on her badge) whips open the curtain and scolds us for sharing a room. The pink-haired wonder doesn't allow any funny business in her shop, or so she says. I can't help but notice the way her eyes linger a tad longer than necessary on my exposed abs. It's a little creepy if I'm being honest.

Olive grabs her pile of clothes and scurries into the room next door as I continue to mumble about being adults and not behaving inappropriately. I can hear Olive giggle as I slide into my first outfit, a bad John Travolta in *Boogie Nights* with brown bell bottoms, a hippie vest, and a flower-print bandana.

Olive must have stepped out because I hear her say, "Sam, you ready?"

I pull back the drape closing my room, and I'm instantly transported to heaven. Olive is in an orange jumpsuit with pink flowers that's so snug it's like a second skin. "You look, uh, that's hot as hell," I mutter, appraising the outfit that leaves little to the imagination.

"I really wish I could say the same, but I'm thinking maybe seventies is not it." She tries to keep her lips in a tight line but a smirk sneaks past them. I take three steps toward her and scoop her up, blowing raspberries on her neck.

"I said no funny business," Sally shouts from outside the fitting area.

Reluctantly, I set Olive down, and we hustle back into our respective dressing rooms. After several nonstarters, I slip into a three-piece gray suit that's supposed to make me look like that one guy from the TV show *Schitt's Creek.*

"Sam, put on that suit and get out here," Olive chirps as the idea of us being Moira and Johnny finally clicks into place in my brain.

Seconds later, I slide out of the dressing room and she appears in a black dress with a white ruffled shirt. She's gorgeous in anything she puts on, even a ridiculous Halloween costume.

"What do you think? If I throw on some fake eyebrows and trim the beard, it could work," I say.

"Yeah, it could work." She shrugs, turning to go back and change out of her outfit.

I pause for a second, weighing my options about disappointing Sally. When I finally push the curtain aside and slip into Olive's room, she's pulling the zipper of the dress down. I place a hand on her back, taking over the task. "You shouldn't be in here," Olive whispers.

I ignore her and kiss her neck as she shushes me lightly. My hands dip into the dress, sliding it off her body, then I quickly unbutton the top, sending it trailing to the floor.

"You're exquisite," I say softly, pressing kisses across the back of her neck and down to the top of her shoulder.

She's facing the mirror in nothing more than a black lace bra and panties. The sight of myself wrapped around her, those perfect lips of hers opened just slightly, makes my cock bounce behind the zipper of my pants.

"Shh, baby. You can't make a sound," I warn.

My fingers trace the changing emotions blazing across her exposed tattoo. In some ways, I know I shouldn't even look at it. It's not like I don't know what her body needs and when it needs it at this point. But also, it's sorta nice knowing for sure, like having a visual reassurance that we're on the same page.

I dip my hand down into her panties, sliding my fingers over her soaked center. I swipe one finger over her clit while dipping another deep inside of her. Olive's breath hitches, and a low groan catches in my throat. I lean into her further, my lips over the shell of her ear as I whisper, "Can you be silent, baby?"

Olive nods, but there's a hesitation in her eyes. Each time she notices me looking at her arm, her hesitation seems to deepen. I lock eyes with her in the mirror, trying to reassure her that she is my focus, not the tattoo. I pull my finger out from between her legs and push it into her mouth. Olive sucks tenderly, licking it clean. I slide my hand back down her belly and work her clit between two fingers, rolling it and applying perfect pressure. I suck on her neck and use my free hand to play with her nipples. Olive arches back into me, closing her eyes briefly until the tension builds. Her arm illuminates in flashes of fireworks and pops of colored confetti. I don't want to look, but it's impossible to ignore. I slip two fingers deep inside her, pumping in and out until her legs shake and she begins to cry out. Quickly muffling the sound with my hand over her mouth, I kiss her cheek and remove my hands, stepping back so that I'm no longer touching her. Olive mimics my move, stepping back and slumping against me. She's sated and breathing deeply from her orgasm.

"We, uh, we better get changed before she comes back," I whisper, sliding my fingers still soaked from her into my own mouth. Olive flushes, her cheeks and chest turning a bright red.

She spins to face me. "What about you?" she asks.

"I'm good. I'll just go change and meet you out there." I would love to continue this and take her right here, right now. But I'm already pushing my luck with Sally, and honestly, watching Olive come is more beautiful than anything else in the world. I'll never look at this store the same.

As I exit her dressing room, I can't help sneaking another glance at her arm. New additions have popped up as permanent fixtures: a pumpkin muffin that makes me hard each time I see it, and a beautiful cabin with a woody backdrop that feels like it could be my home. Back in my own dressing room, I pull on my clothes quickly. There's a guilty feeling gnawing at my stomach. I know that Olive has spent most of her life trying to be what everyone else wanted her to be (and failing, her words, not mine). And based on the way she's been covering up her tattoo more around me, I get the feeling she thinks I'm using her tattoo to do the same, to become what she wants me to be. But it's not that at all—sure it's helpful, but it's also fascinating. There isn't a doubt in mind that without it we'd be exactly where we are right now.

I slink out of the changing room and head toward the shop counter. Olive is already at the front, talking to the older woman about our costumes.

"Oh, I have the perfect eyebrows in the back," she coos, walking toward me and pulling me back to where I came from. The look on my face makes Olive giggle. I had no warning, just an old lady with pink hair leading me toward her back room. I'm not sure what Olive signed me up for, but hopefully it's innocent. The only person in here I have eyes for is her.

Sally leads me into her office. She digs around in a desk, then hands me the bushiest pair of eyebrows I've ever seen. "These will be perfect for your costume," she says, turning and exiting just as quickly. I follow, finally making my way to the front of the store. Immediately, I can sense something is off. Rather than saying anything, Olive hands me a flyer with one hand and I place my credit card on the counter for Sally with the other. I can hear the way Olive swallows hard when I'm reading the paper. Neither of us say a thing while we wait for our items to be packaged up.

Once we're back on the sidewalk heading toward Olive's cottage, I speak first. "So, Irina's going to be at the Halloween Bash." It's not a question, just a simple statement.

"Looks like it," Olive says, a deep breath whooshing out of her.

"For what it's worth, I don't think you need to find her. I mean, aside from the people you've deliberately told, no one knows about the tattoo. It's not like it's changed your life in any way other than physical appearance," I mutter.

She stops walking. "Sam, it has changed my life, changed me. I don't know what's real or what's this stupid curse, anymore."

"No, you're right. I'm sorry, that was insensitive. Of course it has changed your life, I just meant that I care for you either way. Going to see her is dangerous, look what happened before," I defend. I mean, yeah, it has changed her life in that she is marked with signs of, from what I can tell, our relationship, but is that really such a bad thing? Does she not trust what we have together?

I don't want to fight with her, but she won't ever tell me exactly what she's thinking. I know she tries to keep her emotions close to her chest, to not become too much for me to handle. But from my perspective, I want everything about her. I want her funny sarcasm, her too-fancy-for-Mage wardrobe, her messed-up mother, her wild friends, all of it. The good, the bad, the ugly.

Twenty-Nine

Olive

It's Practically Magic

8.5 Hours Until Midnight

"What time did they say they were going to be here?" Sam asks, pulling me closer to him under the covers of my bed.

"Five, I think," I reply, scooching back against him, the feel of his naked body pressed against my skin soothing me.

"It's only three thirty. You know what that means . . ." Sam peppers kisses along my shoulder.

"Yeah, that I need to shower and start getting ready because it's later than I thought."

"Not what I was hoping you would say, but okay." Sam blows out a breath and rolls onto his back taking most of the covers with him.

"You're insatiable." I roll with him, grasping for a bit of warmth as I place a quick kiss on his lips.

Sam spent the night after he got off work yesterday. We christened every available surface in this place at least twice and then again after breakfast this morning. I can't deny that there is chemistry between us. Sex with Sam is the hottest thing I've ever done. And it never gets boring. He's always trying new things and working to learn what I like best. I don't think I could deny him, even if I wanted to. But right now, the anxiety of knowing I'm a few short hours from facing Irina again, a few hours from making a potentially life-changing decision, I guess that's the mood killer I never thought I'd have.

"I promise it'll be worth the wait." I wink at him, hopping up from the bed. The lie churns my stomach. I doubt after he finds out I plan to go see her that he will want anything to do with me.

"I'd be celibate if it meant I could spend every day with you, it's fine. Just go get ready so we can have some fun with our friends." Sam lifts up, scooching toward the edge of the bed and hugging me around the middle.

"That's a lie, but okay, Sam." I chuckle as I shake my head and go to shower. Somehow, he always knows exactly the right thing to say. But I'm naked, so maybe my arm told him what I want without my consent.

An hour later, after showers are had and costumes are put on, I walk into the kitchen and find Sam, who very much looks like Johnny Rose if he had a beard, mixing up what appears to be a cocktail.

"What's this?" I ask, peering around him into the glass pitcher he's stirring.

"I'm not sure what to call it, but it's basically hooch."

"What the heck is hooch?" I ask, hovering my face over the pitcher to sniff the concoction.

"It's like . . . Didn't you ever go to parties in college where they mixed a bunch of alcohol with fruit punch?" Sam asks.

"No? I don't think so." His eyes nearly bugging out of his head when he realizes I have no clue what he's talking about.

"What are we saying no to?" Ariella's voice chirps from the entryway.

"Nothing, I was just—" I step around the corner to greet my friend and am stunned. How the heck could this have happened? "Who are you supposed to be?" I blurt out.

"No fucking way. This is so perfect," Ari sings.

Sam follows me and immediately starts laughing. It's a deep, throaty laugh coming from his belly, and all I can do is join him. My best friend is standing across from me in exactly the same costume. We are both Moira Rose.

"I didn't know, you didn't tell me," I mumble between wheezes.

"Hey, I was just getting this from the car . . ." Howie announces, waltzing in with big bushy eyebrows and dressed in a suit that couldn't be a more perfect match to Sam's.

"Bro, you look great," Sam quips, walking over to Howie to give him one of those handshake hugs that men do. I can't help but roll my eyes.

"What happened to 'no one else will be dressed like us'?" Howie asks Ariella, pinning her down with a stare.

"I mean, I didn't expect them to copy us, but it's kind of funny. I'm actually really happy about this development. It'll be a great conversation starter at the party," Ari justifies.

"Come on, Sam made hooch. We are going to need it to help explain our matching outfits," I say, motioning for the three of them to follow me into the kitchen. I grab four glasses from the cupboard and fill them up, passing them out so we each have one.

"To a witchy night and no one getting cursed," Ari toasts, raising her glass as I glare at her. She just had to throw that reminder in there. I can't seem to escape it for more than three minutes at a time. My heart races. I desperately hope I'm getting rid of a curse tonight and not adding a new one.

After two drinks each and lots of laughter, the hooch is gone and we are ready to head out the door. I walk into my bedroom to grab the flyer for Irina's shop and tuck it into my purse. I wish I could avoid this, but reality is a bitch. It's now or never. Howie startles me as I turn to make my way back into the hall.

"Hey, sorry. Uh, did you see the flyer?" he asks.

"This one?" I pull it out of my purse and unfold it, handing it over to him. At the same time, he pulls one out of his pocket.

"Yeah, looks like we both found one. Are you going to go see her?" Howie asks.

"Yes, but I don't think Sam wants me to. He doesn't think I need to change anything." I give Howie a look that I hope conveys my feelings on the situation.

"Ari and I will go with you. Sam will be okay. When we see the shop, you can just explain it to him, and if he's worried, he won't need to be because I'll make sure you're safe."

I start toward the bedroom door but stop. "Wait. Why do you want to go?" I eye him suspiciously. I won't let him get cursed by her. I refuse to allow this to happen to anyone else.

"I'm not . . . Jesus, the look on your face. I'm not asking her to help me with anything. Ari and I just don't want you to go alone," Howie declares.

"Okay, no, you're right. Thanks for offering to go with me." I smile softly at him. Howard is a good friend, maybe one of the best I've ever had. I am so thankful I met him and that I can trust him and Ari with this.

I nod my agreement slowly then walk past him, joining Sam and Ariella by the front door. We head out, a pit of dread filling my stomach as I flip off the lights and lock the door behind me. I know in my soul that tonight is going to change everything. I want this thing gone, but I'm afraid that it'll cost me Sam, that it'll cost me everything.

The four of us crunch leaves with each step we take toward Mage Hollow. I've avoided smashing them for the entire time I've lived here, but something about today feels like I have permission to break things. The irony isn't lost on me.

"You okay?" Sam asks as he threads his fingers through mine.

"Yeah, I'm good. You?" I don't look at him as I ask.

"You're going to be shocked by the number of people. It's double the amount that come for Hollow Hearts." Sam is digging, desperate to make a conversation, and I wonder if he can tell my mood has shifted. He can't see my arm, but does he know I'm feeling pensive anyway?

We round the corner into Mage, and I notice instantly that he wasn't kidding. There are swarms of people in costumes trailing up and down the street, weaving in and out of shops. There must be thousands of ghosts, goblins, and witches all ready to celebrate the holiday. The energy is magnetic, but how many of these unsuspecting strangers will wake up tomorrow with a curse they didn't know they were asking for? I guess that's not fair—I did know, but I didn't know all it would entail.

We move among the people, careful not to lose anyone in our group as we work to enter Union Tavern. The plan was always to grab some food before enjoying the real party, but the odds of getting a table look slim to none based on the number of people standing in the entryway.

"Howard, can you pull some strings, or is this a lost cause?" Ari asks, batting her ridiculously long fake eyelashes at him.

"Probably not. My uncle wasn't thrilled that I wanted the night off. I doubt he's going to do me any favors," Howie retorts, looking at his shoes in what I suspect is guilt.

"I have some food at Eerie. I thought maybe this would happen so I grabbed some subs and threw them in the fridge just in case." Sam motions for us to follow him back out into the masses.

We weave through the crowd once more, taking triple the normal amount of time to walk the block to his business. Sam's hand never leaves mine and it brings me a sense of calm. A peace in my soul that I know he doesn't want anything to happen to me. I feel nauseous. The guilt at what I know I'm going to do eats at me.

We push into the tattoo shop, and Sam quickly locks the door behind us before approaching his fridge and pulling out four carefully prepared hoagies.

"Where did you buy these?" Ari asks, looking over the Saran Wrap packaging suspiciously.

"I didn't say I bought them, I picked them up from Mabel." Sam smiles, a deep but semi-guilty grin. It's kind of adorable how close he is with his mom. I mentally add that to the list of reasons why hurting him, which I know is inevitable, is going to be even harder than I could imagine.

"Your mom is the best. I might have to start dating Max just so I can get the food hookup," Ari says as Howie's face turns three shades of green.

Poor Howie. I nudge him with my foot and shake my head to let him know she's full of shit. I want to throttle her. She has a perfect guy right in front of her and she doesn't even see it. Meanwhile, I'm over here trying to determine if mine is really into me or if he's just with me because I have the ultimate cheat code etched on my skin. I'm going to have a very stern conversation with her the minute we are alone.

"Anyway, what do you want to do when we're done here?" Sam asks, his mouth half full of his Italian sub.

"I thought the idea was to mingle? Out there." I point at the hoard of people on the other side of the large glass windows.

"I mean, yeah, it is. But there's also a bunch of house parties, the shops run specials, I wasn't sure what the plan was." Sam takes another bite of his sandwich and chews thoughtfully.

"I usually like to walk around, people watch a little. And then typically I go to the hockey party. But we can do whatever. Shopping isn't great due to the lines," Ari explains.

"I'm good with anything," I say. Howie nods in agreement, but I don't miss the meaningful look he shoots in my direction.

Ten minutes later, we clean up from our meal and head back out into the crowd. We make it a short ten steps before Sam's parents and sisters stop us to chat. Then, we follow Howie and Ariella over to talk with Tony. In no time, an hour has passed with light conversation and several barbs about our matching costumes. The sun dips below the horizon, and with each second, my existential dread thickens like a swarm of bees in my belly just waiting to consume me.

Howie suggests we walk to the end of the square. I know where he's headed, but Ariella and Sam don't seem to pick up on it. It isn't until we are approaching the small brick building that sits on the outer edge of the square that Sam realizes where we are going. There's an unmistakable purple neon sign glowing with the word *tarot*, and it flashes at the same inconsistent pace as the first time I saw it.

"No, no, no, no. We're not—you're not actually doing this, are you? The last time you ended up in the emergency room. I'm not going to stand by and watch it happen again," Sam says, stopping and turning to face me. His face looks determined in the dim glow of the streetlamps.

"Sam, I . . . I have to." He barely listens to my reply. Instead, he looks at Howie and Ariella and quickly tells them to wait there as he pulls me away and around to the side of the building. Over my shoulder, I share a look with Ariella, begging her with my eyes to wait where she is. She nods, a sullen look plastered on her face.

"Sorry, I just need to talk to you. Alone," Sam says, meaningfully.

"I know, but you have to understand, I have to do this." I wrap my hands around my belly, the cool air nipping at my skin through the paper-thin fabric of my shirt.

"Why?" Sam takes a step back and crosses his arms.

"Because it's not me, it's too vulnerable. Everyone can see too much of my thoughts and feelings. I can't be this person anymore." My voice cracks at the explanation and tears threaten to leak from my eyes. I look up at the stars that are beginning to pattern the night sky. I wish I didn't have to do this.

"That's bullshit. You act like you've changed so much as a result of this thing, but really, you haven't shared any more with me than you've wanted to. There's still so much I don't know, so I guess I just don't understand why you believe that this thing has really made that big of a difference." Sam wilts, I can see his frustration. It's time to fess up.

"Sam, you're wrong. I know you think that I haven't shared a lot, but I have opened up more to you than I've ever opened up to anyone. In the past, I never went on more than three dates with someone because I didn't want anyone to see the real me. I've never told anyone about my parents or how they treat me. I've never let anyone get close to my friends. You don't see it because to you, I-I look normal right now, but this is not me. This is the version of me that has no choice but to tell you things because you can see it, every day you can see it," I explain.

"I don't believe you. I'm sorry, but this is just an excuse. You're running away because you're scared and nothing more. We went on dates, you told me things before I ever even knew about the tattoo." Sam reaches out to pull me into a hug, but I stop him by putting a hand on his chest and pushing him gently away.

"Sam, I told you that I want to fall in love with you, and I meant it. You are everything I've ever wanted, *everything* I've dreamed of having . . . But if I don't do this, if I keep this curse, I will never know if what we have is real. I'll never know if you're really this wonderful, or if you're just able to do and say the right things all the time because you have my personal guidebook painted across my arm."

"I haven't, I would never use it like that," Sam denies, shaking his head.

"You have. If you're honest with yourself, you have used it time and time again. To see what I like in bed, to see if I'm okay or comfortable. I've watched you do it, and the reality is that I can't even blame you. I'd probably do the same. But wouldn't it bother you to be with me and never know if it was the real me or the version that Irina created of me? Wouldn't you question if I was telling you things because I genuinely wanted to instead of feeling like I had to?" The wind picks up around us, blowing leaves around our feet and causing me to shiver.

"No, I honestly wouldn't. I know the real you, Olivia Bowman. I know you better than I know myself. I'm in love with you." His voice is threaded with anger as he crosses and uncrosses his arms and starts to pace the alley we are standing in.

"You're not in love with the real me. You're in love with a version of me who's open, exposed, and frankly, too vulnerable. Ask anyone who knows me well, this is not me. I care for you, and I hate that I'm hurting you, but it wouldn't be fair to keep this curse and live out our lives together never knowing if what we had was real. I won't keep you just because I want to when it isn't fair to you. I care for you too much to make you live a lie."

I can see the resignation as it blooms on his face. He isn't going to keep fighting me on it. He can't win this, and I can tell he knows it. But that doesn't make it any easier. Sam steps forward and pulls me into a hug, I sink into him, letting the cedar-cinnamon scent of him waft into me like a soothing balm. I nuzzle into his chest for a few minutes, willing myself not to cry, reminding myself this is my decision, before he pulls back and presses a soft kiss to my forehead.

"If this isn't the real you, then tell me who you are? Tell me what is true . . . Because from where I'm standing, I can't imagine everything we've shared being a lie." Sam's voice cracks.

"It wasn't a lie—"

"If it wasn't a lie," Sam interrupts, "then what's the big deal? So you try to please your mother, you put yourself in a little box to make her happy. That doesn't mean that this version of yourself isn't real. I'd argue this is the more accurate version, the Olive I know who's strong and smart and funny and beautiful. Just choose her, choose the version of yourself that belongs with me. For fuck's sake, Olive . . . pick me!" he shouts, tears streaming down his face in a mirror image to my own.

"I can't," I say. My voice is barely audible. Maybe he's right, maybe I can be brave and vulnerable, maybe I am strong enough to stand up to my mother and to embrace my flaws. But maybe it's all fake, maybe I only feel this way because of the tattoo, because I can visualize my feelings and make sense of them. And how will I ever know if I don't remove it?

"I will love you for the rest of my life and the one beyond this existence. I will love you with every breath and fiber of my being, every version of you, in every lifetime. You can't take that away from me. But I know now that I can't make you love me back," Sam says, no louder than a whisper. He wipes his red-rimmed eyes on the sleeve of his suit jacket briefly before glancing at me one last time and walking away.

As I watch him leave, a scream that sounds like it's from a wounded animal rips out of me. I crumple to the cobblestones in agony. I think I just made a huge mistake, but I didn't have a choice. I'm so frustrated that I didn't have a choice. Irina left me no choice. Ari and Howie rush over to me quickly. Ari sinks to the ground, wrapping an arm around my shoulders, whispering, "everything is going to be okay, Ollie."

Thirty

Sam

The Breakup Bender

Sometimes walking away is the hardest thing to do, especially when every bone in your body is screaming not to. I couldn't stay, she didn't want me to stay. And I refuse to stand idly by and watch her repeat the same mistakes she already made. I guess the argument could be made that I helped her look for Irina, that I went to the cottage. But this is different—Olive knew she was there tonight, that seeing her would decide a fate that I believe was already determined.

The thing is, while I enjoyed watching her arm paint her feelings into a vivid picture, it wasn't ever something I truly used to my benefit. Looking back on it, outside of sex, I often didn't even think about her tattoo being there. Also, as the oldest child, does she not think I've had my own pressures to be perfect throughout the years? My own set of expectations to deal with? I understand that Olive has parents who never told her she was valuable, never loved her unconditionally. But isn't that the exact same way she treated me in the end . . . like being with me had stipulations?

I take the steps up to my house, my gut churning with each one. I don't want to be here, to step inside and confront memories of the time we shared in this place. But I also can't remain as Johnny Rose forever. I have to manage my way through it. Turning my key in the lock, I push inside with one singular focus—grab a bag, a few changes of clothes, and get the fuck out.

Hustling through the house, I slide on a pair of black denim jeans, a T-shirt, my leather jacket, and some boots. Grabbing a few extra outfits, I snag my helmet from the hook by the door and race back out. Olive and I only spent one night here, but I can feel her everywhere. Until I'm ready to move on, I'm avoiding this place. Call it denial, but I know it'll take a while for it to sink in that it's over between us.

I sling my clothes into the saddlebag of my Harley, tug my helmet on, and peel out of the driveway. My initial thought was to go to Xavier's, then I remembered that Cami probably isn't up for a wallowing house-guest. Going to Mom's isn't an option. She would demand every detail, and parts of this I can't explain to her. So, with nowhere exactly to land—my siblings would also turn me into Mom—I take the on-ramp heading toward Golden City. It's directly south and larger than Mage Hollow by at least ten times. I won't know anyone there.

I'm not much of a city guy; I prefer the solitude of my cabin (which would also remind me of her) and the tiny town I grew up in. But I've been to the city on occasion for hockey, and right now anything different sounds like exactly what I need to clear my head. It's not a far drive, just thirty miles of cool wind whipping in my face and the rumble of my bike's engine vibrating between my thighs. Plenty of time to burn off some of this nervous energy and lean into drinking my feelings.

Spotting a sports bar on the first blue exit sign for Golden City, I pull off the highway and follow the arrow pointing to the left. It's not hard to spot, with a big neon sign glowing Sports Bar in the window. There are several cars in the parking lot, always a good sign, so I proceed to park close to the door.

Pushing my kickstand out, I step off my bike and place my helmet on the seat. I take a deep breath, smoothing a hand down my face, realizing I forgot to remove the fucking eyebrows. Peeling them off and tossing them in the trash can by the door, I step inside. It's not fancy, which is perfect for what I need.

A brown-haired ball of energy blazes past me with a tray of food in her hand, saying, "Have a seat wherever," before continuing to a table full of people. Instead of choosing a booth, I do what I came to do and belly up to the wooden bar. A few minutes pass before the same woman slinks behind it, approaching me.

"Can I get you a menu, or what are you drinking?" She places her hands flat on the bar, leaning toward me, I think to take in my tattoos. Or maybe just me in general.

"Irish whiskey, neat. No food."

Her eyebrow pops up and I notice, objectively, how hot she is. With tattoos of her own, curves that could kill, and an adorable smile—if I wasn't in love with someone else, I'd probably ask her out. "Who hurt you, stranger?" she asks, shifting to put her balled up fist on her hip.

"How do you know anyone did?" I'm taken aback by the question. I must look awful for it to be this obvious. "I could just be here for a drink."

She moves to grab a rocks glass, pulling the green bottle from the shelf behind her and pouring two fingers. Instead of placing the drink down in front of me, she runs it under her nose, taking a minute to smell it.

"I've been doing this far too long. I know a broken heart when I see one." She finally sets the glass down and slides it to me. I can't help but grin at her. She's kind of funny with her sassy attitude.

"Why'd you smell my drink?" I lift it slowly, mimicking the move she did while savoring the smoky aroma.

She laughs, and it's half-hearted at best. "Because I can't drink on the job, and it felt like I might need to for this conversation." She nods toward the customers out at the tables. "I'll be back and then you're gonna tell me what happened."

I sip my drink, slowly at first, but once the smooth amber liquid hits my throat, I down the rest. There's a hockey game for the Golden City Flames playing on the TVs that hang above the bar. Shaking my head, I watch Drew Anderson float across the ice like he was made to do it. I hate to say anything about my brother that's less than stellar but watching Golden City's star on the ice—I don't know if Max will ever achieve his dream. I'm not sure he could keep up at that level, and my heart aches just thinking about his disappointment.

The bartender slides back in front of me, filling my glass and winking flirtatiously. A weird guilty sensation creeps into my belly. I should be with Olive right now, not sitting in a random bar. "So, what's the deal, she cheat on you?"

I huff a laugh. Honestly, that would be easier to explain. "Nope, just couldn't choose me at the end of the day," I say, swallowing hard, then tossing back the drink she gave me and tapping my finger to the rim for a refill. "What's your name? I feel like I should know who you are if I'm going to pour my heart out."

"Brooke, and what does that even mean? Did you give her an ultimatum or some shit?" The sassy woman refills my glass and waits for an answer. I guess I sort of did, but it's more complicated than that.

I shrug. "Maybe, fuck if I know . . . It all happened so fast. One minute we were celebrating Halloween, and the next she was accusing me of only being with her because it's easy." I know I'm making this situation sound a lot simpler than it is, but there's only so much I can say without bringing up the Irina thing.

Brooke sticks a finger in the air and says, "Hold that thought, table eight's food is ready." She rushes out from behind the bar, and I'm left with my thoughts. I meant what I said to Olive, that I'll love her for the rest of my life. At thirty-two, I've dated, I've seen what's out there, and what we have is special. I know with my whole heart she's my person—which makes it all that much worse that I'm not hers.

Shaking my head, I stand to go to the bathroom and realize the three drinks I've had are starting to hit me. I'm not wasted, but I can feel the warm buzz sinking into my veins. I handle my business quickly, but when I come back out, the brunette bartender is sitting in the barstool next to mine with a beer in front of her.

"Thought you couldn't drink while you're working," I say, sliding back into my seat. The jukebox is playing Bon Jovi, and she's swaying a little to the beat.

Brooke takes a sip of her beer, then leans back in her seat. "Just got off, and man, am I thankful."

"Tough night?" I raise an eyebrow at her. She seemed to be the only one running ragged around the place while the other servers stood idly.

"Yeah, my best friend was supposed to be working"—she takes another long sip of her lager—"but Alex is busy falling for a hot as fuck hockey coach and needed the night off for his game." She nods toward the TV where the coach of the Flames is giving a postgame interview.

"No way, Monte? She's dating Coach Montgomery?" I ask the questions a little too quickly, giving away what Bridget would refer to as the man crush I have on him. I can't help it, he's the best in the league.

Brooke scoffs then says, "Not you too. What the hell is wrong with everyone? I mean, the man has an ass, but it doesn't mean you *all* need to kiss it."

Her assessment makes me laugh, a roaring, belly-twisting bellow. This girl is a fucking trip. When I stop wheezing, I concede, "That sucks that you had to cover for her."

"Nah, I'd do it any day. She desperately needed to get laid. Speaking of that . . . tell me what exactly happened with the girl, and maybe your name so I don't keep thinking you're a stranger."

I take a deep breath. "My name is Sam. And, uh, basically I fell in love with her, but she questioned if it was real or not. I guess she couldn't trust what we had, she couldn't admit to loving me back, so I walked away."

"That blows." Brooke places her hand on my arm, pity marking her face. "She's an idiot. I mean . . . what kind of girl lets a guy that looks like you leave her bed?" It's not really a completely fair assessment, she doesn't know the whole story, but I'll give her a little credit. At least some women aren't afraid to hit on a man—that counts for something.

"Um, thanks, I think." I chuckle to myself, spotting the other bartender and holding my drink up for a refill. She tops it off while giving Brooke a disapproving scowl. "I don't think she likes you very much," I mumble to my new friend.

"That's just Birdie, she hates everyone, especially me. Last month she told our boss I was flirting too obviously with the customers and that the tips weren't fairly split because of it." She rolls her eyes and finishes her drink, sliding a ten across the bar. "Can I be held responsible for being friendly when her problem is more her grumpy attitude than anything else?"

I grin at her. I appreciate that she didn't call out that Birdie is twenty years her senior or that Brooke's own looks could factor into it at all. It tells me she's a decent person. She isn't mean-spirited, which is hard to find these days. Although she is far more direct and fierier than Olive, she reminds me of her in a way. She has kind eyes and—fuck—there I go thinking about Olive all over again.

I sip my drink before answering, "No, you shouldn't be. So, what advice do you have for me, Brooke the bartender, who's an expert on broken hearts?"

"Oh, not a single word, I'm the last person who should be giving dating advice. I always say if you can't get under the one you love, get on top of someone else." She takes the glass from my hand and swallows the remaining three quarters of it in one go. "But since you've been drinking those all night and are clearly still in love with this chick, I will for once practice self-restraint and refrain from volunteering."

I'm stunned by her response. I wouldn't have accepted the invitation, for the same reason she isn't offering. But I'm not sure what my drinking has to do with it. "I get the me being-in-love thing, and I am with Olive. I might need you to explain the other comment though, about my drinking, just so I know."

"Two words—whiskey dick." Brooke stands, smiling at me and patting my shoulder. "It was nice to meet you, Sam. You should probably call a ride share. Or there's a hotel two blocks from here. Take a left out of the lot. Can't miss it when you're walking." She heads toward the entrance but stops short. "Hey, Sam . . . maybe you should try to see where she's coming from. If someone gave me an ultimatum my first instinct would be to tell them to take the bridge. But after some time, some clarity, I might change my mind, and I'm thinking if this Olive is so special . . . she probably will too."

Thirty-One

Olive

You Son of a Witch

4 Hours Until Midnight

It doesn't take long for me to lose my shit on Irina. Howie, Ari, and me, are about two steps into the shop, nearly colliding with a young woman who looks suspiciously like Bridget's ex. With one hand, I brace myself on Howie, and with the other, I grab the woman's arm.

"Do not walk out of this building. Turn around and ask her to undo whatever it is that she's done. I know you think this is fun, I did too. But you will regret it," I warn.

The woman looks stricken, like I've slapped her. *Good.*

"Now, I don't need the theatrics, Olivia," Irina says, her voice reprimanding me. She flicks a wand and purple sparks flash through the air, spinning the stranger around three times before righting her. "I undid it. Now leave," she shouts at the woman—or maybe me?

The woman jolts past Howie, Ari, and me, pushing out the door and kicking it closed behind her. Irina walks gracefully to her chair and sits, waiting for me to say something it seems. Her cauldron bubbles suspiciously over the fire, black liquid spilling over the edge with a gurgle.

"I need you to undo this." I pull my sleeve up, showing her the tattoo that weaves around my arm. Her eyes sparkle at the sight of her work, further infuriating me.

"Are you sure that's what you want?" she asks, rolling her eyes like I'm nothing more than an inconvenience. Three chairs appear across from her, and she motions for us to sit. Ari bristles by my side, glancing between Howie and me, but we do as she commands and take our seats.

"I've never been more sure. Just do it," I shout at her. A shred of doubt creeps in momentarily. *Is this really what I want?*

"Well, I should warn you . . ." Irina starts to say, but Howie interrupts her.

"No! You don't get to warn her about anything. You're done playing mind games with her. We all know the truth. You might be able to make other people believe in your bullshit, but not me. Just change her back to normal, you—you son of a witch!"

Irina cackles loudly, a shrill, somewhat evil-sounding laugh that echoes in my brain. I want to leave, to never see her again. She's ruined everything for me, and she thinks it's all just a big game. Instead of doing anything, she just sits there, staring at us and cracking up.

"Irina, please. I can't live like this. I'm begging you," I plead. I could keep living with this thing, but nothing about my life would feel authentic. Maybe Sam was right in that I have the power to choose my fate. But if I keep it, I'll just be fitting myself into another little box, I'll be open with my emotions and choices because I have to be, not because I truly want to.

Suddenly Irina stops laughing, stiffly sitting in her chair and eyeing me suspiciously. It feels like minutes pass as we wait in this silent standoff, but finally, she speaks. "Okay, Olivia. I'll change you back. But don't pretend you don't love him. Don't pretend that any of this emotional turmoil is my fault. All I did was help you even when I shouldn't have." She flicks her wrist, and the cauldron bounces and shakes, the roaring fire underneath racing up the sides in shades of blue and green while colorful liquid churns within, splashing to the floor.

Is she serious? This entire thing is her fault. If I'd never met her, then I wouldn't be in this situation to begin with. I would have continued living my peaceful, albeit somewhat lonely, life. I never would have been given a glimpse of what love could look like. But she meddled. She demanded I tell her my story, my problems.

"Irina, don't act innocent. You knew things about me before we ever spoke. You plucked me out of a crowd of hundreds of people and decided that I would be your next victim. You saw my pain and thought it was funny to mess with me. Well guess what, I tasted the sun. I saw what love looks like, and you ripped it away. I will never be the same, and that's your fault—but I won't mess with other people like you do, to make myself feel better. I can choose my own fate, I can be whoever the hell I want to be." I stand abruptly, walking as fast as I can to the cauldron to ladle my own cup of magical tea. I sip it down in one long glug before turning to look back at my friends and Irina.

Howie smiles at me with a pride in his expression that I can only assume is the result of me standing up for myself. Ari shouts a "Hell yeah!" and promptly grabs onto Howie as a rat scurries across the room. Irina, on the other hand, looks sad. There are tears in her eyes, threatening to fall at any second. For a brief moment, I feel bad, like maybe I took it too far.

"Olivia, before you leave, let me share something with you," Irina pleads.

"No, we've heard enough out of you," Ari says, wrapping an arm around me and steering me toward the door.

I reach for the handle when we get close, but the lock clicks into place. My breath catches in my throat. *This is it, this is how I die.* Howie comes up behind Ari and me, hugging us both. His hands are shaking, and I can tell he's actually scared. At least I'm not alone.

"I have to tell you this, before you go." Irina's hand clasps my arm. There's a tenderness to her touch. "I know you don't believe me when I say I wanted to help, and honestly, I wasn't going to. Not until my sister encouraged me. The thing is, I was a lot like you when I was younger. I never wanted to open my heart because if I did, it meant I was giving someone the power to break it. I understand you more than you think. By not opening up, though, not being vulnerable after I got burned by love, I cast myself into a pit of despair and a life of loneliness. The point of your tattoo was to help you understand that it's okay to be vulnerable with the right person. You found your person, Olivia. I didn't have anything to do with that, and what the two of you shared was real." Irina lets go of my arm, and I notice the tattoo fizzling away. In an instant, my skin is back to normal, as if the tattoo was never there, and my heart shatters into a million pieces.

"Ollie, Ollie, where are you?" Ari shouts.

"Urghhh," I groan, shoving a pillow over my face and pulling the covers up over my head. Maybe if I hide, she won't know I'm here.

"Ollie, come on. You need to get out of this bed." Ari pulls the comforter off and flings it to the floor before plopping down beside me.

"I can't. I don't know how," I mumble, tears once again slipping down my cheeks. I've cried so much in the last six days, I'm not even sure how I have any fluids left in me.

"Come on, Ollie. Talk to me, I still don't know what happened with Sam. I can't help you if I don't know, and I can't bear to see you like this any longer." Ari lies down beside me and wraps me in a tight hug. It feels good to be wrapped in someone's arms, even if it's not Sam's. At least for a moment I'm not alone.

"I walked away, I can't believe I walked away. I didn't have a choice, but it hurts so bad," I choke out, sobbing into my pillow.

"Did you love him?" She squeezes me a little harder when she asks.

"Yes, and I still do. But I never told him that. I just, you know, I'm not good at this type of thing. How was I supposed to know that what we had was real when everything was clouded by the curse, by wearing my heart on my sleeve?"

"What did he say when you told him that you couldn't do it, that you had to get the curse to end?" Ari asks, brushing hair off my forehead tenderly and wiping my tears.

"That's the worst part, he looked so sad. He asked me to choose him, to choose myself. And then when I said no, he told me he would love me forever, that he'd love me even in his next life. He was all in, and I threw him away. I let my stupid fear cloud what we had, but I did the right thing. If I didn't get Irina to remove the tattoo, I never would've known it was true love. He will never forgive me."

"Ollie, of course he will. That man loves you beyond measure, beyond reason. I can't believe that there's a world in which he would turn you away if you told him you made a mistake."

"That's the problem. As much as I'm hurting, it wasn't a mistake. I'm glad I don't have to see everything I feel painted across my arm. I'm relieved I don't have to reveal anything I don't want to anymore. And even if he took me back, the real me is not the girl that he fell in love with. The real me sticks to her three-date rule and routinely disappoints everyone." I slough Ari off, standing to walk to the bathroom.

"Can you shower while you're in there? You stink!" Ari shouts as I leave the room. Nothing like a bestie to call you on your bullshit.

I use the bathroom and take a minute to look in the mirror. My hair is a rat's nest, my eyes are permanently puffy from crying, and I hate to admit it, but I do stink, badly. I move to the shower and turn on the spray. Once it's warm, I step in and let the water wash over my skin. Closing my eyes for a second, it feels nice, like a cozy blanket wrapped around me. But when I open them to grab the shampoo, a fresh blast of salt goes straight into my heart when I see Sam's bodywash sitting on the ledge.

Instead of washing quickly, I sit down and clutch the bottle to my chest. The scent of it wafts in my nose and tears pour from my eyes. How will I ever get over him? How will I ever do anything again without having him to call or text or talk to? Is this what I deserve, to be lonely and miserable?

Ari pounds on the bathroom door.

"Ollie, hurry up and get out here or I'm going to call Anne," she threatens.

I stumble to my feet, turn off the spray, and wrap myself in a towel. I don't think she'd actually do it, but if there's even a small chance she'd involve my mother, I have to put a stop to it. The woman has been relentlessly trying to reach me for weeks, and a call from Ariella is not the way I'd like to reconnect. I pull the door open quickly, and Ari doubles over in laughter.

"So, this is funny? My heartbreak amuses you?" I sneer at her.

"No, but I knew that would work. Get back in there and use soap this time, but hurry up. I have big things to discuss with you and Chinese food to eat while I do it." She snaps her fingers at me, and it's clear she means business.

I shouldn't do it, but I use his soap. I love the scent, and if I can't have him, at least I can have this. Finishing quickly, I get dressed in a pair of sweats and wrap my wet hair in a towel before meeting Ari on my couch. She has a carton of lo mein waiting for me. I dive in as soon as she hands it to me.

"I think you're wrong," Ari says around a bite of Mongolian beef.

"Wrong about what?"

"I think he did know the real you, I think we all do."

"You do, but no one else does," I counter.

"That's a lie. A story you've told yourself to avoid being scared. I can prove it." She picks up her phone and hits call, placing it on speaker and setting it on the table.

"Hello?" Howie's voice rings out, making my heart melt. He's a great friend. After we left Irina's, he brought me home and stayed with me for the first two days, trading off with Ariella when he had to work. He's come by to check on me since, but I've not been answering the door.

"Howard, I'm with Ollie. You're on speaker, and I need you to confirm something for me. When did she tell you the first time about her parents being assholes?"

"Um, I think it was within five minutes of actually talking to me. It was the first day you came in for lunch, Ollie. Before I even knew you were friends with Ariella, before you even knew my name."

"See, Ollie, you told Howie something deeply personal before you even met Irina. Okay, Howie, that day you hung out with Sam for drinks when her parents were in town, did Sam say anything about them?" Ari asks.

"I don't remember exactly, but he did seem to know about them. I think he mentioned being worried about how hard Ollie's mother is on her," Howie says.

"You hadn't shown him that tattoo at that point," she tells me. "You told him about Anne because you wanted to, not because you had to."

"Okay, I hear what you both are saying, but that doesn't mean that when he sees the parts I haven't shown him that he won't run the other direction. What's he going to do the first time I have a meltdown prepping to see my parents or when I work long hours because I can't stand the thought of disappointing a customer," I retort, sipping my Diet Coke.

"Olive, there's no guarantee he will stay, you're right. But there's also no guarantee that he won't. Sam is a good man, and you are an amazing woman. Sometimes we have to risk it all, and I know you know how to be brave. I've seen you forget fear and take back your power. You did it when you faced Irina like a badass," Howie explains. I wish he was here, I love that guy so much.

"I just, I don't know. Hey, can we finally talk about what Howie called Irina when we were there?" I ask, trying to lighten the mood.

Howie's groan trickles through the phone as Ari, laughing hysterically, says, "He called her a son of a witch." Howie and I laugh right along with her. I have tears streaming down my face, and Howie is wheezing.

I'm so thankful I have Ari and Howie in my life. It doesn't take away the ache from losing Sam, but it does help it sting a little less.

"Okay, Howard. Thank you for helping me prove a point. We are going to go drink our sorrows with a few bottles of wine now," Ari coos.

We say our goodbyes and she hangs up the phone. I move to take the Chinese leftovers to the kitchen and grab a bottle of wine. Plopping back down on the sofa, Ari eyes me.

"So, the real problem here isn't you, and it isn't Sam. It's your mother," Ari says, matter-of-factly.

"My mother?"

"Yes. You are scared to open up because she has torn you down for years. You've never met her expectations, and that pain is bleeding into your relationships."

"Not our relationship," I deny.

"Yes. Even ours. How many times have you called me to apologize for shit that I didn't even think twice about? How many times have I had to convince you of how others see you or that you're a good person? I mean, for fuck's sake, you were worried I was going to tell her I caught you slouching in your perfect lipstick shade before the festival." Ari grabs the wine and takes a long pull. "I want to tell you to go get your man, but I can't do that until you deal with Anne. That man loves you, and he will take you back, but when he does, you have to be all in."

I wonder how long she's been sitting on that. How long has she wanted to tell me to confront my mother? She's not wrong. I know deep down it's the scars from my childhood that leak onto everything else. But I also feel ungrateful saying that. I never went without as a kid, I lived a privileged life.

"I'll try to talk to her."

"Good, I can be here if you need me."

"No, I think I have to do it alone," I say, taking another sip of wine.

"I'm proud of you. Now, should we watch *Top Chef* or *Barbecue Showdown*?" Ari asks, flipping on the TV while burrowing up next to me and pulling a blanket over us.

This is why she's my best friend. She knows exactly what I need and when I need it.

Thirty-Two

Sam

Three Beers Deep

"I understand, I'm sorry, Terry. I'll see you next week," I say weakly into my phone before laying my head down on my desk.

He was going to come in for a few minor touch-ups from the work we recently did together. But my heart isn't in it. To be completely frank, I haven't tattooed a single piece I've cared about this week. I should care about all of them, but the little flash art that walk-ins pick off the wall is all I've been able to muster since Halloween.

I'm still confused and hurt. It didn't feel like a breakup. I've survived enough of those. Things with Olive were different, and this hurts more because of that. Like a limb was amputated from my body, and now, I have to learn to walk around without it forever. It sounds crazy—how could I love someone this deeply so quickly? Somehow, I did.

And that's not even the worst part of the whole thing, living without her. It's by far more painful that she believes I don't know her, that I was taking advantage of her curse to be a perfect boyfriend, not that I'm just a good and caring person. I realize that she has been through a lot, but does she not get how fucked up that is? She basically accused me of being fake, a showboat, a master manipulator. If I didn't care about her so much, I'd be pissed enough to last a lifetime. It was that first night—running off to Golden City, chatting with the bartender—that helped me gain a little perspective. But when I got back to Mage the next morning and a whole other day passed that Olive didn't come try to talk to me, I think that's when I finally realized it's over for her.

Shaking myself from my depressing thoughts, I stand and stretch for a moment before locking the front door and flicking off the open sign. I walk to the back, grab a six-pack from the fridge, and spread out in the recliner I have in the break room. When I installed the TV and placed this cozy blue leather chair in the corner, I imagined this room would be used on the days where I had long appointments with gaps in between. I envisioned it being a relaxing space, not my new living situation as it's become this week.

Someone pounds on the front door.

I check my watch: It's a quarter till eight, and while the sign says I close at eight, there isn't enough time to squeeze someone else in. That's a lie, I have worked way past closing, but I'm not going to when I feel like this. I've never felt like this before, completely alone, lost.

The knock echoes through the space again as my phone rings and my brother's face lights up the display.

"Max?"

"Open the door, asshole," my brother spits out.

Shit! He sounds pissed. I hop up and sprint to the front to let him in.

"Where the fuck were you?" he shouts, shoving past me and into my shop.

"I've been here. Where was I supposed to be?" I ask, taking a second to recognize his freshly showered appearance and team gear.

Fuck! It was his opening game. The realization that I missed it makes me feel even worse than I was already feeling. I've never missed one before.

"My game, you know the season home opener, the one I got a hat trick in? Why didn't you come?" Max's head hangs. He's disappointed in me, I can tell.

"Max, I wish I had an excuse. I forgot, and I'm so sorry. It won't happen again."

"How?"

"How did I forget?"

"Yeah, because I told Olive about it, and she wrote everything down. How did you both manage to forget? Neither of you showed." I'm relieved he didn't say she came, that would have hurt even worse, I think.

"Uh, well . . ." I run a hand through my hair and think of how to break the news. "We broke up. I haven't talked to her since last weekend."

Max doesn't say anything, he just walks toward the back and grabs a beer from the pack sitting next to the recliner before taking a chair and sliding it into the break room.

"Have a seat. Tell me everything," he says, gesturing for me to take my place in my comfy chair. His anger over me missing his big night seems all but forgotten.

"This is going to sound nuts, and you can't tell Mom. You can't tell anyone, ever," I warn him.

"Okay? Go on."

"Olive was cursed by Irina—you know, the famous witch—during the Hollow Hearts Festival. It sounds insane, but she cursed her to wear her heart on her sleeve in the form of a tattoo." Max is looking at me like I need to be committed, but I continue anyway. "I didn't believe it when she first told me, but then she showed me. The tattoo changed with every emotion or thought she had. It was wild. But Olive hated it. She searched and searched for Irina to get rid of it, which honestly, I still don't understand. On Halloween, she saw Irina's shop appear again, and when I tried to stop her from going in, she ended things."

"Why did you try to stop her?" Max asks.

"Because the last time she got close to Irina, Olive ended up in the emergency room. And because I didn't really think it was a big deal. I mean, I have tons of tattoos, and no one that cares about me ever pays attention to them. She acted like the tattoo made her too vulnerable, but really it was covered most of the time."

"So, she dumped you because you didn't want her to remove it? Help me out, I'm a little confused."

"No, she dumped me because she said I didn't know the real her. She said the real her isn't vulnerable and the only reason I loved her is because I had the cheat code for making her happy. Olive said if we stayed together, she would never know if what we had was real. I would never know if she was opening up to me because she wanted to or if it was because she had to," I explain, a long sigh leaking out of me as I finish.

"You know that's bullshit, right?" my brother asks, taking a pull of his beer.

"I mean, yeah, of course it is. But that's what she believes. Olive thinks I'm manipulative to the point that I would use this thing that made her vulnerable to my advantage."

"I don't think she actually believes that. It sounds like she was scared. I mean, who wouldn't be? If that happened to me, I'd freak the fuck out."

"That's what she said. She made it seem like she never would have fallen for me without Irina's interference. And do you know what the worst part of the whole thing is? I wouldn't have done a single thing different, even if she never had the tattoo. I fell in love with her, and I tried my best to show her that, but it wasn't enough."

"Sammy, you were enough, you still are. I know it doesn't feel like it right now, but she's going to come around. She was in love with you, too, I could see it," Max reassures me.

"Nah, I don't think so. She went to see the witch, and I haven't heard a word from her since. I've walked past her house a few times this week, and it never looks like anyone's home. Beau said she took an extended leave. I think she's g-gone . . ." I choke out the last word, tears beginning to streak down my face.

"Nope, let's go. Get up, we're going to Union. You aren't sitting here and wallowing." Max stands, snapping his fingers at me.

"I can't, what if she's there? What if she's with someone else? I can't even go home," I admit, covering my face with my hands.

"What do you mean you can't go home?" Max demands.

"Too many memories. I've been sleeping here."

"Get the hell up, right now!" Max shouts. "You have two choices: You can go with me to Union, or I can call Mom."

"Fine." I stand and chug the remainder of my beer before grabbing a second and sucking that one down as well.

We head out into the back alley, and the cool November air bites at my skin. I tighten my jacket and wipe away any signs that I've been crying. Max leads the way for a few steps before I muster my courage and catch up, syncing our strides.

"Okay, if she happens to be in there, which she won't be, I will make some sort of distraction so you can duck out and go back to hiding at the shop," Max rattles out, strategizing how we can handle this without causing me further emotional damage.

I appreciate the effort he's making, even if I don't feel like drinking with a crowd. Max is a great brother, always there to pick up the pieces when one of us needs him to, not that I've ever needed it before now. I guess I've taken care of him enough over the years that we are finally evening the score.

Max clutches the handle and opens the door into Union. For a Friday night, it's remarkably slow. We walk to the far end of the bar and slide onto two worn black stools. Howie is working. I notice the pity in his eyes as he looks in our direction and holds up a finger to tell us it'll be a second.

"Do you think he knows anything?" Max asks, pointing toward Howie.

"Yeah, he knows. I think he went with her to see Irina," I say, groaning a little. Howie is the other person I didn't want to run into. I'm embarrassed about how everything went down, that at the end of the day she didn't pick me.

Howie approaches, slinging a bar towel down in front of us before leaning in and placing his forearms on the bar. "Sam, Max, what can I get you guys?" he asks.

"A pitcher of beer. I need this one to be at least three beers deep before I take him home." Max pats my shoulder before giving it a gentle squeeze.

Howie nods and moves to grab the pitcher, filling it with ice-cold beer before returning to set it in front of us. He reaches into the cooler below the bar and pulls out two frosted glasses. Max wastes no time pouring, and I begin with a long gulp of the cool skunky liquid before looking Howie in the eyes.

"Have you talked to her?" I ask, knowing I shouldn't.

"About fifteen minutes ago," he replies, that same pitiful look bubbling on his face again.

"Well, at least I know she's alive and well." I chug almost my entire glass of beer.

"She's alive, but I wouldn't say she's well," Howie says before turning to help a new customer at the other end of the bar.

"What the hell does he mean, she's not well?" I ask, looking at my brother.

"She's probably heartbroken," Max replies, drinking down his own glass and refilling both of ours.

"She's not heartbroken, she dumped me."

"Doesn't mean she didn't break her own heart in the process. Don't be an asshole. She loved you, no doubt in my mind," Max retorts.

"She definitely loves you," Howie says, placing a hand on my shoulder as he walks past me into the back.

Max and I each drink down two more glasses in silence. He pretends he's watching whatever basketball game is on the TV overhead, and I internally spin out. Why do they both insist Olive's in love with me when she made it very clear she isn't? She acted like we didn't know each other at all. She hasn't reached out since Halloween, and frankly, the more I think about everything, the angrier I get.

I'm not manipulative. I would never use her or do something to hurt her. She made it seem like I was a dumbass bad boy who only treated her kindly because I had something to gain. Never mind all the times I went above and beyond to make things special for her, or the times I was patient when I knew she was holding back.

"Do you want another pitcher or food?" Howie asks as he approaches.

"I want to know what you know. Why did she do it? What happened when she saw Irina? Does she honestly believe I manipulated things with her?" I rattle off a slew of questions.

"Let's go out back." Howie gives me a stern look, like I should know better than to talk about this so openly.

Max and I follow him outside despite the protest in my belly. I don't want to hide anymore. I hate secrets and lying. I don't want to go into a back alley and whisper. But Howie pushes open the rear door and we file out, standing in the cool dark space.

"Look, Sam. Olive is my friend, one of my closest friends. I want to help you, but I need you to know that while I appreciate how close you and I have gotten, I'm on her side if I need to be." He shifts nervously.

"Howard, answer his fucking questions. He deserves to know," Max says, a murderous look on his face.

"Okay, but Olive needs to explain most of the details. I'll give you the basics . . ." I nod and signal for him to continue.

"Olive grew up never feeling adequate, made to believe she wasn't good enough. Those feelings have made it really hard for her to open up to people, and she doesn't believe she's capable of it. I don't think any of this has anything to do with you, though, and I know she's in love with you."

"No, she's not. So what happened with Irina?" I ask, sloughing off his assessment.

"She is, if she wasn't she wouldn't have spent the last week in bed crying. I've been the one there, wiping her tears and making sure she eats. If you want to continue this conversation, we are going to get one thing straight. You are not going to tell me how she feels or what she's going through. I slept on her bedroom floor for two days straight just to make sure she was safe, so I knew she wasn't alone," Howie warns.

My heart plummets into my stomach. I want to be the one to soothe her, to be there for her. I nod for him to continue, committing with a simple move of my head that I won't assume what she's going through.

"When we saw Irina, Olive was so brave. She demanded what she wanted and stood up for herself. Irina confirmed that she didn't play a part in your relationship with Olive. But the bottom line is that Olive needs to confront her insecurities on her own. I know there will come a day where she comes to you. The thing you need to ask yourself is if she's worth the wait, if she's worth dealing with all of this. She doesn't think you will wait for her, doesn't believe you would want to."

I'm speechless. I told Olive I would wait for her forever, that I'd love her in this lifetime and the next. I wish she'd believed me.

My phone beeps inside my pocket, capturing my attention. I grab it and read the message from Xavier.

Xav

It's Baby Time!

Fuck! Not that I expected my best friend's pregnant wife to schedule her birth around my breakup, but I don't know if I can deal with this right now. I haven't even been home in a week. What good will I have to offer my friend in my current state? Remembering how close we are and that being there isn't optional, I send a quick reply.

On my way!

"Thanks, Howie. I, uh, I gotta go," I say, flashing the screen at Max.

Howie nods at us and heads back inside as Max and I sprint back toward Eerie. My best friend is having a baby. There's nothing else in the world that matters right now.

Thirty-Three

Olive

Two Moms Make It Right

"Momma, can we talk?" I blurt out when my mother answers her phone after the third time I've called. She's been trying to get ahold of me for weeks and then when I finally call, no answer until it's clearly emergent.

"Olivia? Why are you calling me so early? Are you okay?" she asks.

I glance at the time and realize she probably wasn't expecting a call at seven in the morning on a Saturday. I don't feel guilty though; I've never called her like this. One time is the least she owes me.

"I'm fine," I choke out, my voice shaking with nerves.

"You most certainly are not fine. What's going on?" My mother has been activated. I can hear it in her voice that she's ready to battle with whatever has upset me. It's ironic really—she upsets me more than any-one, but she's also fiercely protective.

"I, uh, I don't know how to say this, but I think I'm in love." I rip off the Band-Aid quickly, fully expecting her to react with rage or disappointment.

"You are?" I can hear her take a deep breath. I'm just waiting for her to tell me how disappointed she is. "That's great, hunny," she says instead, her voice carrying an air of relief through the line.

"What?" I ask, stunned by her reaction.

"That's great. I'm happy for you. I've been trying to call you, to talk about—"

"I know, but I thought it was to yell at me, and I just couldn't, Momma. You're not angry? It's not with Theodore," I explain.

"Olivia, I have spent the past few weeks since you kicked me out thinking. I owe you an apology. I have spent most of my life trying to keep up with expectations. Your Nana never approved of me, and I think I spent so much time trying to be perfect for her, I lost sight of reality. I pushed you so hard because I thought if she saw any flaws, she'd insist we weren't good enough for your father."

"Momma, why would you not be good enough?"

"I am good enough, I just didn't see that for a long time. When I met your father, I was a poor waitress working long hours to put myself through college. I didn't have anything to my name, and I think Nana wanted him to pick someone who was more like he was," she explains.

"But you made me feel like a failure for so many years, like nothing I did was good enough. And you have literally been trying to pick my husband for years. I hurt someone I love because I was scared of never being enough for him." The words catch in my throat as I say them. I'm glad my mom is taking responsibility for her past actions, but that doesn't help my current situation.

"Olivia, I'm sorry. I know I hurt you over the years, I know I was hard to love, but you have never been anything but perfect. I think honestly, hunny, I was jealous of you. You're smart, kind, and funny. I wanted to be like you and when I couldn't, it made me mad. I don't expect you to forgive me, but if I learned anything the day you kicked me out, it's that walking away instead of fighting for the people you love is never the answer. If you love this man, you need to fight for him. You deserve to be happy, princess."

"Thanks, Momma," I say, almost a whisper.

I can't believe she's admitting all of this, that she's actually apologizing. I feel like I'm in the twilight zone or something. I've spent my whole life under her thumb, letting her dictate my decisions and how I felt about myself. I walked away from Sam because I couldn't stand the thought of being vulnerable with him, of having my heart displayed on my sleeve just to be picked apart.

"Tell me about this man. I need to know who he is and what he's like," my mom says. I can tell she's hesitant, but why wouldn't she be. Things have not been great in our relationship, and we've never been the type to over share. She has zero information on Sam, but there's more I need to know before I tell her.

"I'll tell you about him, but can I ask you something first?"

"Always."

"How did you do it? I mean, when you thought you'd never be good enough—how did you continue to be brave anyway?"

My mom laughs, a throaty but delightful sound before she answers, "I didn't have a choice. I loved your father more than I could explain, and the thought of having even a moment of happiness with him was more important to me than the fear of what would come if he decided I wasn't enough, or if he listened to your nana."

"And you just went on, trying to mold yourself, even if it meant being someone you aren't? Just so you could have that love?" I question.

"Olivia, I didn't really change that much. Of course, I wanted to be perfect, and in the moments where we needed to be, I was, and I forced you to be too. But in the quiet moments where it's just he and I . . . I'm the same goofy, down-on-her-luck waitress that I was when we met."

I'm shaken to my core by her admission. It's not like I haven't seen that side of her before, but as the years went by, it seemed to show up less and less. I remember catching my parents slow dancing in the kitchen once when I was maybe ten. My mom didn't have makeup on and it shocked me. Part of me feels guilty, like maybe she stopped showing me that freer side of herself because in some ways my need to strive for perfection added to her insecurities.

My momma and I talk for a little while longer, mostly about Sam. I fill her in on what transpired between us, leaving out the cursed-by-a-witch part because that may be a little too much for her to handle over the phone. I don't know that I fully forgive her yet, but I am reassured that most of my insecurities were born out of her deep-seated fears and that I am not in fact a failure at literally everything in life.

When I hang up, my thoughts immediately race toward making things right with Sam. I know without a doubt that I love him. If the last week of misery wasn't enough of a clue, it's the little things. Like wanting to tell him about my mom, wanting to talk to him about the meaningless thing that happened on *Top Chef*, or wishing I could give him a hug right now. I realize that those small things are what matter, the moments that are so insignificant you'd never know they were important until they're gone.

I rack my brain while showering, desperate to come up with some way of showing him how sorry I am, a way to tell him that I'm in love with him. But my mind keeps taking me back to the cabin and the pumpkin muffins. That was the night I started to cover myself back up, to hide who I was. Yet, it also was one of the most special memories we share.

Sam went to so much trouble to make the place beautiful, and I still can't think of those frosted muffins without blushing.

Once I'm done getting ready, it's decided. I get changed and whip up a batch of the muffins. While I'm waiting for them to bake, I call Ari. She answers on the first ring.

"Tell me you've decided to go get your man!" she shouts.

"I have. I'm making him muffins right now. Then I'm going to head to Eerie to see him."

"Yes. Good girl. Did you talk to Anne?" Ari asks.

"Yep, and she admitted that she was wrong the whole time. She told me that she always had high expectations for me because she never felt good enough for my Nana. She even admitted she used to be hard on me because she was jealous," I explain, giving her the high-level details.

"Holy shit. That's some fucked-up family drama. But I'm glad she admitted that you aren't the problem."

"I'll say. I'm still scared though. What if Sam turns me away?" I say softly.

"He won't, but if he does, then I'll be waiting for your call and we will drink our feelings while internet stalking people that we used to know." Ari chuckles to herself.

"Thanks, Ari. The oven timer is dinging. I gotta take these out before they burn. I'll let you know how it goes."

"You're welcome, Ollie. I love you forever."

"I love you too."

An hour later, the muffins have cooled, I've added the frosting and packaged them up, and I am ready to go. I step off the front porch of my cottage, taking a second to look back at the once-beautiful decorations that Sam placed. The flowers are wilted, and the pumpkins are speckled with black spots as they begin to rot. It's like a funeral, and I hope it's not indicative of what is waiting for me at Eerie Ink.

I take a deep breath and walk toward Mage Square. I honestly don't know what I'm going to do if he turns me down. I'm finally ready to open myself up, and it's really scary to think that I might have missed my chance at a happily ever after. I still can't believe that I thought the tattoo was the only reason we were so good together, that he was using it to give me what I wanted. It seems silly, the more I overanalyze it. How could he have used it when half the time, it was a myriad of emotions whipping around and random objects that didn't make a lot of sense even to me? I guess that's what having your life turned upside down does though—makes you question anything and everything.

I approach Eerie, and the lights appear to have been turned off, the open sign dark against the glass windows. I press my face against the cold door, trying to see if I can spot anything indicating Sam is here, but I don't. It's unusual for him to not be working on a Saturday. Maybe he stayed home?

I retrace my steps, walking past my cottage and toward Sam's. I'm outside of the cemetery when a car slows behind me, and I pick up my pace as my heart races. A few seconds later, a black sedan pulls up next to me, window rolled down, and Sam's dad, Patrick, says, "Hey, Olive. Headed to Sam's"?

"Oh, hey. Uh, yeah, I was hoping I could talk to him. Do you know if he's home?"

"No, he's at the hospital. Come on, I can give you a ride," Patrick says. His eyes are so kind, full of compassion. With how nice he's being, he must not know we broke up. *Wait, did he say Sam is in the hospital?* My heart clenches as I jog over to Patrick's car and pull the door open.

"What happened? Is he okay?" I huff out.

"Oh, sorry. He's fine, Xavier's baby's coming." Sam's dad smiles, and relief rushes through me.

"That's great, but I probably shouldn't be there. Can you just take me home?" I set the muffins on my knees as I reach to buckle my seat belt.

"Nope, I can't take you home. I know something happened between you two, and if I take you home, you will sit and wonder all day where things stand. I won't take you to the hospital if you don't think it's the right place to talk to my son, but you aren't going to sit and worry alone either. Mabel is baking today. She will appreciate the company."

Ugh, this man. This is where Sam learned it from. Patrick showed him how to be kind, how to be sweet. My heart melts, and I can't stop myself from hoping it works out with Sam even more. I want to be with Sam, but I want to keep his parents, too.

"Okay, I see how this works. Let me practice my groveling on Mabel," I say, winking at him.

"Now you're learning. Mabel will be far tougher than Sam. I'll only be a scream away, young lady," Patrick coos, winking right back.

We both laugh before falling into a comfortable silence. A few minutes later, we pull into the driveway and I hop out, making my way to the front door. Before I reach the top step, it swings open and there stands Mabel with her hands on her hips, frowning at me.

"Mabel, I'm in love with your son," I blurt out awkwardly.

"Well, duh. I'm frowning because you waited a whole week to admit it," she chastises me.

"It's, um, I'm complicated. But I'm sorry. I'm so sorry, and I just want to talk to him so I can tell him how I feel," I say, rushing the words out as quickly as possible.

"You will get your chance, I promise. For now, you and I are going to bond over baking and undo all that garbage your mother put in this beautiful head of yours. Come on, my sweet little belle." I guess Mabel must know more than I thought about my mother.

Several hours later, after baking nearly enough pastries, cookies, and bread to feed Cami and Xavier for a year, as well as deep diving into my childhood, I'm exhausted. Mabel and I discussed just about every topic under the sun, and while I thought it was going to be difficult to open up, she made it feel so easy. Each time I'd hesitate, she would remind me that I didn't have to tell her anything, and that alone allowed my heart to feel in control.

We talked a lot about my mom, and Mable helped me to see things from my mom's perspective. It's not much different than my own and how I was afraid of Sam not wanting me once he learned of my flaws. Did my mom go about things the right way? No, of course not. But Mabel reiterated that most of the time when the people we love hurt us, it is more about what's going on inside of them than it ever is about us.

I glance at the clock and notice it's nearing five. I'm not going to stick around and invite myself to stay for dinner. It doesn't seem like Sam will be stopping by anytime soon. A pang of sympathy for Cami strikes me. She must be having a heck of a time in labor. I hope everything is okay.

"I think I'm going to head out," I say, grasping Mabel's hand and giving it a light squeeze.

"Okay, sometimes these things take a while. Sam's going to stop by and grab this stuff when he leaves the hospital. Did you want me to tell him you were here?" Mabel asks.

"Yes, do you have a pen?" The idea of leaving him a note feels a little lame, but I want him to know I'm ready to talk when he is.

Mabel digs around in a drawer full of random items and pulls out a pen and some paper. I take them from her and sit down in the dining room to jot out a quick message.

Sam-

I know I hurt you and I'm sorry. I would like the chance to talk, just one chance to tell you how I feel. Please come over tonight when you get home. I only need a few minutes.

Love,

Olive

I fold the note and put it on top of my box of pumpkin muffins before heading back into the kitchen. I set the box on the counter and look at Mabel meaningfully. She doesn't have to say anything, I know she understands what to do. As I grab my bag and turn to leave, she stops me with a hand on my arm.

"Come here, Olive." Mabel pulls me into a hug and I melt into her. "It's going to be okay, I promise," she says, stepping back and offering me a small smile.

"Thanks, Mabel. I hope you're right."

Thirty-Four

Sam

A Baby and a Little Magic

"How much longer do you think it's going to be?" Bridget asks, standing to pace the waiting room for the millionth time.

"I have no clue. I think it can take a while when it's the first one." I shrug and sit back in the pleather torture device otherwise known as a hospital chair.

"Are we planning to just camp out here forever, or is there a cutoff to this?" Max asks, yawning into his fist.

"We've been here all night and all day. You really want to tap out when we have to be getting close?" I ask, looking at him like he's lost it.

I didn't ask either of my siblings to sit here with me, but they insisted. Max because he said he didn't want me getting emotional and calling Olive without sleeping on it, and Bridget because she said she cares about Xavier as much as I do—that one's a lie, but she does look at him like a big brother. Either way, at least I'm not waiting alone.

Sitting here going on twenty-four hours has given me time to think. I understand why Olive was scared, but I am pretty disappointed that after everything she still wasn't honest with me. I told her how much honesty meant to me, yet she was too afraid to admit that she felt like I was using her tattoo, to admit that she felt vulnerable and manipulated until the very end.

Max and I talked briefly about what Howie said. It does make sense, but it still hurts. I love her so much, but that doesn't mean she didn't hurt me. It doesn't give her a free pass on not believing in me.

The doors whoosh open into the lobby and out walks Xavier with a big grin on his face, pulling me out of my thoughts. He looks happy and tired, and I'm relieved.

"It's a girl!" he shouts gleefully.

"Oh my gosh, yes. I bet she's perfect," Bridget gushes, running up to give him a hug.

"She weighs nine pounds, eleven ounces and has a full head of hair."

"That's a toddler. No wonder it took so long," Max huffs before chuckling to himself.

"How's mom doing?" I ask, pulling my best friend into a tight squeeze.

"She's good, man, so tough. You holding up okay?" Xavier asks, gripping my biceps and looking deep into my eyes.

"Yeah, I'll be alright." He knows about what happened with Olive. I talk to my best friend every day.

"Give her another chance if she asks for it, okay? Promise me," Xav says sternly.

"I don't know if that'll happen, but okay," I respond hesitantly, questioning why he would say such a thing when all he should be thinking about is the newborn baby and wife he has to take care of.

"I think it will be before you know it. Just trust me. Now, do you want to meet your niece?" He slaps me on the shoulder and leads us back to the room where Cami is lying in bed, holding a beautiful bundle of joy.

I never was sure I wanted to be a dad, but the moment I lay eyes on this little girl, she looks right at me and my heart melts. I love her, and I'll do anything she asks for the rest of my life. The thought makes me laugh out loud.

"Why are you laughing at my daughter, Samuel?" Cami asks, a sternness to her brows.

"Oh, I'm not. I'm laughing because Xav and I are so screwed. She's going to get asked on so many dates, and I'm going to want to chase them all away," I explain.

"Nope, she's not allowed to date, ever. She is going to live with her mother and me until she's at least forty and then there's the convent." Xav says it like he's serious, but I can tell by the goofy grin on his face that all it will take is one little smile from her and he will jump to make her dreams come true.

"What's her name?" Bridget asks.

Xav and Cami exchange a look, before turning to me with cheesy grins.

"Well, we are pretty sure we have one picked out, but we want to run it by you first," Xav says, coming around the bed to stand next to me and slinging an arm around my shoulders.

"We would like to name her Samantha. Sammy for short," Cami announces.

It feels like the ground beneath my feet quakes, my knees are weak. Tears stream down my face as I quickly cover it with both hands. I've had a shit week. I've been at my lowest emotionally, but this reminds me that I'm never alone. I have a found family in addition to my actual one.

"I-I don't know what to say," I choke out. "Give me my baby, Cami," I demand, holding my hands out to grab the cutest little bundle I've ever seen.

"Wait, you're serious? Why him?" Bridget asks, smirking at the scoff that rips from my lips.

"Very funny, clearly they want her to be cool like her uncle," I spit out, heading to a chair to sit and rock Sammy.

"Should have gone with Maxine if that's the case," Max throws in.

"We chose you because you're the best friend a guy could ask for. When I was hanging on by a thread after the accident, you never left my side. You're my brother, and I hope she grows up to have your generosity, your kindness, and your huge-ass heart," Xav explains. There isn't a dry eye in the place when I pry my stare off the baby and look around.

"Speaking of his heart, are you going to show him?" Cami asks, picking up Xav's phone from the side table and shaking it back and forth.

"Show me what?"

"So, remember how I said that Olive was going to come around a lot sooner than you thought? Well, she spent the day with Mabel, and I got this message about ten minutes after the baby was born," Xav says, pulling up a picture and showing me.

It's a note, handwritten and held open by my mother's hand. There's a message from Olive saying she is sorry and wants to talk. Below that is another message from my mom that reads, *Go get my daughter-in-law back or you're out of the family*, with a heart next to it. I laugh, a deep, rolling belly laugh that startles Sammy and causes Xav to lift her from my arms.

"Wait, is it funny?" Bridget asks, clearly confused.

"Your mom is funny," Cami confirms as Xav hands her the phone to look at the picture. Max shakes his head and starts laughing right along with me when he gets a glimpse.

"What are you waiting on?" Cami asks.

"I, uh, yeah. I don't know . . . I'm gonna go."

I stand and head for the door, stopping only to briefly admire my namesake once more before waltzing out the door.

"Bring her with you when you come back tomorrow," Xav bellows after me.

I hit the elevator button approximately twelve times as the anxiety of waiting to hear what Olive has to say eats a hole through my brain. I'm in love with her, hopelessly and irrevocably. Am I upset by what she did, or rather, how she did it? Yes. But that doesn't mean I don't want to be with her.

Once I'm on the first floor, I all but sprint to my truck and slide in, firing it up and speeding out of the parking lot. The trip to Olive's is less than ten minutes, but I don't know how long she spent at my parents' or when she was expecting me. The sun has set. I glance at the clock on my dashboard, noting it's just after eight.

I turn onto her street and am floored with the sight coming into view. It's like the very first time I saw her at home, when I delivered the Reuben after watching her leave Union hungry. She's swaying slightly on the swing, her strawberry blonde hair almost twinkling in the light that hangs above her porch.

I pull up to the curb and park, shutting off the truck. Before I get out, I take a deep breath. I know what the letter said, but I don't know what to expect her to say. She could want to talk, to resolve things—but there's a lot of hurt too. I'm hurt. Mustering my courage, I slide from my seat and approach. As my feet hit the first step of the porch, Olive and I make eye contact.

She blows out what sounds like a relieved sigh and says, "Thank you for coming."

"Well, to be fair, no one says no to Mabel . . . But of course, I came." I attempt to throw a little humor into the mix. The tension between us is so thick you could cut it with a knife, and deep inside I think she needs a moment of relief as much as I do. Taking her in as I cross the remaining distance, I notice her eyes are sunken like she hasn't slept well and her nose is a little pink like she's been crying.

"I-I'm so sorry, Sam. I was so stupid and scared, and everything was so chaotic. It wasn't your fault. You did everything right, and I hurt you. I didn't know if you were coming, and I just, I don't know what I'm doing," she says, her words barely audible as they float across the night air.

I slide next to her on the swing, wrapping her in a hug and kissing her forehead. "Hey, it's okay. I didn't make you feel safe, I made mistakes too," I say, leaning back a tad so I can look into her eyes. "I told you I'd love you forever and I meant it . . ."

"But I hurt you. I didn't trust in us, believe in what we had," Olive finishes the statement I was going to make. She shivers a little, her bottom lip quivering from the cold night air.

"Let's go inside. I want to talk about this, but I can't focus when you're freezing and I'm worried about it." It's true, we have shit to work through. Shit that won't get accomplished if I'm stressed over her body temperature.

We stand, making our way indoors, and Olive and I settle into the couch, her crisscross applesauce in the middle, facing me, as I sit on the end and look toward the fireplace. In the silence, it feels like minutes pass, although I'm sure it's merely seconds.

"Sam, you did make me feel safe. I'm sorry that I made you feel otherwise. It's just that my entire life I've been told—"

"Stop, you don't have to tell me anything you're not comfortable sharing."

"Yes, I do. I want to. When I was growing up, I was never good enough. I tried so hard to meet expectations, but no matter what I did, there was always room for improvement. Growing up that way made me afraid to let anyone in. I always thought that if I did, they would see me and realize that I wasn't what they wanted. When I went with Irina that first time, I told her I wanted to wear my heart on my sleeve. She did exactly what I asked, but then I freaked out. All these doubts and insecurities crept in on top of me already feeling crazy out of control from what was happening physically," she says, looking at me tentatively.

"I understand that, I do. I can't imagine how you must have felt, still feel, having grown up like that. But I don't understand why you thought you couldn't talk to me, or why you thought I was using it to my advantage."

"I guess it was that first night, when you were gauging my reactions in your bedroom. I loved it, but it also made me wonder, is this just a fun game? Is he only into me because I'm easy to read, literally? And I know now that's not the case, that it was my insecurity, but that's how I felt . . . and each time I noticed you glancing at my arm, the fear festered until it consumed me and I couldn't see anything else."

I take a deep breath. I understand what she's saying, but it still hurts. I wish she would have just asked me.

"How do you feel now?"

"Well, I had a long talk with my mom, and I realized that I was never the problem. Not that I'm perfect, but she took her insecurities out on me. And then I talked to your mom and realized that everything I felt in my heart about you all along was true. You are kind, generous, caring. You make me laugh insanely hard and can sass me right back when I get testy. You are the most talented man and work hard for everything you have. Basically, when I close my eyes at night, you are everything I've ever dreamed of having in a partner. I love you, like truly madly deeply. I'm hopelessly enamored with you."

My heart melts. She loves me. I grab her by the waist and hoist her into my lap, nuzzling my nose into her hair and inhaling my favorite strawberry scent.

"I love you too. More than you will ever know, in this life and the next. But I need you to promise me something." I sit back so I can look into her eyes, grinning a little at how adorable she is.

"Anything, I'll promise anything," she rattles out.

"Oh, really?" I wink at her.

"Okay, maybe not anything, but most things," she relents.

"Promise that if we do this, you'll be in it for the long haul. I can't handle losing you again. And promise that whenever you feel unsure, you'll come to me and let me remind you that I'm never leaving," I say, pressing a soft kiss to her cheek.

"I promise I will never leave. I promise I'll always tell you how I'm feeling. I will wear my heart on my sleeve for you. I promise to cherish the little moments, the mundane and seemingly meaningless times that come and go without even making a blip. I promise I'm going to make you meet my parents and marry me. I promise I'm going to have your adorable little babies, and I'm going to spend every Sunday baking with your mom. I promise that I will love you forever, in this life and the next."

I lean forward pulling her into a kiss. It's soft and tentative at first, but she swipes her tongue across the seam of my lips and it quickly turns passionate. We are exploring each other thoroughly when Olive breaks away from me, heaving air.

"Sam, I, oh my God. My arm, it burns," she says, rubbing at it fiercely.

I grab her arm to inspect it, but in the blink of an eye, it transforms. Where minutes ago there was nothing, now there is a beautiful road map. At the top of her arm there's a small heart, then a pile of books with BKB written on the top, a sign that reads Flashing Ahead, and Boo the ghost surrounded by pumpkins.

"Olive, I think it's . . ."

"It's our love story," she confirms.

Below Boo, there is a tiny movie screen with *Practical Magic* etched on it, a replica of my cabin, and a pumpkin muffin. The whole thing is pieced together with pumpkin vines that twist and tangle effortlessly. And finally at her wrist, written in script, it says, *She wore her heart on her sleeve, and they lived happily ever after.*

Epilogue

January 16- 11 Weeks After Halloween

"Hey, baby." I lean forward, pressing a light kiss to Olive's lips. I'm seeing her for the first time today and can't help but notice she's far more dressed up than I instructed. "I thought I said comfort."

"This is comfortable, and it's not like you gave me any idea where we're going," Olive says, rolling her eyes playfully while smacking my arm gently. She has on a flowing skirt with a sweater tucked into it, not the jeans I had pictured. But then again, when is she ever underdressed? I love that she doesn't worry about fitting into the situation as much as she once would've, and Anne will appreciate the outfit.

I clear my throat, a lump of nerves settling in. "Uh, we . . . Let me try that again. You look beautiful, as always."

Her cheeks turn a light shade of pink, and I run my finger along the blush.

"I just need to get my shoes on. I'll be right back." Olive turns to head toward her bedroom and I follow, detouring to the kitchen to put the flowers in a vase.

I'm filling the vase with water when she wraps her arms around me and lays her head between my shoulder blades. "I missed you today," Olive whispers.

I spin around, setting the vase down with one hand as I pull her chin up and lean in for a kiss. After several minutes, we break apart, both of us heaving for air. God, this woman is everything. I'm not sure I'll ever have enough of her. But right now, we have a schedule to keep and a big night ahead of us. Nothing about pulling this off was easy, yet every plan I've put in place was worth it.

"Olive, as much as I want to say fuck the date and spend the night showing you just how much I missed you, I have it all prepared, and I think you'd be sad to miss it."

She huffs a little, pouting her lip out for a brief second before winking and smiling at me. "Okay, okay, let's go." Olive pushes past me, stopping for a second to smell the flowers I bought her. "These are beautiful. They remind me of fall. Thank you." I don't reveal that I intentionally requested them for that very reason. (Beatrice Bushnell is finally an Olive fan—it didn't take much convincing.) I simply nod and kiss her cheek before guiding her to the truck. I help her in, and she scoots to the center seat. Such a small thing shouldn't give me comfort, but it does. I know we haven't been together that long, and we went through a lot—it would be weird if I wasn't a little scared about how she's going to handle what's about to happen.

"Sam, where are we going?" she asks, peering curiously out the window. Mage Hollow isn't a big place, but there are essentially two neighborhoods you'd want to live in—the one we already do, and the one where Ari and I grew up. Both touch Mage Square, being conveniently walkable.

I glance at her, nothing but love and admiration in my eyes. "If I told you, it would ruin the surprise."

She doesn't respond. Instead, she squeezes my hand and scooches a little closer to me. I'm shocked she isn't asking more questions. She's a runner—I know she caught on to my random tour of town three turns ago.

Abandoning my stall, I pull into a stone driveway. It's technically aggregated concrete, but it looks like pea gravel with warm tones that create a classic appearance. In front of us is a sprawling sage-green Victorian home with a large wraparound porch and a paned-window front door that's painted black.

Olive gasps audibly. "This house is beautiful. Whoever lives here probably thinks we're nuts. How many times did we drive past?" she asks, fluttering her lashes and stifling a laugh.

"The O'Reilly's," I retort, not giving life to the joke she made. Olive knows me well enough at this point to sense I'm nervous. But she's playing along, so I don't wait for her to question if I'm referring to a family member or ask me anything else she could have cooked up in her mind. Instead, I hop out of the truck and round the front to open her door. Olive doesn't say anything, she simply grabs my hand and walks with me up the steps. She starts toward the porch swing, but I stop her.

"Wait, baby. Can you sit right there for a second?" I ask, motioning to the top step. She looks confused as hell (it's frankly adorable), but she does it anyway. "Would you like a turkey Rueben?" I ask, waving the brown bag I grabbed from the backseat of the truck when I exited.

"Sam, what? It's like forty degrees. Why are we eating on the porch of someone else's house?"

I settle onto the bottom step the way I did that first time I brought her food. "Do me a favor and just go with it," I say, moving to pull the box

Howie assembled from the bag. I hand her the Styrofoam container and motion for her to open it. As she takes the first bite of her sandwich, I start talking. "I have spent a lot of time planning tonight . . . And while we didn't meet on *these* steps, I didn't think that you'd be up for flashing the town again." Her eyes bug out a little as her cheeks turn rosy. "But also sitting on steps, even if they're different ones, with this sandwich is where I felt like you started to let me in. It was short-lived, since I messed up and called you princess, yet I still remember thinking that maybe if I played my cards right, I'd be lucky enough to see how beautiful you were on the inside."

"Sam, uh ma gahd," she says around the bite in her mouth. As she chews happily, I push back from the wooden slats and drop to one knee.

"Olivia Anne Bowman, when you came into my life with a flash, I knew instantly that I'd never be the same. I've never met anyone exactly like you. Baby, you see the best in everyone around you, and my happiest moments have been watching you discover all the amazing parts of yourself." I clear my throat as tears start to fall from both of our faces and Olive abandons the sandwich to its container. "I don't need to tell you all the ways or reasons I love you just because this is a big moment. I do that every day anyway. But I will say this, watching you learn to be vulnerable, to wear your heart on your sleeve, has changed me. It's shown me that even when the odds are stacked against us or wild and unexpected events occur, we will always find a way to weather the storm if we stick together. It's shown me that being open and honest with the right person means you can never go wrong. But mostly, it's shown me that you truly are the most genuinely beautiful person on the inside and out . . . Will you marry me, have babies with me, and grow old with me in this life and whatever comes after it?"

"Oh my gosh! Yes! Of course, I love you so much." Olive stands and pulls me to my feet, kissing me deeply, like even though we can do this for the rest of our lives, even that won't be enough. She drops her hands from my chest, and I take the opportunity to slip a key into her palm. She takes a step back and looks from it to me and back again.

"Sam!" She practically shouts, "Did you buy me a house?"

I reach behind my neck, scratching my hair lightly. "I mean, technically I bought it for both of us, but yeah."

She launches back into my arms, kissing me once more.

"I lov—" The door opens with a thud against the side of the house.

"Uh, shit, sorry. I was just coming to see if you'd gotten here yet," Ari stammers, causing us both to laugh. That girl has always had impeccable timing.

"It's fine, Ari. Look!" Olive holds up her hand to show off the vintage gold ring with an oval-shaped diamond shining brightly. "We're getting married."

"Ollie, I love you, but why do you think I'm here? Come on, everyone's waiting." She tugs my future wife inside, and I follow, stopping only for a second to look at the night sky and send up a silent thanks to Irina. As much as I have a love-hate relationship with magic, I'm grateful my future wife finally learned to wear her heart on her sleeve.

When we get inside, Olive is immediately swept up by our family and friends. Her parents and mine are the first to hug her, offering congratulations. Then there's Xav, Cami, Howie, Ariella, and my siblings. Olive shows off her ring, and champagne is passed around our new kitchen. Anne even comments about how beautiful the decor is, causing Bridget to beam in delight. The night feels almost perfect as I clink glasses and exchange a kiss with my girl, but I notice Max trailing out to the backyard with his head hung low.

"Hey, I'll be right back, I gotta check on Max," I whisper in Olive's ear. She nods and smiles up at me, turning to talk to our moms as I exit.

Pushing my way onto the back deck, I find him with a half-empty glass of bubbles sitting on an Adirondack chair. "You good, bro?"

"Yeah, uh, congratulations . . ." He takes a long sip, draining his glass. "Happy for you both. At least one good thing happened this week."

I move to sit next to him, waiting to see if he'll say anything else. When he doesn't, I jump in. "Max, look man, I know this wasn't what you wanted, but the doctors are serious. You're missing six games this time just to heal your noggin. What happens if you continue and the next time the damage is worse?" Max can't keep playing hockey. We both know it but that doesn't make accepting it any easier. I understand where he is, walking away from the game sucked for me too. But I had tattooing to fall back on—Max has never wanted anything else.

"I don't fucking know. That's the problem." His voice cracks with emotion. "I don't know who I am without it."

I stand and grab his hand, pulling him up so I can give him a hug. "That's what we're here for, to help you figure it out. I love you, bro. You're not alone, now or ever."

He shakes his head, clapping me on the back a few times. "Thanks, man. I love you, too. But we, uh, we should probably go in there because I'm pretty sure I just saw Mom and Anne yelling at each other through the window."

"Oh shit! Let's go save my girl."

We hurry inside only to discover that both the moms were acting out some scene from the latest soap opera they've been watching. I'm relieved that they aren't actually fighting, but part of me thinks it would have been a good excuse to kick everyone out. I slink up behind Olive and whisper in her ear, "What are the odds we can get everyone to leave soon?"

"Pretty good, watch this," she says, before spinning in my arms and kissing the daylights out of me. I hesitate at first, caught off guard by the blatant display of affection, but then she sweeps her tongue over my lips and I'm powerless to deny her. I'm not sure how long it takes for it to get awkward, but I do hear Ariella telling everyone they should let us celebrate in our new house alone. After hearing several agreements, we separate just long enough to say goodbye to our family and friends.

When Ariella, the last to leave, closes the front door behind her, Olive turns to me again. "I can't believe you bought me a house and asked me to marry you."

"Honestly, I'm just glad you said yes. I know it's quick, but I've never been more positive about something in my life. You are my life. It's not just your heart you wear around. Mine is on your sleeve, too."

Acknowledgements

Another one down . . . it's hard to believe, honestly. But at the same time it feels like this is exactly what I'm supposed to be doing. This story began as a dream, and the support I've had along the way has been nothing short of one either. As always, I'll do my best to thank every person who helped along the way, but if I missed you (consider this similar to a Grammy's speech) I'm so sorry and thank you!

First up forever and always—Cory—believe me when I say that I know you and the boys have missed home cooked meals, moments hanging as a family on the couch, and probably have had to rewear dirty pants a time or two while I wrote this book. Thank you for loving me through the moments I've taken to disappear into the writing cave, and supporting my dreams always. You are the perfect plotting partner (yes, I have the voice recordings to prove it) and the best main male character in real life that a girl could ask for.

Special shout out to L & G for always cheering me on. I desperately hope I'm making you proud and that one day you'll admit I'm a little more cool than skibidi.

Sarah—we did it! I say "we" because this book wouldn't be a single step above a potato chip read (as you lovingly say) without the hours of painstaking review and feedback. When I was six, Dad & Gretch gave me the best birthday gift a girl could ever ask for and hunny—that's you! From voice recordings, plowing grapes on New Years, and eight million comments—working on this project with you has been the highlight of sisterhood. I love you and trust your judgment beyond measure. Thanks for always hyping me up... now get to speakin!

Cassandra—are there words to describe our friendship outside of destiny or kismet? I'm forever thankful that you didn't give up the first, second, or maybe even third time your DM went unanswered. While it's admittedly sometimes hard to scale the walls I put up, you grabbed a grappling hook and launched yourself right into my life—and I'm so glad you did. From random internet author friend to certified bestie and business partner, none of this book or any of the next would be possible without your encouragement and advice. I will forever finish your thoughts, sentences, be the Suze to your Babs, and stand by our shared love of the color emerald green.

Annie—fancy meeting you here, again. From the moment we met working on CK, I knew that you were my girl! My cheerleader, the world's best dev editor, my voice of reason, my partner in sussing out everything from plot holes and character arcs. You've guided me on how to invest my time as an Indie and to make this a flourishing career, which is not in your job description but absolutely appreciated. I live for your voice memos and the way you make me laugh without even trying. You were my very FIRST call when I woke up dreaming about a witch that cursed a girl with a tattoo on her arm, and your enthusiasm for this story is one of the main reasons it exists today!

Maggie—oh my sweet, Maggie! I'm not sure there is a good way to quantify our friendship, but I'll do my best. You are the teacher, the master, the one who is always in my corner saying, *hey, did you think about this?* From podcasts that guide me on writing for the ID to YouTube's on writing romantasy—being your friend has made me a better writer! But it's also taught me that sometimes there really are people in the world that want the best for you. You never gatekeep! You are always there in my corner cheering me on, lending an ear, making me laugh, and I only hope you truly know how much I treasure our chats and having you in my corner.

Bri—I'm going to take this moment to say thank you for finally teaching me the proper use of an em dash. You are the reason this book has commas in the right place and proper grammar in general. But more than that, your support and cheerleading is always so appreciated.

Sam—holy artwork, Batman! I can't even begin to describe the talent you have. Working with you to bring these characters to life has been nothing short of amazing. Your artistic prowess is unmatched! Thanks for riding out my scattered thoughts and random color suggestions.

Amber—you are a social media goddess! Thank you for all the help making beautiful edits and posts for this book. Without your support, readers might not know this exists and I can't tell you how much I've enjoyed working together.

Let me just take a minute to give a standing ovation for the magnificent, Breanne Randall. As a baby author, I spend a lot of my time researching, reading, and generally fangirling over the authors that are living out their dreams and what that must be like. But, never in my life did I imagine that sliding into your DM's would result in you actually responding. I can't put into words how thankful I am that you took time out of your busy schedule to read my book and blurb it for me. You are the realest for supporting me when you had absolutely no obligation to do so . . . I will never forget it, and I still can't even believe it happened. THANK YOU!

Stef, Jessie, Whit, Mal, Abby, Lainey, Lindsey S., & Jules—y'all are quite the crew! The world's best BETA team, the hype squad, the ones I know are looking out for me and finding all those typos or plot holes so that the readers don't. I'm endlessly appreciative of your love, your support, and your ability to point out my flaws in a kind albeit constructive way.

Lemmy! This book would not have ARC readers without you—but more than that, I would be struggling to find stock photos and sifting through Canva templates to make inspired posts. The resources you bring to the table have made my life so much easier and I am so thankful to call you not only my ARC management extraordinaire, but my friend!

To my family—from asking about my progress, to proofreading and purchasing—you never cease to amaze me with the way you show up when I need you! Y'all are the real heroes of this story, the ones who've dried my tears, answered late night calls, and spent hours pouring over a spicy manuscript even if at times it made you uncomfortable (looking at you Mom and Dad).

A & M—there will never be enough words for either of you! My soul sisters, my best friends, my greatest supporters. I love you forever, in this life and the next!

Finally, to YOU, the readers... Thanks for once again taking a chance on me. For ARC edits, beautifully written reviews, and the love you show me day in and day out. By the time this book releases I will have gotten to squeeze some of y'all in real life, and I can't describe what that alone means to me! You are the reason I do this... why I will continue to write and share my stories.

Thank You!

KC

About the Author

Corporate Girl turned author, Kelli Cooke writes vibrant, funny, and authentic love stories. As a hopeless romantic, Kelli strives to bring a creative twist on what love looks like in real life infused with the kind of comedy that will keep you laughing long after finishing her books. While comedy and feel-good emotions are the stars, she also focuses on threading in raw emotion and hopes to impact hearts for years to come. When she's not writing, she can be found chasing around her two kids or binge watching a show with her husband. Kelli never expected to become an author but has embraced harnessing her creative ability and adores sharing her vibrant tales with her readers.

Check out Kelli's other novel, Coincidentally Kismet, on eBook, Paperback, and Kindle Unlimited.